CHASERS

CHASERS

A NOVEL

LAURENCE MICHIE

V-RAN
DOLPH
BOOKS
HADLEY, MASSACHUSETTS

CHASERS

Copyright © 2013 by Laurence Michie

Contact: vrandolphbooks@gmail.com

ISBN: 978-0-6158171-4-9

Acknowledgement --

The italicized segments in Chapters Ten and Eighteen are quoted from *The Works of Jonathan Edwards,* Yale University Press.

for Virginia

‹ *Chapter One* ›

JASON WAS HUNTING TOO far south. He knew it was dangerous, especially in full daylight, but the harsh winter had driven the deer out of the hilltowns and down toward the Hamp, where foraging was a good deal easier. Jason was a cautious man and a good woodsman, so he thought he could avoid trouble. He had hunted this far south before.

As he made his way the hills leveled off and the land sloped down toward the Hamp. He wouldn't chance hunting in the flatlands, not by himself. Too far to carry deer meat back anyway. He superstitiously patted his pocket. Four cartridges. One in the rifle. Should be plenty to guarantee food, Jason thought. He was tracking deer now, and if two of the five cartridges fired, he'd be sure of bringing back meat.

It was late in the winter, very late. Though the frost was as hard as shale back in the hills, it was mud time here in the woods of the lowland. Mysteriously shaped spreadings of dirty snow lingered wherever there were shadows. Gray snow remained under the protective boughs of hemlock and curled out tentacles from the thick tangle of brambles that in a few months would gush with blackberries. The sun was still high, though Jason already had eaten his midday biscuit. Only half a day behind him back in the hills, winter still had a fierce lock on the land. Here, at least at midday, there was a scent of spring. He was glad he had not worn his bearskin. He left it behind because he could keep warm by staying on the move, and its bulk might be uncomfortable if he had venison to carry. But this far south, he blended into the mud and dirty snow perfectly just as he was, wearing a black, long-sleeved cloth coat and a dark cap that Felicity had knitted.

The deer tracks led Jason to a slope on the hill where he could see a far distance south, and he cautiously eased into a hemlock's shadow and fell into a crouch, his heavy long rifle cradled in his arms as he opened his eyes and ears to the rolling land before him. He had to be sure there were no Jonnies around before he shot a deer. No good having to abandon a kill or, worse yet, be killed himself.

Jason relaxed in his crouch, letting his eyes roam. He was looking for nothing in particular. It was a matter of staying alert for movement. Any movement. He'd wait at least as long as it took for the shadow of a maple branch down the slope to reach a boulder that was in his line of sight. When that happened, if he had neither seen nor heard anything to give alarm, he'd seek to kill a deer. If there were Jonnies around, he'd know it by then.

It was cold in the shade, but Jason didn't shiver. He scanned the scene before him, especially the old road that snaked all the way south to Hamp. That's the way the arrogant Jonnies would show themselves. They wouldn't bother with concealment.

But soon Jason's heart thumped and almost stopped. He heard a sound that he had heard only twice before. It was the roar and whine of a motor. The Jonnies didn't have motors. This was Russ!

Jason instinctively drew himself closer to the trunk of the hemlock, exaggerating his crouch as though he could reduce himself to an imperceptible form in the landscape, no more remarkable than the many rocks that jutted out of the hillside.

He clutched the rifle to his chest.

The noise, very faint at first, rapidly became stronger, and suddenly in the distance Jason could see a speck like a grasshopper suspended above the earth, but moving rapidly toward him, following the route of the road as though it had giant invisible grasshopper legs galloping over the ancient, frost-heaved and overgrown pavement. The grasshopper had a motor, Jason knew and the sound grew closer at the same rate the grasshopper loomed bigger.

At a crossroads less than a kilometer away, the grasshopper suddenly halted in air and began settling to earth by the few ruined buildings there. Jason expelled his breath harshly and realized that he had been holding his breath. If the grasshopper had come any closer to him, he might have panicked and run, though he knew that was the worst thing to do.

He watched with fascination as the grasshopper eased to the ground, the pounding thrum of its motor's stroke slowing and changing pitch. It was no danger to Jason at this distance, but he had never seen Russ engines this close. He noticed the grasshopper had a wing above it, rotating with a magical speed that now was slowing. Imagine a bird flying with one wing!

Jason had barely begun to wonder what a Russ flyer was doing at the group of abandoned buildings in Jonnie territory, but he found out almost at once. The wind carried a "pop" to his ears, then a string of sharp rifle shots. Puffs of smoke drifted out of the abandoned buildings, and the grasshopper, which hadn't quite touched the earth, suddenly jerked upward with a loud whirr of its engine. Jason looked on in horror. There must be Jonnies in those buildings, and they were shooting at the Russ!

The grasshopper skittered erratically, as though tossed by the wind, and Jason could hear the fearful unstoppable noise of a spraygun. In one second, Jason was sure, the spraygun had fired more bullets than the pops of the Jonnies, and bigger bullets, too. The noise was much clearer. But the grasshopper wasn't staying to fight, unless retreat was a Russ trick of some kind. The grasshopper began streaking up the road toward Jason, and it was moving with the incomprehensible speed of Russ flying things. And Jason saw why it was fleeing. The grasshopper continued to rock erratically, and smoke was beginning to stream out behind it. Almost at once the grasshopper was passing over Jason, still moving at great speed, but shaking with mechanical failure. The machine was no higher than three tall trees above him, and Jason saw a sudden lick of flame shoot out of the grasshopper.

A different noise caught his ear, and he glanced back at the ruined buildings. Jonnies were pouring out of hiding—perhaps as many as fifty of them. Jason could hear fragments of their shouts and see them shaking their rifles above their heads in the characteristic gesture of Jonnie triumph. Jason flinched as he heard the screech of metal and then the roar of an explosion behind him. The grasshopper had cleared the hill and then crashed. Jason trembled with the fear of Russ retaliation—the many stories of implacable vengeance were terrifying. And another glance toward the Jonnies told Jason that he could afford to be a passive spectator no longer. At the sound of the explosion the Jonnies had started to trot uphill toward the wreck.

Jason had come through the shadows and depressions in the ground, and he began returning that way. He also was headed toward the crash, but the Jonnies wouldn't be looking for footprints here, so he didn't need to be cautious, not yet. They'd count the Russ dead and take what they could. The Jonnies didn't want a hilltowner, not today. They would take one if they found him, however, so when Jason reached the woods again he'd be careful.

Jason's light-footed, alert trot wove down a gully, behind an outcropping of rock and over the crest of the hill. Now he had the hill between him and the Jonnies for a safe length of time if they stuck to the roadway, as they generally did, and Jason would be well away by the time they arrived. He saw three deer dart into a copse within easy rifle range, and he regretted his need to dash back the way he had come. There would be no meat to bring home this trip, only news of strange and dangerous happenings.

He could smell an awful kind of smoke, and as he rounded a bend in his trail he saw the flaming wreck, barely two tree lengths away and squarely in his path. No one could be alive in that fire, but he stopped and nervously hefted his rifle anyway. He feared coming close to the Russ, even dead Russ. Jason looked for a way to bypass the inferno of the grasshopper without coming near its heat. But to his right was a sheer icy cliff, too dangerous to climb, and to his left a deeply shadowed field fell toward the roadway, two hundred meters of crusted snow marked by nothing heavier than rabbit tracks.

Jason resumed his trot, hurriedly retracing his morning's cautious trail, but he couldn't take his eyes off the burning helicopter. It was gigantic—much larger than he had thought. Even destroyed, it was magnificent, frightening and past understanding. The strange markings were already burned off the metal, and a large pine next to the wreck was ablaze from the fire. Jason stayed as close to the cliff as he could to avoid the heat. The Jonnies would be disappointed. No Russ body or booty could survive such intense destruction.

With great relief, Jason finally passed the wreck, jumped over a stream, and headed at a faster pace for the woods beckoning beyond an ancient pile of boulders where once a building of some kind had stood.

"Halt, Chaser!" The deep authoritative voice from behind him froze Jason. Locked in place by sudden terror, he didn't even move to turn around and see who spoke.

"Face me, you treacherous swine."

Jason turned, still clutching his rifle but with no thought of using it. He felt that his eyes must be bulging out of his head. This surely was a Russ, the first Jason had ever seen at close quarters. The man looked quite normal, however, and that was something of a disappointment. He was about Jason's age, and of approximately the same physical dimensions. But the Russ had straight, straw-colored and rather unruly hair—he evidently had lost his cap. Jason noted with some curiosity the fair complexion of the Russ. Jason and the others in his family had dark coloring and facial features that seemed formed for the very purpose of mirroring dark and worried thoughts.

"I suppose you Chasers thought you'd kill us all and simply take what you could salvage," the Russ said in a bitter tone. "That is the basest sort of treachery, agreeing to meet me and then ambushing me. I ought to kill you where you stand." He was pointing a handgun of some kind at Jason.

"Uh, uh, naw," Jason managed to say. "I didn't shoot you down. Saw from the hill back there. Jonnies, they shot you down. Headed here now. That's why I'm runnin'."

The Russ snorted. "Why would you run from your own kind?"

"They're not my kind." Despite his fear, he couldn't keep the contempt out of his tone. "They're Jonnies. They'd as soon kill me as you—that or take me to Hamp, and I'd rather be killed." He looked wildly back at the path he had traveled. "I saw em comin' this way. We both better run."

The Russ snarled a word Jason didn't understand. "I'm not afraid of that rabble," he said. "They'll take one look at my uniform and they'll fall in line." But he began to look thoughtful.

"They shot at you in that machine," Jason pointed out, shifting from foot to foot like a small boy with a full bladder.

"Can I run now? They'll kill me even if they won't kill you." His eyes kept straying back to the place where he knew the Jonnies would appear.

"Very well," the Russ said with a show of manly reluctance. "Perhaps it would be better if I took no chances." He had been half sitting on a protuberance of rock, but now he stood somewhat stiffly and straightened his collar. His uniform as well as his face was marked with smoke and grime, though Jason could see no wounds or signs of blood. "My name is Captain Aleksandr Iosifovich Brukov, and I command you in the name of the Russian Imperial Mission to offer me your full assistance. Otherwise I will kill you."

"Then hurry," Jason said. "I know where to go." Jason turned, suddenly trembling with the need for motion again, his fear of the Jonnies overwhelming his awe of the Russ.

"Hold on. You'll have to help me." Brukov hobbled toward Jason. "I must have turned an ankle." He was favoring his right foot.

"Surprised you lived," Jason said with a glance at the incinerated flying machine. "Here lean on my shoulder. We have to hurry." He offered his left shoulder to Brukov's hand.

"You may keep that ridiculous rifle," Brukov said, "but no treachery. This will make you look like my auntie's pincushion." He held up the Pushkin Series 2100 machine-pistol, which he had transferred to his left hand. It was powered by a slender gas cylinder suspended beneath the barrel, and each clip held two hundred plastic alloy pellets. It was extremely accurate and could indeed perforate a human target.

"I don't want to hurt anyone who hasn't hurt me," Jason said. "I just want to get away. Be quick. Don't step on snow. Jonnies won't notice mud tracks. Once they see that fire they prolly won't even look for you."

The pair hobbled to the stream and across it, trying to

become accustomed to the team concept of walking. When they reached the line of trees Brukov said, "Can we stop here and watch from hiding? I'd like to see these 'Jonnies' of yours."

"On a ways there's a spot. Up the hill."

"Of course," Brukov said. He didn't like to show the discomfort caused by his ankle. At least it didn't appear to be broken.

Jason adjusted his pace up the trail so that Brukov could limp along beside him. After the gusts of fear, confusion and dismay since first hearing the giant helicopter, Jason felt unaccountably light-hearted. He somehow felt confident that the Russ with his mysterious weapon and his complete self-assurance was more than proof against the Jonnies. So what if Brukov didn't even seem to know what Jonnies were? Anyone who could fly one of those machines could handle Jonnies. Jason felt almost tender toward Brukov. He wanted to be protected by this powerful man.

It took only a short time to reach a bald spot on the hill where the still-burning grasshopper could be seen. Brukov immediately appreciated his new companion's military instincts. The vantage point offered a good view, but did not invite return observation, and from where they sat on a rock, inconspicuous in the shade of the forest behind them, they had control of high ground with command of the trail they had used. They could not be easily outflanked as the terrain on either side of the trail was both rugged and thickly overgrown with brush.

"Here they come," Jason said almost at once. He nodded down toward the diminishing flames of the flying machine, and Brukov saw a ragged band of green-clad men crossing a field of snow toward the blaze. They were proceeding cautiously, fanning out to encircle the wreck.

"Fools," Brukov snorted. "They were so eager to assassinate me that they opened fire before we cut the engine. Another moment and we would have had no chance to escape."

"I saw you turned on the spraygun," Jason said shyly. "I thought that would kill em all."

"I imagine we frightened more Chasers than we killed. The craft was swinging like a leaf in the wind. Well..." he said abruptly, "they're obviously just going to warm their hands around the fire. Let's be going."

"Hold a bit." Jason remained intent on the scene below as Brukov rose and tested his ankle again. "Might as well be sure they don't pick up our trail. There's still a lot of daylight left and this is a better spot to use your spraygun than any place along the trail." Jason nodded respectfully at the machine-pistol and Brukov almost laughed out loud. The ignorant Chaser obviously thought the helicopter machine gun was the weapon he used as his sidearm.

"I have something even better if they come after us," Brukov said. A prayer of praise rose to his lips in thankfulness for the Imperial Mission regulations that he had so often ridiculed. He had counted on the helicopter armaments and the skills of the six men he commanded but now he would rely on the weapons he carried only because regulations were precise and unbending. He patted the three bombs in the pocket of the duty uniform, just short of battledress, that Mission personnel had to wear outside the patrolled borders of Co-ops. He thought it was best not to explain to this Chaser just what the weapons were or how many he had. The fellow seemed trustworthy enough, but Brukov had just had a near-fatal demonstration of the trustworthiness of Chasers.

"Get ready," Jason said grimly. "Jonnies on this side saw something. Look, they're talkin' it out now." He nodded toward the distant scene below them. Brukov could see that there was a conference of some sort underway with a couple of men pointing in the general direction of the trail the two fugitives had taken.

A slight figure at the center of the meeting finally waved the mob toward the trail. The green-coated figures advanced like a pack of wolves on the tundra, Brukov thought. He saw his new Chaser companion looking at him hopefully, as though any representative of the Russian Imperial Mission could protect him even against these odds.

Well, so he could, Brukov thought. It was part of his assignment to encourage that kind of respect and dependance. What children these Chasers seemed to be! "Go back into those woods so you avoid injury," Brukov told Jason. "Shout if you see them coming before I do." He didn't want one of these savages seeing him operate the weapon. They could learn to imitate very readily. That had been one of the lessons repeatedly stressed by Colonel Obolov during Mission Orientation.

Jason obediently retreated to a post behind a giant sugar maple, but he continued to watch Brukov intently. Jason still felt an odd sense of unreality. But here it was happening, sure enough. He knew he was not back in his camp, tossing under a bearskin and wrestling with visions that came to him in his sleep.

Brukov took out one of the bombs and activated the miniature gyroscope. He estimated the width of the trail that the Chaser mob would be funneled through and adjusted the angle of explosion. The bomb was perfect for the situation. Once it landed it would blast out a tiny hailstorm of shrapnel down the trail.

"Jonnies!" came the yell behind him as he completed activation of the bomb. He saw nothing at first; a moment later he heard a scrambling on the wooded trail and caught a glimpse of movement. The whole mob would be right behind, Brukov was sure. With the classic underhand lob mastered by every cadet at the Academy, he carefully lofted the bomb high in the air. He heard with irritation an amazed cry from his companion behind him.

The bomb landed on target and detonated at contact. The precision aiming of the gyroscope sometimes malfunctioned, and Brukov was leery of them ever since an Academy accident involving one of his classmates. This bomb was flawless and projected the shrapnel exactly in the narrow, concentrated pattern that had been set on its controls.

The withering bits of whistling metal had the effect intended. Cries of pain and terror could be heard over the final sputterings of the bomb, and the survivors were running back as fast as they could scramble down the trail.

Brukov limped toward Jason's hiding place with studied unconcern. "Do you think that will hold the savages for a bit?" he asked, unable to suppress a superior smirk at the incredulous gaping of his companion.

Jason was silent for a long moment, then barely grunted assent. He was seeing a lot today he had never seen before.

"Now," the Russian said briskly, "you may call me Captain, or Captain Brukov, as you prefer. And what is your name?"

"Jason Pembroke, Cap'n." He still was staring back at the trail where such swift carnage had occurred.

"Tell me, Jason, from your knowledge of these people..." he nodded back down the trail, "will they still pursue us or will they retire to lick their wounds?" Brukov continued to hold his machine-pistol, but he had already decided that Jason was no real threat. The poor fellow probably thought that anyone who could fly in a helicopter and throw bombs was nearly invincible. As, in fact, he was, thought Brukov.

"That'll stop em," Jason said. "Soon as they dry out their britches they might be back for wounded."

"But they won't follow us? How long will it be before they do this britches thing?"

Jason laughed. "Sorry, Cap'n. I don't think they'll follow, but no sayin' what a Jonnie will do. There's daylight left. We should hide till dark. Jonnies think night is Devil time. They won't be in the woods then."

Brukov looked up at the sky. "This will be a dark night," he said. "How will we move?"

"Oh, I know the way pretty well," Jason said with the air of one indulging in understatement.

"Very well, then we stay here until dark." Brukov prepared to sit and take the strain off his ankle, but Jason immediately shook his head.

"No" Jason said. "If they catch sight of us they might go crazy. I know a place. Not far. It'll be safe to wait there, at least if you've got more of them things like what you threw at the Jonnies." He grinned at Brukov, who said nothing. He simply sighed and leaned again on Jason's shoulder as they took ten steps and were wholly swallowed up by the forest.

‹ *Chapter Two* ›

JASON FOUND A HICKORY BRANCH with a knob at one end. A big-bladed knife suddenly appeared in his hand, startling Brukov, and with one practiced whack Jason cut the branch to perfect size for fitting under the Russian's arm. The rough-and-ready crutch was perfectly adequate for the circumstances, and the two men moved through the woods cautiously.

The path followed by Jason was lazily circuitous, but Brukov quickly realized its advantages. For one thing, hills, trees and rocks always provided cover while affording them views before and behind. For another, the winding path managed to carry them over rough terrain without providing any major obstacles or sharp grades. Before approaching wooded clumps of trees and brush that could invite an ambush, Jason silently halted Brukov and slipped off the trail, looping around the place of potential concealment and finally appearing on the trail ahead of Brukov, once again motioning him forward.

They had traveled a very short way, but taken considerable time to do it, when Jason struck off on a tangent to the path. A tiny stream, noisy with self-importance amid the placid scene of snow, spruce and silence, provided an alternate trail that left no tracks. Since the last snowfall there had been just enough traffic on the trail they had taken that their own foot prints couldn't be distinguished. But if they struck off across a meadow or through the trees, anyone following, even one not a woodsman, would tell immediately that they had diverged from the trail.

"Careful, Cap'n," Jason said, offering a hand to Brukov, who shook him off and picked his way with the crutch and one good leg. They stepped on flat stone washed clean of snow by the stream, and they were able to keep their boots fairly dry. Often solid flat ice along the edges of the stream offered a comfortable path for short distances.

Despite the body warmth generated by hiking, Brukov was considerably colder than he was at the start of the walk. The sun was well past midday and the shadows were lengthening. And despite the long time they had been walking, the Stavrogin helicopter could have covered the distance in the time it took to say a short prayer, Brukov was sure. The two men had made a steady climb away from the lowlands, eased by the gentle meandering of the path. The snow was deeper and more pervasive here.

Brukov had not raised his eyes since being led onto the stones of the stream, as the crutch made his stability extremely uncertain. Now, however, they had rounded several bends of the brook, and Jason had decided they were no longer in danger of being tracked, so they climbed onto the frozen bank. Brukov's breath was taken away by the sight. Spruce and hemlock boldly dotted the field with a brilliant green encrusted with snow and ice, and sprinkled among the evergreens were dozens of white birch, some of them leaning almost to the ground like a worshipper before an icon, some bent with age and split by dark lines of disease, some merely standing proud and vulnerable. The trees, the snow and the cold reminded Brukov of his grandfather's country home outside of Moscow, where a forest of evergreen and white birch had been tended by the Brukov family since the coming of True Russia. The hills, however, had a different character here, and though they had their charm,

Brukov felt in his breast a sharp longing for the wide plains and infinite horizons of his homeland. But this at least would do; it certainly was an improvement over the Co-ops of Chicago and Cleveland.

"Almost there, Cap'n," Jason said. "Hold a bit."

Brukov sighed and leaned heavily against the crutch, resting his ankle as Jason reconnoitered. Brukov admired the beauty of the field and chanted under his breath from the Roll of Humility, the prayer that the Elders of Crimea had devised to offset the complacency and self-esteem they detected in the Roll of Thanksgiving. Church rhetoric in True Russia had rapidly created a large and still-growing set of prayers, some of which seemed to appear almost spontaneously, entirely new but instantly recognizable as a deeply satisfying expression of a people's worship. Now even rural children with little or no education could recite the whole enormous prayer book, so deeply was it tied to daily life, and so instantly could even the ignorant Russian kulak recognize the wisdom and sureness of the words.

Jason returned, appearing abruptly from behind a nearby tree, and now he seemed relaxed. Apparently he thought there was no danger near.

"Come now, Cap'n. We'll rest till full dark."

Brukov resumed his hobbling and Jason fell in step beside him, again trimming his long stride to match the injured Russ. "We're not far from camp," Jason said. "Not much to worry about, not if the Jonnies are gone."

"Not much? There are other enemies here?"

"Not much," Jason repeated. "Bad dogs and whoever might be out and decide you've got something he wants. There's where we'll stay. Keeps out the wind." They approached a crumbled structure that once had been a silo. Its base was still intact, a circle of deteriorated but still-solid stones. They came to the entrance and Jason looked in warily. "Sometimes trouble with rats here," he explained. He threw in a stick and they heard scampering. "Not bad," he said. "Have to stay at the opening anyway."

Brukov entered the dark room and put his back to the wall near the entrance, then slid slowly to the ground, gingerly protecting his injured ankle as he put his legs out before him. "Even rats can't make me stand up any longer," Brukov said, finally allowing his voice to show his fatigue.

"Can't chance a fire," Jason said, also slumping to the ground inside the door but keeping a steady gaze on the field where they had left their tracks. "Can't let em catch us here. Jonnies never come this far off the road, but still..."

"Oh, we don't need a fire," Brukov said. "I have a heat tab." Jason looked on with wonder, but asked no questions as the Russian officer extracted what looked like a button from one of his many pockets and pulled away a piece of wire running through it. The chemicals were smokeless and odorless and caused no danger of fire. They simply radiated heat. It was so cold that Brukov and Jason had to huddle close to the heat tab to warm themselves. "This will last for about two hours," Brukov said. "Will that be long enough?"

"Sure," Jason said, though he wasn't at all sure what the magically equipped Russ was talking about.

Brukov laughed. "I was told in briefings that some of the Chasers of this region were laconic," Brukov said. "Men of few words."

"Well, you talk funny too," Jason said. "I never heard talk like that."

Jason warmed his hands, his eyes trying to understand his companion but frequently checking outside to make sure there were no intruders.

"I suppose my funny talk, as you say, is because I speak a variation of your language," Brukov said. "I've picked up yours pretty well. I speak English, which is slightly different from your version. I studied in England for a period, and my first tour with the Russian Imperial Mission was also in England."

"They talk that way there?"

"Well, I also have a slight Russian accent." Brukov relished this rustic interrogation and couldn't keep from smiling.

"And three names, too," Jason said.

Brukov laughed out loud. "Yes. Aleksandr Iosifovich Brukov. I am proud of my name. But even you have two names, and perhaps a third you didn't tell me."

"Just two," Jason said. "One more than anyone else in camp. My sister's idea. She always wins any argument, so I might as well not argue. Felicity wanted two names, wanted both of us to have family names. Pembroke, she decided. Makes use of it, too."

"Very sensible," Brukov said. "Families need to have names. We are proud of our names in Russia."

"Just words," Jason said absently, and Brukov felt anger flash through him involuntarily. Men of History were constantly battling the outrageous, almost provocative ignorance and insensitivity of the savages they had to deal with.

"I have many things to ask you about besides your name," the Russia said somewhat sharply.

"I don't know much." Jason said it with such resignation, shaking his head, that Brukov again took pity on him. And after all, the fellow had been shrewd enough in the woods to help him escape.

"Tobacco?" Brukov asked, offering a cigarette.

Jason hesitated only a moment. "Believe I will," he said, taking the cigarette and examining it closely. "They got these little smokes down to the Valley," he finally said. "They don't last long. Got a pipe back to the camp."

"So you do grow tobacco around here?" Brukov lit both their cigarettes.

"In the valley where the farms are. Jonnies don't like smokes, but some of the farmers grow it anyway. We trade for it."

"And these Jonnies... who are they?" Brukov wished he had more closely questioned the Chaser who had arranged the meeting that had been an ambush. But the Russian experience was that Chasers always could be bought cheaply. Their material greed was boundless, and Russian Imperial Mission power was so overwhelming that Brukov hadn't even considered the possibility of treachery. His excessive confidence had cost the lives of his men and the loss of his helicopter.

"Tell me about these Jonnies," Brukov said.

Jason shrugged with unconcern. "People down at the Hamp. They believe in religion. They got good bullets." He looked up slyly. "You saw that," he said.

"What kind of religion?"

"Just religion. They kill for it. Mostly folks stay in camps up in the hilltowns. Jonnies'll come and kill and take everything you've got."

"I had assumed..." Brukov said, beginning to realize that both his assumptions and his briefings were sketchy, "I had assumed that all the Chasers outside the Co-ops were essentially alike."

"Naw," Jason said, relaxed and unconcerned. "Nobody's alike. Only the Jonnies. They're all alike. But there ain't many people up in the hilltowns." His voice again was slow and thoughtful, a little sad. "Not many. Some went to the Jonnies. Some went to Boston. Hoping it's safe in the Co-ops."

"It is safe in the Co-ops," Brukov said, returning Jason's shrewd appraising stare. "All the Co-ops are safe. But you people who are left aren't safe. Why do you stay? It can't be easy in this climate, and not with these Jonnie raiding parties. Why stay?"

"Couldn't say." Jason shrugged. "Might be better here than somewhere else, I guess."

Brukov had removed his boot and was wrapping his swollen ankle with a firm elastic tape. He was excited by this discovery of Jason and the Jonnies, all Chasers but all quite different. Even in the Co-op of Chicago he had begun to suspect, but had hardly dared to think it, contrary as it was to accepted Russian wisdom. But what if it were true? What if the Chasers were varied in their beliefs and at least moderately complex in their social organizations. What if all the Russian generalizations about Chasers were simply based on ignorance? Brukov could make a career out of stirring that pot. He grinned at the thought of the outrage his fellow officers would express at such an idea. To them, Chasers certainly were all alike—none of them half the value of a good horse or a hunting dog.

"There. That should hold it," Brukov said, pulling his boot back on and standing to test the ankle. It hurt, but he thought he'd be able to limp along at a moderate pace.

"I'm interested in old weapons, Jason," Brukov said. "Mind if I look at your rifle?" Jason silently handed over the rifle, first glancing out again at the darkening landscape. The Jonnies wouldn't be following anymore.

"Very heavy," Brukov said. The feel of the rifle was good, like the ancient hunting rifles his grandfather collected. The barrel was stamped "Remington," presumably an old Chaser gun maker, and Jason had kept both the machine-tooled metal and the wooden stock polished and in good condition. It was a bolt-action weapon, which marked it as extremely old despite its continuing everyday use, and Brukov noted that it was equipped to take a clip of cartridges, though none was in the breach. He worked the bolt and extracted the single cartridge.

"Why only one shot?" Brukov asked, looking first at the rifle chamber and then at Jason, but he already guessed the answer.

"Right springs are too hard to come by," Jason said, echoing what he had been told by Billy, the man in camp who took care of steel. "What we can get from one place or another we use for the firing pins if we can make em fit." Jason paused "Besides, using a clip just jams a gun. Not even half the bullets go off and a lot of em ain't too good. Just jam. This way you just pry one out and put another in. Lot simpler that way."

"All your cartridges are this bad, eh?" Brukov asked, speaking mostly to himself. The bullet was misshapen and badly fitted, and the casing was battered. The rim was bent, and obviously the casing had been used many times before. "You save all your shells for re-use?"

Jason nodded. "Hard to come by," he said and then paused, "...not like your spraygun, huh?"

Brukov laughed, patting the machine-pistol in its holster. "No, not like this," he said. He thought of the two hundred pellets packed into the Pushkin's handle. The engineering was so reliable that there hardly ever was a jamming, even squeezing off clip after clip at full automatic. A soldier only had to stop to change the compressed gas cylinder every ten or twelve clips at normal pressure. At full pressure, a cylinder would last only two clips, but the pellets had such velocity that two clips could cut a hole in a brick wall. It was a very dangerous weapon, one that was restricted to Imperial Mission officers. They weren't issued at all in Russia.

"Want a biscuit?" Jason asked, pulling a cloth wrapped lump from his pocket.

"Ah... no, thank you," Brukov said, eyeing the leaden baked dough with suspicion. "I'll just take a capsule." He reached into a breast pocket, removed a plastic envelope, took out a pill and swallowed it as Jason looked on with fascination.

"That really food, Cap'n?"

Brukov smiled. "Let's say it's nutrition designed for Imperial use in situations such as this. The capsules hardly take the place of caviar and sour cream."

Jason nodded as though he understood. "Soon it'll be dark," Jason said. "Ain't far to go, but we got to be careful, it'll take a while."

"You don't have many questions, Jason. I think in your place I'd be intensely curious."

"About what?" Jason had reclaimed his rifle and sat with it cradled in his arms as he gazed steadily out of the door crudely cut into the ancient silo.

"About the Russian Imperial Mission, about me, about what happens next. All those things." Brukov warmed his hands over the heat tab, already insufficient as the cold clamped down on the hillside.

Jason shrugged. "The Jonnies shot at you the same as they shoot at us. People in the hilltowns know better than to shoot at the Russ. You people never made trouble for us. You're the first Russ I seen up close."

"So people in the hills just want to be left alone?"

Jason relaxed as though a great truth had been stated. "That's it," he said, nodding sagely. "That's surely it."

"You must be like your ancestors," Brukov said. He had been studying texts diligently since coming to the Americas, popularly known as Chaser Two, but his duties left little time and he had only been in Chaser Two for a few months. His classes at the Academy had concentrated almost exclusively on Chaser One, Old Europe, with the Americas largely ignored. Industrial ingenuity and energy for one short period before the great famines, with political ascendancy for the same brief period. That was practically the sole theme sounded in teaching about Chaser Two. And, of course, the erratic political opposition to the Second Enslavement. Brukov wished he had taken some of the unpopular courses concerning the subject. Too late now.

"Felicity," Jason laughed. "You sound like Felicity.

Ancestors." He laughed again, pleasantly, as though fondly indulging a rather simple friend. "Felicity's smart, but she's sure wrong-headed." He seemed blissfully unaware that his words might have insulted Brukov.

"It must be dark enough to leave," Brukov said coldly. He must remember to be correct, absolutely correct, in his dealings with Chasers. A single Imperial Mission officer could handle any number of Chasers, as had been proven time and again, but formal distinctions must be maintained in order for discipline to be unquestioned.

"Sure," Jason said, standing. "Dark's falling." He took a step out of the silo and stood motionless, sniffing the air, searching the tree line with his eyes, opening his senses to whatever impressions he might instinctively draw out of the air. There was no feeling of danger. The clouds were thick and unbroken. No smell of snow, but the clouds would keep the night dark. He himself would have waited until much later, just to be safe, but he could tell that the Russ was getting restless. He wondered if the whole Russ race talked so much and had so little patience.

‹ *Chapter Three* ›

IT SEEMED TO BRUKOV during the next few hours that they had walked backward in time from early spring into the middle of winter. He felt his body involuntarily shrink, as though drawing into itself to ward off the cold, and his lungs protested against the temperature of the oxygen they inhaled. Had it been a cloudless night, Brukov knew, even more of the earth's heat would fly away, a wind might spring up, and his limping journey into these alien hills would seem like a perfect torture.

As it was, he steeled himself as a good soldier must, and blessed the quality of his winter-issue Imperial Mission duty uniform.

It was too dark for Brukov to check his compass regularly, as no reference points could be distinguished, so he trusted to Jason and kept his Pushkin machine-pistol at the ready. The crunch of the frozen snow marked their pace as they cautiously moved through the woods, and even without compass readings Brukov could tell that they were proceeding circuitously. Jason moved with great sureness, but so slowly that Brukov had no difficulty in maintaining the pace, despite his protesting ankle and the steady uphill grade of their path. Dogs or coyotes were heard occasionally, awakening in Brukov faint stirrings of ancestral fears—Russians respond reflexively to suggestions of night journeys across frozen snow amid the sound of wolves. But they saw no animals at all, and Jason seemed completely unconcerned, so Brukov bore his anxiety with composure.

"This is the last real hill," Jason said quietly.

"Good," Brukov said. "I'll not be sorry to end this hike."

"Want to take a rest for your ankle?"

"No. Let's get it over with." Brukov began to realize how exhausted he was. Since he had last slept, he had been shot down in a helicopter, hurt his ankle, fought off a horde of barbarians, and walked for miles through glacially frozen woods. It was the very stuff of survival training at the Academy.

After the steepest climb of the journey they finally broke through a dense grove of oak and cedar trees and into the beginnings of a town.

"Everyone's asleep," Brukov said when they stopped so he could regain his breath, "apparently including the guard."

"This ain't camp," Jason replied. "This is Ash. Ain't no one here. Camp's a little on."

Brukov tried not to show his disappointment that the painful trek had not yet ended. As they continued along the now-level ground, the Russian could see how the gathering of buildings that had once been a town had been named. The deep darkness of the night had prevented him from seeing at once that all the houses were burnt-out shells, crumbled and useless. They passed one structure that seemed to be still standing and complete, though in the dark it was hard to be sure. They were at a distance from the buildings, still hiking parallel to the old road, easily distinguishable between the rows of houses despite the snow. Jason wanted to avoid meeting anyone else, and Brukov could tell that it was a habit of caution that had been hard learned and was now deeply ingrained.

On the other side of what had been the town of Ash, they crossed another old road, one that had been marked by considerable human traffic since the last snow, though no vehicles had been on it that Brukov could discern from the tracks. This really was the wilds of Chaser Two.

Through the biting cold they trudged, Brukov concentrating on the next step, then the next, praying the Roll of Penance as he walked.

Then up a gentle hill and through a curtain of trees they came to what Jason appropriately had called a camp. Brukov's powers of observation were clouded by fatigue and pain, as well as the starless night, but his training as a soldier forced him to notice a random scattering of huts dotting the snow in a clearing just far enough into the woods to escape casual detection.

"Lo, Jason" a voice said. Startled, Brukov jerked his head toward the voice and noticed a shadow detach itself from a tree and take a few steps toward them, a rifle in seeming carelessness angled in their general direction.

"Lo, Hammon. Just checkin' to make sure you're awake." It was the standard joke of hunters and others returning to the area at night. Hammon almost always was the self-appointed guard. For some reason he could sleep comfortably only during the day, Jason told the Russian. His nocturnal restlessness had been of considerable aid to the camp more than once.

"What game this time, Jason? Don't look like no deer to me."

Despite his fatigue, Brukov bristled at the vulgar jocularity, but he held his tongue.

"Someone needs rest for a sore ankle, Hammon. Sleep's what we both want." Brukov could read in Jason's calm words a decision not to get into a discussion about the fact that his companion was a Russian. Brukov's uniform probably was indistinguishable in the dark, and in any event, this Hammon fellow probably had never seen such a uniform before. In a way, Brukov thought with some amusement, Jason is protecting me. As he has for the entire journey of a few kilometers and many long hours, Brukov reminded himself, and he was almost touched by the thought.

The guard simply gestured at them with his hand and melted into a tree again. Brukov hobbled after Jason, who moved more rapidly and with less tension now that he was in his own encampment. They came to one of the huts and Jason tugged at a rope next to the door. It evidently activated some sort of signaling device within the building.

"Felicity will unbar for us," Jason said, then nodded his head toward the east. "Gettin' ready to crack dawn," he said.

Brukov looked up and saw that it was now possible to discern a lighter shade above the line of treetops. There was a knock of wood from within the cabin and the door abruptly opened.

"Hurry on," a voice said from within three layers of bed-clothes wrapped around her. "Don't lose what little heat we have. No meat, Jason?"

"Didn't hunt much. Got a Russ, though," He nodded toward Brukov. "Cap'n, this is my sister, Felicity."

"Honored," Brukov said with a bow. Only the wood stove that she had poked and stoked back into quick life provided light in the single room of the hut, and Brukov couldn't even see the woman's face.

"Sleep's what we need," Jason said.

"You been out all night?"

"All night."

"I'll stay up then," the woman said. "It's almost time to get up anyway. You use my bed." She looked at Brukov and nodded toward a disheveled cot. Out of the hood covering her head he thought he saw a glint of curiosity in an eye caught by the fire's blaze, but he merely mumbled something under his breath, hobbled to the cot, eased his ankle up so he was stretched out, and at once fell asleep, fully clothed.

‹ *Chapter Four* ›

HE AWOKE IN HIS underclothes, his boots removed, rough woolen blankets uncomfortably warm. He could feel her stare even before he saw the girl on the padded bench near the stove. Her eyes were fixed on his with such intensity that Brukov felt sure that her gaze hadn't wavered for hours.

"Good morning," the Russian said, throwing the blankets to the foot of the bed but keeping the bottom sheet, evidently some kind of flannel, so that he wouldn't be exposed in his underwear.

"You're the first Russ ever been to camp," she said in a flat tone, obviously uninterested in polite chatter. "You speak our language." It wasn't really a question.

"Yes. I take a certain pride in it." He didn't want to confuse her with facts beyond her grasp, but the truth was that most Imperial Mission officers, more military men than Men of History, learned only a few phrases of pidgin English, enough to manage in the Co-ops. English was considered decadent, perhaps even evil, by many Russians. But Brukov wanted to understand Chasers, not just manipulate them. Too many Russians, even Men of History, discounted Chasers. The deeply satisfying fulfillment of True Russia was still in an early stage, and few of those participating in that fulfillment were interested in dead civilizations. But a few Russians, Brukov among them, sensed that Chasers had more to offer than a supply of servants and machinery.

"You can read, too," she said. Again it was a statement of fact.

"Certainly I can read." Brukov laughed. "This is an unusual conversation so soon after waking."

She wouldn't be deterred. "Nobody here can talk any different than I'm talking right now. And nobody can read."

"Would you mind turning your back while I dress?"

She laughed abruptly, the first break in her intense monotone, and Brukov was surprised at both the unaffected delight of the sound and its well-modulated quality. It was the laugh of a person of breeding, almost a Russian laugh, and it took Brukov off guard.

"Are the Russ all shy?" Her face now was animated and the glint in her eye had become a sparkle. The thin, dark, almost witch-like face that had been peering at him had taken on life. She was not pretty, he thought, but she might be attractive.

"We are all taught modesty, particularly in the presence of the opposite sex." He wouldn't bother to explain the lashing prayer of the Roll of Concupiscence, whose abjurations of physical display barely stopped short of demanding facial veils. Every school child trembled at the terrible threats of the Roll of Concupiscence.

"To please you, then, I'll turn my back," she said. "But I did undress you, you know. I looked real good, too."

Brukov felt his face blaze with color, much hotter than the wood stove warranted. "Please do turn away."

She apparently had decided the joke was over. She simply rose and said matter-of-factly, "I'll stir up some food for you. Jason's still asleep." She walked to the stove and began poking a wooden spoon into an iron pot that she slid to the center of the hottest section of the stovetop.

Brukov hastily drew on his uniform, first trousers, then shirt and his duty jacket to make sure all his gear was in place. Nothing had been tampered with. Even his Pushkin machine-pistol was securely holstered. Jason was on a cot across the room, snoring lightly.

"What time is it?" Brukov asked absently, then punched his chronometer to see for himself. Thirteen twenty-seven.

"A little after midday. Here's some food. Jason brought you back instead of meat, so you'll have to make do with oats and bread."

Brukov hesitated a moment, wary of Chaser food. He had plenty of his food capsules left, and they provided sufficient nutrition. But he didn't want to insult his hostess and the "oats" smelled good. "Thank you. I am very hungry. Ouch," he involuntarily cried out, surprised at the sharp pain in his ankle as he moved toward the small deal table where she placed the bowl, a loaf of bread, a small wooden spoon and a knife.

"Hurt bad?"

"I had forgotten how tender it is. It will be perfectly fine in a day or two." Better not show weakness when one is alone in a Chaser camp, he thought. Certainly not until he had a chance to get the feel of the place. Co-op Chasers usually were docile enough, and Jason had been benign, but Chasers had destroyed his helicopter and crew and there was no telling what the disposition of Jason's associates might be. Brukov sat and tentatively tasted the food, which proved to be a delicious kind of gruel not unlike a Russian peasant dish.

"What's your name?"

"My apologies," Brukov said, pushing back his wooden stool, rising to attention and bowing formally. "Captain Aleksandr Iosifovich Brukov of the Russian Imperial Mission." He regained his seat.

"How very wonderful," she said, and seemed to mean it. She sat on another stool across the table from him and continued to watch him closely. "My name is Felicity Pembroke. Do all the Russ have three names?"

"Yes, most of them," he said, cutting off a chunk of bread that seemed darker and more substantial than anything available in the Co-ops. "We are very proud of our names, foolishly proud at times. There is a thriving business in Russia of tracing family names. Some go back to before the first enslavement."

"What was that?" Her eyes had the glitter of excitement in them.

Brukov laughed. "This is very good bread. Almost like what we have in Russia."

"What about enslavement?"

"We had what we call the Two Enslavements before the emergence of True Russia." Surely there could be no harm in discussing common history with a Chaser woman? He tried to consider any possible reasons to be wary and could think of none. But he was a cautious man, and it might be faintly uncomfortable, even blasphemous, to talk about Holy Russia with a non-Russian. She was the first Chaser he'd met to show any interest.

"I don't know any of what you say." Her voice was under tight control. "I want to know all of it. Is an Enslavement why you're here? We've never had a Russ around here before."

He laughed at her burning seriousness and her obvious curiosity. "Now I see the truth of the old saying, 'The Star-Chaser looks for the absent deer while the Russian eats the rabbit.' You Chasers really do shoot off in all directions. We Russians are a steady flame."

"You should be careful of calling people 'Chasers.' A man got hit the other day for doing that."

"What?" Brukov looked up from wiping up the bowl of gruel

with a piece of bread.

"It was Morg," Felicity said. "Morg was in Boston Co-op some while ago," Felicity continued, "and he picked up some ideas. A fellow from another camp came by the other day and they were talking. The fellow wanted to go hunting. Morg's as good a hunter as Jason, and the fellow wanted Morg to go hunting with him. Morg said if he went he wanted more than half the meat because he's the better hunter and the fellow kind of laughed and said, 'Ain't that just like a Chaser,' and Morg didn't say anything, he just real quick got even redder than he always is and hit the fellow with his fist and walked away. The fellow finally got himself up and just went away without a word. Morg's no one to fight against."

"Well, you outfought him," they heard a voice say. Jason was sitting up and stretching, unselfconscious in his tattered underwear. "He never had a chance against you, Felicity."

"Mind your own business or keep your own cabin," she said, flashing with anger and indeed looking as though she could outfight most men, despite her slender frame. She seemed furious at her brother's interruption, and Brukov noted the possible implied relationship between Felicity and Morg. But for now he wanted to overcome this confounded Chaser habit of shooting from one subject to another without ever explaining anything fully.

"But why would this Morg be angry at being called a 'Chaser'?" Brukov asked. "After all, that's what he is, just as I'm a Russian. 'Star-Chaser' is just an easy way to describe you people west of Russia. It's not pejor... there's nothing bad about it. It's even rather affectionate. 'Chaser' simply refers to the way you people are. Why would that anger anyone?"

"Everthin' sets Morg off," Jason said as he fastened his trousers and approached the stove to fill his bowl with gruel. Felicity's ferocity obviously had long since ceased to impress him.

"Perhaps he was mad because the Russ decided the name he would be called," Felicity said with renewed tartness. "But he told me once that he hated being called 'Chaser' in the Co-op. He said the Russians there made him feel like dirt, talking away in their own language, laughing at people, talking our language so you couldn't understand it and calling everyone 'Chaser'. He said he never wants to hear that word again. Morg hates the Russ."

"Well, I don't know what you're talkin' about," Jason said, using a foot to drag a stool to the table while he held a full wooden bowl in both hands, "but you can call me 'Chaser' anytime you want, Cap'n."

"Do many others in the camp feel the way Morg does about Russians?" Brukov asked.

"Don't worry," Jason said quickly. "Most of em don't care and none of em has a spraygun."

Brukov said nothing in reply, but glanced again at Felicity. She thought a moment and then quietly said, "They're afraid of Russ. No one wants to take a chance on getting hurt. They won't like you, maybe, but they'll leave you alone."

"Including Morg?"

"Morg is a coward," Felicity said with contempt, her dark angular features visually framing the scorn of her words.

"I never saw anyone who got so hot about everthin' in the world," Jason said to Brukov, half apologizing for his sister. He laughed in an odd, shy way, glancing at his sister, who pointedly ignored him.

"That was a good breakfast, Felicity," Brukov said with a slight bow.

"Thank you... Aleksandr." And she too made a formal movement of an indeterminate but unmistakable nature.

"Felicity," Jason said, a warning tone in his voice.

"That's perfectly all right," Brukov said, quickly making a

decision that he'd have to drop some formality if he wanted to get closer to these people. Only his fellow officers, family or fiancée in Russia called him by his given name, which had a special resonance because he was named for the first saint of True Russia, but the rules of civil conduct could be adjusted for the realities of Chaser Two. He felt faintly, but deliciously, wicked about his decision to allow himself to be addressed familiarly by inferiors.

"He calls you Jason and me Felicity," the dark girl said to her brother in a tone of stubborn logic. She turned toward Brukov with a smile and said, "It's a pleasure to know you, Aleksandr."

"And I am grateful for the hospitality shown me by you and your brother, Miss Pembroke."

They all laughed, Brukov not the least, flushed by the sudden pleasures of unexpected comradeship and charmed by the girlish delight Felicity took in being addressed formally.

Their enjoyment was interrupted by a rap at the door. "Jason, you in there?"

"Oh, flup," Jason said with resignation in his voice. He rose with effortless fluidity from his stool, went to the door and unbarred it.

"Sam the bullet-maker," Felicity said quietly.

"Come in, Sam," Jason said. A short, fat man who seemed to Brukov to look like a character actor from a Chekov play burst into the room in an obvious state of some agitation.

"Hammon says you didn't get meat," Sam said, waving his arms awkwardly. "Did you miss? What about my bullets?" He abruptly stopped his ranting as he saw Brukov.

"Slept late," Jason said. "Had to eat before I took em to you." Jason reached into a pocket and extracted the cartridges, examined them somewhat ruefully, them dropped them into Sam's open palm.

The bullet-maker was less aggressive after seeing Brukov,

however, and he made conciliatory noises. "It's only that someone else may need em before you go out huntin' again, Jason. I need my meat," he added, patting his ample stomach in a weak attempt at self-deprecating humor.

"Sure, Sam. See you before I go out again. Get you some meat next time." He made no attempt to introduce Brukov or to explain his presence. He ushered the bullet-maker out and barred the door.

"He seems a nervous fellow," Brukov said.

"He's seen Russ before," Jason explained. "If I said I was goin' to keep the bullets, he'd say, 'You do that Jason,' and run out the door." He gave a short laugh.

"Even that inferior grade of cartridge is hard to come by, eh?" He noted that Felicity snorted with contempt at his question.

"That's the only kind of bullet in the hills," Jason said. "Sam knows how to load em. He gets powder down to the Valley. Quite a trader, Sam is."

"What does he trade with?"

"Potato lightnin' mostly. Potatoes are about the only crop in the hilltowns. Best one, anyway. Jonnies only drink water, at least they say so. They go hard on farmers if they catch em with a still. Sam moves his around out in the woods so even I can't find it. Jonnies don't come up here very much anyway."

"Potato lightning," Brukov said, shaking his head. "What an amusing name. It must resemble vodka. I'll have to try some."

"There's a crock full over in the corner," Felicity said. "But Jason, don't you get him started. You're enough trouble by yourself." She turned again to Brukov. "What did you say potato lightning was like?"

"Vodka. We call it our national burden."

"It's just a Russ drink, then?"

"Yes. Often made with potatoes, and all too often in hidden distilleries. We call that kind of vodka 'samogon'. But it's a little too early in the day for me to drink."

"It's too early for everyone," Jason said. "Potato lightnin' takes a little time gettin' used to. Strangers sometimes drink a little too much." He didn't want the Russ to get a crock full and wave his spraygun around. It wasn't hard to imagine, given what strangers sometimes did after their first encounter with potato lightning.

"It sounds like quite a drink," Brukov said.

"Jonnies sometimes kill drunks," Jason warned. "It's against their religion."

"Jonnies are the ones who ought to be killed," Felicity snapped. Brukov could swear that the color of her eyes changed as anger instantly swept away the playful glint. "That's what you ought to be doing," she said to Brukov. "We can't do it. Our people don't have the strength." Her voice was deep with scorn. "The Russ have the guns, the engines, the army. They should kill the Jonnies."

"Perhaps we shall," Brukov said. "After all, they almost killed me. They did kill my men and destroy Imperial Mission property. But I am not the one to decide the fate of the..." he forced the strange word from his tongue, 'Jonnies'. My superiors make such decisions. In fact, the attack on my helicopter may already have brought considerable retaliation."

"If that means thumpin' Jonnies, I hope not," Jason said. "Just make em meaner to us."

"You two get out of here while there's still light," Felicity said abruptly, grabbing the utensils from the table. "I'll clean up your mess. Jason, take the Russ over to Billy's place. Look around some if you want, but go to Billy's. Astid left the other day and Billy says the extra bed's just going to get in his way. You can borrow. I've got some meat buried in the snow, but tomorrow or soon you'll have to go out again. Better get those bullets back from Sam. Now go."

The two men, recognizing the force of her will, rose at once, put on their coats and left.

"Don't mind Felicity," Jason said, standing outside the door as he blinked and squinted to accustom his eyes to the sunlight. "She's always tight. When someone crosses her you could light a fire with her eyes. No one ever saw a woman cause so much trouble," he added with a sad resignation that seemed comic to Brukov.

"It doesn't bother me all," he said. "Besides, you can always marry her off and get rid of her."

"She already married once but she came back," Jason said, and his tone persuaded Brukov not to pursue the subject.

"The camp's larger than I guessed last night," Brukov said, measuring the scene before him with a practiced eye. The cabins, almost interchangeable one-room log affairs, seemed to be scattered at random, but Brukov's training let him see at once that they formed a protected, irregular-oblong common where people could conduct their public business and socializing with easy access provided only from the two ends of camp. Brukov and Jason had entered the night before from the south, and the aching muscles in his thighs reminded the Russian of the gentle but protective slope he had climbed. In the sunlight it looked like the most pleasant and bucolic of scenes, but the trees near the camp provided a clear field of fire into the extensive meadows between the camp and the abandoned town of Ash. The northern end of the camp provided only a narrow trail that quickly wound out of sight, bordered on one side by a rocky cliff and on the other by dense woods. A small but swift-flowing stream cut through one corner of the camp, providing an adequate water supply. The camp obviously couldn't be defended against any determined assault, but it did provide a margin of safety in an apparently lawless area of Chaser Two. Probably safer than many of the Co-ops, Brukov ruefully conceded to himself.

"Lo, Marth." Jason waved to a woman walking toward the common. A pair of five-year-olds, the only children in sight, darted around her skirts, sneaking glances at the stranger. Brukov was to note time and again that the inhabitants of the camp, with the notable exception of Felicity, either had no curiosity about him or actively worked to stifle it. It was a habit of in-bred complacency that the vigorous young Russian found both irritating and inexplicable.

"How do you get by on such little ammunition, Jason? I'd think you'd need to stockpile some, if only for self-protection."

"Hard winter, Cap'n. I try to stay ahead. Got to. But Sam didn't get much powder this winter. Us here in the camp got to get more and more meat to trade for bullets, and game got scarce for a while. A couple of deer will get me ahead again."

"And these cartridges are so unreliable. It is to pray to think what could happen when one of those pathetic things misfires."

"Only got to worry if you're shooting at a bear or a man. If it's a man, chances are, he's got a bad bullet too. I never go outside the cabin without this." Jason patted the large but well concealed knife that had so startled Brukov the night before. "Had to use it on live animals once or twice," he added with a sly smile crossing his dark, angular face. Jason had the same features and even the same expressions as his sister, Aleksandr noted, but the brother's uncomplaining and uninterested demeanor was transformed in Felicity into an excited, mercurial, unsettled and unsettling intensity. The trustworthy stolidity in Jason was a raging and unpredictable fire in Felicity. Brukov could feel that curiosity and intensity in her, and the strain of volatility troubled him. "This is Billy's?" Brukov asked.

"Yup." Jason agreed, rapping with unexpected force against the door of the cabin, one of the rare two-room buildings in camp.

"In," a high voice came to them from the cabin, and Jason opened the door and led the way inside.

Billy was a wiry man of medium height and obviously in a state of nervous disorganization. Jason didn't bother to introduce the Russian officer, but Billy seemed to know who he was and to accept his presence.

"Jason!" Billy exclaimed with relief. "I was just goin' for you. Astid left. Said she was goin' to Boston Co-op." He was stuffing various fabrics and small items into what looked like a canvas rucksack. "I'm goin' after her."

"They was married," Jason explained to Brukov, and then said to Billy, "Not a good idea, Billy. Can't do somethin' like that. Maybe she won't like Boston and come on back."

"I don't care," Billy said. "I thought how to talk to her. I'm goin' to follow. Always had her own bed anyway."

"That's what I come over for, Billy. To borrow. I'll swop."

"Sure. Look after this place while I'm gone and you can have it. If I get her back we won't need no two beds," Billy said rather grimly.

"Well," Jason thought for a moment before speaking further. "We'll talk when you get back."

"But you will look after this place? I'm leaving soon as full dark comes. Don't want to travel in daylight."

"I'll watch the cabin. How long you be gone?"

Billy shrugged. "I guess till I find Astid and talk to her."

"Bad idea, Billy."

"Will you or won't you?" The wiry man asked, stopping to look at Jason and ready to be angry.

"Sure. Can I show the Cap'n your steel?"

"I'll do it," Billy said with a sudden switch of mood. "I'm ready and can't leave yet anyway." He glanced at the Russian officer and quickly looked away.

"In here," Billy said. The workroom was the larger of the two rooms, and it was overcrowded with metal objects. "I'm the steel-man," Billy said proudly, but it was obvious that for the people of this settlement, 'steel' was the word used for anything metallic.

The shop was tidy despite its lack of capacity, with all the objects sorted according to size and, sometimes, function. The largest item was an ancient gasoline engine in one corner, smartly polished despite its utter lack of utility, and the smallest items probably were the tiny finishing nails that were heaped in a crock. There was every size in between, and Brukov was particularly amused by a stack of truck wheel rims near the door. They were engineered to a standard that had long since been discarded.

"Quite a collection of memorabilia you have here, Billy," Brukov said with condescending admiration.

"I keep it all cleaned up whether it's worthwhile or not. Hardest work is the guns. Got to fix em when they break, and that's not easy. Not with all those little screws and pins, and the bullets got to fit just so." He led the way to a small arsenal of firearms—only a few side arms, Brukov noted, and no automatic weapons. Many of the guns were in a state of obvious disrepair.

But what really caught Brukov's attention was a trio of shotguns heaped together on the floor. "Look at those beauties," he said.

"Nah, they're no good," Billy said with disgust. "Found em in a cellar over to Ash. Shot and shell, too." He motioned to a set of small kegs and a large carton next to the shotguns. "Big disappointment. No riflin' at all left in the guns. Couldn't hit a wall with em. Shells way too big, not even steel. Fit the chamber but the shot's all wrong. Too small. Sam the bullet-maker checked. No good at all, he said."

Brukov bent over the guns, suppressing the impulse to laugh out loud at the fool. It was apparent that no one in the settlement knew what a shotgun was. No rifling indeed!

"Let me just take a look," Brukov said, and Billy motioned him on with an air of resignation.

One of the shotguns was indeed useless. It was an antique double-barreled model, apparently with Damascene barrels. Brukov's grandfather had told him of the type known as Damascus steel. Very valuable collector's items, but unsafe to shoot. The other two shotguns appeared to have been well tended by Billy, and when Brukov checked the pump action of the 20-gauge, it operated smoothly. He then picked up the other gun, a 12-gauge automatic. It had a five-shot magazine and was remarkably similar to his grandfather's favorite hunting weapon. There were spots of rust, but the gun seemed salvageable.

Uninterested in Brukov's scrutiny of worthless guns, Jason and Billy began discussing one of the rifles against the wall, Jason with an eye to purchase. Brukov checked the kegs. Each held a different size of shot. He then fumbled open the carton and found the nicest surprise yet. The shells, as Billy had said, were not metallic—they were plastic, and of relatively modern design. The loads were the same kind as his father used—the kind that needed only to be tamped into the shell. Shot went on top, then a plastic wad and a crimp. At the back of the carton was a long row of the plastic wads, packed up against a metal device that looked like a corkscrew. One turn of that and the plastic shell was perfectly crimped. Brukov closed the carton and decided to say nothing for the moment.

"Problem is, Billy, I ain't got much meat lately. Hard to pay what I don't got." Jason eyed the rifle with sad longing.

"Well, I took too much time fixin' it to let it go cheaper."

"I know, Billy, I know."

"Would you mind, Billy," Brukov interrupted, "if I looked at those old guns while you're gone? I'd like to experiment with them."

"Welcome to em."

"Thank you, Billy," Brukov said with his air of princely condescension, which more fascinated than offended his unpolished listeners. "I think I might render them operational."

"They work now, if that's what you mean," Billy said, uncertain how to address this visitor whose wrath must not be incurred, no matter what. Everyone he had talked to said the stranger was best handled politely and quickly. The less to do with the Russ the better. "I worked on em this winter," Billy added. "Just some rust left to take off. But them shells don't make sense. Too big. And no riflin'. Someone been to Boston Co-op told me you people paraded with fancy guns." He had been looking away as he talked to Brukov, but now he stole a quick glance. "Maybe they're somethin' like that, fancy guns but not to shoot with."

"I think not," Brukov laughed. "But thank you for letting me inspect them."

"Will you help me with the bed, Cap'n?" Jason asked.

The two men went back into the living area of the building and began appraising their job. Jason left the bedding intact on the mattress, and after eyeing the rather wide wooden frame of the cot, the two men simply tipped it on its side and walked it through the door, angling the burden appropriately to let the legs of the bed clear the door frame.

Although the bed was relatively light and Aleksandr was fit, his ankle still was troublesome, even with its support tape, and the Russian was hard pressed to keep pace with Jason, who ambled at the same pace as if he were carrying his rifle, not a large piece of furniture. At least the common across which they walked had been cleared of most of its snow, but the brilliant sun did not disguise the fact that the cold still had bite to it, and the drifts outside the camp testified to the harshness of the lingering winter.

Practicing the stoicism so praised at the Academy, and occasionally chanting under his breath from the Roll of Penance, Brukov managed to stumble along at the same rate that Jason strolled. Felicity was outside picking up stove wood, and when she saw them coming she prepared the way by holding open the door.

"Over there by the wall," she instructed Jason. "I moved the stools. No, the other way, with the head against the wall." The men seemed resigned to comply with her will in the matter of arranging the crowded cabin, and they mutely obeyed her orders.

"Did Billy bargain over the bed?" she asked, but before her brother could compose his slow speech, there was a sharp rap at the door of the cabin. The door immediately opened from the outside. Felicity had hardly a chance to move toward the knock.

"Sorry," Billy said as he came in and closed the door against the rush of cold air that followed him. "Jason, I can't wait. Goin' right now." Indeed, they saw, he was carrying his rucksack and rifle. "Take care of the cabin, then."

"Sure," Jason said, and without another word Billy was gone.

"He's going after Astid," Felicity said, shaking her head.

"Told him it's a bad idea," Jason said with regret.

"They weren't what you'd really call married," Felicity added.

"A bad idea," Jason said with finality.

"What's all this about?" Brukov asked when he could contain his curiosity no longer.

"No good to go after a woman," Jason said unhappily.

"Women and children go where they want," Felicity said before Brukov could express further puzzlement. "A woman can't be held," she added with firm satisfaction.

"Not even a married woman?"

It was Felicity's turn to show puzzlement, but before she could say anything, Jason broke in. "Let's go, Cap'n. I want to check Billy's latch. Fool prolly left the cabin door open. You can look at them old rifles."

Brukov could hardly refuse to accompany the eager fellow, so with a parting glance at the dark, intense eyes of Felicity, he followed Jason out the door. His questions could wait until later.

The door to Billy's cabin was tightly shut, of course, and Jason pried open the door and gave the premises a quick but all-encompassing survey. The camp was safe enough from theft, as a rule, but Billy's guns in particular were valuable. Jason didn't want any misunderstandings. In their very different modes of thinking, both Jason and Aleksandr were arriving at the same conclusion and rejecting it for the same reason. It would be easy and comfortable for Brukov to bunk in Billy's cabin, giving added protection against the unlikely event of an outsider penetrating the camp. Only an outsider would steal, as everyone in the camp knew too well the possessions of everyone else. But the reason that the thought of Brukov's occupancy of Billy's cabin remained unexpressed was simple: Neither Jason nor Aleksandr was sure he wanted the other out of his sight for any length of time.

"Well," Jason said at last, "I've got to get some wood in. Billy said it would be fine if you fooled with them rifles."

Jason left and Aleksandr, feeling foolishly conspiratorial, strode quickly to the shotguns. With the help of rudimentary tools he found hanging above a workbench, plus his Imperial Mission multipurpose pocketknife, he first disassembled the 20-gauge pump-action shotgun. There were spots of rust, particularly around the muzzle, but Billy had clean oil on hand—bartered from a more settled community, Brukov supposed. The camp steel-keeper had indeed maintained the guns in respectable condition, even though he thought them worthless. He hadn't even cannibalized any of the springs.

Aleksandr reassembled the 20-gauge and checked the action,

then swabbed out the bore again. It seemed to be in perfect working order.

He turned to the 12-gauge weapon, hefting it appreciatively, and repeated the mechanical inspection with much the same result. It was a solid, dependable old shotgun—though he couldn't be sure, of course, until some rounds had been fired.

He made a space on the workbench and lifted up the carton of shells. This was the exciting part, considering Jason's tales of rifle ammunition that was almost worthless. Aleksandr glanced through the instructions printed on the inside top of the carton. The routine was familiar. But, he remembered, the Chasers in this community could not read. If they tried assembling the materials in the usual way, they wouldn't know to remove the safety tab from the ends of the powder packs and if the tabs were left on, a misfire would be certain.

Everything seemed to be in order. He lifted up the surprisingly heavy little keg of No. 8 shot—he was sure there were plenty of game birds in the area, even if it was the wrong season to hunt them, and No. 8 was the right choice, he thought —and began making shotgun shells. He proceeded slowly and awkwardly at first, but soon developed a smooth rhythm. He popped the safety tab off a powder pack, then inserted the load into a plastic shell. At the end of the metal crimper was a perfectly sized tamp, and Aleksandr used it to firmly push the load into the shell. He then scooped in the shot, snapped a plastic wad off the strip that had been accordioned up in the back of the carton, inserted the wad over the shot, positioned the crimper and gave it a vigorous turn. The result was a perfect shotgun shell. He made ten for the 12-gauge and ten for the 20-gauge. Plenty for a start, and Aleksandr rapidly wearied of repetitious tasks.

He could hardly wait to take Jason out into the fields tomorrow.

The job done, Aleksandr debated whether he should leave the shotguns and ammunition in Billy's house, where there was at least a remote chance of theft, or remove them to the protection of the Pembroke cabin. Against all common sense— after all, he had permission to use the guns and Billy would be gone for days, apparently—he decided to leave the weapons in the workshop until he and Jason were ready to hunt. The rigid canons of the Roll of Material Integrity were too lively in his conscience to brook even the hint of violation.

The Russian meticulously tidied the workbench, straightened his uniform, and glanced around both rooms of the cabin before leaving. He latched the door as Jason had shown him.

It had been a bright and moderately warm day, the first such in some time, according to the pleasantries Aleksandr had heard exchanged in the camp, but now night was coming on and the bitter chill had set in again. He hadn't noticed the falling temperature while he had been intent on his chore, but now he longed for the warm stove he knew Felicity had been stoking all day.

When Aleksandr approached the Pembroke cabin, he was startled by a scene that might have illustrated one of his childhood history books. These Chasers were bewildering in their atavism. Jason was cutting wood into lengths with a double-edged axe. Not only did the community lack even a single Lasersaw, which were quite common now even outside Russia since the safety devices had been perfected, but apparently even the old-style power saw was unknown here. Because there were no sources of power, of course, Aleksandr realized at once.

Despite the cold, Jason was wearing no coat, only his heavy linen shirt, and that was damp with perspiration. He barely looked up as Brukov approached. "May I help you with anything?" he asked with some trepidation.

"You can split and haul what I've chopped if you want," Jason said in a tone of voice that left the decision of how and where to do the chore entirely with the Russian.

"I'd like to," he said, but without enthusiasm.

"Felicity will show you the maul," Jason said without looking up, the regular heavy stroke of his axe biting out wedges of wood with practiced precision.

Aleksandr entered the cabin, quickly shutting the door behind him against the cold. The room was warm and the scent of cooking food was a delicious perfume to the Russian, who suddenly realized how hungry he was. He had eaten nothing since the gruel.

"Lo," Felicity said, shaking a pan over the stove. "You figured out all Billy's guns?" Her look was one of carefully controlled interest.

"The ones I'd like to use," he replied. "Jason said you'd show me the 'maul' I'm supposed to help him with."

"Right there by the door," she said, nodding toward what looked like another axe. On closer inspection, its head was much heavier.

"You ever split wood before?"

"Well, not personally. But wood is burned in Russia, I assure you."

"We're out of seasoned wood and have to burn green. We split it now just to get it down to stove size." She pointed to the chunks that had already been split, "You can have Jason show you how."

"Nothing easier," Aleksandr said, and returned outside to the cold he had so happily left.

"Just split those pieces and take them in to Felicity," Jason said, not missing a stroke with his axe but nodding toward the two-foot-long logs he had scattered around him.

Aleksandr hefted the maul, which was surprisingly heavy,

and tentatively let it fall along the length of a log. He heard a short laugh "Got to stand em up, Cap'n," Jason said, grunting as he lopped another piece of oak onto the ground. "That should be enough. Tree's been down awhile, so it should burn." He wiped his brow with the back of one sleeve, lifted his axe, and went into the cabin, leaving a rapidly freezing Russian staring at a supply of wood that should heat a small cabin for a week.

Well, Brukov reminded himself, Russians barely blinked at tasks that would paralyze other men. Aleksandr smiled at the thought of demonstrating to these Chasers what an Imperial Mission officer was made of.

Propping one of the larger two-foot pieces of oak in the ample snow, Brukov took careful aim and swung the maul in the same kind of effortless loop over his head as Jason had used in chopping the wood. But the maul was much heavier than any axe Aleksandr had ever handled, and the planned smooth stroke ended more with the maul swinging Aleksandr than the other way around. The ten-pound head glanced off the side of the wood, knocking it flat again, and sliced through the snow, narrowly missing Aleksandr's left shin.

"It is to pray," he cursed in Russian under his breath. He lifted the maul head and stared thoughtfully at it, as though careful examination might lead to greater rapport between man and tool. With a sigh, he bent over and righted the log, planted his feet carefully, and swung with a very deliberate aim. This time the steel wedge hit squarely where he intended. It sounded with a dull wet thud, even seeming to rebound a bit into the air.

Aleksandr stared at the offending log as though at an insubordinate enlisted man. Then he sighed, leaned on the maul, and considered the beauty of the snow-laden forest beyond the camp. Finally, his frustration calmed, he again planted his feet and lifted the maul over his head, this time grunting with the force he imparted to the wood-splitter. He concentrated fiercely on the exact center of the log, and was rewarded by seeing the log part with a splendid rending noise. In fact, he had been so forceful that the maul buried its head in the snow that had braced the log.

"Praise!" the Russian rejoiced. The tree that Jason had segmented was not an overly large one, so Aleksandr thought he could dispense with splitting each log into four pieces. Two would do. Confident now and sensing the satisfaction that such mindless labor could bring, he positioned another log and brought the maul over his head with great enthusiasm. But this time he lunged, and the head of the maul went just beyond the log, so that the handle was all that hit the wood. The nasty jarring sensation was of less concern to Aleksandr than the thought that he might have damaged one of the Pembroke family's tools. Fortunately the maul seemed still whole, the handle unsplintered. He gathered himself to try again, already puffing a bit from the effort. He could feel the beginning of the dampness of sweat on his upper back.

Eventually, after more misses than hits and after discarding some logs as too hopelessly knotted to be split, Aleksandr found a steady and generally successful rhythm for his swing, and he began to enjoy the work. Despite the rapidly declining temperature, his coat soon was off, with only his shirt and the padding of his Imperial Mission vest between his torso and the elements, and his breathing was in great hungry gulps.

Aleksandr was physically fit. Imperial Mission field officers had to be. Even so, the unaccustomed strain of splitting wood told on him quickly, and after working his way through about half of the wood that Jason had chopped, Brukov decided that Russia's honor had been upheld. He put his coat on again to protect against the freezing of the sweat on his shoulders and back and he began gathering the firewood.

"Just put them in there," Felicity said, motioning toward the wall near the stove.

"I split about half the wood Jason chopped," Aleksandr said, not sure whether to be proud or defensive.

"That's all right," Jason said vaguely. He was bent over the table, reassembling his rifle, which he had thoroughly cleaned. "Felicity will do the rest tomorrow."

"Well," Brukov said, then decided to say no more. He simply trudged in and out of the cabin, bringing in the wood as quickly as possible. Could a mere wire of a girl actually do work that was so strenuous? But by now, Aleksandr was prepared to believe almost anything about these semi-savage Chasers.

Brukov dropped the last of the split wood on the pile, then threw off his coat and slumped onto a stool with an exhalation of completion.

"Been a short day," Jason said, snapping the bolt into his rifle as he finally was satisfied it was clean. "Tomorrow we'll get an early start, see if we can get some deer. Bring your spraygun if you want. That should get em."

"What will you do for bullets?"

"Oh, I got em back from Sam before I cut the wood. He's not so bad, just wants his meat. Can't blame him."

"He might not want to go hunting, Jason," Felicity said, nodding toward Brukov. "Maybe he's got to go back where he came from."

Felicity spoke from the stove without looking up, but the tension in her voice was apparent. It would never occur to Jason to wonder what Aleksandr's plans were, although Felicity practically vibrated with curiosity.

"I'd like to go hunting," Brukov said, "but not with your rifle or with my machine-pistol. I'd like to try those shotguns I worked on today."

"You think those things 'll work?" Jason gaped at Brukov, and his tone was not so much skeptical as downright astounded.

"They're just a kind of gun Billy didn't know much about. They're in good condition and I loaded up some ammunition today. I assume you have a multitude of game birds around here?"

"We got birds," Jason said, "but the only ones we ever get to eat are whatever chickens we can save from the Jonnies. Lot of fat birds around, but hardly anyone ever gets one. Some try trappin'. Waste of time. Some time you get one sittin' for a rifle shot."

Aleksandr grimaced. "That's hardly my notion of how one shoots game birds. We'll go out tomorrow and I'll show you how it's done."

"I'm serious... Aleksandr," Felicity said, now addressing him with a direct stare that reminded him of one of his schoolteachers in Russia. It was a look that demanded an answer, and a well-considered, satisfactory answer at that. "What are your plans? Will other Russ be coming here? How long will you stay?"

"Well," Aleksandr replied, stretching his legs out toward the fire and speaking casually, though in fact he was wary of compromising any aspect of the Imperial Mission.

"I think it unlikely they would have put out a search patrol right away, probably not until they have thoroughly examined the crash site and cleared up the men and machines." That much he said for Felicity's benefit, but certainly the patrol couldn't have reached the site of the attack until dark, and the Imperial Mission put troops into potentially hostile or otherwise dangerous areas only during daylight hours, except in extreme emergencies. Captain Aleksandr Iosifovich Brukov in peril did not constitute an extreme emergency. "Furthermore," he said to Felicity, "my locator was lost when we crashed and I was tossed out."

Perhaps he shouldn't have mentioned the tiny transmitter all officers wore in the field? Well, the Pembrokes wouldn't know what he was talking about anyway.

"They'll think you're dead when they see that wreck," Jason said, seeming to relish the thought of the incinerated helicopter being examined.

"Oh, no," Brukov laughed. "They have ways of checking. They'll be looking for me." He wanted that fact to be firmly established, though in truth he wasn't as confident as he sounded.

"So they will come here?" Felicity asked.

"I doubt it." He had no idea where his compatriots might search, but it was likely they'd concentrate on the place Jason called the Hamp, where the people called Jonnies evidently were headquartered. "But I'll be able to find them without too much trouble," Brukov said. "We have procedures."

His ankle, which had been relatively painless and had hobbled him very little all afternoon, had begun to throb again as he sat, so he limped over to his bed and began to unwrap the bandage. Perhaps it would be good to let it free for a while.

"So when your foot is fine, you leave?" Felicity was relentless.

"I expect so. There's a minority opinion among the Imperial Mission officer corps that we have all too few contacts with Chasers. I've already found out there's some truth to that. So my time here with you is hardly wasted. I'll return a more valuable officer. Besides, I need to decide what to do about those Jonnies. I need to formulate recommendations." He gently rotated his bare foot, and his ankle, swollen and discolored, protested. He winced, but managed not to cry out. The bandage had done a good job of support.

"I'll tell you what to do about them Jonnies," Jason said. "Just turn them sprayguns on em. Do everyone a favor."

"We want to cooperate," Alexandr said, "not annihilate."

"What's annihilate?" Felicity asked quickly.

"Doing what Jason wants. Killing them all."

"They want to do the teachin' themselves, you know," Jason said. "And they don't want no co-op at all."

"Jason's right," Felicity said. "He knows his Jonnies."

"Food's startin' to smell good, Felicity," Jason said, "and it's plenty dark outside. Time the Cap'n found out about potato lightnin.'"

"Excellent idea," Aleksandr said. "Just the thing in a warm kitchen at the end of the day."

Jason brought two cups to the table, lifted the earthenware jug, pulled the stopper and then poured generous splashes of the almost colorless liquid. He capped the jug and handed Brukov one of the cups.

"No drink for Felicity?" the Russian asked courteously.

"I haven't learned to like it yet," she said from the stove.

"Got nothin' to do with likin'," her brother said, more to himself than to either of the other two people in the room.

Aleksandr stood. "To your hospitality, for which I am grateful."

Jason responded. "To your sprayguns, and may they ann... ann..."

"Annihilate," Felicity said.

"Ann-I-late the Jonnies," Jason concluded with dignity. They both drank, the Russian tentatively, the Chaser with thirsty exuberance.

The crudely distilled alcohol was imperfectly filtered, Aleksandr knew at a taste, and the slight but unmistakable difference from vodka was unpleasant to one accustomed to the more civilized drink. But he gulped in air after he took his first sip and felt the potent liquid scorch his throat.

"Flup," Jason said, smacking his lips.

"It is to pray," Aleksandr agreed, taking another sip, this

time a larger one. The muscles that already were tender from his chore of supplying fuel would not be bothersome after a cup of potato lightning. He opened his mouth to remark on the Russian custom of downing vodka with tasty morsels of food, but he recognized in time that the Pembroke household was unlikely to have a ready supply of caviar.

Another long pull apiece and the small cups were empty, a void that Jason filled in his efficient but unhurried fashion.

"We can eat when you're ready," Felicity said.

"In just a bit, then," Jason responded, settling comfortably onto his stool, his elbows on the table, his hands cradling the cup between them. "Well, how do you like it, then?" he asked Brukov, with the sly, indirect glance to which all these Chasers except Felicity seemed addicted.

"It's different from any drink I've had before. Probably a bit like the privately made stuff at home, though I've never had any of that. It's powerful, I'll give it that, and you'll notice I didn't refuse a second cup."

"People always say you Russ got lots of courage," Jason said solemnly.

"Why, Jason, I do believe I detect a trace of mockery. Whatever faults we Russians may have, and we sometimes concede one or two, as a race we are noted as excellent drinkers. Excellent." As though to demonstrate, he lifted his cup to his lips again.

"We had some glasses, but Sue took em with her." Jason's voice was sad, but Aleksandr couldn't tell if it was the loss of Sue or the loss of the glasses that caused the mournful tone.

"There was another woman here?"

"Yup," Jason responded. "I was married. She left, though."

"She didn't like me here," Felicity said.

"No she didn't," Jason agreed amiably. "Too hard to live that way, she said. She just wanted to get around some, too."

"But you were married, too," Aleksandr said to Felicity. "There seem to be as many divorces as marriages among you Chasers." After all, Aleksandr thought with a slight blur of understanding—after all, divorce was almost unheard of in Russia.

"We don't do it like in the Co-ops," Felicity said. "No papers. Here a woman moves in and you're married. She moves out and you're not."

"Hard on a man like Billy," Jason mused.

"Hard on you, too," Felicity countered.

"Hard on most everyone," Jason agreed. "Hard on Morg, too."

Felicity flushed lightly and Aleksandr saw a spark in her eyes, a literal flashing such as one reads of in books but rarely sees. Once again, he thought how truly remarkable it was in a Chaser, considering the limited emotional resources of the race.

"Morg is all talk and acting," Felicity said. "What's hard on him is not being as good as he says he is."

Brukov was struck by the youthfulness of her face when it relaxed its usually stern expression into animation and her features became lively, as now. "Excuse my rudeness," he said to her, "but how old are you?"

"Nineteen."

"Three years younger than me and she treats me like I was five years younger than her," Jason grumbled, but affectionately.

"That's very young." Aleksandr was a little shocked, though he knew that Chaser manners and morals were a prime reason that the various Councils of Elders were so reluctant to let the Imperial Mission work closely with foreigners. In the Co-ops, and especially within Russia herself, the Chasers were held in check. Many Russian men had Chaser mistresses, of course, even in Russia. But Russian women were protected by the Church. Never could one behave even remotely like these unconcerned libertines of Chaser Two.

The shock showed on Aleksandr's face, and Felicity laughed out loud. "A full-grown woman around here, that's what I am. Have been for years. Old enough for the Russ in Boston, too." She smiled boldly at Brukov, sensing he would be embarrassed and defensive in the face of such immodesty.

"One more cup," Jason said, and followed his own order.

"We're eating now," Felicity said with firmness. "While you can still taste it."

"Flup," said Jason, contented despite his sister's firmness.

"We are very strict about marriage in Russia," Brukov said. "The Church rules are explicit and severe. A girl your age might still be in school."

"Ha." She busied herself with the food. She ladled stew into three bowls. Jason meanwhile produced the same hunting knife that once had so startled Aleksandr. He deftly sliced a loaf of bread into large chunks.

"It smells delicious," Aleksandr said, not to be polite but because it was the truth, and he was suddenly very hungry. In the presence of heathen, he silently recited the brief version of the Roll of Thanksgiving.

The stew consisted primarily of potatoes and venison in a thick dark sauce—a hearty peasant dish of strong flavor. The bread was whiter and of a finer texture than the comparable Russian peasant bread, but the Chaser version went well with the stew.

"Them things in your pocket you eat as good as this?" Jason asked as he hunched over his bowl.

"This is much better. Much better indeed. My compliments to the chef."

"You sure talk funny for having the same language," Felicity said, but she blushed slightly anyway. What a strange creature this Russ was, not at all like the ones she had seen in Boston. He had the same arrogance and superiority, but he was a little softer, a little more open. Imagine one of the Boston Russ eating a meal in their cabin! Of course, she reminded herself, this particular Russ had little choice.

Aleksandr raised his cup. "This helps me talk funny." Jason laughed with his mouth full, and Brukov politely looked away.

"So Russ people go to school when they're nineteen?" Felicity asked as casually as she could.

"Not all of them. Many leave school at age twelve. They have learned all the Church Canons and Rolls and Doctrines. And the rudiments, of course—how to read and write and do sums. Some of them learn history," he added with a touch of wryness.

"They know how to read and write by when they're twelve," Felicity said, with a kind of bitter wonderment in her tone.

"Oh, long before twelve." He smiled assent as Felicity offered to fill their bowls again. "The religious training takes the most time," Brukov added.

"And then some go to more school? Who decides that?"

"Oh, it's very complicated," Aleksandr said, speaking as though to one of those children. He pushed his stool back from the table and crossed his legs, leaning on the table with an air of contented relaxation. He hardly protested at all when Jason silently filled his cup again. "It depends on family and scholarship. Those with a religious calling go on to study under one or another of the Councils of Elders. All of them have schools. Very strict, though I've heard the rules aren't always enforced as they used to be."

"But people like me, for instance," Brukov continued after a sip from his cup, "we study to become a Man of History, a secular student. But most of the children after age twelve go into apprenticeship or work with their families. Our families are much larger than what Chaser families seem to be. Our families are more strictly organized, too."

Aleksandr could see by Felicity's look that she had never heard of anything like what he was telling her, but her dark angular face with its alert kaleidoscopic eyes showed that she absorbed much of what he said, though eagerness to hear kept her from interrupting to ask questions and find out the meaning of words. Crude native intelligence was apparent in her. Brukov had seen very little of it in Chaser Two, while in Chaser One it was commonplace. Probably because it was encouraged there.

"And the people who aren't Russians? The Chasers? Do any of them go to school too, or is that against the law?"

"Oh, yes," Brukov laughed. "Those who are trained are invaluable. Engineers. All our factories. Police. Army. Much of our bureaucracy. All our domestic servants, of course."

Even Jason took note of that. "You got Chasers in the Russ army, even in Russia?"

"Indeed. Many of our best troops are from Chaser One."

"Put a Jonnie in your army and he'll shoot you in the back," Jason said, and Aleksandr made note of the fervent comment, although he laughed to indicate that he could have no such concern.

"We haven't done much training over here," he said. "You people have been left largely to yourselves."

Felicity would not let any ripple on the surface of the conversation distract her concentration. She was avid for Aleksandr's casual knowledge. "I don't understand," she said. "Chasers are allowed in Russia?"

"Position, power, all that. Yes. They're not Russian Communicants, of course. They are strictly controlled and must do as they are told. But they're quite good at technology, and the Elders discourage Russians from that. They don't even like us to use the stuff, much less make it."

"What stops them from shooting you in the back the way Jason says?"

"Oh, there's very little trouble," Brukov said. He didn't like all this talk of Chaser violence against Russians. "The Chasers can never agree among themselves on anything, and they're generally quite happy to let their betters decide things. They're wonderful people, really. I don't know what we'd do without them, though there are always some Elders who don't want to have anything to do with them at all." Aleksandr noted with some amusement that his speech was slower and a bit slurred.

"Then who does decide?" Felicity asked. "These Elders or the Army or what? Jason, don't give him any more of that, it's bad enough you're taking more and you'll both be sick."

"Chaser can't tell a Russian what to do, right, Cap'n? Jason winked as he tipped the jug, which was significantly depleted.

"Right, Jason," Aleksandr laughed, "I'm sorry, Felicity, what was it you asked?"

"Russia. Who runs it? Elders or Army or what?"

"Well, the real division... not division, disagreement. Different way of looking at things. There's no real disagreement, we're all one in True Russia." He drank from the cup and felt the pleasant burn. But he began to feel very weary and he surprised himself with a huge yawn. "Pardon me," he said.

"Chasers aren't supposed to know who runs Russia, is that it?" The girl wouldn't let up!

"No, no, no, not at all. There are two types of Russians. Some emphasize religion and nothing else. They follow the Councils of Elders. And then there are Men of History, like me." He put his finger proudly on his chest. "Not just army. We don't disagree on religion. We just think there are other things in the world, too."

"So who makes the decisions?"

"Every Russian has his say. Somehow it gets sorted out. Elders do what they must and we do what we must. We have a saying, 'Only God rules Russia.' We say that when we try to figure it out." He again yawned extravagantly, and the stool suddenly wobbled. He landed on the floor, surprised but unhurt. They all three laughed.

"Here, Cap'n" Jason said, helping him up. "We're up early tomorrow to hunt. Better get some rest."

"Compments to chef," Aleksandr muttered as he leaned on Jason and tried to chart his course for the bed. He fell asleep before he got there.

‹ *Chapter Five* ›

BRUKOV AWOKE ONCE DURING the night with a lurch, an abdominal spasm that shifted immediately into regurgitation. He managed to lean over the side of the bed. Almost at once, hands on his arm began pulling him from the bed. Strong hands, but not as strong as Jason's. The pain in his head, sudden and unbearable when he staggered to his feet, forced him to keep his eyes shut. He was propelled in a stumble toward the door, and he leaned his sightless head against the wall as the latch was undone. Just in time. He kneeled into a snow bank and vomited again. And again. His head began to clear. The frigid air felt good on his head, but he began to shiver fiercely. He opened his eyes long enough to see Felicity in the moonlight, holding the door closed behind her and watching him. As he looked up, she said, "Get it all out," and reentered the house, guessing the humiliation he felt and could not tolerate. Just as he began to feel marginally better and started to recite the Roll of Penance, his stomach without warning constricted violently again and sent forth a stream of noisome liquids, though less than earlier. His stomach was almost empty by now. He felt he had no coordination, no physical strength, no mental concentration. He shook with cold and his body's poison, and the bolt of pain drove through his head again, forcing his eyes shut. It was as though a gigantic ruffian were beating him, refusing to accept his acknowledgments of defeat. He could feel sweat on his forehead despite the bitter cold. Once more a spasm wracked his body, though this time nothing at all came up. The muscles in his chest and stomach were sore from the abuse.

The door opened behind him. "Come in now or you'll get worse sick." Felicity's voice was firm but not unkind. To his dismay, Aleksandr needed her assistance to get to his feet, and he still could not walk properly. She guided him through the door. There was a dark patch on the floor next to his bed where Felicity had already scrubbed the wood free of the filth he had spewed. He fell into bed and she drew the covers over him. "Sleep now," she admonished. He had time to hear Jason snoring across the room before merciful slumber took away his torment.

ALEXANDR GROANED, newly returned to his wakeful misery.

"Still not either alive or dead, eh?" Felicity asked with an almost tender playfulness. Brukov groaned again in reply. "Captain Three Names of Russia," she chided him. "Mister Man of History." He could not find his tongue even to beg for mercy.

Felicity laughed at whatever expression was on his face and brought him a cup. "Here," she said, "I've been waiting for you to wake up. I do the medicine in camp, so you can trust me." The cup was filled with an herbal drink reminiscent of tea, strong and flavored by aromatic leaves. He sipped at it gingerly, though a sharp pain had shot through his head again when he sat up to drink. She handed him a chunk of bread. "This too," she said. "It'll help your stomach." He obediently gnawed at the bread, was pleased at the taste, and in terror felt his gorge rise and then settle. The hot herbal drink was wonderful, and he wanted to ask her where she got it, but the words wouldn't come out of his mouth.

He finished his tea and bread and sank back, immediately asleep again.

ALEKSANDR'S HEAD was a little clearer when he next awoke. If he didn't move he could almost pretend he didn't have a headache. His stomach was relatively quiescent. Muscular soreness seemed to be virtually absolute, but that could be explained. After all, within the space of forty-eight hours he had been in a helicopter crash, split what seemed like a forest of wood with a ten-pound maul, and drunk a liter of strange vile alcohol that had made him drunker, and sicker, than he'd been since he had graduated from the Academy of History. He considered which Roll to recite and toyed with the idea of going through all the major Rolls during the day as a reminder to himself not to fail his calling and his responsibility to True Russia.

His musings were interrupted by Felicity, who noticed that he was awake and who came to sit on the bed beside him. With surprising gentleness, but with a smiling amusement that warmed and transformed her severe facial features, she said, "You look much better now, poor man. You must promise not to have anything to do with potatoes ever again." She even reached out to push a lock of damp hair from his forehead.

"You have the right to mock," he said. Even speaking required movement, and the movement brought the sharp rebuke of pain. He could not avoid grimacing.

"I don't mean to mock. But you must know that Chasers do think of the Russ as a mighty race who walk upright, not crawl and vomit."

"How poignant."

"I would like you to tell me the meaning of all the words you use that I don't know. I am ashamed."

He looked up sharply at those words, which were spoken in a tone of simple fact, and he saw that she was indeed ashamed of her ignorance.

"At the moment," he said in a voice that was nearly a whisper,

"I am using the word 'poignant' in the sense of 'painfully affecting.'" He couldn't resist the self-mockery. "It usually means something rather sweet and endearing."

She laughed. "Poignant. How poignant. It's hard to say."

"You have it right."

"Can you sit up? Here, let me help you." She propped a pillow behind his back as he dragged himself forward in bed so he could lean against the wall. Felicity went back to the stove and poured something into a bowl.

"Where's Jason?" Aleksandr finally had mustered the energy to look around the cabin.

"After deer. He figured you wouldn't want to try out those new guns today after all."

"Smart fellow. What's this?" She approached the bed carrying a crude tray. "Some soup. A little more bread." She placed the tray carefully in his lap and then drew up a stool to sit on while she watched him eat.

"I'll trade for the food," she said.

He looked up, startled. "Trade what? For what? The nearest place you can use Russian money is the Co-op of Boston. I don't have any money to speak of anyway."

"I want to know how to read."

"To read?" His head throbbed with a reminder to speak softly, if at all.

"You know how," she said with a passionate urgency in her voice. "All you need to do is get me started. Once I know the first part I can teach myself."

"You don't even have anything to read..."

"That's not true," she interrupted with a rush. "There's a whole building full of books in Ash. Most of them didn't burn. It's a stone building. I took a book to teach myself, but it didn't work. It makes me so angry. I thought if I just looked at the pages long enough I'd begin to figure it out."

"I doubt that anyone could learn to read by that method. But your spoken English, at least, seems to be better than the other Chasers around here."

She smiled with pride, and Aleksandr saw again how young she was. "I listen to what sounds good," she said. "I can tell... at least sometimes I can tell. When people who talk good come to camp, I listen real hard. You talk good, I can tell that. When Morg and I went to Boston I listened hard there too."

"Someone in the Co-op could have taught you how to read."

Felicity's features again collapsed into a thundercloud.

"That's what I went for, that and because Morg thought he could be a big man. But they just laughed at Morg, and he couldn't do anything about it. And they only wanted me for cleaning, and the men wanted me for something else. They said they'd teach me to read, but I could tell. They only wanted to teach me what I already knew. Someone like me wasn't worth the trouble of teaching how to read."

"Well, perhaps I'll take a look at your book," he said. "But not now. I couldn't see it." He handed her the tray.

"No no no," she said, eager to please. "When you feel better. I won't take much of your time. Just get me started."

"Well, we'll see." He was much more comfortable now, and perhaps another nap would complete his cure, but there was a necessity that troubled him. Felicity evidently realized what he was thinking.

"Go in the bucket out back if you have to," she said. "You can make it that far, can't you?" Her smile teased him.

"I'll try, but I can't promise." He put on his boots but did not lace them, and he put only his coat over his underclothes. He noted with some surprise that he already felt less self-conscious about performing such intimate activities in the same room as a young woman. He was gaining new material for those long debates he had with his fellow Men of History about how quickly the veneer of civilization could be rubbed away by barbarianism. He tottered outside, unsure of his equilibrium at several points, but he managed to do what he had to do, casting his eyes about furtively to assure himself that he wasn't being observed. Chasers were quite casual about such matters. He retraced his route, gratefully hurrying back into the warmth of the cabin. There had been no sun in the sky, and a cold mist hung in the air and promised to close down visibility altogether, but he reckoned the time as about midday—perhaps he was influenced in his estimate by the fact that he had just eaten.

Brukov wobbled back to his bed and sat there a moment, hanging his head and not yet troubling to take off his coat and boots. Perhaps a bit more rest would do it... perhaps.

He kicked off his boots and shed his coat, putting it on the bed as a blanket. He was still cold from the outdoors, and suddenly very sleepy. He paid no attention to the domestic noises that Felicity was making across the room, but curled into a ball beneath the covers.

JASON'S RETURN woke him. The hunter burst into the room with an excited clatter, and another man followed quickly behind him.

"Got meat, Felicity," Jason fairly shouted. "Deer hanging outside, gutted and all."

"I'll cut it up tomorrow. Hello, Hop. You get deer too?"

"For sure," said the newcomer, a short, heavily bearded fellow who revealed a powerful frame as he doffed his somewhat bizarre coat of mixed fur and cloth.

"Hop got more than deer. We're goin' right out again."

"Eat first," Felicity said.

"Well, fine," her brother agreed. "I'm hungry enough."

"You too, Hop," she said, ladling food into bowls and casually tossing a chunk of bread across the table to Jason. She nodded toward Brukov. "We'll eat later."

"Well, thank you," Hop said, and sat down without further discussion. Both men ate with enthusiasm, but neither displayed any acquaintance with the standards of etiquette.

"Why do you have to go out again?" Felicity asked once her service chores were completed.

"Hop spotted some Jonnies," Jason said between bites.

"I was down to the Valley the other night," Hop said. "Farmers say the Jonnies are all excited." He glanced at Brukov. "The Jonnies say they thumped the Russ. The Russ were back today in them flyin' things."

"Helicopters," Jason said proudly.

"Right," Hop continued. "They didn't get near the Jonnies in them flyin' things, though. Jonnies are all excited. They figure the Russ they didn't kill got picked up by the flyin' things, but they're beatin' on folks so they never even smile at a Russ. Comin' now is a night patrol. Hardly ever see a Jonnie out at night. God must be mad." He guffawed, despite the food in his mouth.

"Sure must be," Jason agreed. "God always tells Jonnies just what to do."

"They think the Russ are all beat up and won't never come back," Hop said with the characteristic sly Chaser glance at Brukov.

"It sounds as though these Jonnie people are very wrong about a number of things," Aleksandr said. He still felt crippled by the potato lightning, but at least he was able to pretend to good health.

"How you feelin', Cap'n?" Jason asked.

"Fine now. Is the camp in any danger from this patrol?"

"Naw. Hop and me 'll go fix that, won't we, Hop?"

"Sure. They got good bullets but they can't tell between a tree and their own backside, special at night."

"If we got to," Jason explained, "we'll pop one or two from

the woods and make em chase us. They'll get lost and cold and start fightin' with each other. Happens ever time if you catch em early on, before they get where they're going."

The simplicity of Chaser tactics, like the simplicity of Chasers themselves, was staggering. "If you like," Aleksandr volunteered, "I'll hide out in the woods until they're gone."

"Naw, Hop and me 'll keep em away."

"Better go do it," Hop said, pushing his stool back.

"Gotta stop at Sam's and get bullets," Jason reminded him.

"Sure. Let's do it." Hop said.

"Right. You got enough food and wood, Felicity?"

"Plenty. Be careful."

"Sure."

"Thanks for the food, Felicity," Hop said as he hefted his long barrel rifle.

And then they were gone as suddenly as they had come.

"How are you really feeling, Aleksandr?"

"Oh... better. Wide awake, at least. Not up to calisthenics."

"What's that?"

"Exercise."

"Don't worry, I'll get the wood in."

"Oh, I..." His protest died in his throat as she briskly opened the door and left, returning with wood—probably wood that she had split that afternoon as he slept. He watched the carrying process three or four times. He felt foolish, but made no further offer to help. At this point he felt he could ill afford to add insincerity to his other sins.

Her chores at last finished, and the stove stoked, she said, "We never should have let you drink potato. I'm real sorry. So is Jason. We're neither one of us good at saying it."

"I assure you, any fault is my own. I am not the first Russian to rue the day that someone thought of distilling the tuber's nectar."

"There you go again," she said in amazement but not in

rebuke.

"My turn to apologize," he said.

"You know, you'll really feel better and sleep better tonight if you get up and get dressed. Take a walk so you don't just dry up from the stove heat."

"You may be right." He pushed himself up until he was sitting on the side of the bed. Not too bad. He was a little lightheaded, but he supposed that was the least of the symptoms to be wary of. He did notice a new nuisance. Since infancy, he had bathed daily, and daily donned fresh clean clothes. His Chaser orderly in the Co-op of Cleveland had been meticulous. Brukov's present condition was deplorable.

He looked up at Felicity. "Are there washing facilities in camp?"

"Sure. For people and clothes both. But you'll have to wait until tomorrow."

"Not a moment too soon." Slowly, with gestures that seemed thoughtful rather than crippled, he climbed into his clothes.

"Do you want to eat?" Her voice had a tone of true solicitude in it, and Aleksandr suddenly was aware that she had nursed him with skill and care.

"Not just now, thank you. I think I'll take your advice and go for a short walk first. And thank you so much for looking after me," he added warmly.

"You're most welcome," she said, and blushed with a sudden pleased smile.

"Would you like to come on the walk with me?" He gestured gallantly toward the door.

"Yes, sir, but I fear I must stay here and tend to my chores."

"A most elegant speech," Aleksandr said. "You listen well.

"Stay inside the camp," she said, regaining a brusque tone. "Just in case."

"Ah, yes, the Jonnies."

"The Jonnies."

"I'll be perfectly safe." He smiled and patted his Pushkin machine-pistol.

The cold night air was a shock at first, but soon he found it bracing, and he realized that it was in truth considerably warmer than the last two nights. Rain evidently had fallen during the day, and some of the snow had melted, so the weather must at last be improving. He slowly circled the inside of the camp, and he apparently was the only one out strolling, though he suspected that the camp guard, Hammon, and perhaps others like him were watching the stranger from the shadows, with wariness if not with true curiosity.

He did indeed feel better now, and the poisons fleeing his body left in their stead a new confidence and growing excitement. A plan was beginning to arrange itself in his head. There was no reason why Aleksandr Iosifovich Brukov had to content himself with the routine accomplishments of an officer of the Russian Imperial Mission. That meant doing what he was told for a few years and not making major mistakes, then returning home to an administrative post, supervising Chasers who were more able technicians than he. Perhaps a job at the Academy or one of the related universities. Proper marriage to his beloved Lyalya. Children, of course. Society and prayers. The eternal squabbling with the various Councils of Elders.

He still could do all those things but wished to stamp a mark of distinction on his service record so that he didn't owe all to his name, his commission and his grandfather's wealth and prestige. He could have prestige of his own. When people said the name Brukov, it would be Aleksandr Iosifovich they meant. And the way to accomplish all these things, he was beginning to believe, was by becoming the first Man of History, the first Imperial Mission officer, to live among, organize, and bring peace to the benighted Chaser Two nonconformists who lived their squalid lives outside the Co-ops and outside the Shared Grace of Holy Russia, as represented by the Imperial Mission.

It need not be a lengthy task. The difference between the Russian civilization and this sink of barbarism was so great that its impact, in his person, must be immediate, profound and irrevocable. True, the differences among Chasers, the varieties of their manners and morals, were bewildering at first. To understand fully would require time he didn't have and effort he didn't want to make. But such understanding, he believed, was unnecessary. What was important was to display the banner of True Russia as a living presence rather than a distant object of fear. Then even the most backward Chaser must recognize and welcome the standards set and assigned by the Imperial Mission.

Aleksandr could tell that Jason and Felicity and their clan were decent and worthy, however simple they were and despite the ignorance and squalor that characterized their pathetic little society. He, Brukov, could help channel that basic decency and worth in such a way as to better their lives and further the goals of the Imperial Mission.

Such thoughts of his own heroic and benevolent future did much, along with the crisp night air, to clear Aleksandr's head and improve the disposition of his stomach. By the time he had slowly gone around the common he felt very nearly healthy again.

When he returned to the warmth of the cabin, the smells of food were more welcome to his nostrils, and he ate a moderate amount of the hearty peasant fare. Felicity, who had eaten in his absence, simply watched him with noncommittal interest, allowing him to eat without demanding that he simultaneously converse.

After satisfying his appetite, Aleksandr thanked his hostess for the meal, rearranged himself on the stool, and gave a contented sigh. Immediately the light in Felicity's eyes brightened.

"Will you teach me now?"

"Ah, well... I will not be at my most brilliant." As it happened, however, his reluctance to undertake kindergarten pedagogy was offset by his vanity. It might prove amusing to play Pygmalion to Felicity's Galatea, he thought.

"All I want is a start," she said, her voice strained with the effort of keeping it free of a tone of supplication.

"Of course, of course. Bring me your book and we'll see where to begin." Her angular face widened into a delighted smile and she shot toward her bed as though her slender frame had been a coiled spring.

"Here," she said, pulling up a stool beside him at the table. "I tried and tried, but I couldn't figure out where to start." Aleksandr had to stifle a laugh. The book was an English-language translation of Dostoevsky's *Crime and Punishment*.

"How did you happen to pick this one?" he asked.

She shrugged, already defensive. "I didn't know what any of them were. I liked the picture." There was a dust jacket still on the battered old volume, and the piercing eyes of Raskolnikov peered out.

Aleksandr tapped the book cover with his right index finger. "We read this book in school in Russia. It was written during the First Enslavement."

Felicity's eyes were almost frightening as they glittered. "I want to know! I want to find out these things. Just start with the first word in the book and tell me what it is, and then the second word. I'll learn. I promise I won't waste your time."

"You certainly have a good attitude for a student," Brukov said, hoping to calm her intensity with a leavening of humor. She would have none of it.

"Be serious, Aleksandr. Tell me honestly if there is a Russian law against telling me these things. Are they secret? If so, tell me. If no, teach me."

"Of course reading is not a secret," he said, trying for a

soothing tone that did not patronize. He failed. "As I told you, we encourage Chasers in their learning. They are very valuable. Some are great scholars."

"Then why don't we know how to read here?"

"Some people in Chaser Two do know how to read, at least in the Co-ops, but Chaser One is much closer to Russia, so we have kept learning alive there. People in Chaser Two once knew how to read. I remember a study we were shown in one of our culture classes at the Academy. I don't recall if it was from Old Europe or Chaser Two, but I remember that it showed the way a people could unlearn something. It was plotted on a graph—I'm sorry, you don't know what that is, but it is like a picture and it showed how fast something could be unlearned by a people who had all the learning in common. What happens with something like reading is that first the standards are relaxed a little, but no one notices; then, within a single generation, a large number of students no longer meet even the lower standards, and the curve drops faster and faster. That kind of unlearning can only happen when the political and economic life of a people—how they live together—gets worse and worse, too. As I recall, the population of an area can go from eighty percent literate to ninety-five percent illiterate in three generations."

"I want to go the other way. I want to understand what you said."

"Well," Aleksandr said, "it won't do to start with this book. Your suggested word-by-word method would be very inefficient. Tomorrow we'll go to the place where all the books are and see if we can find a more suitable volume." He saw her expressive face collapse into offended gloom. Her straight dark hair seemed to surround her face like the clouds around a thunderstorm. "But we can make a start tonight," he said quickly. "I don't suppose you have a pen and paper?"

She shook her head blankly, but the destructive expression

left her face at the promise of a prompt tutorial. Aleksandr withdrew a map marker from the breast pocket of his tunic, then opened the back of the Dostoevsky volume. There were unused pages there, and Aleksandr carefully tore out one of the sheets.

"Now," he said, "We begin." He smiled at her, but her concentration was entirely on the blank page before him on the table.

He went through the letters of the English alphabet, Aa, Bb, and so on, before he said another word. Then he made her recite them after him, touching each letter in turn on the page as she did so. He explained that capitals are for proper names, the beginning of sentences and some other uses she would discover in due course. And then he printed at the bottom of the page: Felicity Pembroke. And beneath that he printed: Aleksandr Iosifovich Brukov.

"Those are our names," he said.

"I have two, you have three." She took the map marker from him and copied at the bottom of the page, slowly but with a firmness of line: Felicity Pembroke. Her smile would have put to shame the noon sun on a cloudless day.

"Excellent, Felicity. Now tell me what letters of the alphabet are in your name?"

Thus began the education of Felicity Pembroke, nineteen, a nonconformist Chaser who, if her studies succeeded, would be the first member of her community to either read or write.

‹ *Chapter Six* ›

"LATE START FOR huntin', Cap'n. Better get up. Felicity wants you clean."

Aleksandr was fully awake at once. His night's sleep had been so firm that he hadn't heard Jason return to the cabin, and now the aftereffects of the horrid alcohol were entirely gone. He felt strong and ready for adventure.

"How did you and Hop do with the Jonnies?" he asked.

"Never came near us. Back in time for a good night's sleep."

"He brought some eggs and milk, too," Felicity said. She couldn't hide a mood of cheerful excitement, though she tried to be as severe as usual. "We'll have some cakes to eat," she said, "but first you wash. Jason, take him to the smokehouse."

"Very brisk marching orders for so soon after rising," Aleksandr grumbled amiably, yawning and stretching.

"Here," Felicity said, ignoring him, "put these on after you wash. She threw him a crude but clean set of underclothes. "And bring those longjohns afterward so I can wash them," she said.

"This casual treatment is hardly that which normally should be accorded an officer of the Imperial Mission," Aleksandr said as formally as he could manage under the circumstances.

"How poignant," Felicity replied.

Aleksandr abandoned the discussion. He dressed discretely

and followed Jason to the smokehouse, a low-roofed shed next to the brook on the downhill side of the camp. Smoke was, indeed, billowing from its chimney, but smoke also billowed from virtually every cabin in camp, so the distinctive name of the building was not apparent.

"This is where we smoke our meat and do our sugarin'. Do our sugarin' in those big steel thin's." The vats weren't steel, but Brukov didn't want to correct his guide.

"You just missed sugarin'," Jason said. "We open up the roof then for the smoke." He pointed up and Aleksandr saw a pulley system that indeed could lift a large portion of the roof to allow smoke from the fire beneath to escape. "Always got plenty of hot water here. Tub's the last run-off before the brook."

The system was designed just that way, with the large drum of perpetually heated water available for any number of chores, including baths. It was hooked up to an old bathtub at the lowest corner of the shack, and the drain apparently did go right out into the camp's stream. Aleksandr was relieved to see that the bathtub appeared to be clean. "Very nice," he murmured.

"Let go a bath, Judd" Jason called across the length of the shack to a man tending the fire. A tall and friendly looking man waved back and opened a valve on the side of the hot-water drum. "Just get undressed and climb right in, Cap'n. Soap's on the table. Just pull the plug when you're done and I'll see you back at breakfast." With a wave at Judd, Jason left the smokehouse, and Aleksandr stripped for his bath.

By now the Russian had concluded that he had little to fear from the Chasers of the camp, and nothing at all to fear from the brother and sister who were his hosts, so he simply relaxed, hummed the latest stroza tune from Russia, and enjoyed his bath. It would be a fine day.

It was, in fact, a fine day, he thought as he strolled back to the cabin. The sun was grudgingly shedding some warmth as it cleared the trees at the lower end of camp and the smell of a promised spring was in the air. It was the wrong season to go looking for game birds, but Aleksandr was sure that the local feathered population was plentiful and he was equally sure that game wardens were scarce in Chaser Two. He smiled at the thought.

He was still smiling when he entered the cabin.

"You musta been dirty for sure," Jason said. "I'm awful hungry and Felicity said we had to wait for you."

"You'll enjoy the food the more for a slight delay," Aleksandr said, not apologizing a bit.

"That's what I should have said," Felicity joined in from the stove. She had started pouring batter the moment Aleksandr entered the room.

There was a pot of strong herbal drink on the table, a platter of smoked sausages and a basket of corn muffins. Soon Felicity began dealing pancakes onto their plates, and Aleksandr saw Jason reach for a crock. "Maple syrup from the smokehouse," he explained.

After a day of illness, Aleksandr's body yearned for nourishment, and the sensory appeal of the food was such that he barely paused between mouthfuls. Felicity looked on with amused pride as the two men bent over their plates.

"Well, I think I killed whatever was hurtin' inside me," Jason said at last, pushing his plate away.

"That was truly excellent," Aleksandr concurred. "Most unusual. Certainly the best Chaser Two meal I've eaten."

"Ha," Felicity said, vastly pleased. "You must not have been hungry until this morning. Now it's my turn." She poured more batter and began fixing pancakes for herself.

"Hop got some tobacco down to the Valley," Jason said, explaining the pouch he withdrew from his pocket. "You're welcome if you've got a pipe."

"In my coat, if it's not broken," Aleksandr said. He had exhausted his supply of cigarettes, and the taste for tobacco was suddenly powerful. The stubby pipe he carried in the field was indeed intact, and the two men stuffed their bowls and lit up with twigs from the stove.

"How luxurious," Aleksandr said, and quickly defined the word to satisfy the sharp glance from the cook.

"Not bad," Jason said. "Tobacco's hard to come by."

"Is this locally grown?" It was passable tobacco, but not at all comparable to one of the rich mixtures he favored.

"Down to the Valley," Jason said. "Lot of crops there. Good farms. Jonnies eat good."

"All the farmers are Jonnies, then?"

"Oh, I don't guess most are. Farmers are good folk, not crazy like the Jonnies. But the Jonnies got the guns and good bullets."

"So you people here can get things down there too?"

"If we come at night and the farmers ain't too jumpy. But we ain't got much to trade, and that's a long walk. Potatoes and potato lightnin'. Farmers got to hide lightnin' from the Jonnies. Syrup. Small thin's. Farmers got most of what they want."

"Are you two going to hunt," Felicity asked as she finished her own breakfast, "or are you going to sit around all day smoking and watching me work?"

"That sounds the way Sue used to talk," Jason said.

"Sue was right."

"I think we're no longer welcome, Jason," Alexandr said. "And I am eager to test those shotguns."

"Don't be too long," Felicity said. "Get back while there's plenty of light so we can go look at the books in Ash."

Moving with sluggish contentment after their heavy breakfast—Jason even had fried eggs along with his pancakes—they collected the guns and ammunition from Billy's cabin.

"Any relatively open places around here where we can scare

up some birds?" Aleksandr asked.

"Off-year potato fields up to the top of the hill," Jason said. "Wind keeps most the snow off. Whatever sun we get melts most the rest."

"Sounds perfect. Lead on."

"Let me stop at Moe's and get Smoke." Without further explanation, Jason turned toward a cabin. Aleksandr's mystification was soon ended as his companion promptly appeared with a lurcher bounding happily before him. The mongrel's coat was a streaked gray and black. "Smoke's always chasing birds out of the brush. Moe said it would be all right."

"He's a fine looking dog," Aleksandr said.

"He don't bark. Hard to keep a dog around here if they bark."

They set off up the hill in back of the camp, Brukov's bad but tightly wrapped ankle causing him little difficulty. It was a long hike, but the upgrade was gentle for the most part, and Jason set a relaxed pace. He said the dog would know if there were any Jonnies around.

At last they reached spacious fields. The temperature was mild, and Aleksandr had worked up a sweat from the hike, but he left his coat on against the possibility of a chill. The bright sun and clear air turned the scene into a vivid nature picture, each detail of sky and tree and bush unnaturally sharp and striking. Aleksandr's chest swelled with satisfaction as his eyes, no longer bounded by the hills, took in the sweeping vista and uncluttered horizon offered by the vast fields. Patchy with snow, they were bordered by other fields that were several years along in second growth, tangled with brush, saplings and brambles. Those neglected fields sloped down to where the forest proper began.

"Sit here, Smoke, till we tell you to move," Jason said to the dog, who obediently complied, but with his tail still wagging and his tongue rolling about in anticipation.

"Now, Jason, load up through there." Aleksandr had assigned the Chaser the 20-gauge pump action, and he loaded his own 12-gauge automatic as he watched Jason try to master the unfamiliar mechanics of the shotgun. They had relied on Aleksandr's machine-pistol for protection on their journey. "That's right. Now let's take a couple of practice rounds to get familiar with the arms," Aleksandr said. "I'll go first." He wanted to go first to allay any fears that Jason might have of the strange weapons that Billy had been so sure were useless if not dangerous. There was a long-forgotten scrap of lumber leaning against a windbreak tree, one of a twin line of trees between which a rutted road still ran, and Brukov carefully sighted on it. It was only twenty meters or so away, and a section of wood flew into the air as the shotgun roared.

"Seems to work," Jason commented, almost bursting with excitement. "Now I'll try mine." Following Aleksandr's instructions, he gingerly worked the pump, observing the smooth action as the shell popped into the chamber, and then he made the same piece of lumber jump. He smiled broadly. "Little different kick than my rifle. Shame to waste the bullet. Hate to do that. How close together do those little balls stay when they go through the air?"

"The way your weapon is choked, and at the distance that board is, the pattern is about this big," Brukov said, holding his hands in a rough circle. "It gets bigger the farther it goes. Big enough to shoot birds, which you couldn't do with your rifle."

"You really think all these shells will fire?" Jason pumped another shot into his gun, looking again at the mechanism with wonderment.

"Absolutely. How well trained is Smoke here?"

"He runs through the brush and chases em. He'll spot em for you first."

"Will he bring birds back after we shoot them?"

"If he finds em, he'll prolly eat em."

"Can't have that. Well, maybe after one or two he'll be full and leave the rest to us. Let's get started. Remember to shoot in front of the birds. They move fast."

Jason nodded assent. "Go, Smoke."

The dog bounded happily to his feet and trotted toward the brush, the two men holding their shotguns at the ready following slowly behind. They walked side by side and had agreed to shoot according to whose side the bird rose on, rather than alternating shots.

Almost at once, Smoke began the routine that Aleksandr soon learned by heart. The dog froze in an atavistic parody of a point, appeared to concentrate very hard on some imponderable canine calculus and then ripped into the brush in a furious, silent chase. A grouse broke out of the tangled growth with a familiar sound of rapid wing flutter. The bird was in front of them, low and fast, in Jason's line of fire. He didn't shoot. The bird had melted back into the landscape before he had his shotgun at his shoulder.

"What happened, my friend?" Aleksandr asked. He would have liked to try the shot himself.

Jason grinned hugely. "So that's the way it happens. I'll learn. Plenty more birds."

Aleksandr laughed. "Plenty indeed. I forgot that you haven't hunted birds before."

They continued their stroll through the clumps of brush, and almost at once another grouse broke cover. This time it was in the Russian's field of fire, and with a smooth motion he raised the shotgun and squeezed the trigger. The bird jumped in the air and fell like a stone. Aleksandr felt the familiar glow of pleasure at a good wing shot.

"You know how to shoot with more than your spraygun,

Cap'n. Look at Smoke go."

The dog tore off in a blur of speed—he looked like his name. "His first meal of the day," Aleksandr said with a laugh. He still was so pleased with his shot that he didn't mind the loss of the bird.

"Looks like I was wrong about Smoke, Cap'n."

Jason nodded toward the dog, trotting briskly back to them with a slight cant in his stride. His jaws were lightly clamped over a plump but very dead grouse. He came directly to the men and dropped the bird at their feet, wagging his tail furiously and looking up in an obvious appeal for approval.

"That's excellent, Smoke," Aleksandr said, patting the woolly head. "Very professional. I wish I had a reward for you."

"I brought some biscuits for hunger, Cap'n," Jason said. He withdrew one from his coat pocket and offered it to the dog, which jumped in the air to take it from his hand.

"He doesn't look like any bird dog I've ever seen," Brukov said, "and he obviously hasn't been trained, but it's just as obvious that the skills are buried inside him somewhere, and not too deeply buried, either."

"Right, Cap'n." Jason stuffed the bird into a cloth sack that he had brought at Aleksandr's request.

THEY HUNTED THROUGH the midday; several hours was plenty of time to bag enough grouse to supply half the camp, had they the shells to shoot that many birds and the means to carry them. Jason on his second opportunity expertly took a bird out of the air, somewhat to Aleksandr's surprise, as he fancied the sport to be a challenge that had to be mastered over a period of time. Smoke tirelessly and happily alternated between flushing the birds and fetching them with great enthusiasm. The birds were of several varieties, all apparently called grouse by local folk. All of Jason's supply of biscuits went to the invaluable dog, without whose cooperation they would have been hard pressed to retrieve even a brace of the game.

The golden day, the cloudless blue sky dipping down toward the far horizon, comfortable companionship, plentiful game, an active dog—all served to bathe Aleksandr in a glow of well-being. Even his earlier injuries seemed to have faded toward oblivion. The two men briefly exchanged guns so each could get the feel of both; Jason was mightily pleased with his 20-gauge, and Aleksandr for the time being almost believed he was tramping through a vast portion of Russia.

They turned back while the sun was still warm.

"I do believe we got a new food supply," Jason said as they turned onto the path down the heavily wooded hillside.

"It would seem so. Your only fault is that you pass up all but the sure shots," Aleksandr said. You mustn't worry so about conserving..." He stopped as Jason abruptly seized his arm and froze attentively. Was it Jonnies? No, in a moment he heard the same sound as Jason.

"Have to be your people, Cap'n. Want to get into the open so they can see you?"

The beat of the helicopter rotor was drawing closer.

"No," Aleksandr said after a heartbeat's hesitation. "I haven't done my job yet. They won't spot us if we're still under these trees."

"Shouldn't. Here, Smoke. Down." He moved the palm of his hand toward the ground and the dog dropped motionless.

Aleksandr felt the hair prickle along the back of his neck. He was taking a chance, though a small one. He probably could talk his way out of any unpleasantness, but surely Colonel Dalstroi would guess some of the truth, and he could be a hard man. The Imperial Mission no doubt was putting considerable time and effort into a search before deciding Captain Aleksandr Iosifovich Brukov was lost.

The helicopter came into view. If it had sensors on board, he was discovered; but most of the old sensors had been disassembled in anticipation of vastly improved new equipment, which subsequently had twice missed shipping deadlines. The helicopter swung out of sight, then cut back again. Its path no doubt had been plotted exactly by a search officer back in the Co-op of Cleveland. Other helicopters undoubtedly were following other lines on other maps.

The craft disappeared a second time, and the throbbing of its rotor died away. Aleksandr whooshed out his breath. He hadn't realized he'd been holding it in.

"Looks like you did it, Cap'n."

"Yes. For better or for worse."

"Wouldn't hurt to let em know you're alive, would it?"

"They'd make me go back, Jason. I was sent to talk with those people you call Jonnies. I don't want to return to base until I at least can make intelligent recommendations. Otherwise it will be, 'Useless Brukov, can't even overcome a few obstacles. Oh, well, we'll send a more experienced man who knows how to handle these people.' No, I could never face that."

"Whatever you say." Jason shifted the bag of birds hanging over his shoulder. Aleksandr was carrying both shotguns to help split the load, but Jason's burden was more clumsy. "Seems to me," Jason said after laborious reflection, "that means you're goin' down to Hamp to see the Jonnies."

"Correct."

"Sure, but them Jonnies is dangerous, Cap'n. Almost killed you once already."

"I think," Aleksandr said rather stiffly, "an Imperial Mission officer who is on his guard ought to be able to deal effectively with a ragged group of..." He almost said "Chasers," but he changed his wording to "Jonnies."

"Well, I don't know, Cap'n. How you goin' about this?" Jason switched the bag of game to the other shoulder of his lanky frame.

"I'll have to decide. I've been thinking I might take a night trip down there to reconnoiter, perhaps take a prisoner I can interrogate, find out the essentials. Something like that. Should be no real problem."

"Flup. That sounds worse than flyin' a hel-i-copter into the middle of Hamp. Them Jonnies is *mean.*"

"It will work well enough," Aleksandr said with more than a trace of complacency.

"When you think you'll do all this?" Jason's flat tone of voice couldn't wholly disguise his disapproval of Brukov's plans.

"As soon as I'm sure that I can walk long distances with no difficulty. My ankle is much better—just a minor sprain that responds well to support bandages. I probably could leave tonight." He grinned impishly at Jason.

"You're talkin' foolish," Jason said, but the sentence almost ended with a question.

"Yes," Aleksandr laughed. "I am talking foolish. But, to be serious, I must act soon. As you suggest, my superiors are going to have to find out about my activities, and I had better not give them enough time to figure out how to go ahead without me."

"Well, I tell you, Cap'n." He paused.

"By all means, do tell me, Jason."

"It's like this. When you go down to Hamp, I'm goin' with you."

"Why, that's very kind of you, Jason, but I wouldn't think..."

"No talk about it," the grave-faced Chaser said. "It's settled."

Aleksandr sensed that he couldn't change Jason's mind, and he was pleased that he couldn't.

‹ *Chapter Seven* ›

As THEY APPROACHED camp, Jason excused himself—he had several accounts to settle, and the birds in the bag were recognized currency. He took Smoke and the 20-gauge shotgun with him.

The afternoon shadows already were lengthening, so Aleksandr walked briskly back toward the Pembroke cabin. He found himself unaccountably eager to see Felicity again, and his sense of well-being was acute. He found himself chanting the Roll of Thanksgiving in time to his rapid pace.

But when he drew in sight of the cabin he slowed his stride and considered delaying his arrival, as Felicity was engaged in animated discussion with someone by the woodpile. The fellow was large and wore a heavy black beard. Aleksandr had noticed him his first day in camp when he and Jason were walking to Billy's. Jason hadn't waved a greeting to that particular Chaser.

Reminding himself that Felicity was eager to get a book, Aleksandr didn't hesitate long. As he approached the pair, they were in deep argument and paid him no attention.

"You can stand where you want," Felicity was telling the bearded man in a voice that boiled with malevolence, "but I don't want any more to do with you and it's none of your business if anybody's in our cabin or not."

"She stole," the man said. "I want what's mine. I got no interest in her like in you."

Felicity erupted. "Well, I got no interest in you except to see you gone," she said. "Don't come here again. Don't waste my time. I can't stand the sight of you."

Aleksandr, ignored as he stood uneasily a short distance away, again was struck by Felicity's ardor. She seemed to have no pale emotions, no partial convictions. Tides of feelings seemed to flow unpredictably in her personality, and each nuance of belief and thought and emotion registered on her facial features and even in her posture. She would be a great actress, Brukov thought, except that she could never pretend. A most remarkable savage.

The bearded man was trembling with anger and frustration. "You didn't used to say that. You didn't used..."

"Didn't used to, didn't used to!" The mockery in her voice and in her eyes was vicious. "Well, I was wrong. I thought you was a man and you wasn't."

Red rage flamed across the bearded man's face. "Why..."

He balled one hand into a fist. "Hold on," Aleksandr said, though Felicity had not flinched and the Russian suddenly understood that she had backed the bearded man down before.

"Don't you even raise your hand to her," Aleksandr, said in a firm voice. He spoke as though issuing instructions to a raw recruit.

"And this is the Russ they say you've got now," the bearded man said, quick to turn his rage onto an easier target.

"Mind your manners," Brukov said coldly.

"I'll mind you and the rest like you back where you came from," the bearded man said as his face grew ever more red. "You ain't got a bunch of friends around here. This ain't a Co-op. So don't be tellin' me what to do."

The man had a rifle cradled in the crook of his left arm, but presumably his ammunition was as erratic as Jason's.

Aleksandr held the 12-gauge shotgun, but it was out of shells. The Pushkin, however, could riddle the tall bearded man before the rifle could be lifted up to fire.

"He's welcome here. You're not," Felicity said to the bearded man, a taunt that the Russian doubted would calm the argument.

"Well, he's not welcome to me," the man said to Felicity, then turned to Brukov. "You've got guns and you can make fools out of people in Co-ops. But you better not get mighty around here, not with me. Had enough of you Russ."

Aleksandr glanced quickly about and confirmed his instinct: Several Chasers of both sexes had come into the vicinity as if by chance, and they lingered in random ways, unselfconsciously spectators but not wanting to seem a group. Aleksandr knew that it was important to establish himself if he hoped to have any positive impact on these people.

"You're not man enough to talk," Felicity said to the bearded man before Aleksandr could decide how he wanted to control the situation.

"I shoulda broke your head a long time ago," the man said. The words came out of his mouth as a strangled snarl.

"You'll not touch her," Aleksandr said. "If you have some irrational hatred of the Russians, I'm right here before you."

"Right there with guns and no one to stop you from using em, just like all Russ—hiding behind guns."

"Put your own gun down, and I'll put down mine."

Brukov saw the look of disbelief that briefly passed across the Chaser's face. He could also see that as enraged as the man was, and as eager to avenge real or imagined harm at the hands of the Russians, he still had something of the servant's fear of the master in him.

"You've got no guts for it, have you Morg?" Felicity asked quietly, almost in a whisper.

"Ahrr." The man Brukov had already reasoned must be Felicity's former mate almost threw his rifle against the side of the cabin "Now let's see you," he spat at Aleksandr, stoking his rage so his courage wouldn't die. Aleksandr calmly rested the shotgun against a tree and put the Pushkin on the ground, still in its holster. He was as tall as the Chaser, although nothing like as bulky, but the Academy was quite thorough in its training in all forms of hand-to-hand combat, including boxing, and Aleksandr had been a successful pupil. His only real concern was whether Morg was fond of concealing a knife on his person, as Jason did, but even that possibility was a matter for caution, not anxiety. Aleksandr was trained to handle such contingencies.

Hardly had Brukov shed his coat than the Chaser gave an inarticulate bellow and charged. His hands were open and his arms apart as though to grab Aleksandr about the waist and crush him, but Aleksandr had no intention of wrestling with the fellow, who easily could overpower him in a contest of weight and brute strength. Brukov simply sidestepped the charging bull and gave him a sharp jab to the ribs as he passed, a blow that sufficiently imbalanced Morg to send him sprawling, more in surprise than in pain.

"You Jonnie-lovin' finger sucker," the outraged Chaser spat out as he rose and composed himself. "I'll pound you into the snow."

This time Morg approached in a semblance of a boxing stance and Aleksandr, embarrassed by the Chaser's language although he didn't fully understand its meaning, resolved to punish his opponent thoroughly. Brukov easily ducked the roundhouse right that Morg immediately unloosed, and he countered with a quick left jab that made solid contact with he Chaser's cheekbone. Aleksandr heard a soft "oh" from a woman among the spectators, or perhaps several women. It was a light jab, but it left a burning red spot above the black beard, and the pain and surprise only speeded up the angry windmill flailing by Morg. Resolving to be careful of injury, Aleksandr decided to jab to the face with his left, but save the right for the Chaser's massive trunk.

One of Morg's swings glanced Aleksandr on the shoulder, throwing him momentarily off balance, and he had to be nimble to avoid the next blow, which would have caved in the left side of his head, considering the force with which Morg launched his flatiron-like fists. Aleksandr redoubled his concentration on keeping his feet moving, just as he had been taught at the Academy.

Morg's initial burst of rage-fed energy already was flagging, and Aleksandr began to take the initiative. Morg still hadn't learned how to avoid a straight jab, so Brukov smacked him in the nose, and as the Chaser began to wonder at the warm liquid running down his mustache, the Russian punched him solidly in the stomach. Morg's torso was hard, but not dauntingly so, Aleksandr was glad to discover, and the ease with which he used the bigger man as a punching bag was reassuring. He danced away now as Morg whoofed and wheezed at the body blow. Aleksandr didn't want to increase the distant odds against one of the Chaser's wild punches landing. As he moved in to try out a combination of blows on Morg, Aleksandr could see that most of the fight had gone out of the man, whose energy largely had been expended in pointless flailing and whose confidence had been shaken by the blows he had absorbed almost defenselessly.

For the sake of his standing in the camp, Brukov wanted no inconclusive surrender. Such an end could lead, the soldier knew, to the defeated party claiming victory and having others believe him. So Aleksandr, already winded himself and feeling his injured ankle protest the stress his footwork was putting on it, decided that the time had come for the *coup de grace*—one of those innumerable Chaser expressions so beloved by Men of History and so despised by Elders. He backed away from the newly wary Morg, drawing him out in the open, away from the tree that had been near his back, and weaved in a semicircle around the puffing hulk so that the afternoon sun glinted down into the Chaser's eyes.

Brukov dipped his left shoulder in a feint. Morg brought his ham-like forearms up to defend against the expected blow. Brukov repeated the feint. The reaction was a little slower, the defense weaker. Brukov feinted again. But this time it was no feint. He smacked a left jab into the Chaser's right eyebrow, then immediately crashed a right just over the man's heart, two more quick stinging jabs into his face, then a right, left, right into his abdomen.

Morg was doubled over, punched breathless, and his knees were unstable enough that there was a real possibility that he would pitch onto his face in a moment. Aleksandr decided that the slight risk of injury to his hand shouldn't stop him from ending the match with a flourish. Morg's vulnerable jaw was hanging halfway down to his knees as he clutched his stomach, and Brukov leaned into a right cross that was carefully aimed at the ridge of Morg's jawline.

The blow was exact and powerful, and the huge Chaser crumpled into a heap on the ground.

Aleksandr at once began to shake with fatigue and with the release of repressed fear. He struggled to master his emotions, to appear the calm and self-assured victor. He looked at the people standing about, fewer really than he had thought. They were expressionless at the outcome of the fight, and some immediately drifted back toward their cabins. A man Aleksandr recognized as Hammon, the night-loving camp guard, muttered to the man next to him, and the pair, both powerfully built, strolled over to the unconscious Morg. Hammon lifted under the shoulders and the other lifted the legs.

"Figure we'll give him a bath to wake him up," Hammon said by way of explanation to Brukov and Felicity, though looking at neither. They hauled the limp form of Morg away.

"They'll run water on him in the smokehouse," Felicity said. She had stood throughout the fight with her lips tightly compressed, trying to adopt an objective and dispassionate attitude toward the conflict, but her eyes had flashed with each blow that landed.

"That should keep him from bothering you for some time," Aleksandr said. He was still trying to control himself, and he realized that he hadn't been in a serious fistfight, one without boxing gloves and coaches, since he was a child.

"I don't need help keeping him from bothering me," Felicity said. Brukov flared up. "You may not need help, Miss Pembroke, but you certainly did everything in your power to provoke him into challenging me. That was quite a performance of manipulation."

"If you mean I pushed him into the fight, sure I did. I had to know for sure. I almost wish he'd won." Her voice was expressionless, remote. Whatever emotions she was feeling hadn't yet worked their way to the surface.

"You did what?" Walking over to the rifle that Morg had leaned against the wall, Aleksandr's anger already was ebbing. He ejected the cartridge from the rifle. No use taking extra chances.

"I knew you'd beat him," she said. "I knew it. But I had to find out." Her voice still was almost toneless. "I always used to think that Morg was strong, he could do what he wanted, I could make him get me what I wanted. But when he went to Boston, I saw. I saw what the truth really was. The Russ there made us eat dirt, both of us. Nothing Morg could do. He's just like everyone else around here." She looked coolly at Aleksandr. "You Russ do what you want, you got everything, you know everything. You say if something gets done or if it doesn't get done. Morg doesn't have a chance against a Russ. No one around here does. They're no use at all."

"I think you're being rather harsh on your fellow Chasers," Aleksandr said, but he couldn't keep the complacency out of his voice. In fact, he agreed with her.

"They can't see things. Why can't they see anything?"

He wasn't really sure what Felicity was talking about, but he had other things to consider. "Is there really someone in your cabin?" he asked while attaching the holstered machine-pistol to his belt. "Morg seemed very certain."

"Sue was here, but she went off to get her things. She's coming back. She's got no use for Morg and she wants to come back to Jason. I said she could."

"Well," the Russian said. "That was a bit high-handed, wasn't it? Suppose Jason doesn't want her back?" This was a new complication in his life, the possibility of another cabin-mate.

"He wants her."

"Well..." Just then Jason and Hammon came strolling up to the cabin.

"Hear you thumped old Morg," Jason said proudly, his usually impassive features cracked by an irrepressible smile.

"He was bothering your sister."

"He'll come back for his rifle," Hammon said. "We'll head him out of camp the other way," he said as he ambled off.

"Felicity's the only one ever beat up Morg before," Jason said, "and she did it with words."

"Jason..." she said, and her eyes looked like a thunder storm.

"All right, Felicity, little sister, don't get steamed." His tone was amiable and relaxed, and he swung the much-diminished game bag off his shoulder.

"Jason, you've been drinking."

"Not much, little sister, not much. Had a cup or two with Sam when I paid him for the bullets. Paid off half of what we owe with birds, thanks to Cap'n and his guns."

"So they did work," she said with grim satisfaction.

"Brought back the two biggest ones for us." He reached into the bag and pulled out a pair of plump grouse. "Think you can cook these without burnin' em?"

Felicity didn't pay any attention to her brother's badinage. She now devoted all her attention to the birds. "They're excellent birds, Jason... and Aleksandr." She glanced with frank acknowledgement at the Russian. "I'll roast them both for dinner."

"Well, Felicity," Jason said, "we don't have all the cows what farmer Brown's got. One's enough for tonight."

"You have cows here?" Aleksandr asked in astonishment.

Jason almost choked on his laughter. "Just a sayin', Cap'n, just a sayin'."

"No," Felicity said. "Sue's coming back to the cabin. I'll cook both birds."

That sobered Jason with dramatic speed. "You're sayin' Sue's comin' back?"

"You got good ears for a hilltowner."

Jason was silent for a moment. "Well, how do you know?"

"She was here before. Morg came looking for her. I think he was really looking for me. She's getting some things and coming back before dark."

Aleksandr recalled that Jason had said something about the woman Sue being in another camp just over the hill from where they had been shooting. There was a path between the camps that put them within easy walking distance of each other.

"Well," Jason said, "I guess I'm glad." He appeared to be thinking about whether he was glad or not.

"Sure you are," his sister said. "Give me those birds and I'll get to work on them."

Brukov coughed lightly to reassert his presence. "Excuse me, Felicity, but you had said something about going to Ash today to look at the books."

"I want to, Aleksandr." She paused. "I studied the alphabet. But it's getting late and you need some calming down. Take a walk. But stay close. There're Jonnies out on the road." She disappeared into the cabin.

"Umm," Aleksandr said after a moment's surprised silence. "Women."

"Women," Jason agreed, leaning on his shotgun and staring at the cabin door without seeing.

"Perhaps a walk is a good idea, Jason," the Russian said briskly, shaking off his pensive musing. "Suppose you guide me down the road. Let's see if there really are any Jonnies around."

"Oh, they're there. We might not see any, but we might. They're goin' back and forth like mosquitoes on a fat man. But let's go if you want." He straightened with a sigh and headed out of camp, and Aleksandr was left to scramble for his coat and then trot to catch up.

THEY SPOTTED JONNIES back at the road they had crossed that first night between Ash and the camp.

"Waste of time," Jason had complained without really seeming to mind wasting the time when he first picked a station in a clump of trees to watch the road. They were at a safe distance even if detected, and it was unlikely that anyone could see them from the road, not without luck or real effort.

"I want to see these creatures," Aleksandr explained.

"Saw em once. Close, too."

"I didn't know what to look for when they destroyed the helicopter," Aleksandr said. "All Chasers seemed much the same to me, and I wasn't really curious about them but from what you've told me of these Jonnies, they're an altogether different breed."

"Sure," Jason responded, not caring in the least what Aleksandr had said or meant. The sun had melted large patches of snow on the hillside, so it was easy to find a comfortable spot. They were dressed warmly enough for the shade that concealed them.

"Do you want Sue back?" Brukov asked. He had been thinking about that ever since his fight. Despite his curiosity it was not a question he would have dared ask a fellow Russian, it would simply be too rude. But the casual mores of the Chasers, combined with his own desire to understand them outside the Co-ops, washed away any reserve Aleksandr might have had about prying into private matters.

"Sure," Jason replied, and was so evidently confident that his answer was sufficient and complete that Aleksandr's new boldness disappeared at once.

"I see," the Russian said.

"These shotguns carry all the way to the road?" Jason's mind apparently was very far from Sue.

"Yes, but not very effectively. They're generally short-range weapons. Why do you ask?"

"Jonnies 'll be there soon."

Aleksandr looked down the road in the direction Jason's eyes were turned. "I don't see anything."

"You will. First there'll be scouts, one or two each side of the road. Then the rest. Better not move much or talk loud, even this far away."

"I won't." Brukov wished he had his binoculars with him, but they, like his maps, were in the wreckage of the helicopter.

"See?" Jason asked.

"Where? Oh, yes. There they are." By the time Aleksandr saw the scouts, the main body of the patrol was coming into view. As they had been when he first saw them, they were clad in long green overcoats, though of random cut and varying shades. "Is that a uniform?"

"Sure," Jason replied, but Brukov was not at all certain that the question had been understood.

The Jonnies walked briskly, their scouts darting before them. They all carried rifles, though none seemed to be modern. Aleksandr thought he remembered a few automatic rounds being fired at the helicopter, but probably even those were from antiquated weapons. Most of the twenty or so men of the patrol wore fur hats, and all seemed to be bearded.

"Don't look like much, do they, Cap'n?" Jason wasn't whispering, but he had deadened his voice so it wouldn't carry more than a few yards.

"They've got guns and they keep people in your camps worried. They must be something," Aleksandr said.

"Well, yes. They'll take your women and they'll take your food and your animals and anythin' else they want, even but they got everythin' a man could want down to Hamp."

"Is that where they're headed now?"

"That's one of the ways down to Hamp. Hard tellin' where they're goin' for sure."

"And are their coats always green?"

"Farmers down to the valley say their God orders em to wear green all the time, but don't ask me. Can't figure out all the stuff I hear about their God."

"Do you nonconformists who aren't Jonnies, you people who call yourselves hilltowners, do you have a God?"

"Naw. Some do, I guess. I don't know. But naw."

Aleksandr was almost relieved to hear that the people he had lived with were so nearly without religion. Imposing the ideals and disciplines of Holy Russia should be that much easier. But dealing with the Jonnies could be that much harder. Well,

Aleksandr thought, not really harder. After all, the evident truth and power of the Doctrines and Rolls and Shared Grace of Holy Russia were sure to blow away pagan superstition like the wind on the Steppes blowing dust away.

AFTER THE TATTERED rear guard of the Jonnie patrol disappeared down the cracked and overgrown pavement that once had been a highway, the pair of lanky men, one dark and one blond, returned to the camp, chatting of their midday hunting and planning when Aleksandr could make another batch of shells so they could bring in more of the valuable game.

SUE WAS IN RESIDENCE at the Pembroke cabin by the time the two men returned from their reconnaissance patrol, and Aleksandr was both amused and a little touched by the greeting between Jason and his returned mate. The pair kissed, rather like brother and sister, then gave each other a fierce hug and went about their normal household business with elaborate unconcern. They didn't speak to each other until much later, and then it was of mundane matters. Perhaps, the Russian mused, to act the very opposite of the way his sentimental countrymen would act was necessary with such a lack of privacy within a rudimentary society that offered no security. A public display of affection might make one feel too vulnerable to the brutishness of daily life, especially since the local code seemed to allow women to switch men with impunity.

Aleksandr immediately liked Sue and was relieved to see that her presence was likely to cause no strain. She was physically and psychologically the opposite of the Pembrokes. They were tall, thin, angular, dark, serious, grave of expression, sometimes morose, and in Felicity's case, temperamental. Sue was a good deal shorter than Felicity, and when she hugged Jason he had to crane his neck down for his chin to come in contact with the top of her head. She had short streaked-blonde hair that was unkempt, in contrast to Felicity's long, straight, and regularly brushed hair, the one sign of vanity that Aleksandr found in her. Sue was somewhat plump—in the manner quite fashionable lately in Russia, though not to Brukov's taste—her contours were pleasant and womanly, and her ebullience and energy were winning. She easily could have charmed most ordinary mortals even had she been less gratifying to the eye.

"I heard about you, Mister Russ," Sue said. As usual in Chaser circles, there had been no introduction, but Sue had begun to speak to him naturally and without constraint. "You fell out of the sky and broke your ankle, then you made magic guns and thumped Morg."

Aleksandr laughed. "You may call me Aleksandr, or simply Russ, if you prefer. And your summary of my local career is misleading. I didn't break my ankle—in fact, it already feels much better—and the guns aren't magic, they only need properly assembled ammunition."

"Flup, Felicity, listen to him talk." Sue was admiring and mocking at the same time.

"Ain't it?" Felicity asked rhetorically with a note of wistfulness in her voice. She had removed a portion of the top of the stove and was turning the two plucked fowls on the spit, basting them from time to time. There were potatoes in the coals beneath the slowly rotating birds.

"That's all right," Jason said with a nod toward the Russian. "He shoots real fine."

"If you can shoot down grouse with those magic guns of yours, Russ, you're goin' to be in favor around here no matter what," Sue said. "Shoot a few birds every week and thump Morg real regular and everyone'll love you."

Felicity blazed a look of pure malevolence at the unabashed girl.

"Got the jar filled, Cap'n," Jason said, pointing to the large jug that Aleksandr had come to associate with fears of damnation on earth. "Want a cup?" The woodsman seemed tense, no doubt because of the return of Sue, and he plainly was turning to potato lightning for aid and comfort.

"Not just now, thank you, Jason," Brukov said. "I'll have some of your tobacco, though, if the ladies don't mind."

"Sure, smoke away," Sue said, blithely granting permission on behalf of Felicity as well. "You're awful polite for someone strong enough to thump Morg. You could just light up and no one would dare say anything."

Aleksandr, unsure how to interpret her bantering tone, decided to change the subject. "By the way, Sue," he began as he puffed gravely to get his pipe going properly, "I should tell you for the sake of your reputation that this Morg fellow is going about accusing you of stealing from him." A quick glance at Felicity told Brukov that she hadn't mentioned the subject to her brother's mate.

"What?" Sue's eyes grew so wide and flashed such anger that Aleksandr regretted his words. Here was another Chaser woman with some emotion. "That fat, louse-ridden, scraggly-bearded coward! He's talkin' about a ring he gave me, but I won't have talk like that." She seemed to cool off as abruptly as she overheated. "I think what I'll do is go right back over there right now and give it back to him." Jason looked alarmed but said nothing, sipping again from his cup.

"Then what excuse would he have to come looking for it?" Felicity asked. "He just used it for an excuse. Keep the ring."

"I'll take it back. He says I stole!" The final word was uttered with complete contempt, though her anger was gone and already she was saying things the way an actress trying out for a role might, just to see how the words would sound.

"You could take it back, tell him off," Felicity said, "and then you could throw the ring in his face." The two of them giggled. Aleksandr had expected tension between them from what he had heard of Sue's original departure from the cabin, but now the two women seemed quite chummy.

"I'll take it to him and stamp my foot and shove it up his nose!" The pair of young women burst into gales of laughter. Standards of humor here in Chaser Two might be less than polished, Aleksandr thought, though he was wise enough to keep his thoughts to himself.

"It's already dark out," Aleksandr said. "Perhaps you'd better wait until tomorrow to confront him."

"Oh, I'll wait. I won't even give it back. It's mine anyway, so I'll keep it. If the Russ isn't here, then Jason will thump him."

"Already told him once," Jason said, addressing the wall behind the crock of potato lightning, "if he ever wanted to fight me I'd put a bullet through his head. That seemed to take his edge off some." His casual words were accepted as absolute truth.

"Are you goin' to be around here long, Aleksandr?" Sue asked with a polite and pretty change of tone.

"Not as long as I'd like. I'm enjoying myself here, though I fear I do impose on my hosts' hospitality."

Felicity shot him a sharp look.

"You're the only Russ ever been around," Sue said. "Makes people curious, but no one wants to come and stare at you. They'd prolly like to pinch you just to hear 'ouch'."

"Curious?" Aleksandr said. "I haven't had the feeling that many people were curious about me."

"Oh, not to know you or anythin'," Sue said absently, "Just to look at you."

"Sue," Felicity said, "will you come turn these birds for me?"

"Sure." Sue walked over to the stove and took the wooden handles from Felicity. "Some bird," she said, winking at Felicity, who resolutely ignored her.

"I want to show you, Aleksandr," Felicity said as she came to the table where he sat. "If I can use that thing you wrote with." She held out her hand and Aleksandr gave her his map marker. She turned over the sheet of paper on which he had printed the alphabet and concentrated as she bent over it, holding the marker awkwardly between her slender fingers.

"Your first written assignment," Aleksandr said, then fell silent as she lost herself in her chore.

"There," she said at last, and handed Aleksandr the paper.

"Well, let me see." He studied the printing. The letters were awkwardly formed, but each was accurate and in sequence. "Very good, Felicity. That's an amazing amount to learn in one day."

"I can say them, too. I followed when you said them." She took the paper back and recited the alphabet, pointing to each letter as she spoke. She stumbled several times, but needed little prompting from Aleksandr.

"That's truly remarkable, Felicity." The girl was like a sponge for such learning, Aleksandr thought. She certainly was an anomaly among the nonconformist Chasers. It was a sickening waste for her to have reached age nineteen in such a sinkhole of ignorance. "You'll be a very good student, I can see. Tomorrow we must go to Ash and get a book to start with."

"I looked at the book here," she said gravely, pointing at the copy of *Crime and Punishment*.

"No matter how good a student you are," Aleksandr said with a kindly condescension, "You couldn't expect to read that after one lesson in the alphabet."

"No... no, I didn't think so either. But every letter in that book is what you taught me." She looked at him with excitement, her dark eyes deep with yearning. "It's all there. All I have to do is learn how to put them together. Isn't that so?"

"Well, I suppose in a way that's so, but I must caution you, Felicity, it's not quite as easy as all that."

"I'll learn," she said with simple confidence.

"I think these are about ready, Felicity," Sue said from the stove.

They ate well, half a large bird each, burned in places on the skin but moist and flavorful within, baked potatoes steaming hot inside their charcoaled skins, some kind of delicious nut bread that Felicity had devised, and a large jar of red wine she had obtained from a neighbor for the occasion. The wine was raw and inappropriate, but Aleksandr found it very satisfying. He was careful to drink in moderation, despite the temptation offered by the gaiety of the talk at table. Sue's vivacity awoke a sly humor in Jason and brought merriment to the usually stern countenance of Felicity. Sue managed to make humorous even her tale of being chased by a Jonnie patrol after she had been off by herself in the woods. She finally climbed a tree to hide, "and I pulled up my skirt so in case any holy Jonnie looked up he wouldn't sin," a remark that caused Aleksandr to blush at her forwardness but only made the other two laugh.

They finished their meal and spoke of their satisfaction, and Aleksandr again declined an invitation-by-gesture to have a cup of the vicious samogon that Jason apparently found so innocuous. In helping Felicity clear the table, Sue walked past Jason and tousled his hair and he only looked shyly away without a word, apparently conforming to previous courting patterns established between them.

"Is that a guitar you brought with you, Sue?" Aleksandr asked, gesturing toward a battered case sitting next to the equally battered rucksack she had brought with her.

"I suppose so, but don't ask me. I can't play it. Someone offered it to me as payment for food over to the other camp and I took it 'cause it's so pretty."

"May I look at it?"

"Sure. Play it if you know how."

"Let me see." Aleksandr opened the case and withdrew a fairly well made wooden guitar. All strings were attached, a few frets were cracked but still in place. Someone had worked hard at preserving the fragile instrument. He tightened up the fattest string until it sounded about right to him, and he tuned the other strings from that.

"We are a nation of stringed instruments, you know," he announced to the others as he tuned. "The guitar is little known there, though I learned to play it a little. The balalaika is similar, and very popular. It is a big industry now to make balalaika adaptations of stroza concert pieces." Even Jason had been following him with at least mild interest up to that point, but Aleksandr saw a complete lack of comprehension on all faces when he mentioned the stroza. "We are overwhelmed by music in Russia now," he explained. "Almost daily there seems to be a new concert of original music, one masterpiece after another, people say, and everyone argues over their favorites. But everyone loves the stroza. It's fairly new, a huge ninety-string instrument shaped like a tub. It's all wooden, with different layers each giving a different resonance, and the most expensive ones are made out of single tree trunks. My grandfather donated one to his church in Moscow. It has foot pedals, and a master stroza player can make all ninety strings sing almost at once. It is so beautiful that there are new composers every day, each better than the next, it seems. At last we have a replacement for the organ, which now we leave to the Chasers—if you'll excuse the term. There is hardly an organ left in Russia. The stroza is not so loud, but it can fill any church with sound! A great double-stroza made by the master builder Glivinka has just been made readied, according to the news we get here. That makes me very homesick. It is the price we pay in the Imperial Mission, that we cannot be in True Russia for such things." They had all fallen silent, and the two women wore expressions of wary puzzlement listening to him.

"But here. I have it tuned," he exclaimed, striking a few vigorous chords on the guitar. "I am no master, I promise you." As if to demonstrate, he hit a very sour chord, and they all laughed, not knowing if he had done so on purpose.

"Sing, Mister Russ," Sue said. She stood behind the seated Jason and draped her arms around his neck and hugged him.

"Now you've started," Felicity said, "you must finish. Let's hear what noise you have to make."

With a show of offended sensibility, Aleksandr rose to the bait, first thrumming out his regimental marching song, which demanded a regular beat of simple chords and equally regular shouts of masculine courage, a combination that his Chaser hosts evidently found comical.

"More, more," Sue said. "It's wonderful!"

"Yes," Aleksandr, more," Felicity said, "but be careful. We don't want all the dogs howling from here to Hamp."

He sighed sadly. "It is to pray. Then listen to this." He played a ballad he had learned from his teacher in Moscow, and his listeners all nodded, though they could not understand the words he sang in his unexceptional but pleasant baritone. He explained each song after he sang it.

"And now..." Aleksandr said, working hard to find certain minor chords on the guitar that had fled his memory, "I think now I can play you the most popular song in Russia, at least when I left, though the Elders think it trivial. The English is something like this:

> *On the banks of the river whose name I don't know*
> *The poets are naming the names of flowers,*
> *Pretty flowers, and the poets are naming birds,*
> *Pretty birds.*

Only poets know the true names of rivers,
The true names of flowers, the true names of birds.
The only name I want to know
Is the only name with meaning to me,
Natalie.

As the sweet and evocative, sentimental tune died away, the last chord slowly fading on the warm familiar air of the cabin, Aleksandr could see that even Chasers responded to the bittersweet beauty of the Russian music.

"That was fine enough," Jason said. By now Sue was sitting on his lap.

Felicity said nothing, but Aleksandr could see that her eyes were soft, and the playfully harsh comment that would normally leap from her lips simply wouldn't come.

Jason patted Sue fondly. "I tell you, girl, one more sip of potato and that's it, if you'll get it for me."

She rose and mussed his hair. "Be careful it doesn't melt your bones, Mister Big Hunter."

"Only one more," Jason said complacently. "Cap'n, after all that yellin' you must need a little wettin' down."

"He has better sense than you, Jason," Felicity said. She had resumed cleaning the dishes, an activity suspended to listen to Brukov's concert.

"Well," Aleksandr said, "I'll have just one..." He caught the flash in Felicity's eye. "Just one very small one," he added apologetically, and Sue laughed.

As the men sipped at their drinks, even the vivacious and talkative Sue fell into a silence, though there was still a comfortable feeling in the room.

Finally Felicity spoke. "When you finish your drink, Jason," She said evenly, without a trace of special meaning in her tone, "I think you and Sue should go look after Billy's cabin. It shouldn't be left alone with all those valuable guns there."

"That's absolutely right, Felicity," Sue said promptly, before Jason could scratch his head and think of something to say.

And at once Aleksandr understood the comfortable sense of conspiratorial rapport between the two women. He also realized at once, though he hadn't consciously thought of it before, that the plan worked out by the women was exactly what he himself had been hoping for.

‹ *Chapter Eight* ›

IN THE WARM WASH of wonder at the mutual pleasure and responsibility they had accepted, neither Aleksandr nor Felicity was sleepy. She rose to stoke the stove and damper it for the night ahead, and he followed her out of bed. He poured her another cup of wine and she allowed him one more, "and that's all" cup of potato lightning.

Back in bed again, the blanket of bearskins at the ready as the room's warmth began to seep away, they sipped their drinks in cozy familiarity.

Felicity sighed deeply. "So, my Russ lover, what are you doing here with a lowly Chaser? Are you here simply to mock me because I am ignorant?"

"Mock you? What an idea." He nuzzled against her neck. "As if a mere mortal Russian could mock a laser beam. That's what you seem like, you know, so skinny and strong, and your skin so exceptionally white under your clothes after one grows used to such dark hair and such a grave and serious expression..."

"Stop it, Aleksandr." She pushed his hand away. "Right now I want to talk. Or else sleep. But not that."

"I am not ready for sleep, but I think I am ready for *that*, as you call it."

"You told me soldiers are used to discipline."

"You would make a wonderful sergeant."

"I suppose that's nasty."

"It was a joke. But whatever you meant by suggesting I mock you, I deny. Only the gentle mockery of bed."

"Your hand is too cold from that cup," she said, pushing him away again. He settled back against the propped-up pillows with a resigned sigh and sipped again of the samogon.

There was silence for a moment.

"What I mean when I say you mock me," Felicity said at last, "is that everything I want, you already have and don't even think about. All you Russ."

"What do you mean?" he asked, though he suspected that he knew the answer.

"You know everything," she said simply. "You can do whatever you want. You've got power over every thing living and you're able to make the world do anything you want it to do."

"Well," Aleksandr said, shifting in bed a little as he tried to think how he could counter an argument that he felt was essentially sound.

"Why do you even bother to be here?" Her voice had a tone that told him she had asked herself this question many times.

"Such curiosity seems rare among your people."

"They're fools," she said with a gust of contempt that surprised and disturbed Brukov. "Not even Jason thinks beyond his belly and his bed. I thought maybe Morg did, but he was all talk and no brains."

"You mustn't be too harsh on people who haven't even had the advantages available in Chaser Two Co-ops," Aleksandr said.

"These people don't even *want* advantages, they don't think of a single thing except staying away from Jonnies and just getting by."

"You may be right. But after all, what else is there for them?"

"And for me?" There was bitterness, almost a hopeless

bitterness, in her voice. "That's why I want to know what you're doing here."

"Well, my dear, much of what we do is classified."

She glared at him.

"That's nothing against you," he said." Just a matter of discipline."

"Discipline. That word again."

Aleksandr frowned. "It is necessary," he said.

"Huh." She paused, and he could see in the flickering light from the candle next to the bed that her face was furrowed with the effort of marshaling arguments. "I don't ask because I share your bed," she said at last. "You know I'd never speak to others of what you tell me. You also flatter our kind. Most likely no one here would understand. Most likely I won't understand, and wouldn't know what to tell if I wanted to."

"Oh, I think you'd understand well enough, and on your word of honor..."

"I'd die before I spoke!" She hissed the pledge quite convincingly.

"Well, then." He gathered his thoughts, trying to arrange his narrative. Then with a playful shrewdness he decided to exercise power first. "I'll discuss it with you if you'll get up and fetch me another cup of potato lightning," he said, holding the cup out to her.

She snatched the cup from his hand violently and threw back the covers on her side of the bed. "May your nose and the nose of every Russ always run," she said as she vaulted to her feet and strode toward the much-depleted jug. "Tomorrow Jason will be crying that he needs to get this jug filled up again." She returned with the cup. "Now talk." She got back in bed and pulled the bearskins up to her neck, with only her head awkwardly propped up on the pillows.

"I am but one insignificant and rather junior officer in the

Russian Imperial Mission."

"Just tell the truth."

"I can hardly be expected to satisfy your genetically improbable curiosity if you interrupt every sentence."

"I won't even ask what the words mean. Just go on."

"Very well. But please allow me to develop the scope of my story." He took a draught of the raw drink and felt the pleasing burn in his throat.

"As I was saying, I am but a young Captain, and so forth. My job and the job of others like me now in Chaser Two is to try to enlist the cooperation of various nonconformist groups in a plan that has been worked out in Russia. It is difficult to think how to explain this to you." He paused, and Felicity maintained silence.

"I'll try to sketch it in historical perspective, if I may. You remember that I mentioned the two enslavements?" She nodded. "Well, that's what we call the two historical deviations, works of the Devil, according to the Elders. Men of History agree that for centuries... for many lifetimes... the enslavements prevented the emergence of True Russia.

"The First Enslavement was an enslavement of ignorance. A ruler we called Peter, who was mistakenly called "The Great," took our country when it was very poor, when people were every bit as undeveloped as the people in your camp, and made Russia much stronger and much better known."

"That's not enslavement," Felicity said. "That is what we need done here."

"That's why he was called 'The Great.' But it was an enslavement, the First Enslavement, because his progress wasn't Russian, it was a betrayal of the Russian soul to Old Europe, to Chaser One. He even made the aristocrats, the upper class, speak another language, as though the Russian language were something to be ashamed of! All the fashionable ideas—and even clothes and even the teachers of little children—were brought in from Chaser One. But the Russian soul didn't die. It couldn't be suffocated, even in the cities."

"So it all changed when... Peter died?"

Aleksandr laughed. She was paying close attention to his tale, but the startling naiveté of her question was a useful reminder that she knew far less of the world than even the humblest kulak.

"No, unfortunately, it didn't change. There were still rulers, and they followed the way Peter had shown them. You must understand that while our Elders regard Peter as evil, most of us who are Men of History really think he simply made a mistake. He chose the wrong road. But we don't think he was personally evil, just the results of his rule. And he certainly was a very strong man, a genius. He pointed Russia the way it would go for many lives after his."

"Then what ended it?" She abruptly threw back the covers again. "I'm going to have more wine," she said. "Keep talking. I hear every word."

"Fetch me my pipe and that tobacco Jason left, would you?" He suspended narration until she was back in bed and his pipe was packed and smoking.

"Well," he continued, more and more enjoying the sensation of writing on such a remarkably uncluttered blackboard as offered by Felicity's mind. "What ended it? A good question. There were many bumps along the road, but the First Enslavement really was ended only by the Second Enslavement, and it was truly evil, the Antichrist that the Elders call it. It was when True Russia was not only misdirected and confused, as during Peter's time, but was forbidden and hated. Millions were killed even for imagining True Russia. It was called a Revolution, but really it was the final triumph of Peter, because the Revolution was nothing but evil ideas from Old Europe, not the ideas that Peter admired, but ideas that enslaved bodies as well as souls."

"Millions died," Felicity said wonderingly. "That is like the trees in the forest?"

"Yes," Aleksandr said grimly. "Like the trees in the forest."

"And how did that end, the... the... Second Enslavement?"

"Mercifully, let us pray the Roll of Thanksgiving, the Second Enslavement didn't last long. It ended with the Great Famines. They came at the end of centuries—that was a long, long time ago. But with so little food people turned to God and the leaders of the Second Enslavement turned on each other." There were some things that would be imprudent for a Russian to tell a Chaser. "There were small wars, fighting among many people. The same things were happening with Chasers. In Russia the leaders of the Second Enslavement were very afraid, and they finally made the mistake of having troops from the distant provinces firing on Russians. Killing Russians who only wanted food, killing with bullets fired by those who were not even Russians!" He puffed on his pipe and sighed.

"There were many years of fighting and then the Great Famines. Everything fell apart, in Russia as well as in Old Europe and Chaser Two. But finally the first council of Elders convened, and it drew up the first of the doctrines of True Russia, and the Awakening began with what we call the Final Revelation. Now at last God has smiled and we have True Russia.

"But the Elders and Men of History often do not agree and sometimes," he patted her thigh beneath the bearskin, "and sometimes we find that the will of God falls exactly between the opinions of Elders and the opinions of Men of History. That is why we say that only God rules Holy Russia."

"What does all this have to do with why you are here?" She rubbed her head against his shoulder, enjoying the scent of his flesh beneath the scent of his tobacco.

"Well," he laughed, "I know I'm taking the long way around, even by shortening very long stories, but all of it's necessary to tell you.

"You see, all of us in Russia are very conscious of our responsibilities to the rest of the world, to those who are less fortunate. Now we supply much of the food—almost all the grain —to Chaser One. Their Co-ops are almost entirely dependent on us for food. Your Co-ops here in Chaser Two are much smaller and things go along well enough with only a little Russian organization. But we all remember the Great Famines, especially we Men of History remember them—remember in the sense of having learned the lesson. Most Elders believe now that True Russia has emerged, God will never again punish the earth with famine, but even those Elders admit it is possible for God to cause or allow famines again.

"For a long time now, we have talked about storage of foods and development of new grain sources, but we never got far enough ahead for storage and the Elders always managed to win the arguments about development of areas outside of Russia.

"Some Chaser engineers have changed all that, however. We think we have a practical, economical way of distributing the crops from your great grain fields west and south of the Co-op of Chicago."

"Why don't you just fly it out on your helicopters?" She kept waiting for some secret mental challenge to emerge from his narrative, some real puzzle she could marvel at. Instead, the things he was saying seemed to present no problem at all.

"That's very perceptive of you. We have a few cargo aircraft that could carry grain in bulk, but that would cost too much—I don't believe it, but that's what some people say. I believe the Elders are horrified of anything that flies and doesn't beat its wings.

"Do you know what a train is? It's a perfect Russian machine, always solid on the ground and headed on straight tracks as far as the eye can see. Well, now we have a device that can be mounted to a locomotive, the machine that pulls a string of large containers along two tracks, and this device can put down several miles a day of almost indestructible tempered plastic rail, plenty strong enough to handle lightweight boxcars full of grain."

He had seen a prototype of the Railmaker in Russia before his posting to Chaser Two. There had been problems with the chemical mixing machinery, because the relatively new process of bonding and tempering matched grades of plastic had been developed under more controlled conditions than would be possible with a portable production facility in a barbarian wilderness. Nonetheless, the engineering was correct, and the machine proved to develop few problems in actual service. The locomotive pushed the mixing car, whose two funnels extruded the final product—perfectly formed rails that moments after touching the ground bore the weight of the following train. Boxcars full of the raw materials were interconnected and a second train, following behind, could keep shuttling between the base at the Co-op of Chicago and the ever advancing Railmaker. Half the necessary supplies would be stored in the Co-op of Cleveland, so the supply train could use that as base once the Railmaker had passed east toward its ultimate destination—the port at the Co-op of Boston. The Russian Imperial Mission had argued for the still-excellent port facilities at the Co-op of Hoboken, but the Elders balked at the ruins across the river, the grotesque island of man-made stalagmites that the Imperial Mission had flattened as its first priority in Chaser Two. Those decayed hulks of buildings embodied the reaching-to-the-sky sins of the Star Chasers, and no Russian could feel easy while they stood. So it was toward the port at Boston that the Railmaker was to be pointed, rather than have to come so near the reminders of an alien heresy.

"It's hard for me to understand you, Aleksandr."

She wasn't complaining, she was explaining why it took her

so long to think of questions. "Do you mean this machine can just make a trail right though anything, right though the middle of our camp, and along after it will come boxes of grain?"

"That's the basic idea. Not through the middle of your camp, of course. The machine only works on fairly smooth and level ground. And that explains..."

"It takes days to get to Boston from here and you said the grain fields are way away the other way. That will just take too long to move the grain, won't it?"

"Not at all. The laying of the rails will take a long time—at least two years, maybe longer. But once the trains are operating, shipments from the grain farms to Boston should take no more than two or three days. A few more days by ship and the grain will be in Old Europe, or even Russia herself."

"And they sent you here to run the machine that makes the rails?" The temperature in the cabin was dropping rapidly by now as the dampened stove conserved its heat to ration out slowly through the night. Felicity pushed her body tighter against Aleksandr's, seeking his warmth, and feeling again the stirring excitement of his newness, his strangeness, the power that he represented and embodied—power she wanted to envelop and take into herself and become.

"Not to run the machine," Aleksandr said after a pause. He considered Operation Grainrail security. He saw no harm in talking to Felicity, but he wanted to be able to tell the truth—or most of it—to his superiors when they asked him about his exchanges of information with the Chasers.

"Then what?" An arm across his chest, a leg across his legs, she was physically mimicking her desire to absorb him into her own being.

"I'll tell you 'then what' in just a few moments," he replied, turning toward her, stirred by the excitement of her own newness, her own strangeness, and her own special and haunting kind of power, which he couldn't name but which he felt strongly. They came together with a shudder of need and satisfaction.

"And now," he said with a happy sigh, "are you going to get me another cup of lightning?"

"No. Don't you remember just the other day?"

"I'm stronger now. More used to native produce."

"No. It's too hard to remember who you are when you're crawling around on all fours like a dog and throwing vomit out of your mouth."

"What an unpleasant image! You're awfully rude."

"No more lightning. I want you to talk, not to drink. You'd just say stupid things." She snuggled against him comfortably.

"Sleep seems a much better idea than talk."

"Talk." She pinched him on the chest and he jumped with surprise and then laughed.

"Rather than submit to further torture," he said, "I'll talk. But under protest."

"Tell me about the machine and what you're doing."

"Well, where was I?" Pause. "As I started to say earlier, the Railmaker needs a smooth flat surface, and that's the reason for my being in Chaser Two. It was decided after much debate that the new railroad will be based at the Co-op of Chicago. It is now making a rail loop west and south through the grain farms and back to Chicago. Then it will put rails down from Chicago to Boston. The easiest, fastest and cheapest way of doing that, according to our Chaser engineers and the Imperial Mission headquarters staff in Russia, is to put the rails down over the top of the old highway system here. Just level off the debris. There's a fairly straight shot from Chicago to Boston."

"You mean like the big roads going into Boston?"

"Exactly. You people had a very advanced highway system once, one a Russian could envy. Much of it is fairly intact for our purposes. It's unsuitable for its original purposes, of course, but it provides a ready-made roadbed for our Railmaker. Advance construction teams are already at work patching up spots that have been destroyed or weakened too badly. Much of the shoring up will already be done by the time the Railmaker starts east from Chicago."

"If you're here to fix the roads you're not doing much about it."

"Your tongue has a certain bite, my dear, that is reminiscent of some ladies I have known in Old Europe. Fortunately, I was a little more highly regarded by my superiors than to be assigned to a Chaser work team."

"So come to it, Aleksandr."

"So I'll 'come to it.' The fact is, we think we've solved most of the technical problems of the Railmaker and the roadbed but we are concerned about the possible disruptions that could be caused by bands of nonconformist Chasers who might find some reason to hate or fear freight trains bearing the insignia of the Russian Imperial Mission. It's almost two thousand kilometers from Chicago to Boston, and we simply can't police that length of track." He didn't think it necessary to mention the heavily armed guard car that was part of the Railmaker train, and even more highly classified were the contingency plans for punitive raids and the tentative decisions about placement of rail repair centers.

"So it's the Jonnies. That's why you want to see the Jonnies."

"Correct. The rail line will go fairly far south of their base, but evidently they're active that far south. And we have to ensure their cooperation. Actually, not their cooperation. Just that they leave us alone."

Felicity laughed gently into his shoulder.

"For being so smart, you Russ don't know much," she said.

"I've heard your opinion of the Jonnies."

"They already tried to kill you once."

"They're ignorant savages but the situation can be explained to them. We'll demonstrate force if necessary. A few threats, then a few gifts to make them feel better. It's not a hard task."

"Started out hard, though, didn't it?"

"Officers of the Russian Imperial Mission are expected to face danger from time to time."

"Well, I'm not just teasing you, Aleksandr. I'm worried about you. Jonnies are crazy and they like to kill. They think the Russ all ought to be killed."

"I have no doubt of their savagery but I think I can convince them it would be in their interest to cooperate. If they leave the railroad alone and perhaps provide a work crew now and then, we could guarantee them benefits—a few modern conveniences that seem in perilously short supply in these parts. On the other hand, if they hinder us, we'll rapidly make them see the error of their ways." He emitted a satisfied chuckle.

"For someone smart, you sure are foolish."

"Then help me become enlightened." He was surprised to note that he was becoming used to her barbed comments and no longer found them so impossibly insulting. She simply spoke her mind. Perhaps the difference was that he had accepted her right to have an opinion.

Felicity sighed. "You may be hopeless."

"Perhaps. But after all, I know almost nothing about these Jonnies except that they shot at me and that you people in these hilltown camps are afraid of them. I tried to find out more from Jason today, but he seemed to know nothing more than that they're dangerous and will attack a camp only when they have overwhelming superiority and want to exact revenge of some kind. Otherwise, they simply take what they want—including wives, apparently—by scouring the countryside outside the camps."

"That's about right."

"Also they're very religious. Jason knew that much, but he didn't know anything about their religion. Or about their social or political structure."

"The Reverend gives the orders. That's all there is to it."

"The *Reverend?*" Aleksandr didn't know whether to be amused or shocked. The title, after all, was a perfectly respectable one still used by some of the Elders in Holy Russia. That wretched Chaser who supposedly had acted as liaison in arranging for the Imperial Mission to meet with the group of nonconformists had been either duplicitous or an idiot. From what Aleksandr was learning about the Chasers hereabout, the man probably didn't know a thing about the Jonnies. Perhaps he simply was telling the Russ what they wanted to hear. "The Reverend," he repeated to himself.

"That's what they call him," Felicity said. "He runs their religion and everything."

"What is their religion? It might be close enough to true religion that we can establish a common ground. We have what we call Shared Grace. It would make my work much easier."

"Well, I don't know what they call it, but it's very strict. They could kill us for what we're doing tonight if we didn't have the Reverend's permission. The women are supposed to wear lots of clothes, even in the summer, and the men generally let their beards grow. They live off the farmers in the Valley the other side of Hamp. Most of the farmers aren't Jonnies, but they're scared, so they give crops away and the Jonnies leave them alone. Some of the Jonnies smoke, so they let the farmers grow tobacco, but it's done real quiet. They're really not supposed to smoke, but they're not strict on that. Potato lightning is something else. The farmers all trade for it, but if the Jonnies find it it's real trouble. They don't hold with getting drunk."

"Hum." Aleksandr rubbed his nose thoughtfully. "In truth," he said, "the Jonnies may not be so very far off acceptable doctrine. Simply a bit... fervent in enforcing Transcendent Piety."

"What's that?"

"A way of being good that our Elders are always debating. Some Elders believe in the Doctrine of Transcendent Piety, some in the works of Antinomian Law. The average Russian faith is simpler—those are things argued only by holy men."

"And your holy men are like Jonnies? I'm glad I'm not in Russia."

Aleksandr laughed. "I don't think our holy men are like Jonnies. But from what you say, the Jonnies perhaps could see the light shed by our holy men."

"You're purely foolish."

"Ah, the skepticism of women. It is to pray." He pinched the thin thigh resting next to his own.

"Ouch! I guess you're not purely foolish. I guess what it is that you are is poignant. You're just purely poignant."

‹ *Chapter Nine* ›

THE DAYS THAT FOLLOWED were among the most pleasant Brukov could remember. Spring arrived abruptly and with vigor, and the bright splendid mornings pushed the snow back into the shadows beneath the trees. The people of the camp called it "mud time," since the melting snow had that effect, and they gloomily predicted rain that was sure to make walking almost impossible. But the sun continued to shine, and the mud had yet to live up to its local reputation. Aleksandr observed that the nonconformist Chasers of the hilltowns were fond of predicting the worst possible outcome to any enterprise, whether of man's or of nature's. Perhaps the habit of expressed pessimism was a bulwark against their sense of passivity and defeat.

Aleksandr and Felicity finally went to the library, a stone building largely spared by the fires that had ravaged Ash, and the Russian, in the daylight, clearly saw the inscription above the entrance. The town had not been named for its charred remains after all. Once it had been called Ashfield. That fit with what the Russian supposed about the place the hilltown Chasers called Hamp. He could remember from his map that there was a place called Northampton nearby, south of where his helicopter crashed.

A ragged old man had appeared when they drew near the

library. He was called Josh, Felicity told Aleksandr, and lived by himself in the woods, unwilling to join a camp, but Josh loved the library though he could no more read than any of the other Chasers in the area. With his scraggly beard and his mad eyes, Josh proudly showed the newcomers through the small building, entertaining them the while with a unhermit-like barrage of anecdotes. Aleksandr liked the old man.

While Felicity absorbed the attention of the garrulous Josh for a few minutes, Aleksandr found a perfectly preserved English grammar and slipped it into his coat pocket surreptitiously, just in case Josh assumed a proprietary interest in his library. Brukov had been interested in looking for rare books in the unlikely collection, but from a random sample decided that the town of Ashfield had not been the repository of any unusual volumes, or at least none that had survived. There were many empty shelves.

"I was tellin' er," Josh said to Aleksandr when he rejoined Felicity, "Jonnies all over yesterday early, an a Russ air machine come over later an set down, set down right here. I stayed up to the trees, mighty scared I was. They got out with sprayguns an looked round real quick, then got back in the air machine an up they went. Great noise, I say, great noise." The old man had forced his face up uncomfortably close to Brukov's and compounded the closeness by raising his voice and repeatedly touching Aleksandr's arm, the way a drunken kulak might behave on a Moscow street.

Josh evidently wanted some kind of explanation from Aleksandr, but he said only that he doubted the machine would return, hoping thus to reassure the old man.

Nevertheless, Aleksandr was nervous on the way back to camp, and was glad that he had decided to wear a tattered old coat of Jason's over his uniform. He carried the 12-gauge shotgun so as to appear conventionally armed to a distant or casual observer, but he had the machine-pistol under the coat.

Once back in camp, he promptly gave Felicity her first lesson from the book, then set her to copying and repeating the few simple sentences. He then left her and went to Billy's, where he instructed Jason in making shotgun shells. They heard that Sam the bullet-maker was not pleased, but Aleksandr had no intention of stealing any more of his customers. Sue was cheerful and happy to see him and didn't embarrass him with sly questions about him and Felicity, as he had feared, and he and Jason promptly set off for a brief hunt while the light held.

The pattern emerged soon, though it lasted all too short a time. Aleksandr went over a new lesson with Felicity in the morning and then went hunting with Jason. They ate their cold lunches in the fields, sitting on rocks in the sunshine, talking little but perfectly at ease. Despite the predictions, it never rained hard enough during the day to keep them out of the woods and the fields.

By the time they returned to camp, Felicity had mastered her lesson and was furiously struggling to puzzle out the next one before Aleksandr could explain it. He had found a clutch of pencils and a notebook in the library, and she copied her assignments diligently, absorbing the knowledge the way a parched garden takes in rain. She studied a new lesson in the evening while Aleksandr went to have a cup or two of potato lightning with Jason and Sue. It was a life that suited the Russian, and he repeatedly reminded himself that he had other obligations that couldn't be long ignored.

Not the least of his comforts, of course, was the passionate intimacy of Felicity. Stern, unemotional and even cold in bearing, she dropped all reserve in private. She made no effort to check her desires—indeed, seemed incapable of checking them —and she threw the wiry strength of her thin body so wholly into their pleasures that Aleksandr felt overwhelmed by her. He sometimes feared she was transformed into another being and might not regain her former starchy integrity. But she always receded not merely to spent exhaustion, but to a catlike sensuousness that was at once satisfying and demanding, a well of energy that seemed to grow fuller the more it was emptied.

Their most recent evening of intimacy was almost their last, however. Felicity had asked about other women he had known, and Aleksandr had not stopped to think that an unsophisticated nonconformist in Chaser Two might not have the same attitudes as the worldly Chaser One females he had been privileged to know. Consequently, he responded guilelessly to her question and began waxing lyrical about the many charms of his beloved Lyalya, the girl in Moscow to whom he was to be married.

Immediately there was a lightning storm in Felicity's eyes, and she said several exceedingly rude things to Aleksandr before inviting him to leave her bed. The hapless Russian was defense-less against this surprise attack, stammering in confusion and drawing back in horror as though the force of her words were a physical assault, which indeed she seemed about to launch.

He finally succeeded in calming her, however, babbling nonsense in hopes that a quick temper soon cooled, and she subsided to a pout. Chaser One girls knew that a Russian marriage was a very sacred thing, completely different than a dalliance, no matter how serious that dalliance seemed, and certainly no Chaser One girl would take offense at a Russian praising his intended—or so it seemed to the Man of History who was somewhat less sophisticated than he might have supposed. As the storm clouds cleared, Aleksandr vowed to himself never to mention Lyalya again.

That one storm aside, there was nothing but calm and growing satisfaction for the Russian during his stay in camp. Not only did he have the unstinting love of an exciting girl and the joy of a good hunting companion, Aleksandr often found himself strolling around the common of the camp as though he were the mayor, learning the names of the people and exchanging such pleasantries with them as seemed appropriate. They were in no way as cheerful or as sentimental or as boisterous as Russian peasants, but nonetheless Aleksandr gloried in their shy deference and he amused himself with dreams of how he could help his career by helping them.

‹ *Chapter Ten* ›

ALEKSANDR TROTTED BRISKLY across the potato field and back again while Jason held his shotgun. They had as many grouse as they wanted for the day—already the novelty of the game bird diet had worn off for the residents of the camp—and the Russian wanted the challenge of running over the uneven dirt of the field.

"Fine, Jason, I'm fine," he said, puffing only slightly as he returned to his starting point. He bounced happily on his toes in a rustic ballet imitation. "Not even a twinge in the ankle," he said. The bandage had been off for two days, and tramping through the woods and fields with Jason had provided radical therapy.

"Looks like you're ready," Jason agreed.

"No doubt about it." He was ready to try to establish contact with the Jonnies. He had been convincing himself that he needed to fully recover his strength, but for two days he had been perfectly capable of doing what needed to be done. He realized now that while he had been procrastinating, dallying to enjoy Felicity and Jason and the comforts of the primitive camp, he had only postponed the appropriate guilt he should feel at his slackness toward his duty. But now the time had come, and the decision to act freed him from the guilt and made his soul leap with happiness. He recited to himself the Roll of Thanksgiving as he and Jason wandered back to camp, taking their time in the taiga, the virgin forest they both loved so well.

FELICITY WAS STUNNED at their departure. She hugged Aleksandr fiercely; then let him go without a word. She already was managing to read the children's books he found at the Ashfield library, though as she gradually worked out the meaning of the words, she often became furious. She was not a child and did not want to read childish things. Unless she kept herself under rigid control, she grew frantic with the need to read the other books, the ones where she could make out only the simplest words. At times she was almost paralyzed with the conviction that the learning was simply too difficult, she'd never be able to read those books but then her will and her determination returned, and she trembled with the desire to *know*. Now Aleksandr was leaving. But of him she kept, like the undetectable swelling of a belly, the seed of learning. She wanted him back, but he had already given her more than she had dared hope.

EXUBERANT, EXCITED, and supremely confident, Aleksandr left camp with Jason in the early evening. Jason carried the 12-gauge shotgun, with an ample supply of single-slug shells in his pockets. He was better armed than ever in his life. Aleksandr didn't take the other shotgun, now he was concerned with Russian Imperial Mission affairs, and during the day had thoroughly cleaned his Pushkin Series 2100 machine-pistol and checked his other weapons.

"Well, Jason, we're lucky fellows, eh?" He adjusted the blanket-roll over his shoulder. "Old winter is gone away. Even at dark it doesn't get so cold, eh?"

"Um," Jason replied, his eyes ever roaming ahead and to the side, the eyes of a woodsman who had survived for years by being alert.

"Cheer up, Jason. Don't be so gloomy. You're under the official protection of the Russian Imperial Mission. You're the safest man in Chaser Two."

"Flup."

Aleksandr laughed expansively. "You hilltowners are a pessimistic breed, I've learned."

"Not too loud, Cap'n. Never can tell what's lurkin'."

Again Aleksandr laughed, but softer in deference to the exaggerated caution of his companion. "What's 'lurkin' as you put it, is nothing compared to what we are about to accomplish. We're going to tame the ferocious Jonnies, my friend. Everyone will benefit. Russian Imperial Mission property will be able to pass this way without incident, the Jonnies will have enough trinkets and whatever else they may desire to pacify them, and Jason and Felicity Pembroke and their friends will be free to pursue their lives while living in safety. Poof, we sweep fear and ignorance away, and in their place we have peace, prosperity, and the blessings of a God who tests us before rewarding us. It is to pray."

"It is enough to make a cat laugh," Jason quoted back the Russian saying he had learned from Aleksandr, and even the dour hilltowner had to smile at his own wit.

"Truly, truly," Aleksandr said, pressing his advantage. "Haven't we planned it well? Before light we camp in hiding on this side of Hamp, then tomorrow night we go to the Valley to see the farmer Hop told us about. We arrange to meet with these Jonnies, the Reverend himself, and explain that every day there is a sun and every night there is a moon, it is as simple as that."

"Duh duh duh," Jason commented with renewed gloom.

"Simple reasoning doesn't seem to please you Chaser folk."

"Simple's a word we use to mean someone who doesn't think

so good."

"Oh, don't be so grumpy, Jason. Must you always look for the dark side of every question?"

"They shot you down once. They'll do it again, and this time it'll be a lot harder to get away."

"They shot me down because of an unreliable informer, some-one who probably wanted to start bad blood between the Jonnies and the Russian Imperial Mission. We didn't know enough to be wary. Now I know that they are suspicious and violent people, but I think I can explain the situation to them, explain how they have everything to gain and nothing to lose by cooperating with us. Probably they are as tired of constant struggle as you hilltowners are. They'll welcome peaceful mediation."

"Flup." His favorite word was Jason's only comment.

A few kilometers south of Ash, Jason deviated from the trail the pair had followed in their initial retreat from the Jonnies, a memory that now seemed long ago to both of them.

They veered to the east so they could pass well clear of Hamp on the way to the Valley farm. Conversation ended as Aleksandr joined Jason in watchfulness, and the Russian noted with annoyance that he already was beginning to feel sleepy—his body in a very short time had become completely attuned to a comfortable life, a few drinks in the evening, a warm fire, a warm bed and a warm woman. Tramping through the chill of an early spring night in potentially hostile territory demanded different mental preparations altogether.

The huge friendly moon, surrounded by its thousand acolytes of stars, each throbbing for attention, made nighttime concealment uncertain at best. Jason kept them to low ground, to hillsides away from the moon, to shadows barely cast by themselves.

Jason's hand silently halted them in the shadows after they had been walking for some time, and they watched as five figures moved rapidly down the roadbed that paralleled their more obscure path.

Aleksandr whispered, "Jonnies?"

"No, but trouble of some kind, most likely." Jason spoke in a whisper, but with a timbre that plainly wouldn't carry. "They use the road cause they're in a hurry somehow. Figure no Jonnies are out tonight and they're most likely right. If they do run into Jonnies they'll see the scouts first and run off to the woods. Jonnie patrol out at night is out for a reason, and the reason ain't likely to be those scum. Bandits don't fight Jonnies, they look for what they can take easy."

"Did they see us?"

"Don't think so. Might have chased us if they did, cause they got more guns. But like I say, they're in a hurry somewhere."

"Are there many bandits out at night?" Aleksandr spoke in a normal tone as the last of the group disappeared around a bend in the road.

"See some most nights I'm out. Had to run a couple of times. Killed a couple. Mostly they're not lookin' for a man with a gun, they're lookin' for somethin' easy."

They saw several other night roamers in the next few hours, though no groups, only single men or pairs.

"Good night for huntin'," Jason said. He didn't try for concealment, but kept clear of any signs of travelers.

To Aleksandr, the sight of the armed men seemed symbolic and strengthened his resolve to act as the catalyst for peace in the area. Night men, armed, afraid, uncertain, in ignorance as profound as the shadows they sought—there was no reason for such barbarism. The Chasers of Old Europe, after all, were gentle and well-educated—often better educated than Russian peasants. They were valuable, even indispensable, to the administration of both Chaser One and Russia, to technology, to production of all kinds. Certainly these isolated nonconformists of Chaser Two didn't need to live in darkness. Felicity with her phenomenal thirst for knowledge had shown him that they were capable of much more. Circumstances and the mysteries of God had made them ignorant savages, but they needn't remain so. Many Russians, especially the Elders and their followers, would never think to question the mysteries of God, but Men of History such as Aleksandr could sometimes discreetly hope to influence God to alter those mysteries slightly, and sometimes God agreed.

Before dawn they reached a secluded copse protected by a hill in back and with a wide view south toward level land. A small herd of deer had been startled from cover by their approach, and Jason considered that a good sign—probably no one else was around.

"Here's where we camp for the day," he said. "Plenty good. Keep an eye out toward the Valley." But Aleksandr could see that his guide was uneasy. Jason hadn't been this far south before except with the experienced men of his camp who traded with farmers, and even those trips had been few. He much preferred to stay where he knew each tree and culvert.

THE DAY PASSED uneventfully. They shared biscuits and jerky, for although Aleksandr still had some food tabs in his jacket pouch, he no longer felt comfortable disdaining the fare carried by Jason. It was chilly, having to sit without exercise in the shade of the clump of pines. Not for the first time, Aleksandr wished he had salvaged his binoculars from the helicopter. They saw at some distance various signs of traffic on the roads and paths to the south, and even a few horse-drawn wagons passed during the day. Evidently an open commerce of some kind did take place under the domination and protection of the Jonnies.

"That's somethin', them horses," Jason said, nodding toward the distant animals. "Only two farms got em. All of em got sick long time ago, they say. Only a few left. Even the Jonnies can't take these for ridin' the way they want. Need em too much for farmin'."

Aleksandr marveled again at the backwardness of so much of Chaser Two. A fleet of some two hundred Akhmatova tractors was being assembled in warehouses at the Co-op of Boston for delivery to the grain fields once the railroad was available for transport. A few of the machines had already been quietly airlifted out west to get a head start. A single one of those tractors could handle farming for this entire region, Aleksandr guessed, since the population here seemed small. He recalled from his briefings that Jason's information was correct: Disease had wiped out most farm stock of all kinds, and much of the population as well. The tide of epidemics had subsided as abruptly as it had flowed, however, and now medical officials in Chaser One were planning emergency stocks to handle possible future outbreaks, should the economic development of Chaser Two warrant special protection. Projected population growth figures made it seem that the grain fields south and west of the Co-op of Chicago might be vital in another decade. The population of Chaser One was known to exceed ten million people, and they seemed to breed like rabbits. Almost three times as many people were estimated to be thinly spread over the vast reaches of Chaser Two, though the estimates were admittedly little more than guesswork, as there hadn't been sensor flyovers of much of the area.

JOBEY WAS THE NAME of the farmer Hop had told them about. According to Hop, Jobey was discreet in all his dealings, supplied the Jonnies with sufficient food to earn their protection, and yet did not hesitate to trade with hilltowners and others outside the Jonnie fold. Such transactions were strictly forbidden by the Reverend, but Jobey had always avoided trouble, even while bartering Russian gunpowder stolen from Boston. He also bartered sugar, which often came back to him on the other end of the barter transaction in the form of potato lightning, which he traded to other farmers despite the Jonnie laws.

Aleksandr was so restless after a day of enforced idleness—he slept through the dawn hours, but couldn't drop off again after midmorning—that he tried to pressure Jason into leaving their place of concealment before dark. There were no signs of people around, after all, and the earlier they got to the farmer's the better. Jason was unmoved, and it was fully dark before they set out again.

It took them several hours of circuitous walking to reach Jobey's farm. The land was almost flat, which made the trip easy on their legs, but concealment was difficult. Fortunately, the moon was clouded over, unlike the previous night, so there was less fear of detection. Cloud cover or no, Jason was cautious—excessively so, in Aleksandr's opinion—and kept them well off the roads, halting their progress at any sound of unusual noise. The faint haze of light that seeped through the gray heavens allowed them just enough visibility to make their way. A completely dark night would have meant that Jason, unfamiliar with the paths he picked out, would have had to hold them over another day.

They saw the farm from three kilometers away. Jobey obviously had no fear of raids. His days were unimpeachable in their service to the Jonnies, Hop had told Aleksandr; his nights were devoted to the conduct of other business. Now, windows of the farm were ablaze with light, profligate with the kerosene hoarded so jealously back in camp. It was warmer here in the lowlands, and as the wary travelers drew closer they could see that even the barn had lights, though no people were to be seen outlined against the glow. Jason and Aleksandr stood by a tree for some time studying the farm. They finally saw movement in the barn, but there was no activity that seemed of concern.

"I'll go, then," Jason said. They had agreed he must approach the farm first, as though on a simple trading errand, to make sure that there was no danger. Aleksandr settled back against the tree to wait. Some scent on the breeze, some dampness in the air that mingled with the bark of the birch tree he rested against, reminded him of the scents of his youth, and he quickly calculated that now it would be the beginning of the Festival of Awakening in Russia. Incense and church services all day long, the Elders in their brocaded robes. Concerts in the evening, with rival geniuses of the stroza vying to play so well that their names would dominate the conversations at the celebratory parties afterward. Poetry readings in the Hall of True Russia in Moscow. Choirs delighting in the new settings of prayers that the current generation of composers had developed from the chanting of church services. Ritual village dances and the ordination of Elders. The elaborate formal announcements of engagements.

Aleksandr sighed with a lonely ache for his country and his countrymen, for the company of his vivacious, patrician Lyalya, with her wide sweet eyes and her unquestioning devotion. As long as he remained in Chaser Two, he realized, he could never feel that completion of being, that peace of the soul, that he knew in True Russia, where every creature and custom was as familiar as the Roll of Thanksgiving and where the unexpected was good, unexpected only because it exceeded expectations.

Only the thought of Felicity nagged at his longing for Russia. She was the only element in Chaser Two that promised something he wanted but didn't understand, was tantalized by without quite being able to analyze. She was more than simply a Chaser woman, she was the only Chaser mystery he had encountered. There was little among these people to encourage enchantment. He enjoyed Jason's company and he regarded the opportunity to observe nonconformists in their native setting as a remarkably valuable experience, but he needed the company of Russians.

"It's fine." Jason's voice barely three feet away startled Brukov out of his reverie. He cleared his throat and stirred quickly to act as though he had been alert and had watched Jason's progress from the barn, but he suspected that Jason was perfectly aware he had been unobserved.

"No one there?"

"Just Jobey and one of his boys in the barn. He says no one else will be by tonight, and if there is, he'll show us how to get away."

The pair now approached the farm openly and found Jobey leaning against the wall of a pen inside the barn. The farmer looked up with affected indifference as Jason and Aleksandr entered. He simply lifted his hand in greeting, then turned again to the small boy beside him.

"Now, which one do you want, Angel? You got to make up your mind." The boy was excited, in the perpetual motion of youthful happy confusion. "Poppa, I can't tell."

"You got to tell."

"I can't tell, I can't tell." The boy was simultaneously hanging on the wall of the pen and climbing it, arching his back and contorting himself in the way of small boys and acrobats.

"Then think about it tonight. Time you went to bed now. In the morning you have to tell me which one. Off to bed now." He gently nudged the boy out of the barn as the two strangers slowly approached. Aleksandr looked into the pen. A group of piglets was nuzzling up to a sow. Except for the runt of the litter, who was unsuccessfully dashing from miniature curlicue tail to miniature curlicue tail in search of a teat of his own, the piglets were as fat and seemed as content and affectionate as any pet.

Jobey turned to Jason. "I remember you now, you were here once, long time ago. Came to haul back some powder for Sam."

"That's right." Jason shifted from foot to foot uneasily. He hadn't liked the Valley that time, and he didn't like it now.

Aleksandr nodded toward the piglets. "The boy gets one to raise for himself?"

"He'll pick out one we won't slaughter this fall. Good year for pigs. We'll eat good as Russ next winter."

Aleksandr was in his uniform, having resisted Jason's entreaties that he venture forth incognito, and the farmer plainly knew what the uniform meant.

"We ain't goin' to be long," Jason said.

"No," Jobey said, and stood for a moment in unhurried thought. "Well, my youngest already seen you." He thought another moment. "He's not as dumb as he looks, just like me. My oldest boy, Gar, is out to the road like always, so Jonnies wouldn't surprise us, even if they came along, which they won't. So you might come into the house." He ambled off at a deceptively quick pace, leaving the Russian and the hilltowner to follow if they chose. They followed.

The farmhouse was spacious and clean, though furnished with the utmost stark simplicity. The only warmth of decoration was provided by a profusion of rugs on the floor. The furniture itself was wooden and sturdy, but of only passable workmanship. Nevertheless, after the camp, the farmhouse seemed a palace, and Jason was ill at ease. At Jobey's invitation he sat on a chair, but only on the edge of the seat. He was rigid with the desire to behave properly, but didn't know what proper was in these particular circumstances.

Jobey called out to another room, "Am, bring three glasses and the cider." Soon a middle-aged woman, just beginning to add fat to her sturdy farmwife's frame and her hair just beginning to go to gray appeared. She brought in their drinks on a tray. She shyly glanced at Aleksandr, but said nothing. The cider was pleasant tasting and nonalcoholic.

"So," Jobey said, smacking his lips as he finished his cider in one long draught, "what business do you two have with me?"

"First off," Jason said, bending to the rucksack he had dropped at his feet, "we have this." He pulled out a half-gallon jar of potato lightning. The jar was one of the kind supplied by Valley farmers expressly for the purpose of having them returned full of samogon.

"Ah, thank you." Jobey eyed the bottle appreciatively, holding it against the lamplight to check its clarity. "Not exactly a full shipment, but every bottle helps. What can I give you back?"

Aleksandr interjected himself into the bargaining at this point. "All we request," he said, "is some simple information." He noticed that Jobey had slipped the bottle under a small table that had a cloth on it hanging to the floor. The cautious farmer had developed good habits of concealment. "We wish to go into Hamp tomorrow night and find the Reverend, simply for the purposes of discussion. Negotiations. A kind of bargaining. If you can tell us where to find him after dark tomorrow, that's all we require. Naturally, the source of our information will remain confidential." Brukov considered the last sentence for a moment. "We won't tell how we knew to find him."

"So that's all you come for?"

"That's right," Aleksandr said, and Jason nodded wisely.

"You know they're makin' life hard around here lookin' for you. You're the Russ that killed some Jonnies and got away." It wasn't a question. "Reverend wants to talk to you for sure. They think you're gone, but they're lookin' anyway. Russ air machines been around, so they figure one of em picked you up. But they're lookin' anyway. Jonnies get mighty surly when Reverend's unhappy, and he's unhappy." The farmer was a hard, bulky man, not tall but square. He hadn't gone soft and pudgy from all his commerce. And his voice had no friendliness in it.

"I understand perfectly," the Russian said smoothly. "I have no wish to disrupt the lives of those who live in the hills or in the Valley—nor do I wish to disrupt the Jonnies, for that matter. Once I have a chance to talk to the Reverend, I think all our misunderstandings will be put behind us. Because he is... unhappy, as you put it, I would like to arrive unannounced. He might be difficult to approach otherwise." Brukov supposed the irony was lost on the farmer.

"I see," Jobey said. He poured out some more cider into the three glasses.

"Tell us where to go and how to get there, and we'll leave now," Jason said. "No use bothering you any longer than that." He had been twisting and stretching on the chair the way a bored child might.

"I see," Jobey repeated, not wanting to say anything until he had thought it all through. He had never had to think about anything like this before.

"As Jason said," Aleksandr added, "we'll leave your property immediately. We'll be far away during the day tomorrow, and we'll go into Hamp another way."

"Well, it's worth doin'," Jobey said at last, his decision in the finality of his tone.

"Good," Aleksandr said, trying to sound pleased rather than jubilant. He believed that one should never let a potentially troublesome person know that he had been bent to one's will.

"It's late now for a farmer," Jobey said, and Aleksandr irresistibly felt the weariness in his own body. "I've got to be milkin' in less time than I'd like. There's no need for you two to go anywhere. Sleep here. You won't be bothered. Stay inside tomorrow and no one will see you. Then after chores tomorrow afternoon I'll show you just how to find Reverend. Good enough?"

"Good enough," Aleksandr said, though he could see that Jason didn't like the idea of staying on the farm so long.

"Am," Jobey projected his voice back toward the kitchen, and he sat comfortably until the woman appeared. "These two are stayin' tonight and tomorrow." To Aleksandr and Jason he said, "Couple of beds in the spare room. Not much, but not bad. Am 'll show you. I've got to talk to my boy Gar about his watch before I turn in. Night."

As Jobey left, his wife silently beckoned them to follow her, and they soon were in the simple but adequate room, stripping off their clothes and suddenly very tired after the strain of their trip. Jason barely grumbled about the foolishness of staying in the farmhouse rather than returning to a quiet spot in the woods —that bed looked too good to refuse.

BY THE TIME THEY awoke, the sun was well up and Jobey's farm was past breakfast chores. Jobey's wife, Am, stern and seemingly disapproving, brought a heaping tray of food to their room, but indicated the curtains drawn across the window. There would be people around all day. Aleksandr and Jason were to stay out of sight.

The sleep had done them good, and they resigned themselves to a day of confinement, though time soon wore on them. Aleksandr decided to work his way through the entire set of Russian Imperial Mission physical exercises, which Jason readily agreed to learn. The elaborate series of exercises, designed to flex and test virtually every set of muscles normally used in work or war, began with simple and seemingly meaningless warm-up stretches and culminated after numerous intermediate steps in grueling one-armed push-ups and other demanding exercises that could be performed only by the adept. Aleksandr himself usually graded out in the respectable low eighties percentile, while even the fittest and most athletic of his fellow officers rarely exceeded ninety percent. The grading was done partly by a stopwatch.

Aleksandr again marveled at how well Jason learned demanding skills. The Chaser had immediately become an excellent wing shot, and now he mimicked the exercises with fluid ease. His primitive existence kept him in first-rate physical condition—most Chasers seemed remarkably strong—and his native talents were high as well. It wasn't only a matter of superior coordination and acute senses. He seemed to instinctively understand weights, stresses, motions. Without any formal education, and without even a vestige of the fiery intellectual curiosity of his sister, he seemed to have a firm understanding of nature. His facility in the exercises almost irritated Aleksandr, who insisted that the muscular challenges were fiendishly difficult. With his usual passive pleasantness, Jason agreed about the difficulties, though he continued to perform the exercises with the ease and aplomb of an experienced and well-conditioned Imperial Mission officer.

The exercises at least passed some time, as Brukov carefully explained the purpose and method of each movement to an uncaring student body of one.

There was a basin of water in the room, as well as an antique commode whose function was known to Aleksandr only because he was a Man of History who enjoyed studying ancient civilizations, so they were able to make themselves comfortable. Soon enough, another heaping tray announced lunch, and after that it was a luxury to sleep the afternoon away, storing up energy for the demanding night ahead. On rising, they repeated the morning exercises, and even Jason noticed more than one tender muscle, a fact that somewhat consoled Aleksandr.

A few times they heard voices outside, but there were no intimations of danger.

At last it was dark, Jobey had cleared the farm of outsiders, and his middle son, Bo, who had spent the night before with a friend on a neighboring farm, was posted as watchman.

The dinner dishes cleared—Aleksandr and Jason had eaten with the family, though there had been no pleasant conversation during the meal—Jobey was ready to provide his visitors with the information they wanted, and plainly he'd be glad to see them gone.

"Right," he said, fetching a pencil and a piece of stiff brown paper. "Gar here will take you to the start of town." Aleksandr glanced again at the surly youth, who was a powerful looking copy of his father. "After that, you're on your own, and you ain't to mention me, not ever."

"Of course not," the Russian said, but Jobey didn't seem to be appeased.

"The road goes like this," Jobey said, drawing a street map with a surprising delicacy of line. "Gar will leave you right here." He marked an X. "Nobody uses that road much, and Jonnies won't be around at night. You keep goin' straight. You go past a big brick buildin' on the other side of the road..." marking another X, "and up here's a church. That's where Reverend lives, and he don't hardly ever leave there. Shouldn't be many Jonnies around unless he's got a meetin'. Gettin' to see him's up to you. Look good at this here drawin', you can't take it with you."

They quickly gathered their gear, thanked their host and hostess, and followed Gar out into the night. The bulky young man set a brisk pace.

It was not far from the isolation of the farm to the buildings of the town. Scudding clouds in the evening breezes allowed rather more light at times than Aleksandr would have preferred, but the plan was well underway and he dismissed idle regrets as impermissible distractions.

They circled around the first line of buildings until Gar located the road they were to take into town, and indeed it did seem to have fallen into disuse. No people or lights were in view, and Brukov could sense even the silent Jason's approval.

"Here," Gar said in a normal conversational tone, then turned and went back toward the farm without another word.

"I don't feel so good about trackin' through all them buildin's," Jason said softly. "They ain't trees and I ain't used to walkin' through em."

"We're both strangers here," Aleksandr conceded. "But this looks like a deserted area of town, so we ought to be all right. But no more talk."

Jobey's hand-drawn map turned out to have been quite accurate, though Aleksandr had been prepared to puzzle out relations between the drawing and reality. The landmarks indicated by the farmer appeared on schedule, and the street through the buildings was as straight as he had sketched.

But it was eerie business, Aleksandr thought, picking one's way along a street that had been neglected long before he had been born. When the clouds parted and allowed bright moonlight to flood through, the buildings at least provided protective shadows, and the two intruders were careful to make little noise. For all Aleksandr knew, young Jonnie lovers were fond of the dark neighborhood, though the rules of the tribe seemed not to encourage such pastimes.

The cracked and heaved remnants of pavement combined with their caution to make progress slow, but it wasn't long before they reached a corner from which they could see a settled section of the town. Windows of houses were yellow with light, and Aleksandr knew that they would have to pass beyond those houses to reach the Reverend's church-residence.

Surveying the scene from the shadow of a large brick structure, they could see that it was necessary to cross an open square before they could reach the relative obscurity of the complex shadows thrown by the inhabited houses along the street, which ran uphill toward the church.

"There's nothing for it," Aleksandr said at last. "We'll go

together at a fast walk, like two Jonnies in a hurry to get home. Agreed?"

"Yup." Jason had agreed to every crazy thing so far, and he couldn't stop now.

"We'll head for that line of hedges over there." It was hardly a necessary instruction, as there was really only one destination if one were to cross the square on the way up the street.

The two men gave one more long look around, saw no activity and set off smartly across the open space.

IT WAS A NEATLY laid trap, and there was no possibility of either resistance or flight.

As Aleksandr and Jason approached the hedges and began to hike up the incline, there was a rapid stir in the darkness behind the shrubbery and a line of some twenty men arose, their rifles leveled at the intruders.

"Don't move!" a voice commanded, and Aleksandr froze with fear. "Drop the gun!" Aleksandr continued to look straight ahead, but he could hear Jason's shotgun fall to the ground. His own hands were empty.

Two green-clad men promptly emerged from behind the hedges without their guns and trotted into the light. Both ignored Jason and set to work searching the Russian.

"I see we were expected," Aleksandr said, striving to appear collected.

"Shup!" the man said, and he removed the Pushkin machine-pistol, which disappeared into the folds of his coat.

"Easy on the tailoring," Aleksandr said as the other man plunged his hands into the uniform pockets.

"SHUP!" Aleksandr recognized the near hysteria of an inexperienced and terrified trooper. Such people were prone to swift and irrational violence so Brukov shut up.

They removed his two remaining gyrobombs, his identification papers, heat tabs, food capsules, even his pipe. They unbuckled his holster belt and removed it, along with the machine-pistol clips and other paraphernalia. Then they went over him again to make sure his pockets were empty. Satisfied that the Russian had his sting removed, they turned to Jason, whose pockets yielded only shotgun shells and a couple of biscuits. Aleksandr's bedroll and Jason's rucksack they took without examination.

Only now did a thin man, vibrant with nervous energy, come forward with the posture and glaring eyes of someone in complete control of the situation.

"This time the Russ devil can't get away," the man said with smug triumph. Like the others, he was bearded, though his chin hair was wispy.

"You're wrong on fact and assumption," Aleksandr said, gaining composure with each second that passed without gunfire. "I'm not a devil, I'm an officer of the Russian Imperial Mission, and I'm not trying to 'get away.' I'm trying to arrange a meeting with the man who is called 'The Reverend'."

There was a humorous laugh from the Jonnie officer. "You'll see the Reverend soon enough, all right. Now silence!" He motioned to his troopers. "Church," he said, and no further explanation was necessary.

Jonnies were beside them and behind them, close but several feet away and pointing rifles at them, as they marched up the slope toward the church. Jobey's map had been extremely accurate as far as it had gone, but it hadn't included the Jonnie welcoming committee at the bottom of the hill.

Aleksandr sought to reassure Jason. "Don't worry..."

"Shup." A rifle barrel waved at him from a few feet away. Reassurance would have to wait.

The front of the church was dark when they arrived, but they were steered to a side entrance near the back. The troopers kept malevolent watch over Aleksandr and Jason while the Jonnie officer knocked on the side door and then entered immediately. The officer emerged almost at once and counted off six of his men and led them into the church. He emerged again and beckoned to the prisoners. "Come."

They entered a large room that had been two small rooms, one of them, Aleksandr supposed, the office of the church's holy man. A wall had been torn down or burned out. Earlier fire damage was apparent along the back wall, which had been crudely patched with unfinished pine slabs. The room seemed comfortably warm after the chill of outdoors. The wood-stove near the patched pine had open doors and the flames were glowing cheerfully. The far area of the room was arranged as a living space of ascetic simplicity—a bed, a chest of drawers, a washbasin, a small table. The portion of the room in which they were standing was more comfortable, with a divan and two stuffed chairs. As the prisoners entered, the thin officer closed the door behind them and the six troopers, Alexandr saw, stood along the wall, their rifles trained on the two strangers.

The room also had a desk, and behind the desk in a green robe sat the man who unquestionably was the Reverend. Aleksandr could sense the awe and fear in the troopers, and he could see the grudging deference of the officer. He also could see the hard glittering eyes and stone-like features of the Reverend.

Aleksandr tried not to speak until spoken to, and the silence continued a moment as the Reverend examined the strangers. To his annoyance and discomfort, Aleksandr found it hard to stare down the rascal. But after all, he temporarily was in the inferior position; his skills of persuasion would be tested.

"You are the Russ who escaped from the helicopter we shot down," the Reverend said at last. It was not a question, and the tone was quiet and cold.

"Yes, I am Captain Aleksandr..."

"Silence! I don't want to hear the rituals chanted by devils." He spread his fingers over scraps of paper on his desk. Aleksandr could see charred edges—the paper looked like pages salvaged from a burned book. "There are seven men guarding you, devil," the Reverend rumbled. His eyes rolled up and his voice took on an incantatory liturgical tone:

> *The reason why the number 'seven' is everywhere put for*
> *perfection, is because in seven days all things were*
> *perfected and completed, both as to work and rest.*

The Reverend's voice became almost conversational again. "You have no dominion here. I learned the wickedness of the Russ in a Co-op. You are evil, and we shall rid the earth of your stench." Again he seemed to be gripped by a spell:

> *The divine laws and establishments of the Author of*
> *nature are precisely settled by him, as he pleaseth, and*
> *limited by his wisdom.*

EVIDENTLY THE REVEREND considered himself the author of nature, and Aleksandr began to fear that winning his confidence and cooperation would be much more difficult than was thought by the Imperial Mission staff. He began to feel the fear of dealing with a mad man.

"If I may speak, Reverend," he began, and paused. There was no outburst of anger, only a continuing stare very like hatred. "We both wear uniforms and can speak together as soldiers..."

"We are soldiers of the God Jonathan Edwards," the Reverend said. He again touched the papers on his desk, and Aleksandr supposed that they were writings of this god, of whom he had not heard. But savage gods were prolific, he knew, and at least now he could guess at the origin of the term "Jonnies." And the Reverend evidently was a nonconformist Chaser who could read.

Aleksandr tried once more. "But we are soldiers nonetheless, each in uniform." He felt the need to establish an official position as a member of a larger body, and he nodded at the green coats worn by his captors.

The Reverend replied, incantatory again:

> Green, being the most pleasant color, and above all
> others easy and healthful to the eye, is a fit symbol of
> grace and mercy with which God is surrounded, and
> which he most especially doth exhibit unto us.

The final word was pronounced with no little smugness. Aleksandr had difficulty sorting out the Reverend's opaque thinking. The man in some ways sounded as sincere and as confused as a minor Elder in Russia after too much vodka. He decided to begin again.

"I think, Reverend, I may in all due modesty suggest that we, that is, you and the Russian Imperial Mission, may mutually benefit from a policy of cooperation and peace."

The Reverend's voice rolled again:

> One property of a whore is that she commits her
> wickedness in secret under a covert, and hides it with an
> external shew of modesty.

"Now look here, Reverend," Aleksandr began, his temper igniting at the Reverend's insult.

"Steward," the Reverend said to the Jonnie officer, who in one smooth motion pounded the butt of his rifle into Aleksandr's stomach. A flash of pain and he was breathlessly doubled up clutching his belly. Jason stood impassive, gauging the situation and cursing the odds.

The Reverend intoned as Aleksandr gasped to fill his lungs:

> It signifies nothing, to exclaim against plain fact.

The rifle-swinging Steward was too solemn to smile, but he obviously enjoyed Aleksandr's discomfort, and relished having provided it.

The Reverend waited until the Russian had recovered

somewhat before continuing. "You should know, both of you but particularly the Russ devil, that you are to suffer retribution. The manner of the retribution I have not yet decided. I shall ask the advice of the Steward and I shall pray before I make God's decision. This is the God Jonathan Edwards' church, and his will is known here. I must decide," he nodded at Brukov, "whether to kill you or cut off your hands and return you to the devils who sent you, so that you might be a warning and a chastisement to them. And you..." he motioned toward Jason, "if you cause no further trouble, we can probably find work here for a strong young man. But if you cause us any trouble, you shall die."

Aleksandr's face went white at the threats, and he felt his bowels quake.

"Surely," Aleksandr said, spacing his words to make them calm despite his fear and his impaired breathing, "Surely you have heard reports of the Imperial Mission's weapons. If you harm me, a hundred helicopters and a thousand troops will descend on Hamp in the middle of the night. We do not abide organized offenses against our authority." He glanced at the Steward's rifle butt, but there was no word from the Reverend commanding punishment, not yet.

Then the Reverend intoned:

> We have the abundant instruction of perfect and
> infinite wisdom itself, to lead and conduct us in the
> paths of righteousness, so that we may not err.

As fearful as he was, Aleksandr also was building into a kind of confused rage. So much of what the madman said seemed to be a correlative of the religion of Holy Russia, but as seen in a shattered mirror.

After pausing a moment for thought, the Reverend continued:

> If conflict and war be necessary, yet surely there is no
> necessity that there should be more cowards than good
> soldiers; unless it be necessary that men should be

overcome and destroyed; especially is it not necessary
that the whole world as it were should lie in wickedness,
and so lie and die in cowardice.

"But in your prayers," Aleksandr asked, "is it not possible to ask if peace and cooperation with people who mean no harm, who in fact wish to aid you in any way possible, might not be better than antagonism and threats of mutilation and death?" The scalp line of his brow was tingling with the beginnings of sweat.

The Reverend replied:

'Tis fit, as we all should know, that it don't become us to
tell the Most High, how often he shall particularly
explain and give the reason of any doctrine which he
teaches, in order to our believing what he says. If he has
at all given us evidence that it is a doctrine agreeable to
his mind, it becomes us to receive it with full credit and
submission; and not sullenly to reject it, because our
notions and humors are not suited in the manner and
number of times, and particularly explaining it to us.

"But there can be no doctrine of death or mutilation," Aleksandr burst out. He was a Man of History not an Elder, but the profound and unchallengeable truths of Holy Russia coursed through his soul, and the insane blasphemies he had been listening to were so outrageous as to make him forget his fear for a moment. "Many of the words you say are true, but they are applied to a world that does not exist and they are used to justify actions that are unconscionable."

The Steward looked for a signal, but got none.

The Reverend had Aleksandr fixed with his burning eyes:

The tendency of true virtue is to treat everything as it is,
and according to nature.

"I respectfully suggest, Reverend," Aleksandr said with some desperation, "that neither my companion nor I have harmed you or others of your religion. To treat us according to our nature would be not to harm us."

"Silence!" The Reverend roared, abandoning his rigid calm and fairly shaking with anger. "You shot the servants of God Jonathan Edwards from the devil's air machine."

"But they shot..."

"Silence! You will be punished!" His eyes rolled up again:

> *He that in any respect or degree is a transgressor of*
> *God's law, is a wicked man, yea, wholly wicked in the*
> *eye of the law; all his goodness being esteemed nothing,*
> *having no account made of it, when taken together with*
> *his wickedness.*

Aleksandr glanced at Jason, whose eyes were popping with fright and a lack of understanding.

"And as for him," the Reverend said, "he is only a hilltowner. Our soldiers recognize him. Hilltowners are sunk in sin and are ignorant of God and must be purged."

Aleksandr couldn't resist poking at the madman. "The only person around here who recognized my companion," he said, "was the farmer Jobey, who told you we were coming tonight."

"Steward!" Although Aleksandr saw the blow coming and moved away, the rifle butt caught him fairly well on the side of his cheek and he fell heavily to the floor.

The Reverend rose from behind his desk. "You must be punished further for speaking lies about an honest man who is the instrument of God. The Steward will see to that."

He turned and addressed the Steward and the troopers:

> *Let God arise, and plead his own cause, and glorify his*
> *own great name. Amen.*

At this, the steward and the troopers, the latter having neither moved nor spoken during the peculiar interview, shouted as one, 'AMEN.'

Aleksandr's attempt to enlist the cooperation of the Jonnies had come to an end.

‹ *Chapter Eleven* ›

IT WAS MIDMORNING BY THE time Aleksandr awoke. Jason, standing over him with an expression of concern on his face, said, "They sure thumped you some. You able to move around?"

Aleksandr looked up at him. "I'll find out." It hurt him to speak, as his jaw was bruised and the side of his face swollen. He sat up and looked at the small square room that enclosed them. It was a primitive jail, complete with a wall of iron bars, on the other side of which sat two green-clad riflemen. The cell held two cots and a washbasin.

"They sure thumped you some," Jason repeated, somewhat to Aleksandr's annoyance.

"They weren't very good at it, really," the Russian said, breathing deeply as he checked his ribcage. There were no obvious fractures. "I must have passed out rather early on. I don't remember much."

"Well, they got kind of tired of kickin' you when you was already out. No fun anymore."

"It seems you got 'thumped' some yourself," Aleksandr said, noticing the bloody discoloration on Jason's head.

"Well, I didn't like it when they started kickin' you."

"Ah, my friend, your nobility outpaces your common sense. Ouch!" He would have to try to rise from the cot more carefully.

"Guess now you see why I don't have much use for religion," Jason said. He and Sue had been alternately amused and embarrassed by Aleksandr's occasional bursts of vocal ardor for his Rolls and Doctrines.

"I tell you," Aleksandr said, anger momentarily chasing away any physical discomfort, "this is the religion of a madman and a foul imitation of true religion."

"Careful, Cap'n."

Aleksandr's raised voice had been loud enough for the guards to hear, and he looked in the direction of Jason's warning glance, but the two greencoats were themselves exchanging meaningful glances. Perhaps they were ordered to overhear and report, but Aleksandr judged that they were themselves not entirely faithful to the Reverend's religion—it was a glance of mutual guilty satisfaction they exchanged—and they were curious about what the Russian would say next. Later he would have to sound them out, but now he dropped his voice to continue talking with Jason.

"I apologize, my friend, for leading you into this trap. I was far too smug about being able to talk reason with these creatures. I should have trusted your experienced judgment."

"Well, Cap'n, you didn't force me to come along. Fact is, deep down I figured you was right. Felicity says you're better'n Chasers, and Felicity's deep. I figured the Jonnies'd just get the shakes when they listened to a Russ."

"We both know better now." Aleksandr saw that one of the guards left the room for a moment when the prisoners had resumed quiet conversation. The guard promptly returned, but Aleksandr concluded that a message had been passed.

"Well, we're for it now," Jason said, adopting an obscure phrase that he had heard his Russian friend use from time to time.

"We'll see about that." Aleksandr painfully walked to the

wash basin and used a rag there to pat gingerly at the side of his head.

A third greencoat then appeared with a tray containing two bowls, two spoons, and a small loaf of bread. He passed it through an opening that a guard unlocked in the barred door, and the prisoners immediately discovered that they were very hungry. The potato soup was rich but unseasoned and the bread was satisfyingly heavy.

Jason finished his food first. "That farmer Hop put us onto wasn't no good," he said without anger.

"He was just afraid," Aleksandr said. "Afraid and greedy. He's got a good thing going there. The Jonnies leave him alone as long as he's reliable. The Jonnies get all stirred up because some Russian soldier is at loose. From Jobey's point of view, turning me in was a way to get back to business as usual and at the same time earn the gratitude of the Jonnies anew."

"It wasn't right," Jason insisted.

"No. No, it wasn't right. But that's little comfort to us in our present fix." Eating caused Aleksandr a certain amount of discomfort, but he doggedly finished every bite, not simply because he was hungry but because he was conscious of the need to rebuild his strength.

There was a small barred window in the cell, and Jason went to it to look out.

"Nothin' out there now," he said, "but there was all kinds of runnin' around right after dawn."

"Really? I wonder why." Aleksandr raised his voice and addressed the guards. "Why all the activity this morning? What's afoot?"

"Don't talk," one of the guards said quickly and sternly. "Orders are you can't talk to us or to each other. So quiet."

Aleksandr had to suppress a smile. Evidently a Russian was exotic enough a creature to justify disregarding the Reverend's orders. "Very well," he said with studied contempt, then resumed his quiet conversation with Jason.

"I wonder how long we have to work something out," Jason said.

"Probably not long," Aleksandr replied. "The Reverend doesn't strike me as the sort to delay an opportunity for brutality. I have to think." He eased down onto his bunk to rest, flinging one arm over his eyes.

"I'm tryin' not to think," Jason said glumly. "It don't look good for us."

"No, but I'll think of something if I have some time." He gauged that the guards couldn't hear him now "Do you think you could guide us out of here if we could get free? Could you get us into the hills and away from pursuers?"

Jason shrugged. "Sure, if it was night and you could run. But we ain't out and I already tried to bend the bars. Don't work. And them fellows out there got guns."

"Oh, I think I could run well enough. And the bars aren't any problem; I can take care of them. The guards are something else. I'll have to think about that."

"You sure are crazy."

Aleksandr smiled. "I'll explain," he said, his voice dropping to a whisper. But before he could speak there was a commotion at the door of the jail and the gaunt figure of the Steward appeared, accompanied by two more guards, one carrying a canvas-like bag and the other with Jason's shotgun under his arm.

Aleksandr decided to assert himself at once.

"See here, Steward, I protest this treatment. Not only do you beat us, these guards won't even let us speak." He glanced at the guards, but they stared solemnly at him and didn't even blink. They were used to self-control, Brukov decided.

"What kind of treatment is that, to torture prisoners and

then forbid them to speak?"

To Aleksandr's surprise, the Steward had let him rant on without interruption. The Reverend's lieutenant evidently was very pleased with himself, for his furious grim expression had relaxed into a poisonous smile.

"Our guards are the servants of God." His tone was mild, almost friendly, though even more threatening for that. "They are doing their duty, which is to obey the Reverend's instructions that you not speak to others or between yourselves. As to the beatings, if you acted with proper respect and reverence toward God and the servants of God, there would be no need for us to inflict a poor pale reminder of God's wrath on you. Mend your ways and conduct yourself with proper humility, and only the final punishment the Reverend decides shall be allotted to you."

"And when will that be?" Aleksandr tried to keep his voice calm and soldierly, as the horrors threatened by the Reverend suddenly struck him as all too possible.

"Oh, within another day or two. The corruption spread by the Russ devil must be purged." The fury of his words belied the soothing tone in which they were said.

"Why not use the time to let me communicate with the Russian Imperial Mission so you can negotiate the situation?" Aleksandr well knew that such a suggestion was silly, as these mad heathen idolaters obviously were beyond either reason or negotiation, but he felt he had to blurt out something so that the Steward couldn't read the relief on his face when he heard his punishment wasn't to be immediate. He had time, if only one day. Any action had to come at night, this very night if at all possible, or that precious time might run out.

"There is no negotiation with devils," the Steward said. He motioned to the two guards who had come into the guardroom with him.

The pair, who were larger than the other guards and had a distinctly more brutal air about them, began to carefully empty a bag onto the plain wooden table that was the only furnishing in the room apart from the chairs on which the watchmen generally sat. The bag was filled with the material confiscated from the prisoners, and the greencoats arranged the items with an incongruous reverence, as though handling icons of precious antiquity. The Pushkin Series 2100 machine-pistol was the first object to be placed on the table, against which the shotgun was already leaning. One of the Steward's guards gently placed the spare gas cylinder just below the one affixed to the gun, so that the arrangement seemed designed for a photograph. The two gyrobombs, the heat tabs, the food capsules, the holster belt with its spare clips for the Pushkin, his identification papers, his onionskin paper Book of Rolls, which he carried as a gesture of piety although he knew them all by rote, and a few other minor and non-lethal effects that happened to be in Aleksandr's pockets were all individually removed by one guard who handed each item to the second guard for precise placement.

"Now, then," the Steward said in a determined tone, "we want to know how these things work. These two servants of God," nodding at the thuggish greencoats, of whom the two watchmen seemed wary, "are more experienced in retribution than those who chastised you last night. They will help you remember should you forget any information I might want. Do you understand?"

"Even a Russian devil is able to follow such subtleties," Aleksandr said, but the Steward apparently was too thickheaded to be insulted by the sarcasm.

"First this," the Steward said, picking up the shotgun. "We are familiar with this type of gun and these cartridges, but have had bad luck with them."

"We have too," Aleksandr said promptly, forestalling any

possible interruption by Jason. "As you know, they are not Russian, and I have never seen such guns before. My companion said a similar gun had blown up after repeated misfirings. I simply suggested that he bring the gun and the cartridges along, as the Jonnies have a reputation for dependable guns and ammunition. We thought that once I had established good Russian Imperial Mission relations with the Reverend, we might impose upon you for an explanation of the weapon, but apparently it is quite useless."

The Steward peered at Brukov intently, as though hoping to read a test of truthfulness in his features. Aleksandr's voice and expression remained casually sincere, as though what he said was self-evident. He was puzzled for a moment by the familiarity of the look on the Steward's face, and then he recalled where he had seen such an expression. A newly prosperous merchant from the Caucasus had been examining a horse at a sale Aleksandr had attended with his grandfather. The merchant, obviously no horseman, had just such a look on his face as he tried to impress the seller with his shrewdness and his ability to judge the horse's real worth. The merchant came off very badly in the deal, as Aleksandr recalled.

"The man was carrying no other weapon," the Steward said at last.

"He was under my protection—my quite inadequate pro-tection, as it turned out. We expected a friendly welcome and a pleasant agreement on mutual benefits. He had no need to be armed."

"No one walks about without a gun."

Aleksandr put on a show of anger. "I told you he was under my protection, and I bitterly regret I persuaded him to bring no weapon as surely in any conflict we should be outnumbered and a single weapon would be useless. I told him to bring that ancient relic and its supposed cartridges so that the friendly

Jonnies could show him how to use them."

Somewhat taken aback, the Steward seemed convinced at last, though he maintained a knowing skepticism so he wouldn't be seen by his men to back down. Just like the ignorant merchant of the Caucasus.

"We'll leave that for a moment and turn to something you can't lie about, no matter how shameless you may be before God." Against his will, Aleksandr flushed at the repeated blasphemous insults of the heathen.

The Steward gingerly picked up the machine-pistol and admiringly gazed at its intricate steel construction, its hand-tooled wood-and-leather handle. "This is your own weapon. You can't claim it is unfamiliar to you, can you?"

"Of course not. It is my personal sidearm, issued by the Russian Imperial Mission."

"And it is in good working order, I presume?"

"It has been out of my sight and in the hands of untrained personnel since last night, but unless you've tampered with it, it is in perfect working order."

"Well, then," the Steward said, his thin lips pursed with prissy satisfaction, "the Reverend would like to use it himself. Explain it. And be accurate—one of the servants of God will test it first, and if anything goes wrong, anything at all, the wrath of God will be severe, on both you and your companion." The steward dropped his mask of superior calm as he voiced the threat.

"It's not possible for anyone else to fire it." Aleksandr worked hard at being matter-of-fact about the lie, as though he were imparting information that was taken for granted by knowledgeable people. "We have quite advanced technologies, as you know. The Imperial Mission general staff considers such sophisticated weaponry important enough to safeguard against... abuse. For that reason, the handgrips of machine-pistols are electronically coded. Each person's palm prints, lines like these..." he showed the Steward his right palm, "are highly individual. No two alike. There's an electronic sensor plate in the butt of the handle. The gun simply won't fire unless I'm holding it." He had read that Chaser engineers were working on such an idea, though so far the problems had proven insuperable.

The Steward was stunned. "That is not possible."

"It happens to be the truth."

The hatchet-faced Chaser thought a moment. "What if you need to shoot with your other hand?"

"Oh, both prints are coded in," Aleksandr airily dismissed the question.

A pause. Then a glint of shrewdness relieved the puzzled gloom of the Steward's face.

"Then," he said, "You will not object to explaining each feature of this... advanced techgolny..."

"Technology."

"Advanced technology to me so that I can appreciate what I cannot have?"

"I suppose not." Aleksandr was uneasy, not knowing what to expect next.

The Steward held up the machine-pistol as though at a weapons class, though well out of the reach of the prisoners.

"That is a mighty fine lookin' piece of steel," Jason's admiring voice chimed in, and Aleksandr warmed at his friend's intuitive support in a game he couldn't understand.

"The spare cartridges," the Steward said, nodding toward Aleksandr's gun belt, "lead me to believe they are inserted in the butt."

"That's right. They're pellets, really, not cartridges. When the clip of pellets is empty, the clip automatically clicks down and out of the handle a couple of millimeters, so you know you need a new clip."

"And how do you take the clip the rest of the way out?"

"That sliding spring lock in the thumb rest," Aleksandr said, his heart involuntarily racing. The sliding thumb rest had to be pulled back for the gun to fire. That was the second safety that he was gambling would confound the Jonnie. It was also a design problem in the machine-pistol, as there were instances when an excited Imperial Mission officer had ejected his clip instead of releasing the safety—a most unfortunate mistake.

"Could I take the clip out now?"

"Of course. Just press the lock forward."

The Steward followed instructions and was transparently delighted when the clip dropped into his free hand. "And now can I put it back in again?"

"Of course. Just slide it in and it will click into place."

That done, the Steward repeated the process of ejecting and reinserting the clip, just for the pleasure of feeling and hearing the precision-tooled parts fitting together.

"This is the safety catch?" he then asked, pointing to the conventional safety. Aleksandr nodded. "And what is this?"

"That sets the rate of fire. It's on full automatic now. The other settings mean that one pellet will be shot at each pull of the trigger, or five pellets will. Generally we keep them at full automatic."

The Steward was mightily impressed, and obviously trying hard not to show it. "How many pellets in each clip?"

"Hundreds," Aleksandr answered nonchalantly, and the Steward seemed satisfied with that vagueness, as though afraid that too specific an answer might overawe him.

"And this dial here?"

"It sets the velocity of fire. As it is moved farther in the direction of the barrel, the pellets will travel faster and go farther. The setting regulates the pressure from the gas cylinder under the barrel."

"That is what I was going to ask next. You need a second?" He nodded toward the spare cylinder on the table behind him.

"Yes. Depending on how it's used, the cylinder must be replaced from time to time."

"Ah. I see. I see."

"That's real interestin'," Jason said. "You never told me none of that."

"Of course not," Aleksandr said coldly, wagging his hand behind his back as a kind of general signal. He wanted the Jonnies to believe Jason and he were virtual strangers, and that the hilltowner had been pressed into his guide service against his will. If punishment had to be faced, it would be much more severe for Jason if he were considered the willing tool of the Russian Devil.

"So, then," the Steward repeated, "this admirable weapon can only be fired by you." A tight little smile was intended to disconcert the Russian. The Steward had learned his style from the Reverend, but did not have his master's presence or strength of personality, only a nervous energy that seemed to make his skinny frame vibrate.

"Quite right," Aleksandr said.

"Then you won't object, will you, if I point this weapon at you and pull the trigger."

"Well," Aleksandr said uncomfortably, shifting on his feet, to the obvious amusement of the Jonnie contingent, "I don't regard it as very polite, or a wise way to handle weapons, but if you must, go right ahead."

The Steward took a step closer to the cell and leveled the Pushkin at Aleksandr's chest, aiming between two cell bars. Aleksandr tried not to stare at the savage's thumb. It was extremely unlikely that the Steward would draw back the second safety, though sometimes a firm grip on the handle could slide the metal plate partway back to the firing position.

"Now then," the Steward said with a show of pedantic irony, "unless the gun handle thinks my hand is the same as yours, you have nothing to fear. I will pull the trigger now."

With an exaggerated attempt at suspenseful dramatics, the Steward sighted along the barrel and slowly squeezed the trigger all the way back until it was flush against the trigger guard. Nothing happened, and the disappointed Steward lowered the gun with a stab at an ironic smile.

"Well," Aleksandr said, breathing out and visibly relaxing, "I always take the scientists' word for it when they say no two hands are the same, but it's a little more difficult to believe when someone's pointing a gun at you." He could see the two regular guards grinning, although the pair who had accompanied the Steward seemed only disappointed that the Russian hadn't been riddled by his own weapon.

"Your very nervousness convinces me that you have lied," the cold voice of the Steward said. "I will give some more thought to this gun." He looked at the Pushkin wistfully and replaced it on the table.

"It occurs to me," the Steward went on, "that you have explained why the righteous cannot use the guns of the devils, but I do not believe that God would allow such a thing. Indeed, devils may not use the weapons of the righteous, but the righteous should be able to use all instruments, for God created the entire world."

Aleksandr flushed. "Your idea of God may not be quite as accurate as you believe."

"Silence!" The Steward glared at Brukov. Then more calmly, "I will ask you about the guns later. Let us hope you have better answers about some of these other things." He turned his back to the table.

"If you like," Aleksandr said, "I can give a demonstration of the gun to show it works when I hold it. You can have your guards keep their rifles trained on me so I don't aim at one of you." He made it a casual suggestion, as off-hand as possible. Once he had the Pushkin in his hand, he could make sure it was on full automatic, drop to one knee, and spray all five of the greencoats before they had time to blink.

"It is you who are the fool," the Steward said, "not I." He could spare only a contemptuous glance for the Russian. "Now, then, these things." He cautiously picked up a gyrobomb. "Suppose you explain what this is."

Aleksandr hesitated. If his lying became excessively strained, or if he simply refused to answer, very likely there would be more beatings, perhaps severe ones that would make it impossible for him to be mobile enough to escape should the opportunity arise. Yet his mind wouldn't present him with a plausible lie about the gyrobombs. Repeating the handprint explanation for a mass-production item such as gyrobombs would be transparent, and besides, the explosives didn't have extra safety devices. Even a savage could trigger them easily enough.

"Perhaps I can set you on the path of truth," the Steward said with some self-satisfaction. "I have given the matter thought. When my men followed you after we shot down the devil machine, you escaped after some kind of explosion. My men thought you had unleashed the very Devil himself. But I think it was a devil's bomb. And I think these are two more."

Aleksandr reminded himself not to underestimate the shrewdness of the Jonnies. After all, they were of the same race as the hilltowners and even dominated the hilltowners, while those simpler folk already had impressed him with occasional flashes of unexpected intelligence.

"Well, ah," he began, though he had nothing to say. He considered reciting the Roll of Penance.

The Russian's problem was solved by fate, however, and the

Roll of Thanksgiving immediately became more appropriate. For the door to the guardroom abruptly sprang open and a youthful greencoat, much swelled with the importance of his mission, fairly ran into the room.

"The Reverend needs to see you, Steward," the boy exclaimed.

"What for?" The tone was decidedly exasperated.

"I don't know, Steward. But at once."

The Steward turned to his two thugs and lifted his eyebrows in eloquent criticism, though the other greencoats couldn't see his expression. Heathen idolatry could never entirely drive out native politics, Aleksandr decided.

"Very well," the Steward said. "As the Reverend wishes." He turned back to Brukov with deliberate leisure, however, much as a child might express rebellion. "I shall return to question you further as soon as I am able," he said. "I hope your answers are more suitable. I'm sure the Reverend wishes to discuss your punishment with me, and if you have nothing of benefit to offer, I shall recommend that God visit full wrath on the Russ devil."

He turned abruptly and snapped at the two regular guards. "Watch them closely, and keep those things on that table where they are. Don't touch them. And don't let them talk. I'll be back as soon as possible." He stomped away, the messenger before him and the two assistants or bodyguards behind.

When all sounds of his departure had died, one of the remaining guards said, "Don't let him bother you none. Most everyone's out on the road and the Reverend made him stay. Makes him jumpy. Afraid he'll miss something good. Just be sure to keep on saying nothing." His eyes had a twinkle, and Aleksandr knew he was being thanked for his initial complaints to the Steward about being silenced. Brukov nodded with a smile at the guard.

Aleksandr and Jason both sat on the former's cot, facing the wall opposite, not the direction of the guards.

"That wasn't too bad," Aleksandr said in a voice that wouldn't carry, "but the next time it could get rough. I'm not a very good actor, and it's simply impossible to be agreeable to someone as offensive as the Reverend or the Steward. May God choose me as his instrument of chastisement."

"Seems to me old Steward feels the same way about you."

"Ah, shrewdly put, Jason. Bring me back to reality, however squalid it may be."

"I sure can see how Felicity gets all a marvel over how you talk."

Aleksandr laughed. "Talk doesn't do us much good in this particular fix." He glanced again at the guards to make sure they couldn't hear him. The guards were chatting comfortably together, old chums glad of easy duty together.

"You still got a plan?" Jason asked. "It don't look good to me."

"Not only do I have a plan, but our chances are much better now than before."

Jason looked at Aleksandr with a grimace of skepticism. "Flup," he said.

"Just listen before you judge. Fortunately, the Jonnies don't seem to have any prior experience with Russian Imperial Mission technologies, so they don't know what to look for. Also fortunately, all our gear is sitting right there on the table for our convenience."

"Well, then," Jason said, "now you mention it, I'll walk right past these iron bars and pick it up."

"Odd sense of humor you Chasers develop in isolation. But as a matter of fact, we will walk right over and pick it up. I'd rather wait for night, though."

"Well, I don't know what you're talkin' about," Jason said somewhat more hopefully, "but the day's gone on some already.

If the Reverend keeps old chicken-face off us for a bit it'll be dark and most likely they won't be back until morning."

The Steward did look something like a chicken, and Aleksandr smiled at the unbroken irreverence of his companion. "If we have another night here, we should be able to do it. It might mean killing those two, and any other Jonnies we run across."

"They don't seem too bad," Jason said, "but they're Jonnies, so it won't bother me none."

"Good." He glanced again at the guards. "Now, what the Jonnies don't know is that the Russian Imperial Mission expects its officers to run into trouble from time to time, and it provides us with as many tools as it can." He couldn't help being a little pompous, lecturing a Chaser on the superiority of Russians. "Among the tools are the buttons on my tunic. They're perfectly good buttons and perfectly harmless, unless I connect two of them with a thin wire that is woven into my collar." He touched the collar, and Jason could see a glimmer of silver there. "When they are connected, all I have to do is touch this button on my chronometer," which the Jonnies had neglected to take, probably because it had been sufficiently concealed by his sleeve, and he had continued to keep it concealed, "and when I just touch this button the area between the two buttons will explode. I could work it even without the chronometer, but having the automatic trigger makes it easier. The explosion will be perfect for the lock on our cell door. The only danger will be flying metal. There may not be any, but it's a chance we have to take."

"And then we just walk out, and we're free until the Jonnie guards shoot us. That's a real good plan, Cap'n."

But Aleksandr could tell Jason was still listening, confident that there was more to come. There was. "In the heel of my boot there's a small stunner. It will only give us a few seconds, but that's all we need. I considered using it last night after the

Reverend made it plain that he would not cooperate, but there were too many of them for it to work. It has an impact in a radius of about six feet, perfect for the two men sitting across the room."

"It'll kill em?"

"No. Perhaps knock them out. Definitely knock them over and leave them groggy for a few moments."

"Same time your lock bomb goes off. We grab our guns and get gone?"

"Yes."

Jason paused a moment. "Well," he said at last, "if it works, it works. I can see out the window we're on the same road as we was on comin' in, and if we keep on goin' that way we should be headed back toward camp. Sure could stand to spend a night with Sue."

"I doubt that you'd spend long standing," Aleksandr said, and Jason allowed himself a slow grin.

"You're okay to bunk with, Cap'n, but it ain't the same."

"Well, with any luck, one more night here and then we're both back to our women." At Jason's mention of Sue, Aleksandr felt a sharp pang of his own, not just for the warmth and vibrance of Felicity's body, but for the puzzle and challenge and pleasure of her company, for the way she made him explain and then rewarded his teaching, for the way she disturbed him and made him think again about the things he thought he knew. No woman had ever done that to him before, and he realized he already was in danger of becoming addicted. Just thinking about it in those terms made him eager to return to the source, to see if she still irritated and satisfied him so regularly, to see if in his arms she became transformed and in turn transformed him with the excitement he remembered but now seemed so far away, almost as alien as before he met Felicity or even stepped foot on Chaser Two. Ah, the challenges of service with the Russian

Imperial Mission—how many lectures he had heard on the subject by Men of History like himself, and how little did either the lecturers or the auditors understand the variety of those challenges.

"So how do we do all this?" Jason asked, bringing Aleksandr out of his reverie.

Aleksandr explained.

WHEN IT BECAME FULL dark, they relaxed a little. The Steward had not returned, and Jason's instinct that the Steward would not question them again until the next day seemed sound.

The solid but unexceptional evening meal arrived, and when the trays were taken away, there was a logical development, but one that Aleksandr had not anticipated, and one that could prove to be troublesome.

There was a changing of the guard. What's more, the new guards were the same pair of primitive creatures who had been acting as the Steward's bodyguards. There was no sign of camaraderie between the two shifts—indeed, there was no sign that the one pair recognized the existence of the other, though the thugs obviously had contempt for the greencoats they relieved. To Aleksandr, who already had reached some tentative conclusions about the Jonnies and how they could be eliminated as a threat to Operation Grainrail, all signs of disaffection between and among Jonnies were welcome.

Of immediate concern, however, was whether the new guards had been shifted from the Steward because they were experienced in violence and had been ordered to beat or otherwise torture the prisoners.

"Long duty today..." Aleksandr began.

"Shup," was the immediate and snarling response.

The rule that had been ignored now was to be enforced and their escape plans might have to be modified.

The new guards sank with surly resignation into their chairs, not even conversing with each other, but showing no sign of having orders to indulge in sadism. Aleksandr supposed that perhaps the other guards were right, that most of the troops were 'on the road,' so the Steward's bodyguards had to take a shift in the jail.

The Russian looked over at Jason, who from a sitting position on his cot was eyeing the new guards impassively. Aleksandr felt reassured. Even if the plans had to be adjusted somewhat, Jason could manage his part of the job. And if for some reason it became necessary to shoot rather than simply knock the guards unconscious, the deaths of these grim fellows would rest more lightly on Aleksandr's shoulders than the deaths of those relatively decent guards.

Aleksandr speculatively eyed the walls of the outer room where the guards sat. Brick and mortar, nothing to worry about. Ricochets were unlikely with the Pushkin. The pellets were made of what the Chaser engineers called a "plastic alloy," and entire clip-loads were machine-stamped as a unit so that a clip could be loaded and snapped into place in one swift movement. The pellets were perfectly engineered for accuracy, but once they made contact were flattened slightly and tended to spin crazily, causing a good deal of damage. At normal velocity, however, they'd simply flatten up against the brick, penetrating slightly, and get lost if they entered the mortar.

Yawning elaborately, as though he looked around simply from boredom, Aleksandr paced back to his cot and flopped on it as though to nap. His back was to the guards, and with the hand that wasn't cradling the pillow he dexterously removed the black caps on two of his tunic buttons, then with slow movements pulled a thin metal thread from his collar.

Though it took some time with one hand, he eventually managed to insert one end of the metal threads into the tiny receiver connection in one of the buttons, then painstakingly repeated the process with the other. He tested them to make sure the connections were tight. Just the way Colonel Obolov had demonstrated during Mission Orientation.

The buttons now were perfectly safe, but alive, so Aleksandr cautiously put them under his pillow and then sat up, again with a show of bored restlessness, and sat on the other end of the bed. He didn't want to be too close in case he bumped his chronometer the wrong way, or in the unlikely event the button bomb had been flawed in manufacture.

Now it was a matter or waiting.

Jason already was dozing, an outdoorsman used to danger and able to prepare. Sleep now, be rested in the middle of the night, when strength and alertness would be required.

But Aleksandr couldn't sleep—there was too much at stake. It finally had begun to fully sink in that the Reverend meant just what he said. Death or mutilation. That was hard for an officer of the elite Russian Imperial Mission to comprehend. Such things were unthinkable. He knew they happened in the Orient, a far more violent theater of operations than Chaser Two, and even here, there had been a few cases of punitive reactions by natives. After all, they were barbarians. But such incidents were relatively few, and certainly it had never crossed Aleksandr's mind that he could be sacrificed to a heathen god. Firefights such as the one that destroyed his crew and helicopter were rare, but could be accepted as part of the burden of bringing Shared Grace to a benighted people. But execution? Mutilation?

His own welfare, however, was a secondary consideration. The destiny of True Russia, the honor and general reputation of the Russian Imperial Mission officer corps, the completion of the Operation Grainrail assignment with its vast long-term importance, even the welfare of the nonconformist Chasers, who had to be shown the glories and benefits of Shared Grace—all these duties and desires were of overriding importance, as any Russian, especially any Russian officer, would know in his bones without a moment's reflection.

So sleep was not possible for him, and he could only envy Jason's composure and his relative lack of responsibility. If they were unsuccessful, of course, Jason stood to suffer proportionately, and to that extent his complicity with Aleksandr was an extra risk.

Somehow the hours passed. Jason had suggested midnight as the ideal time to act. The Jonnies all would be asleep, and yet there would be hours of darkness left to cover their escape. Aleksandr had agreed.

WHEN THE TIME came, Aleksandr saw that Jason's eyes were open. He hadn't moved. He was waiting only for the Russian's signal.

Aleksandr studied the guards closely. They both seemed to be asleep. Each had his rifle leaning against the wall next to his chair, and each was slouched as comfortably as possible into the ancient padded pieces of furniture, which originally, no doubt, had belonged to some local residence. One of the guards was snoring lightly.

As quietly as possible, Aleksandr took off his left boot and held it in his lap. Neither guard stirred. He unscrewed the heel and let the small stunner drop onto the cot beside his thigh, out of the possible line of sight of the guards. He replaced his heel, then put the boot on again. The light snoring continued, and the other guard showed no signs of consciousness in the lamplight.

Cautiously, trying to make his movements seem as natural and innocent as possible, Brukov reached under his pillow and extracted the buttons and wire. He took them in his right hand while his left palmed the stunner. There still was no indication of unrest by the guards.

Aleksandr rose, and as he did so Jason rose as well. There

was no attempt at conversation and there was no delay. The Russian handed the Chaser the stunner, which looked like a miniature hockey puck, and they both moved toward the cell door. Aleksandr removed the paper backings from the buttons, exposing the adhesive, while Jason dropped his hand between two bars, ready to press the button to activate the stunner and toss it at the guards.

"You two get back to bed." The snoring had stopped, and Aleksandr glanced up to see both guards peering at them malevolently.

"Just restless, I guess," Aleksandr babbled back witlessly. He leaned his hands through the bars above the lock in a clumsy attempt to casually hide the fact that he was sticking a button there.

"Shup!" Now both guards were fumbling for their rifles and struggling to rise from their comfortable chairs. Aleksandr heard the faint click of the stunner being activated.

"Throw it!" he suddenly yelled, jumping back into the interior of the cell.

Jason also jumped back, as instructed, when he threw the stunner, and Aleksandr jabbed frantically at his chronometer. There were two explosions almost simultaneously, though their sounds were very different, and both of the prisoners were knocked off their feet. Aleksandr hadn't calculated that the brick walls would increase the range of the stunner, and the inexperienced Jason had hurried his toss. It fell somewhat short of the guards and landed on the floor, instead of exploding on impact against the wall behind the guards, as had been planned.

Nonetheless, Aleksandr was on his feet at once, and he found his balance after one wobbly step.

The lock on the cell hadn't shattered completely, and Aleksandr threw his weight against it. It gave but didn't break open, and he saw almost in panic that the guards were groggily stirring. One was crawling to the wall where his rifle had landed. Again the Russian threw his shoulder into the door, this time with increased fury, and now it sprang open. He could hear Jason scrambling out after him, but he didn't look. He reached the table in two long strides and grasped the machine-pistol. In one integral flow of small, sharp movements, Aleksandr clicked off the safety, made sure the switch was on full automatic, and jerked back the second safety in the thumb rest. In the second it took him to reach the table and grab the Pushkin he half expected the searing thud of a bullet in his back, but the stunner had dulled the reflexes and coordination of the guards. As he pivoted, his machine-pistol level, he was looking right into the small black eye of one of the guard's rifle, no more than three meters away, and it exploded with a roar just as Aleksandr squeezed off a burst of pellets.

In his panic and disorientation, the guard had jerked his finger and ruined an easy shot. The bullet passed an inch from the Russian's head and smashed into the wall behind him, but the greencoat had no time to express dismay at his own failure, for a stream of small plastic pellets ripped into his chest in a cluster. Several spun wildly through the muscles of his heart, and several more smashed into bone so forcefully that the impact lifted him into the air and threw his body back into the brick wall. By the time he had fallen to the floor, his green coat had become a large cloth bag holding an inert and insensate mass of meat and bone.

Jason was on the floor, out of the line of fire, as Aleksandr had instructed, but as the other guard hurriedly aimed his rifle at the Russian, Jason lashed out with one leg, crashing a foot into the back of the guard's knee. The man gave a sharp cry of surprise and his rifle discharged into the ceiling.

Brukov leapt at the man and grabbed the rifle away. "We have no desire to kill you," he said in a rush of words. "Turn around and be quick." The guard, almost tearful with terror, did as he was told, and Aleksandr clicked on the safety of his machine-pistol and brought it down on the back of the guard's head in just the place and manner that was taught at the Academy. He had never done it before, other than practice, but the result was most satisfactory. The guard crumpled to the floor.

His safety off again, Aleksandr leveled the Pushkin at the closed door of the jail. "Get your things. Hurry, hurry!"

Jason grabbed his shotgun, checked to make sure it was still loaded, and stuffed the extra shells into his pocket. Then he in turn aimed his gun at the door.

"Right," Jason said, and Aleksandr swiftly moved to the table and recovered his paraphernalia. He was in a hurry and didn't need such minor appurtenances as the heat tabs and the food capsules, but he took them anyway, even though a second or two was wasted. He had been issued those things by the Russian Imperial Mission, of which he was an officer, and he would not willingly leave them in the hands of a savage. That training had been long and rigid, and it ran deep in the bones of Captain Aleksandr Iosifovich Brukov.

"Set," he said, stuffing the heat tabs into a pocket. The table of spoils was now bare. "No silhouettes." He rapidly lifted the glass on the two lanterns and blew them out. "Go."

The Pushkin was almost silent, and the button-bomb muted, but the stunner had rattled the windows of the jail and the two rifles had gone off with what had seemed to Aleksandr and Jason deafening roars. How much the sound had been contained by the brick walls they couldn't tell, but both feared that other greencoats were on the way.

Jason opened the door and Aleksandr went out first, his machine-pistol at the ready. There was no movement in the dark. "This way," Jason whispered, coming up beside him. He led off up the gentle hill at a trot. Through the thick white clouds a dull moon diffused a shadowless light, just enough to see by, and the escaping prisoners had no difficulty in plotting their course or in finding firm footing.

Five hundred yards away from the jail the wind carried to them faint vocables of alarm, and then the beautiful solemn tones of a bell followed them through the night and spread out ahead of them as a herald.

"It'll take em a bit to set out even if they guess which way we went," Jason said. "But if we stay on this road, there'll be guards. What say, Cap'n?" They had paused a moment to listen to the sounds behind them.

"Hum. Point well taken." A moment of thought. "We stay on the road. We can't relax until we get at least as far as the hills where my helicopter was shot down, and that's too far to make it before daylight if we start dodging about and circling every shadow. We've got a good enough start."

"Ear elephant."

"What? Oh. How do you mean irrelevant?" It was a word Aleksandr had often used in his evening chats with Jason and Sue, but Jason never could seem to get his tongue around the syllables.

The Chaser nodded back toward where the bell continued to toll. "They'll know somethin's up. They'll be ready."

"Well," Aleksandr said in dismissal, "we'll have to be more ready than they are."

"Then let's go." They renewed their trot. Most of the buildings they passed were long abandoned. Aleksandr estimated the Jonnie community at no more than a few hundred, and their dwellings appeared to be clustered near the church and jail.

They had traveled another kilometer or so when suddenly Jason halted Aleksandr with a hand on his arm. "Hold here," he said. "Thought I saw somethin'." Aleksandr silently complied.

They had come to a point in the road where it bent rather sharply and stretched out ahead toward the roll of the beginning of the hills, but there was a cluster of burnt-out buildings, almost picturesque in their desuetude, standing at the bend of the road.

Jason slipped ahead, leaving Aleksandr behind the dark protection of a towering maple tree. The Russian soon lost sight of his companion, who silently merged into the chiaroscuro landscape.

Aleksandr looked nervously back along the road they had taken. No sight or sound of pursuit, but he hoped Jason would be quick about his patrol. The Jonnies didn't like to be out at night, but the escape of a murdering Russ devil should give them plenty of incentive to overcome their distaste for nocturnal peregrinations. The nerves of the Russ were already twisted tight, despite his attempt to discipline and control the tension, and without drawing deeply from his body's store of adrenalin he couldn't have overcome his aches and bruises so long. Aleksandr lurked passively next to the maple tree, repeatedly checking the blinking figures on his chronometer, cursing to himself in the crude mechanical fashion he had learned from the Chasers.

Just as he was about to step away from the tree and follow his companion into the area of the buildings, he saw two rapid flashes and heard, twice, the accompanying roars that were distinctly those of Jason's shotgun. Machine-pistol in hand, he sprinted toward the buildings, but almost at once slackened his pace as he saw Jason step into the faint moonlight of the road and casually wave him forward.

The sudden rapid exercise abruptly warmed up the Russian, who had tightened with cold standing still in the spring night. "What happened?" He had his weapon pointed toward the ruined buildings from which Jason had emerged.

"Two of em sittin' there with a little fire. Bet the Reverend says they ain't supposed to have night fires. They was talkin' about what the bell meant goin' on like that, and if they ought to put out the fire and sit out by the road. They heard me, or one caught a look or sumpin'. Grabbed for their rifles. Took em both right here." He thumped his chest with his free hand.

"You think it's safe to stay on the road?"

"No more guards, I bet. But if they are followin', they'll be comin' hard now. This don't sound like no Jonnie rifle." He caressed the barrel of his shotgun, then reached into his pocket and brought out two shells. He inserted them into the magazine. The shotgun was the most complex and marvelous machine he had ever used, and he loved it for both its mystery and its dependability.

"Let's move," Aleksandr said as he looked back along the road toward Hamp.

"Make good time on the road," Jason said. "We'll stay on it up to where I know the hills, but if there's noise behind us, just follow me and we'll get into the trees early."

"Good enough," the Russian agreed. They set off at a trot, which they maintained until Aleksandr's lungs slowed them to a brisk walk a few kilometers on. They had passed through several clusters of buildings, but Jason hadn't slowed the pace, confident that there would be no guards, and even if there were, they would have had no warning and be vulnerable to the shotgun and the Pushkin.

"This here's where you got shot down," Jason said as they approached an abandoned village. Walking and puffing, Aleksandr managed to say, "So it is, so it is," but paid the site of the ambush no further attention.

"Time to get off the road and find a place to sleep," Jason said once they were past the buildings. "Won't go past your hel-i-copter unless you want to special."

"No need."

The Chaser led the way into densely forested, steep terrain, marked by moonlight like latticework lamps, slanting at random through the thick cover of limbs only just barely ready to bud. The sky was lightening towards dawn.

At last Jason found them a protected shelter with a dry leafy floor. Their bedrolls hadn't been among the items brought to the cell by the curious Steward, and they had to curl into their coats in imitation of hibernation.

"Thank you, Jason," Aleksandr said.

"What for?" the placid Chaser asked as he rustled in the leaves to find some insulation to conserve his body heat.

"Just thanks." Aleksandr was suddenly swept by emotion at the realization that he could not have escaped from the jail, indeed could not have survived at all in Chaser Two, but for the skill, courage and ingenuity of Jason. By training and experience, the Russians withheld their affectionate sentimentality from the possible misunderstanding of the Chasers, but Aleksandr suspected that the group of nonconformists he had lived with in Chaser Two, with the exception of the emotionally intense and disciplined Felicity, were at bottom as sentimental as his own countrymen, though they labored to show no affection. And he discovered now that he felt bound to them by a commonality that he had never suspected, a commonality that disturbed him as a Man of History and an officer of the Russian Imperial Mission. Not only had Jason shown a rare skill and fortitude, but Aleksandr realized that the people of the hilltown camps were, in their quiet and undramatic way, exemplars of determination in the face of a harsh and uneasy existence in which they were all but defenseless and had no trump to call. Not an easy life, and one that he had been smugly, blindly contemptuous of, as though they were children at a game. He heard Jason begin a gentle snore, at ease as ever in an uncomfortable bower of the forest.

But Aleksandr stayed sleepless yet awhile, more determined than before to repay his Chaser friends, and thinking again of Felicity and the unsettling joy of her company.

‹ *Chapter Twelve* ›

THE SUN STRUCK ALEKSANDR'S sleeping eyes and he woke, but he saw that Jason was already alert and watchful, so he turned on his side and resumed his sleep. Jason would know when to wake him.

By the time he sat up of his own volition, yawning and stretching hugely, it was past midmorning. Jason was watchful, and appeared not to have moved at all.

"A beautiful day, Jason, a perfect day not to be in prison." They had a long view north toward their destination, and east, to their right, but they had slept against a high ridge that cut off their view to the west, where the road from Hamp ran.

"Every day's a perfect day not to be in prison, even when it rains," Jason said.

"A profound observation, Jason, profound. What we need now is a couple of bowls of Felicity's hot porridge. I'm hungry as a bear."

"Sorry the Steward didn't want to know about my biscuits. Didn't put em out on the table. Afraid we'll just have to hold out, Cap'n."

Aleksandr sighed. "Good thing I picked up my food capsules. Have some uninteresting nourishment." He held out one of the pills. Jason glanced at the colored ball with very real distaste, which he rapidly exaggerated into humorous scorn.

"I'll leave that to you Russ devils. Prolly can't eat it unless you got the right hand prints."

Aleksandr laughed. "They're good for everyone except Jonnies." But Jason still shook his head. He'd rather go without food until late that night, when they expected to reach camp.

EVEN THOUGH IT WAS a bright day and they knew Jonnie patrols were active, Jason decided and Aleksandr agreed that they could cover some distance during the sunshine hours. They could pick their way slowly and with care, and keep a hill between them and the main road whenever possible. A pleasant, warm day, no threats in the air, and Aleksandr had to struggle to remember that danger might show itself at any moment.

In early afternoon they were on a fairly good path of the sort that had long been abandoned except by those of Jason's trade. They'd had a long climb toward the crest, still shielded from the west by dense woods, and they now were beginning to test a different set of thigh muscles on the winding descent. Jason suddenly halted alertly, and Aleksandr snapped out of a reverie of Felicity. "What?" he whispered.

"Heard somethin'," Jason said in almost a normal tone. "Stay here while I take a look." He disappeared into the woods toward the west. Aleksandr leaned against a tree, his machine-pistol in hand.

It wasn't long before the Russian heard a finger snap and he glanced from the trail to see Jason in the woods up the slope. He was motioning for Aleksandr to come along.

"Well?" he said as he joined the Chaser.

"You'll see," Jason's expression and tone were grim as he led on. "Follow me and no quick movements."

There was a crude natural line of boulders jutting from the ground where the trees thinned out and the hill sloped toward the main road. Jason placed them behind one of the larger of the boulders. "Just look on down there," Jason said. "No chance they'll see you if you don't jump up and wave your arms."

Aleksandr slowly elevated his head over the boulder and looked down the hill. On the road below there was a long column of green-coated men in ragged formation on the way back toward Hamp. "Biggest batch of Jonnies I ever seen," Jason said. "Usually they keep it down to where they know they ain't goin' to get beat in a fight, so they can keep on the move without any fuss. This bunch is bigger than when I seen em warrin'. But these been warrin'."

"You mean attacking camps?" Aleksandr asked sharply. He looked again at the loosely disciplined stream of greencoats. He could see a cow and three goats being led along. "Those animals. Are they spoils?"

"Jonnies took em from some camp or other. Don't recognize em from here, but I'm a hunter. Prolly wouldn't recognize em up close. But you bet they're from some camp around here. And look there up near the front." Aleksandr's eyes followed Jason's nod toward the head of the column, in sight again around a bend in the curving road. "There's at least three women, maybe four, and some little kids with em. They been warrin', all right."

Aleksandr couldn't make out the hostages at first, but then he saw an unevenness in the sea of green and could discern the presence of outsiders. His eye was not as keen as Jason's, however, and he could not pretend to estimate numbers. "Yes," he said. "More prisoners for their jail."

"They just want the women to be wives and get children. Now I seen how they live I don't wonder they always got people runnin' away and can't get women without stealin' em. And them animals—they don't need them animals, they just want to starve us, but we ain't starved yet, and they been tryin' a long time."

Jason was being uncharacteristically garrulous, and Aleksander could tell that he was badly upset to see the column of Jonnies triumphantly dragging along its captives.

"It's very troubling, Jason, but unfortunately there's nothing we can do—not just yet." Aleksandr tried to be calming without being patronizing. Jason and Felicity, the former by his skills and the latter by her acuteness and capacity, had begun to cure him of his innate Russian Imperial Mission condescension. Not all of it was wholly justified, he had begun to learn.

"Only thing we can do," Jason said, "is get back to camp and make sure Sue and Felicity are all right."

A sudden chill went through Brukov at the grim suggestion of Jason's words. Neither man wanted to waste talk or emotion on idle speculation. "As fast as we can," Aleksandr said.

"Here's what," Jason said. "That's the most Jonnies I ever seen, so there ain't many more around. Maybe a few bringin' up the rear, stragglers or a guard." He nodded down the road, where the end of the column was moving briskly around the last of the bends in the road. "So what we do is cut back the way we came and over to the back road to Ash. That'll take us straight to camp and we can take our chances on movin' in daylight."

After a moment's hesitation while he absorbed Jason's line of thought, Aleksandr nodded. "Right. Let's start now."

They set off with a new urgency in their step, and a concern about what they would find at camp urged them to a brisk incautious pace. They returned to the path they had been following, then angled sharply downhill, almost due east, and soon found the other major road that led to their camp area. Pausing only for a cursory surveillance of the empty road, they strode onto the smooth surface of the paths on either side of the broken pavement and began a rapid walk, each man's long legs setting a pace that threatened to become a trot.

THEIR ANXIETY AND unexamined conviction that the Jonnies were all a mountain away and heading in the opposite direction urged them on, but not without wary alertness. Each held his gun in a ready position, and they traveled on opposite sides of the road, Jason slightly in the lead. Aleksandr was breathing hard and sweating from the brisk pace and the demands of the winding, steadily uphill road. He was almost mesmerized by the mechanical way he kept putting one foot before the other, each step the regulation quickstep stride, as though he were on an Academy exercise with his classmates.

Then suddenly he saw Jason dive into the bushes and down the slope toward the steam that was on his side of the road, and Aleksandr reflexively imitated Jason's mercurial move and leapt into the cover at his side of the road. As he came to rest in the previous autumn's leaves, he thought he heard a sound ahead on the road, undoubtedly the same sound that had precipitated Jason's abrupt scamper. Aleksandr was not adequately shielded from the view of the road, and he desperately twisted his body forward through the leaves until his head and shoulders were behind the rotting trunk of a tipped-over tree. His torso and legs were still exposed, but he froze into immobility, a prickling of sweat popping anew from his pores as he heard the tramp of feet, many feet, already at the spot he had so recently abandoned. There were no shouts or shots. Evidently neither he nor Jason had yet been spotted. He clutched his machine-pistol, determined that at the first cry from the road that announced his discovery he would leap up, spray the clip at full automatic, and dash into the woods. Not much chance, perhaps, but his only hope.

The maddening thing was that he couldn't see the passersby. He heard some coarse laughter and occasional words of conversation, but no sentences he could understand. The unknown marchers had to see him soon, he was so close to the road and so exposed. But he fought against his trembles of fear in an effort to remain perfectly still, as still as the bushes and dead limbs and leaves on the ground along the side of the road.

He heard a clank of metal, a mild oath, the plodding step of what sounded like a large farm animal of some kind. The stream of unseen people continued, and the sweat trickled down Aleksandr's ribs. The sounds dwindled, but Aleksandr forced himself not to be optimistic. Perhaps a squad of green-coats was standing silently over him right now, staring down at him contemptuously. But he still didn't dare look.

Silence. A few birds returned, a puff of wind rustled some leaves. Perhaps it was safe. But perhaps he should wait for a signal from the more experienced Jason, whom he presumed to be also in undiscovered hiding.

Just as Aleksandr was about to convince himself that the dignity of a Russian Imperial Mission officer had been compromised long enough, just as he poised his rigid and motionless arm muscles for a cautiously slow push, he was swept by terror again. More sounds and jangles and indistinct voices from the road, and this time the unseen enemy was running. They had spotted him at last and were returning to make sure he didn't flee! Aleksandr almost jumped to his feet to make a dash for the woods, but luckily perceived at the last moment that the sounds were traveling the same direction as the first group of people and animals. Stragglers trying to keep up, presumably.

Again his protesting nerves and muscles reposed motionless among the twigs and brambles and leaves and irregular batons of fallen limbs that were scattered on the untidy floor of the forest's edge. He was, he hoped, no more noticeable than any other twisted and rotting, lightning-blasted oak limb beside the road.

The rapid steps and swish of cloth receded and even Aleksandr's inflamed imagination could detect no aura of menace surrounding him. But still he waited, a quick student but with scanty experience. Incongruously, perhaps as a reaction to the sudden gusts of fear and relief that had raced through him, be began to doze off.

"Get up, Cap'n." Jason's voice jolted him awake. Aleksandr hadn't heard his friend approach, and in reflex he almost leveled the machine-pistol at him. "Move," Jason repeated. He was ashen-faced and short-tempered, the most rattled Aleksandr had seen him. Aleksandr hardly had time to stretch his limbs before he had to follow Jason at a trot into the woods. Only when they were safely distant from the road did the Chaser stop.

"We'll wait here for night," Jason said. "That was too close."

"It was," Aleksandr agreed with fervor. "I almost got up before that second batch came by."

"Only five and I was watchin' close. We might of handled that, got away before the others came back."

"I couldn't see a thing," Aleksandr said. "I didn't dare lift my head."

"Good thing, open as you was." Jason was still tense and distracted.

"How many of them were there?"

"Almost as many as that other batch. No wonder we didn't get chased from the jail. There weren't none left to chase us. I never seen this many all out on the road. Never."

"I heard an animal. Did they have prisoners, too?"

Jason was silent a moment. "I saw April from over the other camp." That was the way people from Jason's camp referred to the nearest settlement. "Couple of kids I wasn't sure of. That cow was from over the other camp."

By now, Aleksandr was as anxious and as irritable as Jason. The two men passed the rest of the day where they were, mostly in silence, not needing to speak of the similar dark threads that were tangled in their minds.

TORN BY RESTLESSNESS and caution, they forced themselves to wait until full dark.

"Time," Jason finally said. His emotions had subsided to a hard determination. Aleksandr silently followed him back toward the road. Before they reached it, Jason veered off onto one of the slow but little-traveled paths familiar to him, and there were frequent delays while Jason scouted around a corner, behind a boulder, or led them through thick growths around an abandoned farmhouse.

Dawn was already announcing itself by a lightening gray sky when they approached camp. First they noticed the smell of wood smoke on the air. They said nothing. They hadn't seen a single person, Jonnie or hilltowner, since they had thrown themselves off the road to hide from the column of greencoats. But still Jason led cautiously, and despite their mounting anxiety he insisted that they make a half-loop around the periphery of the camp before coming closer to look.

The gray of a misty dawn mixed with the smoldering wood as Jason and Aleksandr finally came to the camp from the rear, down the path that led at the other end to the fields where they had had such pleasure in hunting birds.

They surveyed the scene in silence. All of the cabins, the smokehouse, even the few small outbuildings had been exposed to the torch. Not a single structure was standing—a wall here and there, but no roofs, and no two walls together. Dying flames, not quite sated, suddenly shot out of blackened timbers and then receded, their mastery established. There were no people in sight, though Aleksandr saw one of the Chasers' rough, hand-made boots standing with incongruous dignity on the unscorched grass of the common.

There was misery in Jason's face, and Aleksandr knew the same desolation must be mirrored in his own.

"Them," Jason began the curse, but couldn't think of a

strong enough word to use for the Jonnies.

"Let's look," Aleksandr said, striding with sudden urgency toward the cabin he had so briefly shared with Felicity.

"No use. Wouldn't likely leave dead." But he came to look too. The cast iron stove was still standing. So, after a fashion, were the two bed frames. Aleksandr stared at the smoking remains as though at a deep and hidden symbol that would yield its mystery only after long study, and then only partially.

The words of the Roll of Penance began their mournful rhythms in Aleksandr's mind. They came unbidden, taking the place of any words he cared to say.

"Nothin' here," Jason said. "Be full daylight soon. Still may be Jonnies around."

"We can't just sit hiding in the woods all day," Aleksandr said with some asperity.

"No. Let's look over the other camp. But not on the trail. Follow me." Shotgun at the ready, Jason led the Russian into the woods in a weaving pattern roughly parallel to the regular path. They encountered no one, and at the end they found a scene that duplicated the one at their own camp.

"Flup," Jason said miserably. "I wish I seen all the people the Jonnies were pushin' along. I never seen anythin' this bad. Never."

"Obviously there are survivors off in the forest," Aleksandr said. "Where would they be most likely to go?"

"Higher up. Over to the Camont." He nodded vaguely eastward toward a range of low mountains he had mentioned before as a place where he and Aleksandr must sometime make a long hunting excursion. "Or maybe the other way. Mountains over there, too. But I never been."

Aleksandr bleakly regarded the prospect. "It could be a long search."

"Well, I been thinkin'," Jason paused, as if to review the mental process. "Prolly if we just walk on toward the Camont we'll find someone. Someone's goin' to wait for night and come back to see if anythin's left. Anythin' they can use."

They stood, looking out into the clearing, each trying to sort out the possibilities. Neither spoke.

IT DIDN'T TAKE LONG to find someone. Shortly after leaving the second camp behind, Jason silently halted Aleksandr and stood, his shotgun held loosely but in position for swift use. A bearded Chaser was coming warily along the path.

"Lo, Morse." At the first syllable of Jason's greeting, Morse's rifle sprang up, but at once he saw it was only Jason and the Russ.

"Should be careful callin' out, a day like this." Morse said in mild reproach.

"Any day," Jason said, and spit.

"Day like this more'n most." He was a bulky man whose dark beard was streaked with gray.

"We weren't here," an impatient Aleksandr interjected. "How much of what happened do you know?"

"Well," Morse said with a slow sadness, "not much. I was huntin' over to Coe. That's where people headed to."

"Is that far?" Aleksandr abruptly asked Jason.

"By the Camont," then to Morse, "what they tell you?"

"I only saw Morg. He was gittin' back after checkin' to make sure the Jonnies didn't follow. Morg said they had some warnin' and most folks got away. Some sort of didn't believe and stayed, some was just too stubborn. Some got killed."

"Did he say the names?" Jason asked calmly.

"Didn't ask. He said they got my Ainy and the kids." Morse retained his composure in the Chaser fashion that Aleksandr found so hard to understand. "I come back here to look for myself."

"That's bad, Morse. I'm real sorry to hear."

"Did you hear about Felicity or Sue?" Aleksandr asked,

again unable to restrain himself.

"Didn't hear about anyone but Ainy and my kids."

"Wouldn't chase em if I was you, Morse."

"Well, I don't know." He paused. "Not much I can do. Never is. But I think I'll go take a look. One of the kids might run off when they ain't lookin'. I'll go on down toward Hamp a ways."

"We'd come along, Morse, but we got to check Coe."

"Sure. All the Jonnies back in Hamp by now anyway. Got enough burnin' and women to keep em happy all summer." This last was said with noticeable bitterness.

"Morg say where in Coe they went?"

"Over in the hills by where you can see the valley. Where them farmhouses is for shelter. Good thin' it ain't winter."

"That it is," Jason concurred. "We'll be goin', Morse. Luck."

"You too, Jason." Morse didn't even look at the Russian, but at once headed away from them in the direction the Jonnies had taken, sadness in his gait.

LESS WORRIED NOW about Jonnies, they hurried toward the small mountain that the local Chasers called Camont, where Coe, according to Jason, was a settlement that waxed and waned with variations in the season, fear of the Jonnies, and the inexhaustible whims of hunting and crops. The Jonnies didn't normally range that far—Coe was so distant from the abundance of the Valley farms, and so limited in its own potential for cultivation, that it was considered a harsh and remote habitation, even by the standards of the hardy and isolated nonconformists of Chaser Two. The camps near Ash, which the Jonnies could reach, but only with determination, were considered the safest distance from Hamp and the rich farmland to the south.

They didn't need to go far before they had more news. Halfway to Coe, they came upon a man and a woman sitting with apparent unconcern beside the path.

"You look to be travelin' fast, Jason," the man said with a perfunctory wave as, with the other hand, he lowered his rifle to a rock. He had pulled it into a semi-prepared position as Jason and Aleksandr approached. The woman was nursing a small child.

"You should be travelin' too, Tim, what I hear."

"Oh, the Jonnies didn't chase us. They wanted to burn, I guess, and take what they could find. Maybe they even left enough we can go back in a bit."

"Didn't leave nothin'," Jason said. "We been there. Everythin' burned to the ground."

The man looked thoughtful, though not particularly distressed. "Guess we'll have to build again, either in Coe or back to camp. Don't think I want to stay at Coe."

"What happened, Tim? How many got away?" Jason could not keep the urgency from his voice.

"Oh, most everyone got away, I think. People just sort of said 'Coe' and we lit out. I didn't stay around to see it. Some lingered. We're stoppin' here until the kid feels better."

"Don't help runnin' off in the middle of the night," the woman said.

"No, it don't," the man mildly agreed, then turned to Jason again. "We seen some people from the camp come by here while we wuz laid up. They didn't know much except to head for Coe."

"Did you see Felicity or Sue?" Aleksandr broke in.

Tim thought hard. "Don't believe I did."

The woman added, "For sure we didn't."

"But that don't mean nothin'," Tim said. "People was usin' all different paths."

"I'm surprised with all that burnin' the Jonnies didn't kill more," Jason said.

"Oh, that was Hammon. Like a ghost, that man is. He saw

em comin' and set off shots and lots of yellin'. We just lit out right off, what with the baby and all."

Ordinarily Jason would have grinned at Hammon finally realizing his dream of warning the sleeping camp of a Jonnie raid, but the reality of the destruction sobered him. "Hammon finally got his raid, eh?" Jason said without spirit.

"Hammon and others, I think. I got gone. But Hop and some of the others went out to throw em a couple of shots and slow em down, I think."

"That's the way we always talked about doin' it if we needed to," Jason mused. "Well, thank you, Tim, and be well. Hope the baby's fine." He nodded to the woman, and he and the Russian continued on their way, more worried than ever.

"God knows what we'll find in Coe," Aleksandr muttered. He had hardly absorbed the import of the conversation beyond the fact that the fates of Felicity and Sue were still unknown.

"You better keep talkin' to your God," Jason said. "Maybe that'll help."

Aleksandr was, in fact, rather thoughtlessly dipping into the Roll of Humility as he walked, throwing himself on God's mercy but aware that his heart was unwilling to accept the prayer's words, which yielded entirely to God's whim. Aleksandr could not accept the full range of possibilities, some things that God might have decided would estrange even his pious Russian soul, and the knowledge frightened him.

They crossed a small but roaring stream, using a makeshift bridge that Jason said was necessary only in spring. Otherwise the water was shallow enough in many places to ford by foot. They saw several individuals and small groups of people, most of whom they couldn't identify, but they kept their distance. There was a good deal of wariness in the air.

At last they began climbing hills from the banks of another small river, and Jason was able to point to a cluster of ramshackle buildings in the distance that constituted their destination. Despite their lack of sleep and food, and despite their weariness from the strenuous hike, they picked up their pace, Aleksandr for once not complaining about his strained breathing.

"There are some other old farms around they might be at," Jason said, "but we'll start here. These folks should know, at least." What the two men might find didn't need to be said.

A couple of sullen men Jason didn't recognize were lounging with rifles beside the natural path Jason and Aleksandr were following. Each pair nodded to the other, courteous but cautious. "Must be from Coe," Jason said. "Some live up here. Prolly guards just in case the Jonnies want to try their luck this far."

"Nice of them," Aleksandr said, puffing with the exertion of strenuous walking.

"They ain't thinkin' to throw us out," Jason said. "Sometimes we help em. But they sure don't want to see the Jonnies the way our camp did."

"I imagine not. They live... those houses?" Huff, puff.

"No. Them houses ain't no good. Just good enough for us if camp burns down and it ain't winter."

A group of people gathered by a stream some yards away, and Jason suddenly cried, "Lou. Lou." A woman looked up and came toward them, wiping her hands on her dress.

"Jason," she said, and looked at Brukov. "We wondered if you'd get back."

"We got back. Wasn't easy, but looks like it was easier than you had it."

"We're alive. Got some food and blankets from folks in Coe."

"That's good, Lou. What I wanted to ask..."

"Felicity's up there," she nodded toward the group of buildings. "Biggest house, cookin' last I seen her."

"And Sue too?" The woman thought a moment. "Couldn't say. Haven't seen her and I haven't talked to Felicity."

"Well, thank you," Jason said.

"Be well, Jason." She stood with her arms folded, watching the two tired men hurry up the hill.

They broke into a trot as they neared the house, and Aleksandr took the lead. He threw open the door and ran in, heedless for the moment of the forms wrapped in blankets sleeping on the floor. "Felicity," he yelled, then realized his mistake as groggy complaints arose from the floor. "Sorry, sorry," he semi-whispered as he began a kind of uncontrolled ballet, dancing toward the open door in the back of the large room that must lead to the kitchen. Jason followed behind, managing to seem more composed.

She appeared in the door before he could reach it, and after the briefest of glances she stepped toward him and they collided in a way that most Russian sports would have forbidden as too dangerous to bodily safety.

"And Jason..." Felicity said, opening her eyes while still in Aleksandr's crushing embrace. "You're both all right."

"We was more worried about you," Jason said. He paused. "And Sue."

"Oh Jason." She left Aleksandr's embrace and took her brother's arm. "I don't know what happened to Sue. I'm sorry. I lost sight of her. I hoped she'd show up here, but so far no one's seen her."

Aleksandr quickly spoke up. "But she might easily be here and safe. There is so much confusion."

"Yes," Felicity agreed.

"No," Jason said. "She's not the kind you'd miss in a crowd. Either she got hurt somehow or the Jonnies got her."

"We don't know that," the Russian cautioned. Jason didn't argue, but both Aleksandr and Felicity could see that he was convinced of his belief, and they couldn't find the heart to press the case for Sue's safety, as they both thought that Jason probably was correct. Felicity now stood between the two men, an arm around each.

"Tell me, Felicity. Just what happened?" Jason was calm but coldly determined.

"Let me get you some soup. You both must be starved. Of course I'll tell you all about it. But I must hear from you. What happened to you two, Aleksandr?"

"Jason's right," Brukov said. "First let's hear your story."

"Very well." She led them the rest of the way into the kitchen where she had been working. "Stragglers keep coming in who've had nothing to eat. I'm afraid I've had no more sleep than you two appear to have had." She smiled and rubbed her hand against the blond stubble on Aleksandr's cheek.

"Accommodations here don't seem too private," the Russian said.

Felicity laughed as she ladled out bowls of the thick meaty soup. "Don't worry, my love," she said. "We'll find a place." And Aleksandr blushed immediately and deeply. As though that's what he meant! But of course it was what he had meant. The embarrassment momentarily blotted from his mind the words of the Roll of Thanksgiving, which had been tolling in his head like joyful bells after worship services on a sunny spring morning.

"So tell," Jason said, breaking off a piece of bread as he sat on a bench by the kitchen table.

Felicity paused a moment. "Sue moved in with me in our cabin when you two went off to find the Jonnies." The last she said with a certain complex irony that Brukov found endearing.

"We already knew that," Jason said, beginning to slurp his soup.

She sighed. "Everything was going fine until the Jonnies came."

"You were still awake when they came?"

"Yes. We had stayed up talking. We had the light out, but not for long. It was Hammon who saved us. All his hiding in the shadows every night, I swear I'll never laugh at him again. I'm glad he can't sleep at night and likes to half freeze to death walking around in all kinds of weather." She shuddered.

"What'd Hammon do?" Jason was resolutely sticking to the point. His sister still seemed to be haunted by private and incommunicable memories.

"He spotted the Jonnies leaving the road down by Ash. He ran on back to camp. That's what I heard this morning. It was a moony enough night he could see the metal plate on top of the smokehouse while he was still outside camp, and he shot it the way he always talked about doing. First bullet didn't work. But he got a new one in, and the sound of the shot and the ring of the metal were clear enough to me, but I was still awake. We both jumped up and got on our coats and boots. Sue said if Hammon was just fooling or had been drinking potato lightning, she was going to break his rifle over his head. We could hear some other people stirring outside. We didn't light a lamp. I had the rifle loaded and was ready to go out when Hop came running by. I don't know how he was up so quick. He must have been out hunting and spotted the Jonnies, or maybe he was out talking to Hammon, he sometimes does that." She was beginning to ramble, reluctant to continue the tale.

"So tell, Felicity." Jason held out his bowl for more soup. "If you've got it to spare."

"There's plenty. Aleksandr?" The Russian extended his bowl.

"Well," she continued, "Hop said a whole lot of Jonnies were coming and it looked serious. We should get out and head for Coe, not to waste any time, not to take anything, the Jonnies were almost there. Other people were starting to come out and everyone spread the word. We heard some more shots. Hammon and Moe, I heard later, were down the hill popping at the Jonnies, just to slow them down. They shot back, but Jonnies aren't much use at night."

"Could you see torches comin'?"

"No. They must have had them, but not lighted. They knew they'd find plenty of coals in the cabins.

"Anyway, I went back in the cabin and got my books." She was matter-of-fact, assuming anyone would understand and agree with her decision. She looked at Brukov. "I got another one from the library and I'm working on it." Then to Jason, "Sue just swore and said she'd be right back. She ran off to Billy's cabin."

"Flup," said Jason. "She was so grateful he let us use that cabin she was like a she-bear with a cub, she wouldn't let anyone near Billy's steel."

"That's it," Felicity said. "I yelled after her, but she was already gone. I put the books in my coat pockets and picked up the rifle. When I went out on the common I had the idea somehow that I'd follow Sue and help her, maybe drag her away, I don't know what. But I came out and Judd and Lisa and their kids were running past. Judd just grabbed me and started me off with them. By then there was shooting right outside camp." She paused. "I was scared." She made the admission quietly, and the idea seemed to be one that interested and surprised her.

"With the running and shouting and shooting," she went on, "I had no choice and I suppose I forgot about Sue. I thought she was running too and that we'd meet later. We didn't. No one I've talked to has seen her since the Jonnies came."

"We saw two big Jonnie mobs out on the road when we was comin' back," Jason said. "They both had prisoners, I couldn't see just who. I did see April."

Felicity nodded. "There were two groups. No one had ever heard of anything like it. Before we were even down the hill we heard shooting over the other camp. When we first stopped to rest and looked back, we could see light coming from both camps. So they had torches, all right."

"We came by there on the way here," Aleksandr said. He studied Jason, who seemed to have heard Felicity's story only as confirmation of what he already knew.

Felicity looked steadily into Aleksandr's eyes. "How bad was it?"

"Bad," Aleksandr said.

"All burned," Jason said. "The smokehouse, all the cabins. What they couldn't take they burned."

Felicity's eyes blazed with anger. "They are scum," she said. "We have always lived at their pleasure. Whenever they want, they kill us and rob us, and we survive at all only because they are so careless and stupid. And we can do nothing but run and be afraid. Aleksandr..." she turned to him and he involuntarily drew his head back from her ferocity, "you must do something. You have the knowledge and the power." She suddenly fell silent and seemed to regret her outburst, another of her mysterious, volatile shifts of mood.

"I intend to do something," he said with determination and her eyes flashed again.

"So do I," Jason said. He was calm, but the weariness of recent days seemed finally to have overcome him. "I'm goin' to get some sleep, and then I'm goin' back to Hamp. Find Sue. Like Morse. He's out lookin' for Ainy and their kids. Prolly a few more out lookin'. Well, I'll be out lookin' too. Plenty of shells for the shotgun," he added grimly, a kind of thing he wouldn't have said had he not been so tired.

Felicity was eyeing Aleksandr speculatively. "What do you plan on doing?" Her brother had to wait his turn for interrogation.

"I'll explain to you both," Aleksandr said. "I'll need your

help. As usual," he added with a wry smile.

"Sorry, Cap'n, you'll have to explain to me later." Jason yawned hugely. "You're hard enough to understand when I'm wide awake. I'm goin' into that other room with them other folks and see if I can find me a blanket." He slowly rose from the bench.

Aleksandr nodded in his direction. "Just promise you won't go anywhere until you talk to me, Jason. I'll be going with you."

"Anythin' you say, Cap'n." He left in the midst of another yawn.

"Aleksandr, you can't go back to Hamp now." Her voice was quiet but tense.

"I'm not going to Hamp. I'm going to do something about the Jonnies." He too yawned, and excused himself. "I'm suddenly as tired as Jason. We both had to push ourselves a bit. Look, my love, I'm delighted to see you again and I want to explain everything to you, but I absolutely must have some sleep."

She regarded him in silence a moment, and Aleksandr could see her fighting back her usual ravenous leaps of curiosity, her desire to know everything immediately.

"Very well," she said. "I'm exhausted too. A woman with a cabin up the hill said I could use it for three days. She's gone to visit her people while we're all here on the run from the Jonnies. I gave her Jason's rifle. He'll never use it again anyway now he's got your shotgun." The shotguns were always referred to as Aleksandr's, as though he owned them or perhaps had invented them as, in a way, he had.

The Russian smiled sleepily. "Very thoughtful, my dear. Why three days?"

"I figured by then you'd be here or I'd know you were never coming back."

IT WAS A DECENT LITTLE cabin and Aleksandr slept beyond his dreams. He awoke to the sound of cascading water and discovered Felicity, who was uncommonly conscious of cleanliness for a Chaser, pouring hot water into a tub by the stove.

"Ah, my love," he said, stretching his limbs and luxuriating in the pleasure it gave him, "come to my arms."

"Not until you bathe." Her tone would brook no contradiction.

"Sometimes, Felicity Pembroke, you are far too much of a mother and not nearly enough of a mistress." He sat up as he happily grumbled, looking about the cabin and preparing for a bath.

"In a very short time," she said with cool words and a glance that was anything but, "I'll be all the mistress you're man enough to handle." But her pose dissolved into laughter as Aleksandr jumped from the bed toward the tub as though he had accidentally sat on a porcupine.

"WHEN YOU AND Jason left," she said later as she rested in Aleksandr's arms, "I just knew that you'd never come back. You, Aleksandr. Either the Jonnies would kill you or you'd decide to go back to Russia, and that would be that."

"Ah, but you were wrong, my precious."

"That's when I knew," she said, ignoring his words, "how much I love you, really love you, and that you had left me, I had let you go, and that my life had vanished with you. However long after I lived I would be just like an empty corn husk, walking, talking, smiling, but with nothing inside, not a real person at all, the real person would be far away and lost."

"Hush, darling." He hugged her closer, submerged in powerful and conflicting emotions himself. She was describing his own feelings as well, and they were feelings he didn't know how to analyze. It was nothing his experience or imagination had prepared him for.

"I won't hush. I had nothing but anger and emptiness and the sense that I was missing everything until I met you, and that's all I'd ever have if you left me."

He knew that he should be frightened at her assertion of dependence. He had reacted that way to other women but somehow she was speaking only what he himself felt. In a way he didn't understand, Felicity drew him out of himself, made him larger, more complete, and the feeling was unique in his experience. Through the medium of Felicity's perceptions, so elementally powerful and strange to him, he could sense a compelling new vision of himself and the world, a vision so far unrevealed but undeniable. In a sense, he had been as ignorant as she until they met.

"Felicity, my dear, I love you too," was all the inadequate expression he could manage.

"It is as though you opened a door for me," she said.

Aleksandr smiled with a kind of relief from the confused surge of emotions he felt. He stroked her long dark hair. "That is a terrible cliche, my dear."

"What's a cliche?"

"A saying that has been used so much it's tiresomely familiar and simply sails past people without having the impact it should."

"Well, for me it's not a cliche. It's not familiar. I want it to be a cliche. I want everything I say and think to be a cliche so that I know it's familiar to everyone else, and then I'll be free and nothing will be a cliche. I will annihilate cliches," she concluded with triumphant and only half-intended humor.

"As far as I'm concerned, my love, you have already annihilated cliches."

"So I must know your plans, Aleksandr. You see, I live for you."

"Another cliche."

"But not for me. Not yet. I don't want you to go back to Hamp. I don't want to have that feeling again of everything real deserting me. I can't bear the thought. If you must go, take me with you to a Co-op. I'll be your slave and never complain. Take me even to Russia. I don't care. Jason is all I'll miss, and he loves these hills more than me. If he finds Sue again, he'll be happy. Even if he doesn't, there'll be someone else. But there will never be anyone else for me."

"My darling, you do overwhelm me." She had touched on the things he had feared to think of. What could he do? Ask for a permanent posting in Chaser Two and abandon his career? It would destroy his family. It would not be permitted. Resign his commission and marry Felicity? Even worse, of course. Take her back to Russia as a mistress, marry sweet Lyalya and try to balance the halves of his life? Chaser mistresses were commonplace and generally ignored by Russian society, but they had to be treated with elaborate casualness. None had been imported from Chaser Two that he knew of. That would be making too much of a mistress, declaring her importance in far too public a way.

"I wish you to overwhelm me," she said. "I wish you to take me over, to control me completely. I don't care if you beat me. I just want to be yours."

"I should *never* beat you," he chided with a smile as he stroked her cheek. "Don't give me such thoughts. It is not Godly."

"I wish also to know what is Godly. I will do it for your sake."

"You must do it for God's sake."

"You are my God."

"Felicity! 'In all things amaze our flesh and intellect that her spirit may not be struck dumb or that false gods confuse her tongue'." The words from the Roll of Penance sprang from his lips, changing only the personal pronouns.

"You are not false," Felicity said, though her tone was a little hurt at the fervor of his rebuke.

"I hope I am not false as a man, but as a god, I am false."

"Then tell me what to believe and I will believe it."

"You make a very profound thing sound almost like a whim."

"It is you I believe in, and that is a very profound thing, so naturally I will believe what you believe."

"Even a Man of History must have some doubts about that."

"What do you mean? Tell me what you mean and I will believe it." Now she was almost teasing him.

"What I believe is natural to the Russian soul, and taught in the home and the church and the schools for many years. Our religion is the truth, the ultimate truth that other religions were groping toward for many centuries. Even your hated Jonnies seem to see some of the correct principles in the evil shadows. But even our Elders, even our Council of Councils, can't seem to agree whether it is possible for a Chaser to fully experience what we call Godmanhood."

"Godmanhood!" She was almost satiric in her awed pronunciation of the word. "Does that mean man is God? I may be right to worship you after all."

"Quiet your blasphemy, woman. Godmanhood does not mean man is God, though it is related to the fact that one Man was God. It is a term that was invented by a Russian during the First Enslavement who was groping after the truth that man is the intermediary between God and nature, and that all things must work toward an ultimate unity in God. His name was Vladimir Sergeyvich Solovyov." He rolled the syllables of the name on his tongue, savoring them.

"Between God and nature," Felicity said, musing. "I like that. That is true. I can believe that. Nature we see and know how beautiful and harsh it is. If there is a God, He must be beautiful and harsh too. He looks down on us and steps on us when He is angry that we are ugly."

"It is to pray," Aleksandr swore. "That is a typical kind of Chaser misunderstanding. It really is true that you Chasers are all alike. That's why the Elders finally decided on Shared Grace."

"What's that?"

"All things must be brought into unity with God. Even Chasers," he said with a touch of asperity. "So Chasers are offered Shared Grace. We pray that others may find the harmony of the Russian soul. We originally, by 'we' I mean the Russian Imperial Mission, were supposed to proselytize, to bring God's truth to others. There are some who still believe it is possible. Men of History see tides in history, some even think that the truth of Chaser One, the religion of Old Europe, was once as valid as ours. They argue that, but no one can believe it. Not even Chasers. That faith is dead, there is nothing but a shell of it left, and truth does not die."

"Then they must accept the Russian truth. I will," Felicity said calmly.

Aleksandr sighed. "That is why we call you star-chasers. No matter how often we tell it, you can't seem to get the truth straight. 'He looks down on us and steps on us!' That is not it at all."

"I didn't claim to know anything about God," she said.

"What Russians understand is that God is like the horizon, that is, that is how we begin teaching little children. The horizon is always there and always soothing to contemplate. Always you travel toward the horizon, whichever way you travel, but you never reach it. Always the horizon is far away, but beckoning."

Felicity was thoughtful beside him. "I like the idea that man is between nature and God better."

"That's a start, I suppose. But you must remember the spirit of unity and harmony."

"Aleksandr, what are your plans? Are you going to go to Hamp with Jason?"

"Didn't you say he was coming here later? I can explain to both of you then."

"I'm not afraid to hear it twice. I want to hear it now." Aleksandr stretched beside her in bed, then touched her and waited for the magical responses that delighted him so. "I've been away for days, my love," he murmured.

"Please, Aleksandr," she said, removing his hand. "First tell me your plans."

He sighed with resignation and told her his plans.

WHEN JASON ARRIVED he could see that Aleksandr was happy and that Felicity was not, but he had long since learned not to wonder overmuch about Felicity's moods.

"Come in, Jason, come in."

"Cap'n. Felicity. Brought somethin' to help us think. He held up a large glass bottle filled with clear liquid.

"Our old friend potato lightning, I believe," said the delighted Brukov.

"You go easy on that," Felicity said with her usual minatory intensity.

"Aw, Felicity, a drop or two never hurt."

"Not at all, not at all," Aleksandr interrupted. "Let me fetch the cups myself. Here we are. I presume this is a local product? Let us compare the quality to the brew of your camp." Jason filled their cups half full and they each took a sip.

"It'll do," Jason said.

"You stop far short of praise, my friend. In my opinion this ranks with the finest potato lightning north of Hamp."

"That's what I said. It'll do."

"Ah, Jason, at times I find your wit almost too dry to be perceptible."

"Food's ready," said the deliberately ungracious hostess. The very companionability of Jason and Aleksandr irritated her. But it was an irritability of love and frustrated will, not dislike, so dinner went well and the men tipped up their cups of samogon afterward without much regard for Felicity's pointed disapproval.

"I'm heading toward Hamp tomorrow night," Jason said. "You still want to come?"

"Part way. I want to ask you about some ideas I have."

"Don't know nothin' about ideas. That's your stuff, you and Felicity."

"You'll know about these ideas."

"I will? I'm gettin' more important all the time. You stay around long enough and I'll turn into a Russian, fly in hel-i-copters and everthin'."

Aleksandr laughed. "You're more Russian every day. You've even started to talk more."

"That's Russian, right enough."

"Enough of your insults. Let's talk about my ideas."

"You're a subtle one, Cap'n." Subtle was a word he had learned from Aleksandr, and one he savored. It seemed to him to have endless meanings and possibilities.

"The reason I want to go only part way back to Hamp with you is that I wish to make contact with the Russian Imperial Mission and return to the Co-op of Cleveland."

Aleksandr was gratified at the impact the statement made on the normally impassive Jason. "But only temporarily," he continued. "I'll be back very soon."

"What if they don't let you come back here?" Jason asked, and Felicity made some sort of noise that indicated appreciation of the question's pertinence.

"They will," Aleksandr said with great confidence. "They'll see that my proposal will benefit the Russian Imperial Mission immensely, even as it benefits the hilltowners. For all our wisdom, I realize that the Mission isn't fully aware of the varieties of nonconformist Chasers."

"You lost me there, Cap'n."

"I digressed. The point is that the hilltown camps have recently been taught, and not for the first time, that they can have no security whatever as long as the Jonnies can raid whenever they have the whim. The Jonnies can kill, they can burn, they can take away women and children, and the hilltowners can do very little about it."

"Well, if that's an idea, I guess it's one I already had."

"From time to time, Jason, you're subtle yourself." Aleksandr said, and the Chaser couldn't suppress a self-satisfied chuckle. He took a substantial sip from his cup as a reward.

"You better go easy on that," Felicity said, taking the bottle off the table before Jason could grasp what she was about. "I'm holding this until Captain Brukov finishes his sermon. I want you to pay attention."

"That ain't fair, Felicity. I'm your brother."

"So listen," she said firmly.

Jason glumly resigned himself to his fate.

"Go on, Cap'n. I got nothin' better to do but listen."

"My assignment," Aleksandr continued without further preamble, "essentially is to guarantee goodwill toward the Russian Imperial Mission by the various groups of nonconformists between the Co-op of Chicago and the Co-op of Boston. Other officers are working with other groups, of course. But we wish to establish ground transport from the center of Chaser Two to the ocean. We desire nothing more than to be left alone—just as the hilltown camps seem to desire nothing more than to be left alone."

"That's true, Cap'n, you know it is."

"What I propose to do is to get permission from my superiors to organize... to help the hilltowners get rid of the Jonnies once and for all. We saw for ourselves that not all of them have deep loyalties to the Reverend. They are simply cowed by his power."

"Food they don't have to work for and women who can't walk out on em," Jason agreed.

"Exactly. But what if the hilltowners banded together for once and attacked the Jonnies instead of simply running every time the Jonnies attacked them?"

"Can't be done, Cap'n. People have tried. Don't work."

"Why not?"

"Too many of em and their bullets all work. Hill folk can't never decide how to go about it, and they shoot until a bullet don't work and they give up. Been tried. Don't work."

"But it hasn't been tried with the advice of a trained military officer and with reliable Russian ammunition."

Jason thought a moment, then said, "Ah. And them bombs like you used when they shot you down? And them sprayguns?"

"That depends on what my superiors decide," Aleksandr said somewhat uneasily. He knew that they wouldn't authorize Russian weapons. Ammunition that would fit most of the hilltowner rifles was available and might be approved for distribution to useful nonconformists; weapons, never. "But the Jonnies don't have bombs or machine guns. They can be defeated with rifles. Reliable ammunition. Careful planning."

"You saw those two batches of Jonnies out on the roads. We ain't got near that many men willin' to pull a trigger."

"Perhaps not. But there are plenty of hilltown camps where men are tired of Jonnie raids. They're tired of being afraid, of never knowing whether their women or their property will be taken away by force."

"For sure," Jason affirmed.

"Many of the farmers in the Valley also must be tired of living under the thumb of the Jonnies."

"Not Jobey, though," Jason said, his face darkening as he spoke the traitor's name.

"Probably even Jobey," Aleksandr said. "He's simply making the best of a bad situation. Who wouldn't rather trade freely and be left alone?"

"Them Jonnies know how to fight pretty good," Jason said.

"But they always fight the same way and under self-imposed limitations that are quite vulnerable," Aleksandr said.

"Lost me there."

"Never mind. The point is, I'm quite sure we... the hilltown camps can destroy the Jonnies and make Hamp into a friendly town where farmers and hilltowners alike can go to trade... or to live, if they like."

"And not bother the Russians, you mean," Jason said.

"Exactly. Hilltowners will not bother the Russians and the Russians in turn will not bother the hilltowners.

"Turn Hamp into a Co-op?"

"It's not big enough or important enough," Aleksandr said. He'd have to make plain to his superiors that the nonconformist Chasers obviously had no use for Co-ops. "Simply an open town where everyone can get along."

"Well... it sure sounds good."

"Here's what I propose," Aleksandr said. "While I'm gone, you just spread the word to as many people as possible. Tell them that when I get back I'll explain it all to them. No one who listens will be obliged to go along. But I'll bring back ammunition and anything else I can get."

"I'll talk," Jason said. "Don't know who'll listen."

"Don't worry about that," Aleksandr said confidently. "They'll be interested enough to listen to me when I get back, and the promise of getting rid of the Jonnies will convince them."

"Maybe. Won't hurt to talk."

"So perhaps," Aleksandr said with delicacy, "you would be

well-advised to postpone your trip to Hamp until you can go in the company of a small army of hilltowners."

"Nope. I'll spread your word for you. But I'm goin' to look for Sue by Hamp."

Felicity slammed the bottle back on the table. The two men judged the look in her eye and decided not to try to include her in the conversation. Jason poured the liquid into their cups.

"You'll want to leave as soon as it gets dark tomorrow?" Aleksandr asked, knowing the answer.

"Yup. Come along as far as you want. Don't know how you're goin' to find the Russians, though."

"I don't know either," Aleksandr admitted. "I don't want to walk all the way to the Co-op of Cleveland, however."

LATER WHEN JASON HAD left, Felicity shifted from silent anger to voluble argument. "Aleksandr, there is nothing here for you or for us. You must understand that. Even my brother had no interest in organizing, as you put it. It will be no use trying to make them fight the Jonnies, and you yourself may be killed. Forget all that. If you need to make your railroad safe, a few of your soldiers with sprayguns can kill all the Jonnies in one day. There's nothing here of any interest. Take me with you, Aleksandr. I'll be your servant and never say a word. But all those books and all that knowledge, it's no use here. Both of us must leave and never come back. There's nothing for us here."

"Now, my precious, be calm. Be reasonable. It is true that the creative energy is gone from your people and they are a simple folk. But they can be much more useful to the civilized world than they are. Now they are of no use even to themselves. They can play a part, however humble. Such a part is not to be despised, not by any means."

"They can do nothing," she said in disgust.

"And," he continued unperturbed, "while it might seem

much easier to send in Russian Imperial troops to dispose of the Jonnies, that would be a temporary solution at best. We are trying to establish security for the long term. For that, we need to involve the local people and train them so they will be helpful friends."

"These people are not Russians, Aleksandr. You yourself just said they lack... what the Russians have."

"Creative energy?"

"Yes. I think I know what you mean by that. It is why the Russians are here trying to organize Chaser Two instead of the other way around. It is why we are slaves in the Co-ops."

"You exaggerate, Felicity, but there is some truth in what you say."

"Of course." But now she had grown thoughtful. "If you leave me, Aleksandr Iosifovich Brukov, I shall never learn. I am reading sentences now in the other book from the library. I can understand some of it, but that is not enough. I need to learn from you."

"Felicity, my sweet, I am leaving you for only a matter of days. Then I shall be back in your arms and we shall conquer the Jonnies and decide how we can stay together. I shall teach you just as you have taught me." He stroked her arm, her back, her thigh, and she closed her eyes. She still was not satisfied with his words, but she surrendered to his touch.

THE NEXT DAY, before afternoon naps and farewells to Felicity, Aleksandr and Jason went to see Hammon, who had straggled to Coe after his heroic efforts in warning the camps and then harassing and delaying the Jonnies. He had been wounded in the shoulder and was convalescing at a farmhouse not far from Felicity's cabin. The short, powerful-looking hunter Hop already was visiting Hammon when the Russian and Jason arrived.

"Finally catchin' up on your sleep, eh, Hammon?" Jason asked with great jollity, at the same time raising his hand in greeting to his old companion Hop.

"Lost some blood, but I'll be out again in a couple of days." He was sitting up in bed, and Aleksandr had to fight back the impulse to ask if he could examine the wound. He had training in such things, but the Chasers could be quite put out by any suggestion that their own remedies were at all inferior. Felicity had examined Hammon's wound, and her knowledge of the healing arts seemed extensive.

"He didn't know when to quit fightin'," Hop explained. "Slowed the Jonnies down some, but they decided to take their losses even if it was nighttime. Them Jonnies don't like fightin' at night," he said to Aleksandr, as though the foreigner still needed such explanations.

"Still people in camp," Hammon said calmly. "Had to give em a chance to get out."

"That's somethin' I wanted to ask you, Hammon. If Sue was still in camp. Cap'n and me got locked up by the Jonnies down to Hamp, but we busted out and saw the Jonnies comin' back from the burnin'."

Once again, Aleksandr was amazed at how little curiosity flickered through the eyes of the Chasers as they heard this story. Instead of igniting with excitement and demanding to know every detail, they simply accepted the words as an unremarkable tale that did not concern them.

"We saw they had women and children, and I ain't found Sue."

"Already asked to help you, Jason," Hop said, shaking his head.

"Couldn't see no one to put a name to," Hammon confirmed. "Too busy. Wish I had."

"Well, I'm goin' to look. Far as Hamp if I have to."

Hammon smiled wanly. "Luck to you, Jason. Look out for them bullets. They don't feel too good."

"Want me to come along?" Hop asked.

"Well, thanks, Hop, but I'll be better off alone. Cap'n here's goin' to come part of the way."

That gave Aleksandr the opening he was looking for, and he took the opportunity to explain his plan in as concise and straightforward a manner as he could manage.

"Get rid of the Jonnies," Hop said, aloud but to himself. "Now no one would mind that too much."

"They're too strong," Hammon said. "Runnin' away from em's hard enough, runnin' at em just ain't smart."

"I think it can be done, with Russian bullets and hilltown courage." Aleksandr had already spent considerable time thinking of how to convince the fervently independent Chasers of the camps. "There will be risks, of course. No doubt some will be injured, some even killed. But in the end, everyone will be safe, and the most you'll have to fear in the woods is that Jason will mistake you for a deer."

"I only make that mistake when I want to," Jason said to the laughter of the others.

"I'm not asking you to decide anything now," Aleksandr said. "I have to get back to my people and get permission, but I do ask you to think it over and talk to the others about it."

"Talkin' don't hurt," Hammon agreed, and Hop nodded his head.

IT WOULD BE A GOOD moon for traveling that night, Jason had decided, and he intended to stay on open roads at least as far as Ash and perhaps as far as the regular Jonnie sentry outposts of Hamp. He would trust to luck and his own instinct to avoid trouble on the road. And stragglers from the burned camps probably would be near the roads. It was possible that he might find Sue as easily as that. His source of shotgun shells was gone, but he still had a pocketful left and Aleksandr promised to bring him a supply when he returned to Coe.

Having guaranteed that the idea of a direct challenge to Jonnie dominance would be discussed in his absence, Aleksandr returned to Felicity's cabin for a brief afternoon rest while Jason went to the main farmhouse for a nap on the floor there. They agreed that Jason would return to Felicity's cabin as soon as the sun dipped behind the hill.

It was only when Aleksandr began his tender farewell to Felicity that he realized the extent to which he had come to think of the hilltown nonconformist Chasers as independent rational humans. It would be a shock to return to the values of the Russian Imperial Mission, but Felicity had ceased her pleas to be taken along with him, realizing at last that it was impossible. So when Jason came to collect Aleksandr and say good-bye to Felicity, the Russian was washed by a sentimentality that only the Chasers' stoicism kept him from expressing with rhetorical and emotional excess as he looked into the deep eyes of his lover, now calm and unknowable rather than burning with intensity. He looked anxiously around the cabin, trying to ensure that he would remember it as it was even though so little in it belonged to Felicity. Her two books, the grammar and the child's storybook, prominently placed on the table, touched him to the core of his being. It was much more difficult for him to leave her now than when he and Jason had set out for the Hamp on his wrong-headed, blindly arrogant quest to tame the Reverend. Now he and Jason planned to stay together, to remain within the physical and moral world of the nonconformist Chasers, and to return together to the Hamp. He said good-bye, promising to return in a matter of days with all the ammunition that the ancient Chaser rifles could use in a month of shooting Jonnies.

It was not to be as easy as that.

‹ *Chapter Thirteen* ›

AFTER ALL HIS WORRYING about how to get in contact with the Russian Imperial Mission, after fussing about the perils of trying to walk all the way to the Co-op of Cleveland, Aleksandr found the reunion anticlimactically easy. The first morning of their trek, while he and Jason dozed in concealment only a few meters from the road, Aleksandr heard the regular flutter of a helicopter approaching, and at a fairly low level. At once his own heart matched the beat of the rotor.

"Stay here, Jason." He was almost whispering, though obviously there was no need to be quiet. "Good luck, and I'll see you again in a few days." Jason said nothing, but the two men shook hands with feeling.

Aleksandr dropped the coat he had been dozing in and eagerly dashed toward the road, clad only in his uniform, which he hoped was conspicuous from the air. He reached the road before the helicopter skimmed past, but only just. The crew spotted him, and the machine abruptly halted in midair—to the wonderment and delight of the secretly watching Jason Pembroke. The sleek helicopter swung sideways and the impressive heavy machine gun on that side was manned and pointed in his direction. It was apparent that the helicopter patrol had expected, or at least hoped for, a certain measure of trouble. Aleksandr knew from his own patrols that the psychology of the situation led one to tend to force action if none was apparent, and he hoped that the helicopter crew was at least disciplined enough to ascertain that he was in Russian Imperial Mission uniform before taking target practice.

As quickly as he could raise his hand in greeting, a pair of swarthy Chaser enlisted men jumped out of the settling helicopter and took up the regulation stances of fore and aft cover. They were short and stocky men, and they pointed their deadly Mayakovsky assault rifles toward their potential fields of fire with supreme confidence. His eye caught a unit patch and his guess was confirmed. General Vinogradov at last had succeeded in transferring the Indimex regiment from the Southwest Sector to the Co-op of Cleveland.

Aleksandr walked with calm military strides toward the helicopter, but a Russian lieutenant popped out of the opening and frantically waved him on, calling hurry, hurry, in their native language. So Aleksandr trotted up to the side of the craft and hopped in, almost being jostled by the Indimex sentries who speedily followed him.

"I apologize for my haste, Captain Brukov," the lieutenant said as the helicopter abruptly roared away, the machine-gunner still at the ready, "but since your ship was shot down we have adopted somewhat more cautious methods, and there has been a good deal of Chaser conflict in this area recently."

When he entered the helicopter Aleksandr immediately had recognized Ilya Falike, a young man who had been assigned to Chaser Two straight from the Academy. "A good deal of activity indeed, Ilya, as I have reason to know."

"I'm sure you do, Captain. I cannot speak our relief at finding you safe. Excuse me." He spoke into the microphone on his helmet. "Pilot, call in Captain Aleksandr Iosifovich Brukov safe and healthy, ETA base eleven hundred." Lieutenant Falike smiled at Aleksandr. "German pilot, so your worries are over." The German Chasers made the best helicopter pilots, according to the Russian Imperial Mission consensus, and there were frequent jokes to that effect.

"I see the General got his Indimex troops," Aleksandr said, nodding toward the stocky soldiers now patiently sitting at their assigned posts, cradling their assault rifles. Only highly trained, proven and reliable Chaser troops were issued such sophisticated weapons. A man with a Mayakovsky was a small army by himself.

"Yes," the lieutenant said somewhat uneasily. "They already have proven invaluable." He didn't need to say that unless he meant it, as they were still speaking Russian and it was unlikely the Indimex troops could understand the language of Holy Russia, but nonetheless Aleksandr felt the man wasn't speaking his mind. Junior officers in the Russian Imperial Mission were well advised to practice the virtue of discretion.

The two officers talked for the entire trip back to base, with Aleksandr growing grander and grander in his attitude and his diction as he patronized the awed younger man. The Russian Imperial Mission tradition of officers addressing their inferiors in rank by their first names added to Aleksandr's self-inflation, and several times he verged on making the terrible error of discussing his future plans with the impressionable Ilya. To start such rumors and discussion before his superiors had fully considered his proposals would weigh heavily against him.

HIS NOTIONS OF GRANDEUR were shaken as soon as they arrived at base, not least because the reception he was accorded made him realize how much unnecessary worry and grief his absence had caused his fellow officers. Colonel Dalstroi, the commander of the security detachment preparing the way for Operation Grainrail, embraced Brukov in an emotional bear hug when he stepped off the helicopter, muttering "God be praised" over and over in a half-sobbing voice. There were cheers of joy from the men who happened to be at the base and the other senior officers repeated Colonel Dalstroi's fervent embrace.

They went immediately to the conference center for debriefing. With the door closed behind them, Colonel Dalstroi led them all in kneeling before the icon and reciting aloud the entire Roll of Thanksgiving. By the end, Aleksandr's own eyes were watering.

"And now," the colonel said, rising, "to find out about your adventures and how you survived." They seated themselves around the conference table and Colonel Dalstroi used the intercom to order a samovar of tea. "I'm sure we'd all prefer something stronger right now, but General Vinogradov expects Aleksandr and me for lunch, and we should at least start at his table with a clear head.

"Tea sounds better than vodka to me right now," Aleksandr said. "I haven't had proper tea since my last day at base."

"You have had vodka?" Major Utyosov, the sharp-faced second in command asked.

"Of a sort. The arts of samogon, it turns out, are not unknown to the nonconformists I stayed among."

"Really?" the colonel said. "But please, let us be orderly. Start at the beginning."

"I should like to start at the very beginning. I would appreciate it, Colonel, if you would arrange an interrogation of the Chaser who provided our initial contact. In the light of my experiences, there are many questions I wish to ask him."

"That won't be possible, Aleksandr. As soon as we learned that your helicopter was destroyed, we shot him as a traitor. General Vinogradov's personal orders." That code phrase, said with no hint of insubordination, invariably signaled Colonel Dalstroi's disagreement with the commander of the Co-op of

Cleveland, under whose temporary jurisdiction he uneasily found himself.

"Pity," Aleksandr said in the style affected by Academy graduates who had been allowed study tours in England. "He could have revealed a great deal."

"What were the circumstances where you were shot down?" Major Chernov interjected. Normally the most deferential of officers, the chief administrator of the command now was too eager to hear the tale to suppress his excitement. Captain Nikolai Gvozdev was the other debriefer—he and three others held the same rank as Aleksandr and were in charge of specific Operation Grainrail liaison missions. The other three liaison officers presumably were away from base on assignments or they too would have been present.

"Ambush," Aleksandr replied in the terse style he intended to employ in his discussions of his sojourn among the Chasers and his subsequent recommendations. The Russian Imperial Mission staff tended to be impressed by matter-of-fact decisiveness, and all too willing to bend to its will.

"Use the map," Colonel Dalstroi suggested.

"Very well." Aleksandr stood and went to the wall. He pulled down the relevant map and studied it eagerly. The places he recently had been took on a new perspective. It was a Russian Imperial Mission survey map, so it was photographically accurate, but there were no place names, only referent numbers. "My own maps were destroyed in the crash, so I have to reacquaint myself with the terrain. Also I would like another Chaser map reproduction like the one I had so I can refresh my recollection of town names and the like. "

"We'll order one," Major Utyosov said, "but it will take an hour or two. Why not proceed with this map?"

"Very well. Here is the dominant town, called Hamp locally, originally Northampton, according to my recollection. North of that town, here, is where we were to rendezvous with the non-conformist Chaser leaders. We approached by following the road north from Hamp and followed all standard Mission procedures. We were at ready when we settled down."

"How many Chasers were there?" Major Utyosov asked.

"None that we could see." Aleksandr looked blandly into Utyosov's eyes. The rigid disciplinarian was probing to discover if Aleksandr had in any culpable way been responsible for the loss of the helicopter and its highly trained crew.

"We settled down on full alert, naturally. And thanks to the bloodthirsty enthusiasm of the Jonnies we...

"Jonnies?" Colonel Dalstroi interrupted.

Aleksandr smiled. "I discovered that the nonconformist Chasers exist in a bewildering assortment. They most emphatically are not all the same, however much we may believe otherwise. The Jonnies are the religious sect in control of Hamp —in control of the region, in effect."

"What is the religion?" Colonel Dalstroi asked. A full report would have to be made to Moscow, and Chaser religious tomfoolery was a constant source of strain between the Russian Imperial Mission and the various Councils of Elders.

"Apparently some offshoot of pre-Revelation Christianity. You know how irritating it is to hear savages chanting pious blasphemy. The name 'Jonnies' comes from the creature they worship."

"Bunch of mumbo-jumbo," Major Chernov muttered, and Captain Gvozdev smiled and shook his head in amused wonderment at the strange heathenism of the Chasers.

Colonel Dalstroi sighed. "They sound absolutely foul," he said. "Do you think they would be receptive to Shared Grace?"

"Not the Jonnies. They're quite fanatic about their god—or gods. I confess I didn't get a chance to explore their doctrines very far." The other men in the room laughed.

"How did you learn about them, then?" Major Utyosov asked. "When we digressed from the ambush you were being thankful that they were bloodthirsty."

"Quite," Aleksandr said coolly. Utyosov almost had gone too far and suggested a criticism of Colonel Dalstroi's conduct of the debriefing, and Aleksandr took pleasure in drawing attention to that fact by his response. "In fact, despite our full alert, we should have had no chance at all if the Jonnies had held their fire. But we had barely touched down when they opened fire, primitive rifles only, but quite effective in their own way. They were concealed in this group of abandoned buildings you see here on the map." He again used the pointer. "We returned fire immediately, of course, and Pilot First Class Balgar got us out of there at once."

Captain Gvozdev, who might as easily been in command of the helicopter as Aleksandr, couldn't repress himself at the tale of ambush. "You'll be glad to hear, Aleksandr, that Provisional Forty-three has been rescinded." No more needed saying at the table. The result of some unfortunate over-enthusiasm by several Mission helicopter patrols, Provisional Ukase Forty-three allowed patrols to use rockets or heavier weaponry against Chasers only after first contacting base and receiving permission from Operations. Mission troops had been gravely insulted by the rule, but now they were free to make their own decisions.

"We certainly would have killed a few more Jonnies if we had put rockets on the firing system at full alert, but we wouldn't have saved any lives or equipment, worse luck. We got away quickly, but I could see on the lights panel that central systems had been damaged. Balgar could get only limited altitude, and he tried to shift course, but couldn't manage. It all happened very quickly. We were headed north, tilting and smoking but out of range of the rifles. We finally came to a hill we couldn't surmount. Evidently I was thrown clear, and perhaps momentarily lost consciousness, though in the event my only injury was a badly sprained ankle. I must have awakened at once. The helicopter was in flames, and no one else had managed to get out."

"We examined the wreck, of course," Major Chernov said quietly. "It was the same fuel tank vulnerability noted before in the Stavrogin model." The Russian Imperial Mission had been complaining about that flaw for eighteen months, virtually from the introduction of the helicopter model.

"I am assured that the engineers are working on a modification," Colonel Dalstroi said. "But there's no possibility of an entirely new line for several years. We simply must learn to live with the Stavrogins." He managed a wintry ironical smile.

"I had assumed that some malfunction caused the actual fire," Aleksandr said. "At any rate, I tried to stand, and of course fell down again. Then I propped myself up and managed to limp over behind a boulder. I hadn't any real idea of how far away from the enemy troops we had come, and I didn't have an estimate of their number. As you know, the sensor had been removed from the helicopter. I assume they still haven't been replaced, as I tried to flag a patrol craft from the woods one day and the helicopter evidently had no idea there was a human being below."

"The sensors are still a sensitive subject, Aleksandr," Colonel Dalstroi acknowledged, and Brukov congratulated himself on presenting one of his excuses to his superiors in a way that made them defensible.

"Was your locator damaged?" Major Utyosov asked.

"I left it on board, I suppose, when I was thrown clear. I was running a personal check on equipment when the fusillade hit the craft, and in the confusion I must not have secured the locator. I have no precise recollection of the crash or being thrown clear. At any rate, I did not have the locator when I regained consciousness, or naturally I would have activated it at once."

"We were quite frightened at your disappearance without any base contact, Aleksandr," Colonel Dalstroi said gently.

"I appreciate that, Colonel."

"What procedures did you institute, Aleksandr?" Captain Gvozdev asked. He was acutely interested because his colleague had found himself in a situation they all discussed as a possibility, but in fact was a rarity. All the Mission officers wondered how they would react if they found themselves isolated and under attack in the Chaser wilderness. It didn't happen often—but obviously it could become a nightmare when trying to set up a network of Chaser liaison across such a broad stretch of little-known countryside.

Aleksandr smiled. "It would be an exaggeration to say that I initiated any procedures at all, Nikolai. I had barely recovered my wits when I saw a Chaser coming toward me with a rifle." He relished the horror registered by the other officers in the room. "Fortunately, he was alone, and he was so terrified at the sight of the burning helicopter that I surprised him rather easily."

"Were not the other... Jonnies right behind?" Major Chernov wondered.

"No, and he wasn't a Jonnie, as it turned out."

"Prayers and suffering, Aleksandr," Colonel Dalstroi interrupted, using the strongest oath he permitted himself, "you are deliberately confusing us."

"No more than I was confused, sir. You see, the Jonnies are dominant in the Hamp area, and they most assuredly are not candidates for Shared Grace. But Jason—for such was the name of the man I encountered near the burning Stavrogin—was what they call a hilltowner, one of a group of perhaps several hundred nonconformist Chasers living in small informal camps yet farther north."

"And do they share this Jonnie blasphemy?" Colonel Dalstroi asked.

"They do not. They have no religion at all that I can determine, except perhaps some kind of unstated crude pantheism and the usual Chaser traits of vagueness. They pride themselves on their independence and on the whole they seem satisfied with as uncomplicated an existence as they can manage. But I think they can work together if it is shown to be in their own self-interest, and they seem no worse as candidates for Shared Grace than most of the Chasers I have encountered in the various Co-ops."

"Did the hostile Chasers attempt to pursue you?" Major Chernov wanted to know.

"Yes. But I drove them off and with Jason's assistance managed to get away. He took me to his hilltown camp, and it was there that I was exposed to the true nonconformist Chaser existence. Undoubtedly there is a firm foundation for many of our stereotypes of the race, but those stereotypes can only be seen from a considerable distance. Up close, living with them as I did, they seemed to be a people of considerable individuality and variety, shrewd though not very intelligent—there are exceptions, of course, but there seems to be no tradition of culture among them, as there is in Chaser One."

"And what is their attitude toward Russians?" Major Utyosov wanted to know. By this time the samovar of tea had been wheeled in on a cart that also was laden with pastries, and Aleksandr joined the others at the table.

"Their attitude toward Russians," Aleksandr mused. He of course intended to say nothing of Felicity to any of the Russian Imperial Mission staff, yet everything he said about his adventure brought her to mind. He could almost hear her ironical, disturbing voice in his head questioning each sentence he said, making him seem empty and pompous, shaking his certainty, awakening his physical response to her by provoking and teasing his mind.

"I should characterize their attitude toward Russians as negative but not hostile," Aleksandr continued at last, after a sip of the strong tea. It was delicious. If only humans had the discipline to forgo their pleasures for long periods, how sweet they would be upon resumption.

"The Jonnies are another matter, of course," Aleksandr said. "Jonnies are actively hostile and warlike—I subsequently discovered beyond doubt that their attack on our helicopter was a matter of policy, not a misunderstanding. But the hilltowners simply want to be left alone. They fear us, so they want only to avoid us, not fight us. Their negative attitude seems to stem primarily from experiences many of them have had during short stays in Co-ops. They feel badly treated, degraded, and so return to the hilltown camps, and they naturally associate Russians with the often callous treatment they receive in the Co-ops."

"These people you describe are the dregs of Chaser Two," Major Utyosov interrupted sharply. Much of his previous experience had been dealing with Co-op Chasers. "We have consistently found that ten to twenty percent of the nonconformists who come to the Co-ops in hopes of protection and economic stability and honest employment are unable to adjust to civilized rule. That is common knowledge."

As Aleksandr inhaled to begin a sharp rebuttal, Colonel Dalstroi quickly cut in. "The figures are indisputable, Vladimir. As you say, they are common knowledge. But perhaps Aleksandr had the opportunity to discover some new insights that might even help us reduce that attrition rate."

"That is certainly my hope, Colonel," Aleksandr said, the quick rush of anger already dissipated. "Perhaps the Mission could assist in building some system of education, for example. Chaser Two has not preserved its heritage the way Old Europe has."

"Heritage!" Major Utyosov said with contempt, and

Chernov and Gvozdev laughed in agreement. "False religions and star-chasing, that's their heritage. As Men of History we know that their culture died because it overreached, it was too proud and did not know humility before God. Holy Russia has that precious truth, and these descendants of blasphemers now have the choice of Shared Grace or sinking back into the darkness. That is our responsibility, not offering them an education for which they are unsuited. If they were capable of education they would have preserved some form of schooling, as did the Chasers of Old Europe, who seem to know humility and subservience far better than the savages over here."

Aleksandr realized that he was almost dizzy with the strain of being away from the crude, strange world of Felicity and her fellow Chasers and back in the bosom of the Russian Imperial Mission. After all, it was not many weeks since he might have said the same words that now tumbled with such conviction from the lips of Major Utyosov. He certainly had subscribed to those ideas. But the old Brukov and the current Utyosov were wrong. He needed to devise a line of reasoning that could at least introduce a note of uncertainty into the argument.

Before he could collect his thoughts, however, Colonel Dalstroi smoothly intervened with the good-humored suggestion that a discussion of abstractions be postponed until they could all satisfy their curiosity about the actual events of Captain Brukov's sojourn in the wilderness.

So Aleksandr continued, careful to confine his narrative to indisputable fact and to withhold interpretation. He described the physical and social organization, or lack of it, in the hilltown camps, their armaments and inadequate ammunition, their role as prey of the Jonnies. He mentioned the farmers of the Valley, and went to the map to point out approximately where he and Jason had spent the night at Jobey's farm. Then he described as dispassionately as he could manage his interview with the

Reverend and the Steward, his discovery of their intransigent fanaticism and hatred of all things Russian, their threats—at the mention of mutilation the debriefers expressed shock, then set their faces in lines of determination to deal ruthlessly with such barbarism—and indications of the possible weaknesses of the Jonnies.

Brukov told of how he and Jason escaped from prison, an account that particularly delighted Nikolai Gvozdev, who vowed to remember such tricks if he ever ran afoul of Chasers. Aleksandr explained the raids of the Jonnies against the camps and the displacement of the hilltowners, and how luckily he at last came into the path of a Stavrogin patrol. He carefully did not mention his plan for the liberation of Hamp—that could wait until he had the colonel and general together at lunch.

Major Utyosov questioned him closely about his lengthy inability to make contact with Russian Imperial Mission search patrols. Aleksandr parried his thrusts successfully, while at the same time suggesting rather clearly that he was grateful for the opportunity to study the nonconformist hilltown Chasers over an extended period of time. Major Chernov wanted to know about the people, and Aleksandr described them as decent, incurious, varied in temperament but generally slow to warm to strangers. He didn't speak of the special qualities of Felicity, or mention her at all. Nikolai Gvozdev was absorbed by Aleksandr's accounts of the successes and failures of Mission equipment and procedures, and was delighted by the story of the Chaser ignorance of ammunition and the Russian's godlike ability to make the shotguns work. Colonel Dalstroi, for his part, tried to keep the discussion to the point—namely, how to guarantee the security of Operation Grainrail in the area controlled by the Jonnies. But the colonel quickly understood that Captain Brukov did not want to present any proposals just now—the exhausted young officer needed a good night's sleep in a proper

Russian bed before undertaking such a chore.

"Enough for the time being, gentlemen," Colonel Dalstroi said. "Aleksandr and I must attend upon the gracious member of the general staff who is our host in the Co-op of Cleveland. We'll meet again tomorrow afternoon. In the morning, Aleksandr, I expect you to begin your formal written report. We shall discuss recommendations in due course. Peace in God." They rose, the meeting over.

THERE WERE MANY ways in which the officers of the Russian Imperial Mission disobeyed the rules devised by the Councils for their service abroad, but the methods of disobedience were respectful even when blatant. Rules were broken, but a rhetoric and demeanor of pious obedience was maintained. General A. A. Vinogradov, however, was one of the rare exceptions, a Mission officer who lacked true feeling for religion and had no respect for the spirit in which Mission regulations were formulated. His family's power, bolstered by long years of meritorious service in troublesome areas abroad, ensured one limited command post after another, but he would never advance further, and he would never be offered a position of responsibility within the borders of Russia proper. Tall, heavy and handsome, his white hair longer than usual among senior Mission officers, he had a thick, pendulous lower lip that lent credence to reports of his cruel sexuality among the Chasers he ruled. His lunches, which never began until at least 1400, were famous for ending his workday, and in complete disregard of the spirit of Mission regulations he used his helicopter to commute between Co-op headquarters and the large estate he had restored for his personal use at the edge of a lake some distance from his post.

It was on the general's helicopter and to the general's estate that Aleksandr and Colonel Dalstroi came.

"My dear Constantine! My dear Aleksandr!" the general

shouted out over the dying helicopter motor as the pair stepped onto the sprawling back lawn of the enormous stone house. "Especially my dear Aleksandr! It is so good to see you safe!" He hugged Brukov enthusiastically. "It is such a beautiful spring day I thought we'd have our intimate luncheon outdoors."

It was indeed a warm day, and the sunshine was flattering to the carefully tended lawn, hedges and flowers that fell away from the house in terraces. There seemed to be a regiment of white-coated Chaser servants ready to attend upon them as the general shepherded them into comfortably cushioned wicker chairs.

"Vodka, Horace, Vodka!" the general shouted to his chief attendant, and at once a team began its clockwork movement. A large crystal bottle of the finest vodka was brought to General Vinogradov on a tray, along with three of the small crystal glasses that were all the rage in Moscow when the general was still a youthful student. The general insisted on pouring the first drinks himself. "To Russia!" he toasted as they all clasped their glasses. "To Holy Russia," they murmured in response, and all three threw back their heads. Aleksandr had forgotten how smooth good vodka could be. Potato lightning might as well be considered a particularly obnoxious medicine.

Now a servant stood by each of the chairs with a tray of caviar, sour cream, small sweet radishes, and thin delicate onion biscuits. Horace himself now carried the crystal bottle from chair to chair, replenishing the three glasses, his grave and humorless eyes never meeting those of the Russians. The general at once asked Aleksandr for a recitation of his experience, and the young captain envisioned the disappearance of several bottles of vodka before he could repeat his tale. But the general was interested in only the one crucial point—the Chasers in power were not willing to cooperate. He fastened on that fact at once, questioned Aleksandr closely about it, and then considered that he had learned all Aleksandr had to offer. The general's disregard for embellishment or subtlety left Aleksandr somewhat deflated.

"You're lucky you escaped from those heathen savages with your life, Aleksandr, eh, Constantine?" Colonel Dalstroi said nothing, as was expected of him. "Filthy beasts need a few lessons in Russian, eh, Aleksandr?" He too was expected to remain silent, though respectful nods of agreement were perfectly acceptable. "Well, it's clear what must be done now. This... railroad thing," he said with a dismissive wave of his hand, "is obviously your assignment, Constantine, but your tiny band of peacemaking diplomats will need augmenting, and Moscow already agreed to extra troops on the helicopter patrols after Aleksandr's unfortunate experience."

Aleksandr already was rigid with horror at the direction of Vinogradov's speech. "General, I have in mind a plan..."

"Now, now, Aleksandr, it's simple enough. You notice the Chaser troops on the helicopter that brought you back? Excellent troops! The best Chaser Two has to offer. Been trying to get them assigned to me for months. Already done marvels here." The general downed another glass of vodka and held it out for a refill.

"In fact," General Vinogradov continued, "though I hate to admit it, we were having some problems here. Nothing we could talk about before, eh?" He laughed and indicated the stoic servants, though the Russians were speaking their native tongue. "Local Chaser troops just couldn't be trained to keep things orderly. A few ugly scenes, small-scale disturbances and minor rioting, usually over housing or working conditions, were commonplace in the co-ops, and easily suppressed. It's a different matter with Indimex troops, though. Different matter altogether." He was grinning with enormous smugness. "Now, the Indimex, you see has no particular attachment to his fellow Chasers. No particular attachment at all. A good soldier. Well-trained, if I do say so, from my days in that sector. Tough. Chasers at the Co-op of Cleveland rapidly learned that the Indimex doesn't point his Mayakovsky unless he intends to shoot it. Magical. Overnight, peace and calm."

"General, I..." but Aleksandr got no further.

"A simple matter. We'll load up a few Stavrogins with Indimex troops and hop them over to this Hamp place. I know the Elders don't approve of magic," he added with evident malice, "but then it'll be presto. Just like that. Presto. No more problems. And you'll have your own railroad, Constantine. Don't even have to ask Moscow, not if we agree between us. Less to do with Moscow the better. Half a mind to take my next tour there so I can straighten out those crooked little minds." He restrained himself with difficulty, as he knew some of the servants had a better understanding of the Russian language than they let on.

"General," Colonel Dalstroi said gently, "I believe Aleksandr may have some suggestions based on his firsthand observations of the nonconformist operations."

"Doesn't do to coddle them Aleksandr, that's the key thing," the general resumed. "They're absolutely lazy dreamers unless they're firmly disciplined. Then they make decent enough kulaks. That's what Moscow needs to be told. Shared Grace indeed! It's all a bunch of nonsense made up by monks without experience of the world.

"Well, it doesn't matter, I suppose," he rambled on, their glasses filled again, "why bother to waste my time with those fools in Moscow? For my next post I have my eye on Asia. Devastated areas there are still a pack of trouble, and there's much less grumbling about 'Shared Grace.' I'd go tomorrow if I could get approval to take the Indimex regiment with me. Even the best Mission troops have had trouble in the jungle. The Indimex, he doesn't feel heat. Good endurance. Good Troops!"

"I believe they're used to a far drier climate than they'd find in the jungle," said Colonel Dalstroi, who himself had done a tour in the South Asia Sector and had no desire to return.

"The Indimex, he can take any kind of heat," the general repeated, more to himself than to his audience.

Horace coughed discreetly. "Time for luncheon, gentlemen." General Vinogradov announced grandly, suddenly revived. He hoisted himself from his chair with some difficulty, and it was apparent that he had entertained himself with vodka while awaiting the arrival of his luncheon guests.

It was a sumptuous luncheon for such a small party. Despite being set outdoors, the table was replete with fine linen, china and silver, as well as a small vase by each place setting with spring flowers from the general's greenhouse. The chairs were of ancient Chaser Two design, a style Aleksandr much admired— wooden, high-backed, with curved arms and plush velvet backs and seats. They would bring a fortune in Moscow.

Though only the three officers were dining, servants brought out a roasted duck, a glazed, fruit-studded ham, and a choice sirloin roast of beef. There were silver bowls of vegetables, and General Vinogradov had even managed to obtain a fair replica of Russian bread, no doubt from a bakery devoted to his personal needs. One had only to nod at a servant to have an immediate serving of the food under his custody. Horace himself saw to the pouring of the wine. As usual at the general's estate, the prayer was brief and perfunctory. Tradition reserved dining conversation at Mission tables to the social amenities, which in this case meant monologues by General A. A. Vinogradov on the subjects of the superiority of Chaser Two beef to Chaser One beef, the superiority of Chaser One liquor to Chaser Two liquor, the superiority of Chaser One mistresses to Chaser Two mistresses, the superiority of his own wine cellar to that of any other Co-op commander's, and the unreadable obscurity of the new Russian novelists. Only his vocal contempt for Elders intruded occasionally as a breach of etiquette, and as he was the senior officer present as well as the host, he could scarcely be held accountable, though his open and dismissive criticism of church officials made both Aleksandr and Colonel Dalstroi uneasy.

With brandy and cigars, a postprandial practice despised by the Elders but a Mission tradition nevertheless, the general surprised Aleksandr with a question that almost put him off stride by its swiftness and unexpectedness.

"By the way, Aleksandr," he said, blowing a column of smoke along the current of a sudden gentle breeze, "why didn't you hail rescue helicopters with flares while you were among the savages?" His gaze was cool and level despite the drinking he'd done, and Aleksandr wondered whether Major Utyosov had radioed ahead to the general to plant the question.

"I certainly prayed for them," Aleksandr said with an easy smile. "but they were in my kit in the helicopter. Things were a bit hectic after the fusillade began, and my kit was destroyed in the crash, of course."

"The positive result of his not having flares or a radio locator, General," Colonel Dalstroi said smoothly, "is that he had a rare opportunity to spend time among the heathen—an unwitting anthropological expedition, as it were." The colonel tended to be too intellectual for even Aleksandr's taste, and he feared that the general would be bored or offended but there was no polite way to interrupt.

"For that reason," the colonel went on, "I think it might be valuable to hear what conclusions he drew from his experience and what his recommendations for action might be."

"By all means," the general said. "Of course." His one thrust had been parried, and Aleksandr saw that any response other than a panicked admission of culpability would have been satisfactory.

The general already was heavy-lidded and uninterested, stifling yawns, ready for a nap. He was keeping awake by moving one hand to his mouth with brandy and the other hand to his mouth with tobacco. It was a self-defeating exercise.

"I observed," Aleksandr said, taking the general's words as an invitation for him to explain his ideas fully, "that the nonconformist Chasers are remarkably divergent, and even pride themselves on individuality as well as independence. But there are broad areas of self-interest around which they cluster. The religious fanatics of Hamp, who call themselves Jonnies, pursue their own heathen idol with such fervor and violence that they are the dominant force. They are resolutely opposed to any person or thing Russian, and may be counted on for maximum harassment of Operation Grainrail." The general's attention might be wandering, Aleksandr noted, but he had the full concentration of Colonel Dalstroi.

"On the other hand," the young officer continued, "the independent but peaceful nonconformists to the North have neither the weaponry nor the leadership to manage defiance of the Jonnies on a large scale.

"A third group seems to be the farmers of the area adjacent to Hamp on the south and east. They pursue their occupation, dealing with anyone who comes along, and are largely left to their own devices for the very good reason that their crops are vital to the entire region."

"Sounds like what they need is some Indimex troops," the general mumbled.

"If you'll forgive me, General, I think not," Aleksandr said. "The hilltown nonconformists are thoroughly disgusted with the Jonnies, and I think they're ripe to act. They have an adequate number of men, I think, and there are plenty of working rifles, equivalent to the arms borne by the Jonnies. But they have scarce and extremely unreliable ammunition, and no leadership whatever."

"Can't fight without bullets or officers," the general agreed.

"Exactly. My proposal is that instead of sending Indimex or other Mission troops, we send in a few cases of the proper caliber ammunition, and have me return to organize them into a functioning regiment with a coherent battle plan. I think I could accomplish that with relative ease."

Colonel Dalstroi looked thoughtful, but General Vinogradov spoke first. "Far too complicated and dangerous, Aleksandr." The proposal seemed to have shocked him awake. "For one thing, it's always a risky business arming Chasers, especially nonconformists whom even you describe as independent. Moscow wouldn't like that, I'm certain. Secondly, why bother? We can do it faster and easier ourselves. You haven't seen the Indimex troops in battle."

"First of all, General," Aleksandr said with a bow, "arming the hilltown nonconformists should not concern the Mission. They are already armed, and pose no threat whatever. All we would be doing is bringing them up to parity with the Jonnies, who are potentially a considerable nuisance. In neither case do single-shot rifles constitute a threat to the Russian Imperial Mission troops or objectives.

"As to the question of why we should bother, that gets to the heart of the matter, at least as I see it." For the flicker of an instant he was insanely tempted to say that his rationale was too subtle to explain to the general, but the temptation was quickly overcome and helped him concentrate on making his point forcefully.

"There's no doubt it would be simpler and faster to use Mission troops, Indimex or any other. But I think there are two main arguments in favor of my proposal. One is that we are all aware that Moscow stresses the need to avoid armed conflict with Chasers whenever possible. Indeed, working out peaceful cooperation was my assignment when I went to Hamp. My proposed operation will put only one Russian in peril—myself—and as far as Moscow is concerned the operation can be treated as a conflict between Chaser sects, which is of little interest.

"The other argument is the result of my prolonged experience of living among these people. I may lack the eloquence to convey how firm my convictions are, or how hard-won."

Colonel Dalstroi smiled. "So far, Aleksandr, your eloquence seems not to have deserted you." Even the general was watching Aleksandr with guarded, perhaps wary, interest.

Aleksandr bowed his head in smiling acknowledgement of the compliment. "As you have repeatedly explained to those of us privileged to serve under you in Operation Grainrail, my Colonel, we must be concerned not solely with temporary pacification of the natives, but with building long-range terms of cooperation that can ensure the successful functioning of the railroad for the years God pleases it to run.

"A simple attack by Mission troops against the Jonnies would succeed, of course. But some Jonnies no doubt would survive and reconstitute and they would be more opposed to Russians than ever, and more determined to vex us. In addition, other nonconformists might wrongly consider such an attack as indicating that the Mission is peremptorily bloodthirsty—not a good foundation for building cooperation over the years. We will have rid them of the Jonnies, but then we will disappear again, leaving them with no greater sense of security or control over their own lives.

"But if the hilltown nonconformists depose the Jonnie rule themselves, there will be a sense of continuity and integration. For instance, I have reason to believe that not all the Jonnie troops are zealots—they simply take orders for their own security. If their own people firmly and successfully oppose the Jonnie rule, much of the problem may just melt away, the zealots dead or on the run and the rest happy to settle into a peaceful life. Grateful, furthermore, for the discreet aid of the Russians, and perfectly willing to cooperate, perhaps even actively, in ensuring the security of Operation Grainrail."

Aleksandr and the colonel declined more brandy and, to their surprise, the general took no more for himself. He evidently had reached the saturation point and was ready to succumb to his obvious need for sleep. But he did say, before the discussion was adjourned: "Simplicity is the key. Too complex trying to guess what Chasers will do. Totally unreliable. Quick strike, just like that. Matter of hours. Indimex." Brukov and Dalstroi wisely failed to respond, and mumbled farewells followed.

‹ *Chapter Fourteen* ›

IN THE PRIVACY OF the special passenger compartment on General Vinogradov's helicopter, Colonel Dalstroi allowed himself to suggest that he had been impressed by Aleksandr's arguments.

"After all," he said, "you are the one with direct experience. And the less direct force exerted by the Mission the better. At least, that's what they taught during my days at the Academy."

"The Academy hasn't changed," Aleksandr said, smiling.

"Naturally, I was inclined to agree with the general. It *is* simpler to do the job ourselves. And I wonder about your theory that your nonconformist friends can handle it. I don't doubt your judgment that they're trustworthy, though even Russian prayers have not made Chasers trustworthy in the past. But a failure, an attack against these heathen fanatics that is defeated, could substantially complicate our position."

"Certainly there would be no further argument then against sending in the general's esteemed Indimex troops," Aleksandr agreed.

"Prayers and suffering," the colonel muttered. "They are as efficient as General Vinogradov says. Would that he succeeds in taking them to Asia."

"You find them unworthy?" Aleksandr asked.

"Not at all. Excellent combat troops." Despite the praise,

which he voiced with perfect sincerity, Colonel Dalstroi looked worried. "It's just that here it is possible that pacification should be achieved by more subtle means. The general's judgment is no doubt correct, but I can't avoid the impression that Chaser hostility has been suppressed only temporarily in the Co-op of Cleveland, and may one day manifest itself even more virulently as a result of these very firm methods so prized by the general. But it is his command and his judgment, so no doubt he is correct."

"If the Indimex troops were used against the Jonnies, they might be indiscriminate in their violence?"

"The general would have it no other way."

"Ah," said Aleksandr. "That possibly could be unfortunate. There is no need to use the cane on the child so hard the cane breaks. It ruins both cane and child."

"I perceive that you had the same governess as I."

"And the rest of Russia." They both laughed.

"Well, Aleksandr," Colonel Dalstroi said, "it is a delicate matter. I shall give your recommendations my prayers and my thought."

"You can do no more, my Colonel."

And so some delay was unavoidable. It was no idle joke that "Only God rules Holy Russia." Even in the Russian Imperial Mission, lines of authority, if not responsibility, often overlapped. Decisions were made by a kind of gentlemen's code, and if the directly affected officer were forced to decide quickly, he frequently would defer to other opinions. An officer who insisted on his personality and aggressively promoted his own ideas was quickly marked by the others in the Mission. Careers could end rather abruptly.

As Aleksandr was vividly aware, the Chaser liaison aspects of Operation Grainrail were the direct responsibility of Colonel Dalstroi, but the large Co-ops that provided support men and materiel for Operation Grainrail were commanded by generals, and it was unthinkable that a major decision be made by the colonel alone. It was not at all presumptuous for General Vinogradov to expect, though not demand, to be fully consulted on any proposed military activity that had not been specifically set out in the Operation Grainrail order forms approved in Moscow and provided to each Co-op commander affected.

To the Russian Imperial Mission way of thinking, General Vinogradov and Colonel Dalstroi were exactly equal in considering Aleksandr's plan, and an appeal by either man to superiors in Moscow was all but impossible. For one to attempt to go over the other's head would offend the unwritten Mission code; for them to appeal jointly for arbitration would mark them as inadequate to the demands of Mission leadership.

Aleksandr knew that he couldn't press for a quick decision. Colonel Dalstroi would feel, and be, honor-bound to adopt the general's point of view. Aleksandr was concerned that the longer he was absent from the Chasers, the weaker his position would be with them. Already he missed Felicity, missed her sharply, but he could only hope that soon the general would bow, however reluctantly, to the judgment of the officer who had firsthand experience with the people involved.

THREE LETTERS FROM Lyalya had accumulated. She naturally had not been informed of Captain Aleksandr Iosifovich Brukov's disappearance under such forbidding circumstances. By policy, the Russian Imperial Mission did not inform Russia of speculation or gossip, only fact. Not until he had been missing for six months would Russia have been told of his unexplained absence.

Aleksandr opened the letters in chronological order. He smiled to see himself addressed as "Tita." As his fiancée she was entitled to use his childhood nickname.

My dearest Tita,

How thrilled I was by your last letter! Not only does it soothe my heart, so bruised by your absence, to see the unmistakable dear scrawl of your script, it is so exciting to read your tales of such unimaginable things. I read your stories aloud to Mama and Papa at the breakfast table, though not the parts that must remain known to only us, dearest! They were as thrilled as I. We fear for your very life among those savages, but I swell with pride at the thought of your brave service for Holy Russia. Your story about the ancient Chaser at the Co-op of Chicago who believed an ancestor had flown to the moon had us all laughing so! Chasers can be so charming when they're nice.

Darling, you must be more careful. Colonel Dalstroi is the sweetest of men and the joy of every Russian woman who has a portion of her heart attached to the Mission, but really he should be more prudent with those men we entrust to his care! It seems to me most perilous to venture into the wilderness with so few men on such an uncertain task. After all, the savages you deal with are nonconformist Chasers far removed from even the benefits of Shared Grace, and I cannot but feel that they have only to sense the slimmest opportunity and they will fall upon you with foul intent. I pray each night that you are ever vigilant! But I must not let your dear welfare so capture my mind that there is no room for joy! This land much loved of God fairly bursts with newness each day, and I weep that you must protect us from afar under such dangerous and disagreeable circumstances. You will be amazed at all you must learn when you return from your tour. So much happens each day! Cush (her nickname for her brother, who was a year behind Aleksandr at the Academy) took Mama and me to a concert last night—a new tenor, V. Gamov, by far the best tenor yet! Munakovsky had written a new setting of 'Delivered to Love' especially for Gamov and stroza, and never has there been such beautiful music. All that was after intermission. First there was the Ural Choir of Elders with their strange prayers. Forgive me, my beloved, but I do not always understand such words or such music! The newspapers today all preferred the choir to Munakovsky, however, though they all loved Gamov.

All Moscow is still astir about Plantov's reading last week. It was from his new book of poems that was just published, called 'Patromonies,' and they can't be printed fast enough! Already people know many of them by heart. I'd send the book but Misha borrowed it and perhaps I'll have to buy a new copy. One of the poems, 'Caution to an Elder Tree' is very naughty and has everyone laughing, though it is the sort of thing one shouldn't write about in a letter to an officer of the Russian Imperial Mission!

The Elders are debating about a new Doctrine, as usual, and everyone is very excited about that, but I can hardly understand their arguments—the points seem so very similar to me!

The weather this winter has been beastly, but there are signs now that it is ending, and one can sense that people feel like horses that have been penned too long. They wish to escape and gallop in the fresh air and the open land! But we must wait a few weeks longer, I fear.

Food was very plentiful all winter, though some kulaks apparently did not think so, and there are many rumors about how when my Aleksandr has made his railroad there will be grain to scatter in the streets! They do not mention you by name, of course, but your name is always in my heart and in my thoughts, and I pray always, Tita, love me and love God and all will be well.

    Yours past telling,

    Lyalya

Alone at last, Aleksandr was reading the letters in his rooms in the early evening, before dinner in the officers' dining hall.

He rang for tea, which he decided would help combat the effects of General Vinogradov's table before he had to face more vodka and food. His eyes were misty with tears from reading the first letter, and he composed himself before the Chaser orderly brought him one of the pots of tea perpetually in preparation in the sprawling kitchen downstairs. Only after he had tasted the sweet drink did he open the second blue envelope.

My dearest Tita,

I know that we agreed I should not write two letters to your one, but wait for your reply, as you are so busy and so often away from base, but it seems an eternity since I last saw your dear handwriting and my heart is too full to hold it back from paper! Papa is meeting with some of the Elders of the Council of Councils today, and I think they will ask him to be Minister of Finance, though he is too modest to believe that. Should I write such things to a Mission officer? I don't see why not. Papa is so excited, but he thinks he doesn't show it and pretends to be bored, but he spilled his tea all over the table this morning and blushed and became very angry when Mama and I laughed at him, and of course we just laughed the more!

Cush thinks that some time this summer he may be assigned to Chaser One, and after this winter he is trying hard to get constabulary duty on the Riviera for a year. Imagine Cush handing out tea to fat vacationing Russians! But that's what he wants, he says. He doesn't ever want to be cold again!

Arkansky's new play is quite the scandal here; I can hardly wait to see it! It suggests the possibility that certain Elders in the past may have been just the tiniest bit corrupt, and the newspaper reviewers drew the conclusion, which the playwright subsequently refused to deny, that the same suspicions might be held about certain contemporary Elders. Our poor Elders! I pray for them regularly.

I have dozens of things I could write about, all that is

happening at our house—and at yours, your grandfather visited us a few days ago and was most merry and wonderful—and all that is happening in Moscow and all the witty things people are saying. But truly I write, Aleksandr, only to express my love for you. My heart simply overflows when I think of you, and I think of you always, and each measure of my being yearns to see you, to talk to you, to touch you, to hear your dear voice. For me, marriage will be such a blessed release that I pray God I do not lose sight of the humility of our earthly presence! To you I confess, my darling Aleksandr, I must often pray the Roll of C.—I blush but admit it! I yearn so to hold you! And that is why I could not bear to wait for your letter before writing myself. There are so many things I cannot help myself about, and loving you is chief among them! Hurry, darling—build your railroad and come to me so that God may see our marriage and witness our love.

    Yours forever,

     Lyalya

Aleksandr put the letter down, walked to the window, and stared out sightlessly. He blew his nose, sighed, and packed a pipe with the excellent Mission shag. He poured another cup of tea before turning to the third letter. It was just a note, really, and it bore a very recent date.

Darling Tita,

    Please forgive me for writing another letter and putting you under such an obligation when you are so busy, but believe me, I must. I write to you every day, sometimes twice a day, and simply do not send the letters, but only God rules Holy Russia, and only you rule my heart, as the song so hated by the Elders says.

    But I must write because Cush has heard from a Mission officer just back from Chaser Two that you have been on a long and dangerous assignment from which you have not even yet returned, and the news so frightened me that I am writing now to affirm that I know you have returned or soon will return without

dishonor or injury and with great credit. That knowledge is in my
heart and it must be true because I love you!

God protects you with the armor of my love, and I know that
soon I shall have a letter from your own dear hand.

Forever yours,
Lyalya

ALEKSANDR SAT BACK IN the deep leather armchair and puffed at
his pipe. It seemed to him that all his life he had been resolving
on one course of action only to follow another, and the problem
was not simply a character flaw, it was some other kind of
failure. Perhaps it was a failure to understand other people
adequately. He could decide in his mind just what he thought
and just what he felt, and be perfectly comfortable with his
convictions. Then along would come someone else to raise new
thoughts and feelings—an unexpected factor that jumbled the
entire equation. All those wonderful convictions would vanish,
poof, like smoke up a chimney.

He could picture his beautiful Lyalya, sitting at her writing
desk in one of her simple, fashionable dresses, barely more than
a schoolgirl and writing with such florid naiveté. She was tiny
and fine-boned, a style of slender beauty that Aleksandr and
many others considered exquisite, though he knew that some of
his fellow officers shared the more usual Russian taste for a
greater hardiness of figure.

What a terrible confusion he felt. Felicity had opened a new,
uncertain but exciting world to him with her passionate
curiosity and her bedeviling lack of conformity to any standard
known to Aleksandr. With her he felt the intoxication of his
own mastery, mastery won by knowledge, mastery that enslaved
her with a powerful addiction and released her passions and her
intensity to his benefit, to his service. He in turn became
addicted. And her mysterious perceptions, never correct but

always having the ring of a distant truth, mesmerized him as though they were a labyrinth of mirrors whose secrets somehow were important. He wanted to understand, to gain control of the impulses and forces that gave Felicity such intensity so he could master that part of her too, instead of having always the unsettling, irritating, itch-like worry that her intensity was mastering him.

And then in the midst of such things, when Chaser Two seemed to provide all the uncertainties and challenges that could make life exciting and vivid and when his settled existence in Russia had taken on the form in his imagination of a predictable chess game full of certainty and satisfaction and stable emotions that could never overrun their banks, just then he is surprised with evidence, irrefutable evidence, that his soul is bound in Russia!

The letters of his charming, chattering, romantically lightheaded fiancée were almost more evocative by what they did not say than by what they did. They captured his imagination utterly with the suggestion of Moscow society, the plays and the readings and the concerts, the unending controversy over each new masterwork, the constant squabbles between the Elders and the artists, the Elders and the Men of History, and the Men of History and the artists—many of whom scorn all factions and were loved the better for it.

The very ritual of breakfast tea with the ladies of the household galvanized him. The conversation of equals, the sharing of prayers, the wrenching piety of the church music, the sobs of Russians who felt as one in the new and irresistible bursting forth of their civilization. To understand does not mean the absence of feeling, Men of History were taught at the Academy. The deepest understanding is left to God, and surest knowledge remains just over the horizon for even the wisest. The Russian soul had a contentment in God's knowledge, Men of

History agreed with the Elders, an agreement that spared the torments and errors, the miseries and pretensions that had destroyed civilizations before but allowed Russia, Holy Russia, True Russia, to be the highest expression of God's destiny in man. And man could express that destiny in Godmanhood.

With such confused emotions, Aleksandr more than willingly answered the summons to vodka, where before dinner he could play the returned hero to his admiring fellow officers.

THE NEXT FORENOON, suffering slightly from a hangover but feeling in control of his emotions, which he had determined needed nothing more than time to be sorted out, Aleksandr wrote to Lyalya. An airplane leaving that evening would carry the letter to Moscow promptly.

'My darling Lyalya,' he began, having decided that for the time being he would avoid the word 'dearest,' which he previously favored.

> My darling Lyalya,
>
> I cannot express the depth of feeling I experienced when I found your letters upon my return to base and read your charming endearments.
>
> The rumor your brother heard is substantially true, though I fervently wish Mission officers would obey orders and not spread tales when they return to Russia.
>
> God be praised the ending was happy—I am entirely well and unharmed—but I regret the unnecessary worry you have been caused.
>
> Darling Lyalya, please forgive me the shortness of this note. My duties are pressing my time most severely. I can, of course, tell you no details, except that we are hard at work building what you call my railroad. But know that I am in good health, recite my prayers unfailingly, and think of you now more than ever.
>
> It sounds as though Cush has not changed his ambition of

*living comfortably at any price, and you never did tell me the
outcome of your father's meeting with the Elders. Please give my
love to all, and tell my family that I will write at the first
opportunity, which may not, however, occur until the next phase
of my assignment is completed.*

    *Know that I think of you and count the days until I see you
again.*

    Your devoted fiancé,
    Aleksandr

There. Lyalya would be reassured with this brief note since
he already had the reputation of being an unreliable and unimag-
inative letter-writer. He sealed the letter and called for an orderly.

DUTY ALWAYS PROVIDED the undutiful among Mission officers
with an excuse for not writing their families. In Aleksandr's case,
however, it was the anticipation of duty that provided his
excuse. He was so eager to prove the validity of his plan for the
liberation of Hamp that he somehow set his mind to expect a
continuous flow of action, with him at the center. At once, quite
suddenly, nothing happened.

He finished his debriefing uneventfully, and as soon as the
other officers divined that Colonel Dalstroi was inclined to
endorse Aleksandr's recommendations, they inclined that
direction themselves, even Major Utyosov. All were curious as to
how such an adventure might be conducted, none could be
personally endangered by the project, and the prospects of
Aleksandr's gaining excessive glory seemed more than
counterbalanced by the excellent chance that eventually he
would be forced to crawl back to base, announce his failure, and
ask that the Indimex troops be dispatched forthwith. All these
things, however, remained unsaid.

Still, Mission etiquette required Aleksandr to await a
decision calmly, resigned to accept any eventuality as the will of

God and for the benefit of Holy Russia. He did press, with extreme delicacy, for the assembly of quantities of ammunition of the types that would be required by a Chaser regiment. It would be, he pointed out, merely a prudent anticipation. Colonel Dalstroi agreed, and assigned Captain Brukov the task. After considerable confusion, exasperation and tedium, the cases of rifle cartridges and shotgun shells were assembled, drawing on Mission resources in the Co-ops of Chicago, Boston and Hoboken. It took several days to locate the ammunition, and another week to gather it at the Operation Grainrail base. Meanwhile, Colonel Dalstroi calmly attended his regular meetings with General Vinogradov, where they no doubt discussed everything except the proposed assault on the Jonnies at Hamp.

To Aleksandr, it seemed he should have been back at the Chaser camp two days after returning to base and explaining the situation, though he realized now that his expectations had been based on emotion, not thought. Naturally, it would take some time but this was altogether too much time. He considered asking for permission to make an interim visit to the Chasers, to reassure them that he hadn't disappeared entirely, but of course Colonel Dalstroi couldn't permit that until a decision had been reached.

So, instead, once he had completed the frantic search for ammunition, Aleksandr was at loose ends. General Vinogradov kept an excellent stable, and Aleksandr loved riding, but he did not want to put himself in the general's debt just now. He tried a morning of hunting with a fellow officer who was an excellent wing shot, but Aleksandr was only reminded of much more enjoyable hunting in the company of Jason. He accompanied Nikolai Gvozdev in a Stavrogin to a nearby village of Chasers, but Aleksandr was only an observer and quickly grew bored.

Almost as a last resort, he wrote to his mother, then to his grandfather. Then, more warmly but still with a confused unhappiness that he hoped did not show through the words, he wrote again to Lyalya. In the last mail transport, there had been no letter for him; she would not have received his own. The next delivery would not be for at least another week. Perhaps he would be back in the hills by then, and therefore able to postpone a reckoning with his feelings.

THE HELICOPTER SWUNG rapidly away from the base toward General Vinogradov's estate.

"We must be very courteous, of course, and seem unhurried," Colonel Dalstroi said to Aleksandr, sitting with him in the passenger compartment. "If the general suspects that we must decide, he can simply sympathize and pretend to give the matter more thought. If he delays, he wins his point, and the Indimex regiment gets its slaughter. The more I have thought about the matter, the more I have come to agree with you. The approach you propose is a novel one. If it fails, there is little lost. If it succeeds, you will have made an important contribution to the theory and practice of Chaser pacification. At best, it could favorably change our entire relationship with those to whom we wish to extend Shared Grace."

Aleksandr swelled with pride at the intoxicating words. "It is my prayer, Colonel."

"But I tell you, Aleksandr, we cannot delay much longer. The grain collection is complete, and Moscow wants to start putting down Plastirail eastward soon. They are quite impatient. The machines are ready, the material is at hand, the decision has been made. But they don't want to commit themselves to the start of such a project until the preliminary liaison steps with the Chasers have been completed. I agree entirely, of course, and not simply as a line officer who must do his duty. It will be difficult enough to prepare the roadbeds and put down the Plastirail without uncertainty as to local situations still ahead. There can be no joy in work when progress means only that one is closer to uncertainty and possible conflict. In short, we must be reasonably sure that any Chaser difficulties can be resolved by the security car on the train before we begin. Any delay in construction between the Co-ops of Chicago and Boston could be disastrous, and very damaging to relations between the Mission and the Council of Councils."

"Of course."

"And delays right now are almost as dangerous. The means have been allocated. All is in readiness."

"Of course," Aleksandr repeated unhappily. He could see quite clearly that Colonel Dalstroi was perfectly prepared to embrace General Vinogradov's plan if it came to that. Swift action was imperative.

"Ah, Aleksandr," the colonel sighed with resignation as the helicopter swooped down toward the general's estate, "it's only too bad you didn't bring back a comely Chaser maiden as a present for the general."

"The only ones I met seemed too old for what I understand is the general's taste. Possibly the wrong gender as well."

"Aleksandr!" But the rebuke ended there, and the colonel smiled as the helicopter settled on the lawn.

It was another warm and sunny day, and the general again seated them outside. Though not yet summer, the weather spoke of that season, and the greenness of the lawn and the colors of the gardens were almost languid in their vivid hues. The scene might well have been painted by one of the Old European masters so much admired by the irreverent new painters in Moscow. With his usual insensitivity toward the delicate balance of regulations worked out by the Mission in negotiations with the Elders, General Vinogradov had sprayed his grounds with generous doses of insecticide. It had become almost impossible to sit outside at the base, and it was with guilty pleasure that Aleksandr and Colonel Dalstroi accepted their drinks in the drowsy and stingless air.

"It is so kind of you to accept my invitation, Aleksandr," the general said, his handsome, slightly puffy face genuinely genial in expression. "Constantine and I spend too much time together. We need young blood around."

"It is my pleasure, General."

"I hope so, I hope so." He seemed to Aleksandr to be less drunk than was often the case. "I may even see if I can tempt you away from Constantine once Operation Grainrail is on its way. I hope to go to Asia, of course, if the elderberries don't stick in my teeth." He laughed hugely at his own joke. "We need bright and brave young men over there, real Mission officers who aren't afraid to get out among the savages."

"Everyone agrees that Asia is a challenging assignment," Aleksandr said without enthusiasm.

"Challenge! Yes, that's what we need more of. Too many of our officers wish to spend all day listening to music and reading poetry! We need soldiers, not poets and religious fanatics!"

Aleksandr smiled, though the look on Colonel Dalstroi's face said that he'd heard these diatribes before. "We Men of History believe that Russians have newly discovered their own culture, General," Aleksandr said. "It is natural that they should be avid in exploring all its highest expressions."

"Well, so they say, so they say." The general's bile subsided and he sighed. "At any rate, the only thing I can find of merit in your proposal to foment a revolution within the ranks of the nonconformist Chasers is that it shows initiative and a willingness to face up to a challenge. Mind you, I think it's a harebrained scheme. But at least you didn't come back to base and tell Constantine to send in a regiment while you locked yourself in your room with a book. Books! They should be forbidden outside of Russia." He had managed to work himself up again to the point that he needed another drink, and the efficient Horace materialized as usual.

"I am delighted," Colonel Dalstroi said smoothly, "that the general is becoming convinced of the need to let Aleksandr test his theories. Troops can always be used later."

"I am by no means convinced, my dear Constantine. I only admired the young man's pluck and ingenuity. Such qualities need to be encouraged within the Mission. But I am considering the position. I am considering very carefully."

"I too am considering, General Vinogradov," the colonel said. "It is a subject that demands the most thorough examination. At first, every time I had decided that Aleksandr should be allowed to implement his recommendations, only minutes later I would think of him failing, perhaps being killed, and Operation Grainrail being discredited in Moscow. So I would decide in favor of an immediate dispatch of Stavrogins full of Indimex troops, just as the wise and experienced general suggested. But then I would think, after all, these heathen did shoot down one helicopter. What if their armaments are sufficient to put up a good fight? There could be casualties beyond what we have come to regard as acceptable, and that could damage morale within the Mission as well as inviting Moscow to grumble. Such casualties among Aleksandr's ragtag group of nonconformist Chasers wouldn't even occasion notice, however."

The general rubbed the rim of his glass slowly. "I don't think you need worry about the Indimex troops incurring undue casualties, Constantine." But his tone was not as infuriatingly superior as usual.

"I have considered," Aleksandr said, "if I may be so bold as to enter the discussion when my opinion is already declared, that there is yet another possibility. I have no doubt that these fanatics, these Jonnies, will put up a determined fight. They will have no real chance against Mission troops, especially against Indimex troops. But such a large-scale operation will be examined closely in Moscow. The general has noted that some of our beloved fellow-Russians are not always well-informed about affairs outside their own precincts. They are not at all accustomed to hearing of considerable armed resistance by Chaser Two nonconformists. Thanks to the leadership of the general and others, such things simply don't happen of their own volition. Suppose Moscow becomes frightened? Experienced Mission troops, even Russian officers, might not be rotated out of Chaser Two for fear of uprisings. Certainly troops as efficient as the Indimex regiment would be ordered to stay in place. That could affect your own plans." He nodded toward General Vinogradov.

"Well, um um um," the general said, sipping at his vodka. "Personal considerations of career plans are never sufficient to influence a military or administrative decision, of course, but you do mention potential problems. What is important, naturally, is that Moscow not be deceived into thinking there is more difficulty with the Chasers here than in fact exists. There must be no doubt about the ability of the Russian Imperial Mission, about our ability to handle any contingency in Chaser Two easily and as part of our ordinary routine, our standing orders."

"Quite true, General," Colonel Dalstroi said with appropriate solemnity.

Now they were summoned to table, where the numerous servants once again offered quantities of food.

"The local vegetables are coming in nicely," the general said. "Be sure to try the asparagus. The best I've had since my leave two years ago on the Riviera."

"Ah, there they have white asparagus," the colonel said with fond recollection.

"Yes, white indeed," the general said, as though he were

thinking of an altogether different pleasure.

IT WAS NOT UNTIL after the food and wine, after the elaborate compliments and deprecating acknowledgements, after they had been seated again in the garden with snifters of brandy, that Colonel Dalstroi again opened the subject they had met to discuss.

"I have been thinking, General," he began, as though General Vinogradov's words had been his first introduction to the idea, "I have been thinking about what you said concerning the necessity of Moscow perceiving that our regular Mission procedures are capable of disposing of any eventuality here in Chaser Two."

"And what, my dear Constantine, just what exactly is it that you have concluded?" By now, alcohol again had begun to cloud the general's demeanor and to affect, though slightly, the cadences and pronunciation of his speech.

"Only this, General. Suppose there might be some... impressionable people in Moscow who are not experienced enough abroad to correctly read our situation..."

"Suppose indeed! Bunch of Elder-ridden old women who've never spent a single day in combat."

Colonel Dalstroi smiled, indicating at least partial agreement without committing the treason of a word. "Now, if there are a few who are capable of misunderstanding the situation, and pray that can never happen, you must admit that one misunderstanding or misinterpretation generally leads to another..."

"Come to the point, Constantine, come to the point."

"The point is, General, that you and I both might be judged inefficient at best if we have to throw an entire regiment of troops into full-scale battle against Chaser ragamuffins. Ever since Moscow decided that an admiral was needed to command the Co-op of Boston because the land area of this Co-op is too extensive..."

"I prefer it. The larger the area the better. It only wants firm supervision."

"Exactly! You and I are both aware of that, without question. But Admiral Zeed is not likely to understand our point of view much better than Moscow, and he could get nervous if there were a significant military clash in your jurisdiction and so near to his beloved port."

"Ah, Constantine," the general said wearily, waving his glass in a kind of signal that the point had been taken and further words were unnecessary. "The world is full of fools. Those who do the best work are the easiest to criticize. There you are right, there is no doubt about it."

"So you see," Colonel Dalstroi said, looking at the general and inclining his head toward Aleksandr, "so you see why I grow somewhat more disposed to favor Captain Brukov's plan."

"You have my promise that I shall consider all things with care." And the subject was closed.

TWO DAYS LATER, almost trembling with excitement and frantic that he might be overlooking an important detail, Aleksandr gave a final check to his gear. He was waiting in a hut while the crew completed its tests of the helicopter. It was full night outside. After considerable thought, Aleksandr had decided to arrive back among the Chasers at Coe just after first light.

This time, he was being transported in full battle dress—not much different than the Russian Imperial Mission officers' duty uniform, but somewhat bulkier and designed to carry more equipment. Along with the Pushkin Series 2100 machine-pistol, he had requisitioned a Mayakovsky assault rifle. Twin strips of clips laddered from his shoulders to his waist. Taped in at his right thigh were four flash bombs, and at his left thigh were four similar devices, though of a very different design. They were armor-piercing high explosives known by Mission troops as "slams" because of their force. They could blow apart most armored vehicles. The flash bombs, on the other hand, would light up the place they exploded for about ten seconds, and one kind, the kind carried by Aleksandr, also threw out shrapnel in a twenty-meter radius. Not very deadly, but a good surprise weapon, especially at night.

Both types of projectiles fitted into the Mayakovsky assault rifle without adaptors; Aleksandr was, in fact, equipped the same as the best of the combat troops, though he also carried some officer's gear, such as the Pushkin machine-pistol and his locator transmitter.

The Indimex guards that would accompany him on his trip were outside, loosening their legs before the cramped flight.

The door of the hut opened and Colonel Dalstroi entered.

"I see you are the very image of the invincible Russian Imperial Mission warrior," he said in a tone that bordered on distaste.

"That is my hope, my Colonel." Aleksandr was surprised to see his commander. He had thought the good-byes and prayers they had shared after dinner had been his farewell.

"The transport was late tonight," the colonel said. "You must have been asleep when it came in."

"Trying to sleep," Aleksandr corrected. "At least it's rest of a sort to stretch out on a bed and stare at the ceiling while your mind races and your heart tries to jump out of your chest."

"That nervous, Aleksandr?"

"That nervous."

The colonel sighed. "I hate to add to your discomfort. But there was mail on the transport. Do you want your letters?"

He held out three packets, and Aleksandr with an effort managed not to even look at the handwriting.

"No, sir. I'll read them when I get back." There was a Mission superstition about reading letters from home just before departing for combat. The colonel would suppose that to be the reason for Aleksandr's refusal to take the letters, but really he wasn't superstitious. He simply had too many conflicting emotions and rapidly changing, contradictory thoughts already cluttering his head.

"Of course," the colonel said. "I'll put them in your duty file for when you return. But I hope you don't mind if I share some of the information in a letter I received, nothing personal, I assure you."

The Stavrogin pilot briskly entered the hut and snapped a surprised salute in the direction of the colonel. All the crew spoke German; their Russian was grating but understandable. "Pardon me for interrupting, Colonel," he said. The colonel nodded tolerantly. "But all is in readiness, Captain. We depart at your will."

"All cargo checked?" Aleksandr asked. He had personally reviewed the crates before loading, but still he wanted no mistake. Rifle ammunition of various calibers as well as two crates of shotgun shells was included, as were several crates of the old-fashioned Beefpac rations. Fortunately, the Indimex troops were as averse to food capsules as the nonconformist Chasers, so the more acceptable marching provisions were readily available.

"All checked, sir, and ready for further inspection if necessary."

"That won't be necessary. Get the guard troops on board and prepare to depart. I'll be along in a moment." He resisted the temptation to glance at his chronometer.

"I apologize for the interruption, my Colonel."

"No matter." He sank wearily onto a wooden chair. "Excuse me, but I'm not accustomed to keeping the hours of you young fellows."

"What was the letter you wished to speak of, Colonel?"

"A letter from a Mission friend at Moscow staff. Never mind just who. He was somewhat delicate and circumspect, but I thought you'd be interested. It appears that General Vinogradov had decided long before our last discussion that he would reluctantly approve your recommendation, based on his unfailing respect for the judgment of a line officer."

"You mean all that charade we went through with the general was unnecessary? He already had decided?"

"It appears so." The colonel took a letter from his breast pocket and began referring to it. "He had informed Command confidentially of our plans, and expressed his willingness to go along. But he informed them primarily because he wanted approval in advance for pacification raids at once should your attempt fail. He contacted Command direct because their 'orders' regarding Operation Grainrail are being executed with 'admirable skill and restraint'." The Colonel smiled rather wolfishly, "and, 'since Command gave those orders, Command alone should review them. If Captain Brukov's adventure'—prayers and suffering, that he should call it an "adventure"—'does not succeed in establishing successful liaison with the nonconformist Chasers in question, then the framework of the Operation Grainrail orders will be called into question.' If you fail, he proposes to mobilize his Indimex troops on a fleet of Stavrogins and start with these heathen fanatics you encountered."

"Start with the Jonnies?"

"Yes," Colonel Dalstroi said evenly, "and then work his way back along the path of our liaison efforts, land in force, and eliminate any show of opposition."

Aleksandr was silent for a moment. "In short, if there are no nonconformist Chasers alive, there can be no opposition to the progress of Operation Grainrail."

"I believe that is his reasoning. Something like that."

"And what did Command say?"

Colonel Dalstroi sighed. "You know Command. Nothing was said. They asked for further details about the Indimex training, the availability of operational Stavrogins, and so forth. The usual."

"But?"

"But our friend on the staff thinks that if you should fail, Command will cede to the general's wishes. There's too much riding on Operation Grainrail to take chances. The Council of Councils is monitoring closely, and already wants guaranteed projections for the first shipment."

"How can we guarantee any date when the first foot of Plastirail hasn't been put down east of the Co-op of Chicago?" Aleksandr fought to keep the exasperation and bitterness out of his voice.

"We can't, but the Elders want to know, nonetheless. The Operation Grainrail orders were approved by the Council, of course, but Command will change them fast enough if it seems likely that we'll encounter a series of delays."

"What fool could think that punitive expeditions could do anything other than ensure as much harassment of the rail-laying as humanly possible? Does he really think that a regiment of killers can wipe out the entire population between the Co-ops of Chicago and Boston? It would be a disaster."

"I agree, Aleksandr. But the general does not—if he's even considered the matter. He's simply spoiling for a fight. One where he can turn the Indimex troops loose with full battle license." The colonel paused. "It would be better, Aleksandr, if you didn't use the word 'fool' in a way that might mistakenly be considered as applying to a senior officer. Also, of course, 'killers' is not an appropriate way to refer to valuable Chaser troops."

"Of course, my Colonel." Now he couldn't help but glance at his chronometer. Already it was past the planned departure hour. "One other thing, my Colonel."

"Of course. Then you must be on your way."

"Have there been any signs of... changes... or anything at all noteworthy in the patterns of our intelligence work with the Chasers?" He couldn't think of any way of phrasing the question that didn't betray the sudden and profoundly inadmissible suspicion that had swept over him, the way the thought of an unmentionable sin will sometimes interrupt the most pious prayer.

"Changes in intelligence? You mean from the nonconformists?"

"Yes."

"None that I've noticed. Co-op command is in charge of intelligence in the sector, of course, but we see all its reports. Co-op intelligence staff has been fully cooperative. As you know, they have to be. The Operation Grainrail orders are quite specific. Just what is it you wish to know, Aleksandr?"

"I... I don't know, my Colonel. It's just a sudden feeling I had."

"We've heard nothing out of the ordinary. Don't worry so, Aleksandr." He smiled. "I'm sorry to have put this extra burden on you. I know you would have done your best under any circumstances. But now you must draw on the strength of your prayers and your Godmanhood even more, knowing how necessary it is for many Chaser lives as well as for our plans that you succeed."

"Naturally, my Colonel. I cannot tell you how grateful I am that you gave me this information. I will do my best for Holy Russia."

Aleksandr saluted and left the colonel staring after him as he dashed to the helicopter. The crew impatiently slammed the hatch behind him and the Stavrogin at once lurched into the sky.

Did the colonel guess what Aleksandr had thought? Did

unanswerable Satan put such ideas in his head? Aleksandr groaned beneath the sounds of the accelerating helicopter. He couldn't avoid the thought now that it had been introduced into his skull. The questions wouldn't go away. After all, General Vinogradov controlled local intelligence activities. And there could be little question that in one way or another he hoped the liaison efforts of Colonel Dalstroi's command would fail. How had it been that Aleksandr's first mission to the Jonnies had been so successfully ambushed? And why was the Chaser informer responsible for the ambush so promptly executed, before he could be questioned. Why did the general withhold his consent to Aleksandr's recommendations until the last minute, even though he had made his decision earlier? Was it to build his case for an eventual bloodbath? And, come to that, why had Colonel Dalstroi and Aleksandr met with the general alone? Would it not have been normal for senior officers of the general's staff to be present? Did General Vinogradov fear that his staff analyses might differ from his own? Or did he fear that his staff's attitude or something one of them might say could betray information that General Vinogradov wanted withheld?

Aleksandr shuddered with fear and revulsion and fell into chanting the Roll of Penance to himself. Such thoughts must not be allowed to twist his mind. He must keep knowledge and suspicion apart, or he would be paralyzed with uncertainty. What he now had to do was more important than ever.

‹ *Chapter Fifteen* ›

ALEKSANDR CONTROLLED HIS suspicions of treason. His was not a nature to dwell on dark imaginings or the most vile possibilities of human nature. So now he put his fears aside, not suppressing them—they would be handy for checking against such new facts as came along—but not letting them dominate his consciousness, either.

By the time the helicopter swirled down into the gray mist of predawn light and settled in the clearing near Coe that Aleksandr had selected from reconnaissance photographs, he was able to concentrate on the task at hand. The clearing was close to the camp, accessible though not on any pathway, and not likely to attract the attention of Jonnies who might be in the vicinity.

The crates were quickly unloaded into neat piles. The Indimex guards took their efficient posts as usual, but Aleksandr had explicitly ordered them, in the presence of the helicopter crew, to open fire only on his direct command. He had been alerted by a speculative corner of his mind that two Indimex soldiers with full clips in the Mayakovsky rifles could quickly tear apart any welcoming group from the Chaser camp, and that General Vinogradov could explain it all away as a regrettable mistake.

But now the crates were stacked, the guards back in the helicopter, and the helicopter back into the air before there had been a chance of any misunderstanding. In all fairness, the Indimex guards were, as always, entirely obedient as well as tirelessly efficient. If they were as good in combat as reputed— and a look at their stocky bodies and hard blank eyes made their reputation easy to believe—Aleksandr could appreciate the high regard in which they were held by General Vinogradov and other Russian Imperial Mission officers who had commanded them.

Abruptly the whirr of the Stavrogin departed from his ears even as its embodiment had departed, moments before, from his eyes. Aleksandr sat comfortably on one of the crates, relaxed but alert. His Mayakovsky was on automatic, and if Jonnies or other enemies should happen on him here, he was confident that he would have sufficient time to defend himself.

Soon enough, as the morning mist settled into the tall grass in the form of heavy dew and the sun began streaking into the air dazzle by dazzle, the Russian officer heard the call of a grouse, once, twice, three times, the third edging into an unmistakable human whistle. It was the same whistle Jason had used when first hunting with Aleksandr, and the Russian's heart leapt with delight.

"Made it back after all, eh?" a voice suddenly said from the edge of the woods, and Aleksandr saw Jason walking toward him. He stood up from the crate and would have rushed at Jason to embrace him except for the three other Chasers, none of them known to Aleksandr.

Jason saw the sudden wary look. "These ones just come to see. Whole bunch in camp waitin' to see."

"Well, here I am. It took a good deal longer to assemble the ammunition than I had foreseen. Bullets to fit your rifles are hard to come by."

"Told em you'd be back." His tone tried to express unshakable confidence, but the note of relief was clearly discernible. His Chaser companions affected an elaborate lack of interest.

"These supplies have to be guarded," Aleksandr said. "Will you three stay until we send relief?" The three exchanged noncommittal glances. They hadn't reckoned on their curiosity getting them trapped into work.

"I'll send some other men up in a bit," Jason said. "Everyone 'll want a look."

"Fine with me," one of the men said, and sat on a crate. The other two nodded.

"Good," Aleksandr said, military command in his voice. "Don't let anyone near the crates, and don't tamper with them yourselves. They are all rigged to explode if anyone tries to open them before I've defused them." The first Chaser guard promptly jumped off the crate he'd been reclining on as though he'd been burned. Aleksandr laughed. "You can sit on them, just don't try to open them." Nevertheless, by the time Jason and Aleksandr reached the woods and the Russian looked back, all three guards were still standing, and they seemed more alert for an attack by the crates than by a Jonnie patrol.

"Good thing we were still here," Jason said as they set their strides along the wooded path. "You mighta been sittin' on them crates when first snow come."

Aleksandr laughed. "All I had to do was put out a signal and a helicopter would have come for me."

"Got a new rifle, too."

"Yes." He hefted the Mayakovsky so Jason could get a better sideways look as they walked. "This one can do some tricks you haven't seen yet. The Jonnies haven't seen them yet either."

"Hope we get to fight them Jonnies."

"That's the whole point, Jason."

"You've got convincin' to do. Ain't as many men in camp as we saw in just one of them Jonnie patrols when we was comin' back from jail. And not all of em is willin' to fight the Jonnies."

"They will be willing after I talk to them."

"There's been plenty of talk already, that's a problem."

"A problem or 'the' problem?" Aleksandr asked with a laugh.

"Either one." Jason said with his customary gloom.

"Tell me all about it and I'll make it go away." But Aleksandr couldn't even joke Jason into further discussion just then, and he soon confined himself to describing the ammunition and food he had brought, and promising Jason quick access to the boxes of shotgun shells.

They soon came in sight of the cabin. "Not evicted yet, eh?" Aleksandr asked.

"The woman didn't want to come back with all these people camped here. Can't blame her. Some grumblin' about one woman in that whole cabin while plenty of men sleepin' on the ground, but Felicity says she'll shoot anyone who tries to take it. She ain't even got my rifle anymore, gave it away for the cabin. People here also reckoned they better see if you was comin' back before they mess with Felicity."

"I don't suppose any of them give a second thought to you, do they?" Aleksandr asked dryly.

"Some don't want to mess with me, either. I don't bother with the cabin. Sleep out with the camp men."

"I guess there is wisdom in that."

"Just didn't want to get used to a bed and then have you come back." He grinned enough to allow Aleksandr to see it was a joke—a matter the Russian sometimes had trouble determining where his Chaser friend was concerned.

"Uh, Jason... I don't know how to ask."

"Sue? Well, she ain't here. Guess she's in Hamp. Don't know for sure. Tried for three nights to get in Hamp to look around, but couldn't do it. Jonnies swarmin' like mayflies down there."

"Just a few more days, Jason. You'll be in Hamp and the

Jonnies won't. The cabin door opened before they reached it and Felicity rushed out and flung her slight frame into Aleksandr's embrace with such force he had to take a step back. He feared she would bruise herself against the clips of ammunition hanging down his chest.

"This time I knew you must come back," she said after kissing him fiercely. "There is not so much cruelty possible in the world that you could leave me with the thoughts you started and no one to say them to."

"I told you I'd be back," Aleksandr whispered, his voice suddenly unsteady. He was too much at the mercy of emotions he didn't understand, but which overwhelmed his senses nonetheless. And the feel of her strong slender form beneath his hands, the entirely natural and entirely feminine and entirely irresistible smell of her dark hair, reminded him of how long he had been without her or any woman, had been unable even to think of touching one of the Chaser women back at base.

"Well," Jason said with the uneasy embarrassment of the superfluous observer, "I'll go along. No use talkin' until after supper. Everyone'll be back in camp by then, or most will. I'll pass the word. Plenty of fellas be willin' to stand guard. I'll come by after supper." And he departed without having received much attention from either Felicity or Aleksandr.

"I heard the helicopter," Felicity said, leading him into the cabin and barring the door behind them. "I was still asleep, but I woke up when the sound came along down the valley, and I knew it was you. I stoked the stove and waited."

Clearly Felicity had planned that breakfast could wait, and indeed it seemed that each was incapable of satisfying the need to touch the other. To Aleksandr, old resolves seemed minor and unimportant, while new resolves were imminent, though unformed. His nostalgic, almost patriotic love for Lyalya was swept away, at least for the moment, by the consuming passion of Felicity, which he counted himself lucky to share. Even the Roll of Concupiscence seemed irrelevant, and certainly it did not spring to his lips as swiftly as the kisses of Felicity. The thoughts of home so powerfully stirred by Lyalya's letters seemed distant now. In truth, he had felt a stranger at base, but now a sense of completion washed over him, and he did indeed feel at home again—or not at home, but completed because half of his soul was restored again, the unknowable and frightening and magical half.

A CHILD CAME TO THE cabin door while they were having their eventual breakfast, and Aleksandr saw another following behind. Felicity went to the door and spoke softly to them.

"New admirers of yours?" he asked when she returned to table.

"I'm teaching them to read. In your honor, I've cancelled class until I notify them otherwise."

"Teaching? How very admirable, my dear, but surely your own training is somewhat incomplete."

"I can read easy sentences. I can even read an easy book. I'm just teaching them the alphabet so they can go on the way I did. I can teach that much." She was determined rather than defensive in tone.

"And what do you expect them to do with their new education? Jason and Hop and people like them are the backbone of the hilltown camps. They neither know how to read nor care to learn, I'm sure."

"That will have to change someday. The important thing is to know, and you can't know without reading. That's itched me all these years, always having these feelings about everything in the world and never knowing. Well, maybe I can start to find out now." Her soft voice had built in intensity until Aleksandr again felt the thrill of being within the orbit of her almost palpable will. An exquisite savage, he thought, and not for the first time.

And now she wanted to lose some of the savagery.

"Perhaps knowing, as you put it, will make you more boring, my dear. You'll become like a tiresome Russian schoolgirl, always reviewing her lessons and thinking she's sophisticated and bored."

Ignoring both his condescension and his intended humor, Felicity only said, "I don't know what I'll become, but whatever it is, I must become it."

They had finished breakfast, and Aleksandr rose and took Felicity in his arms. She put her head on his chest, not responding as he wished.

"Aleksandr," she said, "don't judge me from all your knowledge. Just help me gain some of my own."

"Haven't I already, my dear?"

"Yes, and I love you for it. I want to pass it to the children. It's the only way, you know, the only way we'll ever be able to hold our heads up, even to the Jonnies. Jason and Hop and the others may be the best we have now, but the best can be so much better."

"I'm sorry, my love, but I'm exhausted. I must have rest."

"Of course. I'll rest with you. I have so little time to hold you." Once he slept, though, she rose and cleaned the cabin, needing to expend energy and to occupy her hands. Then she practiced reading until Aleksandr awoke again.

"So tell me," he said, stretching luxuriously in bed and showing no signs of getting up, "how are things here? What sort of mood will people be in when I talk to them tonight?"

"Most people want to hear what you've got to say, I suppose. A lot of them think you might be crazy, but they're still mad at the Jonnies and it's getting harder to stay here in Coe. People have to decide what to do, where to go. They want to go back to the camps, but they're afraid of the Jonnies."

"Exactly the reason they should march with me."

"Some say if the Russ would go away, so would the trouble

with the Jonnies. They only raided us because we put you up, some say."

"What nonsense!" In fact, it was uncomfortably close to his own guess. "And the Russ certainly are not going away. We'll be here for a long time to come, and we're the best hope they have of protection from Jonnies and their like."

"You don't have to argue with me," Felicity said softly. "I'm just telling you what some people say."

"I know, I know. I'm sorry. What else?"

"Well, Billy and Astid are back."

"Really," Aleksandr said without interest. "He talked her into returning, eh? Poor fellow must have been miserable to find his place burned down." The Jonnies no doubt had taken the steel-keeper's rifles and whatever else of his stores appealed to them.

"She's the problem. Didn't like it over to Boston. She says real bad things about the Russ. She's telling the truth, too. It's what happened to me when I went to the Co-op."

"I fear some of our policies in the Co-ops need review." He managed to combine sympathy with complacency in his tone. "The percentage of malcontents shouldn't be so high."

"Nobody likes it," Felicity said bluntly. "Some stay because they're weak or lazy, but they all hate the Russ."

Aleksandr laughed. "Felicity, really! You shouldn't judge everything by your limited experience. Or Astid's experience. There are mistakes that need to be corrected. But the socio-economic byproducts of Shared Grace are necessary and valid."

"I don't know what you're talking about, but the Chasers in the Co-ops hate the Russ. That's all there is to it."

Aleksandr sobered a bit. Certainly conditions in the Co-op of Cleveland indicated a considerable unrest. He would have to discuss the situation with Colonel Dalstroi when he had the opportunity.

"But the men here," he said. "You think they are ready to be convinced to fight the Jonnies?"

"Perhaps. Jason and some of the others try to keep them interested. They don't know what to make of Jason these days, though."

"Because of his friendship with me?" That was something that Aleksandr had feared, infecting Jason with his friendship.

"Because of you some, and because he killed a farmer down to the Valley."

"What?" Aleksandr sat up in bed, shocked.

"That farmer down to Hamp." Felicity's voice was elaborately casual. "Jason couldn't find Sue and he couldn't get into Hamp. He figured the farmer was to blame somehow. So he went to the farm and killed him."

"Jobey," Aleksandr said, almost to himself.

"That was his name. Jobey."

"Sometimes you wouldn't think Jason ever got mad," Aleksandr said.

"I know better than that. So do you." Her voice was flat.

"Now I know for sure."

"Some of the people are worried that'll just set off the Jonnies again," Felicity said. "They haven't yet come up this far again, though."

"Well, it's a rough justice, and I wouldn't have done it. But Jason had his reasons. Poor Jobey. There's no doubt he did betray us, but he probably thought he had no choice. The man had a family, too."

"Jason's got a family, too, and the Jonnies don't seem to worry about them. That's what Jason said."

"Well, he's right, of course. But still."

"Anyway," Felicity said, "some people are a little edgy. Some thought you weren't coming back. Some drifted off, some to Boston, some to find a new place. God knows there's plenty of forest. Most want to hear what you got to say, though. Then they'll decide."

"And what do you think, Felicity?" he asked softly.

"Well." She took a deep breath that sounded like a sigh in reverse. "I think we've got to stop the Jonnies so we can get on with living and thinking about other things. I think we ought to let you show the way, because you know things, you know how to do it. And then we ought to get to learning things ourselves, so we know how to do things too. No two people around here think the same way about anything, and no one man can get another to do something he doesn't want to do, but sometimes people have to get together and have one man make the decisions.

"Leadership," Aleksandr said.

"Leadership." Felicity pronounced the word firmly.

"You know, my love, your people had all that once. It's gone."

"It's gone if we ever had it, but it can come back."

"That's not the view of Men of History."

"Well, you can take your Men of History," she flared up. "Something that exists doesn't just disappear. We had it once, you say so yourself, and we can learn it again."

Aleksandr wisely didn't contradict her, no matter how obviously, and how hopelessly, she was wrong. But he understood from her manner that she had reached new decisions about her own people. No longer did she discuss them with contempt. She hadn't mentioned returning to Russia with Aleksandr. Now she was trying to teach hilltown children how to read.

IT WAS STILL LIGHT WHEN Jason came to pick him up, but the evening breeze was cool and already Aleksandr could see a tall column of smoke bending to the wind's will above the place where the meeting was to be held.

Aleksandr looked forward to the challenge of addressing the

prospective warriors. He felt cramped after a long day spent inside, though certainly he had enjoyed Felicity's company. He had even gone over her reading and it was true that she was becoming adept at the basics. The food had been good, and of course it had been marvelous to have her to himself for a whole day, even though he spent a good part of it sleeping. But he easily put those pleasures from his mind now. He was a trained and eager officer of the Russian Imperial Mission, and he had long dreamed of having an opportunity such as the one that now presented itself.

The campfire was flaming brilliantly by the time they arrived, and the men were sitting comfortably around it on stumps and logs, enjoying the end of a day that for most of them had been filled with hard work. And now they were to be rewarded with a special entertainment, something they all eagerly anticipated. There were about a hundred men, Aleksandr estimated, and they all seemed to be cut out of the same hardy cloth as the hilltowners he already knew. There were some women present, though many apparently had chosen not to attend, or had been convinced to stay away for one reason or another. After all, it was a council of war. Many of the men were smoking pipes. There were many crocks and jars being passed around and it would have been foolish indeed to guess that they contained anything other than potato lightning.

All eyes were on Aleksandr, though in the undemanding way of the hilltowners. Probably he could decide to sit and share their drink, and no one would even mention the idea of marching on the Jonnies. Aleksandr picked out some of the faces that he already knew as a way of building his confidence before he spoke. As he stood there, the Mayakovsky over his shoulder, the men gradually stopped all their discussions, and he had their silent attention before he said one word.

"Good evening," he began, not loudly, but with a resonance

that carried. "Some of you have already met me. The rest of you know who I am and why I'm here. But I'll start from the beginning so that everything is clear.

"I am Captain Aleksandr Iosifovich Brukov of the Russian Imperial Mission. I first came among you after the Jonnies attempted to kill me. I escaped from them with the aid of one of your people—Jason here. My aim at that time was to talk to the Jonnies, to try to reach an understanding with them, so that the Russian Imperial Mission and the people of this region could live in peace. It took me some time to discover what you all have known from birth—it is impossible to live at peace with the Jonnies. But I can go away tomorrow and never worry about the Jonnies again. For those of you who live here, however, the Jonnies are a cloud over your heads that never goes away, a threat to your homes and your families and your very lives. They can attack at any time. Because of the Jonnies, most of you here tonight are without homes, and many have lost wives and children. You know all that, of course. But I want you to realize that I know it too, and to realize that the Russian Imperial Mission sincerely wishes that you may live without the threat of the Jonnies and with assurance that the future will be better.

"I know that attempts to stop the Jonnies in the past have failed. There were two reasons for failure. One was the lack of reliable ammunition. I have brought with me large supplies of such ammunition, and of calibers that will fit most or perhaps even all of your rifles. The ammunition is valuable and difficult to find but the Russian Imperial Mission gladly gives it to you for the purpose of establishing peace in this area. Once that peace is established, the Russians will continue to supply you with ammunition for hunting and self-protection. In the camp where I stayed, I had the opportunity to see ammunition being manufactured, and I see that Sam the bullet-maker is here tonight." He nodded toward the dumpy figure, who seemed apprehensive. "He did a wonderful job with the materials he had available, but the proper materials weren't available in sufficient quantities, so even as fine a craftsman as Sam couldn't work miracles." Aleksandr knew he had to be careful not to slight the hilltowners as backward ignoramuses, or he would lose the audience entirely. He knew that Sam and his friends now would be glowing with the praise. The next subject must be approached even more delicately, Aleksandr reminded himself.

"The other problem with your past attempts to fight the Jonnies," he continued, "has been your lack of experience in large-scale military operations. After all, none of you are soldiers, you are people who go your own way and are proud of it. I have seen for myself how difficult it is to change a hilltowner's mind once he has it decided."

The men around the fire smiled and made brief comments to one another. They all cultivated a stubborn independence, and Aleksandr knew he had to play to that pride.

"I couldn't do anything about the way you are, even if I wanted to, and I don't." It was the kind of statement that he had heard in the hilltown camps, and he decided he'd gone far enough in that direction; they'd soon enough detect any false note if he tried to pretend to be one of them.

"But I am a soldier, and I've been trained to win battles against other soldiers. There are more of the Jonnies than there are of us. We all know that. And good ammunition won't make up the difference. They have good ammunition too. We need a plan of operation, and I have one. The plan means getting together in several groups, and it means that everyone in those groups has to agree to take orders, both from the group leader and from me. But that doesn't have to be as bad as it sounds. I'll explain what my plans are before you have to carry them out, and taking orders just means that all of us will be working together."

Aleksandr looked at the men sitting in various attitudes around the roaring fire. It was full night now, but the fire provided plenty of light, and Aleksandr could see that he had the complete attention of the men. As was their custom, they were slowly thinking through the ideas he had presented. He had to be careful not to say so much that they would decide the scheme was too complex to be grasped, and therefore worthless to them.

"I think everything I've said is plain enough. I'll go over my battle plans tomorrow morning with those of you who decide to join me. At first light we'll meet to distribute ammunition, organize into groups, and discuss plans. We won't actually leave here for another three days. We need the extra time to get ready. But bring your rifles to the ammunition storage area tomorrow morning.

"Are there any questions?"

Scarcely had the words left his lips before a short dark woman was on her feet, her very posture shouting of anger.

"I have a question," she said with loud belligerence. "My question is: Why should we have anythin' at all to do with the Russ? At least the Jonnies are people from around here, and we can keep away from em if we try hard enough."

There was a stir among the crowd, and Aleksandr could tell she had struck a responsive chord of some kind. He saw Billy the steel-keeper sitting near her feet, and he guessed she was the Astid who Billy had chased to the Co-op of Boston.

"The reason why you should have anything to do with the Russ," Aleksandr said calmly, "is that we can and will help you get rid of the Jonnies so you don't have to worry about them any more. And then we'll leave you alone to lead your own lives."

"Like you do in Boston?" the woman shouted. "I just got back from there, Russ, and all we are in Boston is dirty Chasers and what we do is what we're told, and no talkin' back, either.

We're just dirt to you."

There definitely was a feeling in the crowd now that Aleksandr didn't like; even the most isolated hilltowner Chaser had heard horror stories about the Co-op of Boston.

"I believe you're right," Aleksandr said. "I perhaps wouldn't have believed you before I lived among you, but I believe you now." He could see people exchanging glances and whispers; he could only hope that he had taken the right approach and was inspiring an army, not a lynch mob. But he thought the hilltown Chasers responded well to truth, and would have shut him off cold if he began to spout the same cliches about Shared Grace mouthed by Russian Imperial Mission officers in the Co-ops. Aleksandr's brother officers believed those words and so had he, but he had come to realize that those words had far different meanings for the Chasers who had to live by them.

"I can assure you we mean well, no matter what you think," he went on loyally, appeasing his Mission conscience before deviating again. "But I understand how difficult it would be for you to accept the standards of a Co-op. I think that is all the more reason for you to band together now to rid yourselves of the Jonnies. Without them oppressing you, there would be less reason than ever for you even to consider going to a Co-op. You'll have peace, be able to trade freely, grow crops where you wish and pasture animals without fear that a Jonnie patrol will take them away as soon as they are full grown."

He paused to let the words sink in. Perhaps he wouldn't convince Astid or anyone else who had direct experience of the Russian Imperial Mission but Aleksandr was the only contact with Holy Russia most of these people had ever had. His heart jumped as a shimmer of light showed him Felicity's face behind the circle of men around the fire. She had come to listen to him!

"Hum." A man near the fire was clearing his throat. Aleksandr recognized Moe, the man whose dog, Smoke, had helped him and Jason in hunting for birds. "Hum," he said again. Everyone waited for him to speak, as they knew he would. "Well, Cap'n," he said at last, "now you mention it, why is it you want to help us get rid of the Jonnies? It's our worry, not yours."

None of your affair, either, Aleksandr knew Moe meant. These Hilltown Chasers were reluctant to share or even admit their problems. Aleksandr paused as though thinking over an answer. He didn't want to seem to have his words down too pat. "It's in our self-interest as well as yours," he finally said. He had already decided to leave mention of Operation Grainrail until after the rout of the Jonnies had been accomplished; no use giving these people too much to think about at once. "We want the countryside at peace. I don't want to get shot down again." There were appreciative chuckles around the campfire. "We want everyone to be free to come and go as they will, to trade and to prosper. That will benefit us as well as you."

"Uh, Cap'n," said a man across the way, someone Aleksandr didn't recognize. "You say we ain't as many as them, and we all know that's true. Say we fight, even say we win. How many of us 'll get killed?"

"No commander has ever gone into battle knowing the answer to that question," Aleksandr said. "I have a pretty good idea, however, based on what I've seen of the Jonnies. They're not used to organized resistance. Hilltown men who do what they're told when they're told to do it will stand an excellent chance of surviving unharmed." In fact, Aleksandr knew, at the first appearance of mounting casualties, his army would melt away, so his prediction had to be correct. Or else he'd be left in the middle of a road facing a couple hundred angry Jonnies by himself.

"Somethin' else, Cap'n," another voice spoke up. It was Hammon, the camp guard, apparently recovered from his wounds. It seemed that those who previously had met the Russian were most willing to question him. The others were still too shy or wary.

"Yes, Hammon?"

"What I wonder, Cap'n, is this. Suppose all you say is true, and I ain't sayin' it ain't, but then there's this. You Russ got plenty of soldiers. You got sprayguns and them flyin' thin's and everythin'. You could use them flyin thin's and sprayguns and between dawn and the first cockcrow there wouldn't be no Jonnies left, just like that."

Aleksandr smiled. "It might not be as fast as all that, Hammon, but it's true we could do it." He paused, gathering his words. "We decided against sending in our own troops. The reason is very simple. We could kill a lot of Jonnies and run the rest out of Hamp, but as soon as we got back in the helicopters and flew away, Jonnies or someone like them could come right back and cause just as much trouble as before. Your life wouldn't be any easier and neither would ours. But if you do the job yourself, nobody between here and the Valley will have any doubt that the Jonnies are gone and that you are determined to keep it that way. That's why we don't want to do it ourselves."

It was the same argument he had repeated many times at base in more sophisticated language, but he had come to doubt it a little himself. Was the real reason, perhaps, that Captain Aleksandr Iosifovich Brukov of the Russian Imperial Mission wanted to make a name for himself, wanted to establish himself as an expert on the inhabitants of Chaser Two and guerrilla tactics there, wanted to ensure a promotion and a good posting at the Academy or on staff back in Moscow? Aleksandr reminded himself to recite the Roll of Humility. One couldn't be too careful, especially about one's own soul.

‹ *Chapter Sixteen* ›

THERE WERE NO MORE questions, and Aleksandr knew better than to linger while the Chasers talked it over. Jason, Hop and some of the others who already were convinced of the need to drive away the Jonnies would be far more effective arguing for war than Aleksandr could hope to be. Felicity and he drifted together, almost as if by chance, for the walk back to her cabin.

"At least we have the three more days together, Aleksandr." She was holding onto his arm as they walked, and she wanted to touch him every moment she could. "I have so much to tell you, so much to ask you about."

"My apologies, my love, but it may be tonight only. I hope we can march tomorrow." He spoke softly, glancing swiftly around to make sure no one besides Felicity could hear him.

"What?" She stopped abruptly, jerking him to a halt.

"Quiet, please. The fact is, I fear the Jonnies might have a spy in camp, and it would be disastrous for us if our plans got back to the Reverend. If there is a spy here, he'll slip away tonight with word that we leave in three days—just what I want." Aleksandr doubted that the Jonnies bothered to spy on the hilltown Chasers. After all, he was never tracked down while living peacefully with Felicity. Jobey had said, on the other hand, that the Jonnies thought that a patrol helicopter had rescued him.

There was the chance, spy or no spy, that the Reverend knew that Aleksandr would finally turn up in Hamp, Aleksandr admitted to himself. There was even the chance that the Reverend and General Vinogradov exchanged information. And that was an even more compelling reason to march at once rather than wait three days.

The further fact was, as Aleksandr knew all too uncomfortably well, he was again indulging that character flaw that had plagued him at the Academy and had since exasperated his immediate superiors: He was changing plans on his own initiative. It had been agreed at base that the Chaser troops would require three days of training. Senior officers often praised his spunk, just as Vinogradov had done, pretending, at least, to admire the spark that made him difficult to tame. But Aleksandr was perfectly sure—had been told by senior officers, in fact—that he had better not ever cause a major bungle through his improvisations. His career could be irreparably harmed. So far he had succeeded in going his own way. After all, the Russian Imperial Mission would be the ultimate beneficiary of his insubordinate conniving to avoid earlier rescue flights and stay among the Chasers, just as it surely stood to benefit by his outsmarting any possible treachery. On his flight to Coe bearing the ammunition, he had decided that it was impossible, unthinkable that General Vinogradov could betray the integrity of the Mission to his own ends and ambitions but he had also decided to act prudently. He could wall off his private suspicion, but still bear its warning in mind.

Felicity had been as intently inward as Aleksandr during the rest of their walk to the cabin, but once they closed the door behind them she spoke as though determined to compress three days into the one night that remained.

"Listen, Aleksandr, my love and my teacher," she said, wrapping her strong thin arms around his waist and pressing her head against his chest.

"I always listen to you, my sweet."

"I don't know if we have but one more night together or many..."

"Many, my love. We'll find a way."

"But whatever it is, you're always going to be part of me, Aleksandr, you have been the light that brought me to life.

"Oh, Felicity, my dear, God did that."

"Then you're are my god, though I know you are not God. But you opened the door to knowledge for me. Until then, I didn't even know what it was that I wanted, only that I was empty and that the emptiness made me angry. Now I am full, in more ways than one." She hugged him again and he laughed affectionately.

"That simply means you are a good and eager student, Felicity, not that I am any kind of god at all. You know how blasphemy upsets a Russian, though bless me quickly, you've more or less accustomed me to it."

"Well, we have so little time now, Aleksandr, I suppose it is best to talk about that. I've got to get it straight in my mind. Your 'Godmanhood' talk, I mean. I don't think the Godmanhood idea can be right."

"My sweet, you should learn simple piety before testing the subtleties of theology." He tried hugging her tighter, but she broke away and sat at the table, signifying that she would not be content with condescension and placating terms of endearment. Aleksandr sighed. Felicity waited in silence. Aleksandr sighed again, this time with defeat. "Felicity, my dear, even Solovyov was wrong about Godmanhood, and he first stated the concept. His mistake was that he looked toward the West to try to find some kind of synthesis... a blending together. We know now that instead he should have looked deeper into the Russian soul. But he lived at the time of the First Enslavement; what is natural to

Russians now may have been impossible for him. At any rate, we have long since discovered that Godmanhood is a gift of the Russian soul. Probably no Chaser, probably not even you, dear Felicity, can ever really understand Godmanhood, because you cannot absorb it into your being. That is why our Elders developed the Doctrine of Shared Grace. It was either that or consign all non-Russians to the darkness, and we prefer to believe that is not necessary."

"Of course not," Felicity said, seeming sure of herself on this one point. "God is God, one for everyone. If God is to be God, He could not just single out the Russians. If He did, He would be a Russian God, but not God."

"You repeat the arguments worked out by our Elders long ago, and after much haggling, I assure you."

Aleksandr sat opposite her at the table, marveling again at Felicity's untutored ability to grasp abstract concepts. He would have preferred by far either holding Felicity in his arms or thinking about how he would proceed tomorrow, but Felicity determined was Felicity irresistible, he had learned. It was less painful to give in sooner rather than later. It saved time. "Do you mind pouring me a small drink of samogon, my love?"

She glared at him as she fetched the cup. The glare meant that he would not be allowed to change the subject.

"Well," he resumed after a sip of the harsh liquid, a taste that was something of a jolt after the Russian vodka he had been drinking back at base, "What you say is true. It's agreed. As you say, God is God. But our race has been blessed with special understanding. It was only after enduring the centuries of the Two Enslavements that we earned a special understanding from God. It is that which we have uniquely."

"A special understanding," Felicity repeated. "You have a special understanding with God. But I feel something else, something that talking with you and listening to all you say about life outside of our camps and Co-ops made me feel. Not something new, really something that was there and that I have become more aware of, something that bothers me. It started by talking to you and beginning to read and suddenly everything started to seem... so much larger. Infinite, that's your word. That feeling made me worship you as a god." She laughed. "I still do. At least I can touch you. But I begin to feel something else, too," she added unhappily.

"Perhaps it is the beginning of Shared Grace," Aleksandr suggested.

Felicity smiled. "Not if you continue to talk of Godmanhood and God being just over the horizon. None of that feeling seems right to me. You Russ and your horizon! I don't think of God when I look at the horizon, I think how easy it would be to walk there."

"And if you got there, still the horizon would be distant. That is the point with God and Godmanhood. It's not really a straight flat path to the horizon, but subtle progress hard for a weary man to discern."

But Felicity plainly wasn't listening to him. She had other things on her mind. "I always had a feeling that frightened me, that I didn't understand, but I think I'm beginning to understand," she said. "Ever since I was a little girl, whenever I would be by myself for a long while and set to thinking, however I started out I would get tighter and tighter in thinking, and everything would come together, everybody and everything, and I'd begin to think I just couldn't go any longer, because if I did... well, I just couldn't. It was as if I'd come to the edge of absolutely nothing, a huge black hole, the edge of a huge black hole. It frightened me, I couldn't stand it; I'd pull back and try to break the spell. But everything there was vivid and exaggerated—exact and not wasteful, too true to be able to bear. I couldn't stand it. If I looked down, I'd just disappear forever. Everything would disappear, fall apart into something else."

"That's perfectly plausible," Aleksandr said. "That's what Russian children in school are taught is the Abyss of Ignorance. It is what man without God is condemned to face, always."

"No," Felicity said firmly, though she had never before heard of the Abyss of Ignorance. "It's not ignorance, more like its opposite. It's only because of my own ignorance and weakness that I can't understand, and because of my own cowardice that I can't bear to face it."

"You're anything but a coward." He reached across the table for her hand, but she withdrew it.

"No, I am when it comes to that. I realize now why I was so bitter but having met you and sensed what I found in you, I think I may be learning to face whatever abyss it is, if not of ignorance. It takes practice. It's a habit, overcoming fear. Looking down."

Aleksandr lighted his pipe. "My poor darling. You will appear very strange always looking down. Look straight at the horizon, that's the proper human way."

His attempt at levity didn't make her smile, but it did prompt her to leap up from the stool and grab the surprised Aleksandr's hand. "Come. Come with me," she said.

She led him through the cabin door and into the night air. The moon was a sliver, barely larger than a nail paring, and the stars competed fiercely for primacy in the inky sky. The campfire was some distance away, so it did not dim the view. The stars were spread out above them in immutable patterns. In a sweep of his eyes Aleksandr took in sprawling Ursa Major and its companion, Ursa Minor, stretching its neck out to Polaris at its extremity. Cepheus was close, hovering near Cassiopeia at the horizon. Vega and Hercules trailed to another of the brightest stars, Arcturus, at the end of Boötes.

"I want you to look up, too," Felicity said. "You call us Star-

Chasers. I can believe we went there."

Aleksandr puffed at his pipe and decided to reply seriously.

"Whole cults of Chasers in Old Europe believe that, it's the one remaining belief that excites them, in fact."

"But you don't believe it?" Felicity trembled with the excitement of what he said, with the possibility that the first sweet flowers, so newly bloomed from her old bitter dreams, were not just hope and imagination but had a past and a future; were shared.

Aleksandr only shrugged. "It's so unimportant. They're certainly clever with tools, the Old Europeans. We couldn't do without them. But they have no sense of organization without Russian guidance. Perhaps in the old days." Again he shrugged. "They have books to prove everything they claim, but many are obviously fiction and the rest are mostly theory. Of course, many entire libraries have been destroyed. But still. The imagination of those Chasers is simply unreliable. They even say Russians went to the stars in the days of the Second Enslavement." He laughed, a short bark that ended abruptly when he realized that Felicity couldn't possibly appreciate the absurd humor of the concept.

"But you don't believe?"

"As I said, it's unimportant. We assume it never happened. It is so fanciful."

"It's the most important thing of all," Felicity said quietly. "It's what the feelings in us are that make us confused and angry, that make all these men dull and incurious. It's because they lost that."

Aleksandr raised an eyebrow speculatively as he cocked his head to one side. "It's true that your civilization is dead, Felicity. There's nothing that either you or I can do about that, it's historically certain."

"But we can do something, or at least we must try. We're going to learn to understand, and by 'we' I mean Chasers. That's what is wrong with your Godmanhood."

Aleksandr felt a chill at the certainty of her tone as she fervently dismissed that which was unquestionably true.

"Man is not some kind of bridge between nature and God. We are neither bridges nor slaves. We are dominant! The only way to live up to God is to struggle against Him. You can only know anything about Him by fighting Him, otherwise He has no reason to appear. There is the abyss below, as you call it, and the stars above, and both are part of the whole, both must be faced and looked at and conquered, God must be challenged and must reveal Himself. If we are destroyed in the process it's worth it, it's the only way we can live without fear and cowardice and ignorance and never knowing anything. We must know everything!"

"I... Felicity." This woman he loved sounded like the Very Satan, and he didn't even know how much of the poison that infected her had been injected into her bloodstream by his own words and ideas. A deep weariness swept over him as he watched her still staring up at the stars, hardly mindful of him as she considered again her heady challenge of God. Aleksandr felt discouraged, and chilled by a certain fear of Felicity, because her passions ran so deep and in such unholy and contrary directions. He thought, and not for the first time, that perhaps there was much about Chasers, even those in Old Europe with their apparent easy subservience and acceptance of orders, that Russians didn't understand and never would.

"Let's go back in, Felicity," he said at last. "It's getting quite cold out here."

‹ *Chapter Seventeen* ›

"QUIET." ALEKSANDR'S FIRM, controlled command had its effect and the clumps of men grouped around the supply crates fell silent in the pleasant coolness of dawn. The Russian had been shaken by his conversation with Felicity, offended by her heresies, which he had somehow nurtured. But he was a trained, experienced, and enthusiastic troop commander, and he now turned with relish to the task of organizing Chaser rabble into a fighting unit. It was the work of a sculptor, shaping that formless mass of able but aimless men into a military organism that would act with one will—Aleksandr's will.

"All right." His voice was clear and resonant, but not loud. It didn't have to be. "I'm not going to ask you to do anything you can't do; and the only thing I'm going to ask you to do that you're not used to doing is to work together." There was a little light laughter. Good, Aleksandr thought, they're willing but a bit nervous; that's the way it should be.

"First thing is, we're going to organize. Nobody's going to have to do a job he's not fit for. If you don't like the group I put you in, say so and we'll find another group. If nothing suits you, stay here. We'll have to manage without you. Understood?" He looked out across the ragged collection of nonconformist Chasers, about seventy-five men. There was no muttering. They just wanted to hear what he had to say next. Aleksandr saw Felicity and two other young women standing behind the men, near a tree. Felicity had forcefully insisted, with the earnest assent of the other two, that all three must come with the men as nurses. Aleksandr reluctantly agreed with her logic, but ordered that they would billet apart from the men and would be stationed well away from any battle. Felicity readily accepted the conditions. Now, he deliberately ignored her. She already was organized.

"Here is how I have planned it." He paused to ensure their complete attention.

"Hop, you pick three men besides yourself. The four of you will be advance scouts." The stocky hunter was surprised for a moment, but then nodded in agreement. He pointed to three men, each of whom had been standing near him, and spoke their names. They all ambled closer.

"That's right," Aleksandr said. "Gather around him so we can all see how we split up. Now you, Mack." Aleksandr pointed to a wispy young man, the last sort to catch the eye of a military recruiter. "You pick three scouts. You'll protect our rear." There was no reluctance in the three men nodded to by Mack. Despite his appearance, he was one of the most respected hunters in the hilltown camps, and noted as a man not to cross. He was reputed to be as skillful with a knife as with a gun. Aleksandr had barely met him, but Jason had strongly recommended him for the job at their predawn breakfast.

"Now, Jason, pick the men you want for a strike force." Jason moved rapidly through the men, making his choices. "You men stand over there," Aleksandr pointed. The three newly formed units now were standing somewhat proudly in their separate groups, and Aleksandr noted with satisfaction that the remaining fifty or sixty men were standing roughly in the three groups that he and Jason had envisioned.

"The rest of you are the main battle-line force. You must act together but there will be times when separate functions will be necessary, and for that reason you need to operate under three separate commands." Alexandr stressed the point for that reason, and also to make sure that all the prominent camps had a place in the leadership.

"The three leaders I want are Fallon, Smit and Dad. Stand by the one you want to serve with, and if there are any objections, let me hear them now." There were no objections, of course, as all three men were respected leaders in their different ways. And very little movement was necessary for the groups to coalesce. Men had been standing near the people they wanted to fight beside.

"I'll explain our plans to all of you, but these three men are the ones I'll be talking to the most. When we have to take up positions, you'll be grouped by unit. And if fifteen or twenty men are needed to do something, I'll just ask Fallon or Smit or Dad, and he and his men will get the job done. All clear?" He paused aggressively, obviously willing to answer questions but also obviously not in the mood to waste time with any foolishness. He could see the newly designated commanders already assuming the postures and paternal airs of leaders. Fallon was a quiet man, thin and dark, but was known for his intelligence and fairness. In his own camp, he was often called "the judge," and he did indeed settle disputes. Those who didn't accept the verdict had to argue it with him, and few relished the prospect. Smit, on the other hand, was a huge blond, and what in repose seemed to be fat proved in action to be well-coordinated and powerful muscle. He was blustery and well liked, though probably too fond of potato lightning. Both Fallon's and Smit's camps had escaped the worst of the wrath of the Jonnies' recent attacks, but they had no illusions about their safety. They knew they had to fight.

Dad, however, was from the largest camp in Coe, and was known for the pacifism of his views. His people lived in Coe to be away from strife, and the other Chasers vaguely thought that Dad's group practiced some old form of religion. Aleksandr had feared they would shun any military service, but it turned out that the latest Jonnie attacks finally had convinced Dad and his people that action was necessary. What they heard from the refugees sickened them, and what they had learned of the religion practiced by the Jonnies only hardened their resolve. At the core of Dad's unit were his five strapping sons, all of prime fighting age, and Aleksandr didn't doubt they'd acquit themselves well. Dad probably was the oldest of the men who would be marching, but like every one of the hilltown Chasers, he was strong, able to hike all day without tiring, and a dead shot with a gun.

"Now," Aleksandr said, smiling for the first time, "believe it or not, we're organized." The men responded with good humor. "Next we have to get our supplies straightened out. That means ammunition, food and medical supplies. I also brought a few rifles if they're needed." He waved over to the women. "Marth, Jen, Felicity. You come over here too."

He looked briefly at the crates. "The ammunition crates are rigged and I'll have to free them," he said. "Then Sam and I will pass out the ammunition. Each man will get a hundred-bullet bandolier, and I think I can fit all your rifles. If not, Billy will issue you a new one. Each bandolier has slots for three food tins, and you can stuff two more in your pockets. Five each will have to do, so don't waste them. Marth and Jen will pass out the food after you get your ammunition. Felicity, you check the medical supplies and figure how to split them up with Marth and Jen."

Aleksandr had a couple of men separate the crates and he then knelt to defuse them. It was a simple matter, involving only the removal of a wire that would elude a quick inspection, but the bomb in each of the crates could blow the contents, and any people nearby, to bits. Aleksandr was careful to be brisk in his movements and show no concern in front of the men.

"All right," he said when the last wire had been pulled, "line up in your groups and we'll get you equipped.

Sam, whose own bullets were so dreadfully unreliable, was gripped by a kind of awe as he pulled out the hundred-cartridge bandoliers and dispensed them, one to a man. Brukov kept up a casual chatter with both Sam and the men, and he made a point of mentioning to Sam that the ammunition distributorship in Hamp and the hilltowns naturally would be his for the asking when they defeated the Jonnies. Some form of barter or payment could be worked out, Aleksandr told the suddenly fascinated fellow, so that the Russians could keep up a regular supply of reliable cartridges for the hilltown men. The men already had exclaimed over the clean brass-and-lead perfection of the new cartridges, and Sam knew that never again would they willingly settle for his make-dos. He didn't commit himself, but he was thinking.

Billy the steel-keeper, who had impressed a suddenly meek Astid that morning by telling her that he was marching to Hamp whether she waited for him or not, was only a few meters away, inspecting the new collection of rifles, and he took a sharp interest in what he overheard. Aleksandr had intended him to, of course. He had selected the old but serviceable firearms because he knew that they were familiar to the nonconformist Chasers. He could have included clips, but the hilltowners were used to single-shot efficiency. Besides, he had been well drilled by Colonel Obolov before being posted to Chaser Two. Give them as few armaments as possible, train them in their use as little as possible. Aleksandr thought a single-shot capability was sufficient; after all, that was all the Jonnies had.

But the rifles held a powerful attraction for Billy, as Aleksandr had guessed, and so did the idea of holding a Russian franchise, though Billy wouldn't have known the word.

"You should consider that too, Billy," Aleksandr said rather carelessly. "That might solve some of Astid's worries. You could have the advantages of living in a more settled place than a camp, do a good trade in rifles, and not have to put up with the restrictions of a Co-op."

"Well, I'll talk to her," was all Billy said, but Aleksandr knew that for one of the hilltowners those words were a large concession.

"The fact is," Aleksandr said, knowing that other of the men were listening and soon would discuss the matter, "we're going to need people to settle in Hamp and help run things there once the Jonnies are gone. It won't just be a matter of Sam's bullets and Billy's rifles. The farmers are sure to want supplies from the Co-ops, too. A lot of business will get done." He let the subject end there, and he stood aside while the Chasers all got their gear. Aleksandr suppressed a smile at the painfully obvious chain of reasoning being begun by those who had heard his words. Probably none of them had thought forward to the consequences of their war against the Jonnies. They simply supposed that if they won, life would go on as before, but with less worry. The Russian Imperial Mission knew better.

Felicity approached him now, shy before his authority. "There seem to be plenty of bandages, Aleksandr. I don't know what some of the things are."

"I'll show you soon. I ordered only the most basic supplies, and they ought to be sufficient for minor wounds. We don't have surgeons available for anything worse, anyway. I'll supervise you when the time comes. If I'm still there," he added with a wintry smile. It was the old dogged mournfulness of the Russian soul that made him say it, that and the desire to see Felicity's reaction.

"Oh, Aleksandr, don't say such a thing." She glanced around to make sure no one else was paying attention to them, though of course everyone wanted to hear everything Aleksandr had to say just now.

"Just a soldier's joke, Felicity." He was immediately sorry that he had yielded to the temptation.

"You are a soldier," she said with admiration. "I listened to you. I was very proud of you."

"Of course I'm a soldier." He wished to change the mood; he was beginning to feel like a small boy being praised by his mother. "Divide the medical supplies with Marth and Jen. We haven't much time." He turned away, not rudely but with the decisiveness of a busy officer. He loved her, and he alternately wished to be with her forever and never to see her again. The unknown is so much more difficult to cope with than the known, and Felicity was deeply unknown to him, never more so than when they were most intimate. Yet she excited and thrilled him as no woman ever had. He began to recognize that he was growing weary of the contradiction, the tension; it could dominate him, and he mustn't allow that.

He barely heard her say, "Yes Aleksandr," as she walked away. Already he was concentrating on what needed to be done, and done quickly.

"All right, listen!" He jumped up on one of the now-empty crates. Silence fell at once. "As soon as you have your ammunition and your rations, go on back to camp and have your midday meal—and say good-bye to anyone you're leaving behind. We're marching after you eat."

He felt the exhilaration of an illusionist producing an object from thin air. The men were incredulous. He held up a hand. "I know I said it would be three days. But in fact there's no need to delay, is there? If any of you can think of a reason, speak up." There was no challenge.

But suddenly Fallon, conscious of his new leadership duties, spoke up. "Why did you say three days, then?" It was as much as he was liable to say for the day.

"As a precaution," Aleksandr said with some satisfaction. He had been fed the line as if Fallon had been rehearsed for a Moscow stage. "It is possible—not likely, perhaps, but possible—that the Jonnies have a spy or two among us." Again there was an outburst of muttering that Aleksandr quickly silenced by raising his hand.

"Probably some men left camp right after the meeting last night?" Aleksandr made the statement into a question.

"Sure," Hop promptly said. "But lots of us talked about skippin' war and goin' huntin'. Nothin' wrong with doin' what you think right."

"Nothing at all," Aleksandr agreed. "But what if one of those men didn't go hunting but headed back to Hamp to report to the Jonnies? He'd get there by tonight, and I don't think the Jonnies would want to wait for us to come down there. They know where we are, and they'd think they could take us by surprise—just like they've done before." He paused to let them talk it over briefly.

"Why not wait for em?" Dad spoke up. "My boys and I know every rock in Coe. We could lay for em."

"That's good thinking," Aleksandr said. "We're going to do something like that. I'll explain it all tomorrow, but we can't do it here for two reasons. One is that we have women and children here, and there are other camps in Coe as well. The Jonnies fight hard. There's no reason to risk your camps." Dad nodded in vigorous agreement with that reasoning, his sons watching his reaction to see what their own opinion ought to be.

"The other reason is we can't be sure they know we're getting ready to march. Maybe they don't have any spies." As the men thought it over, Aleksandr indulged himself in a nasty wry thought: And maybe General Vinogradov is simply a degenerate, not an egoist willing to subvert the aims of the mission for his own gratification and self-promotion. Aleksandr quickly cleansed his mind.

"We have to go part of the way toward Hamp, prepare to intercept the Jonnies, and then if necessary move on to attack. As I said, I'll explain the details tomorrow. But you agree with me?" He looked toward the group leaders, and it was at once apparent that there was general agreement, though the nature of the hilltowners was that they'd have to think it over for a while.

Just to seal their loyalty, Aleksandr added, "I'll promise you two things. One is that our battle plan will be simple and effective. You've got a right to expect that. The other is that if our first engagement with the Jonnies is a disappointment to you, if you lose your taste for fighting, I won't try to stop you from going on home." He knew he couldn't stop them anyway; that's why the first fight had to be successful but it might ease their complicated Chaser sense of loyalty if he said it at the beginning. And they did seem gratified by the promises.

With supplies distributed and the excess cached, Aleksandr, Felicity and Jason were the last to return for lunch, and barely an hour remained before assembly. Felicity held to Aleksandr's arm, smiling to herself and, at moments, oddly for such a stern and furious girl, blushing and having to restrain a laugh. Aleksandr and Jason, intent on their plans, didn't notice.

HARDLY AN IMPRESSIVE number, Aleksandr thought as he cast a critical eye over his troops self-consciously shifting their new bandoliers and shuffling their feet and glancing from Aleksandr to their group commanders.

"All right, marching orders!" Silence was immediate and profound. "Hop's scouts go first. Stay on the road. One man on point, two more at an interval but in sight of the first, one trailing in sight of the second and in sight of me. He'll signal back any encounters." Aleksandr had rehearsed a few simple hand signals with the scouts; they didn't need instruction beyond a common agreement on hand code. "I'll signal forward any halts. I'll march at the head of the column with Smit and his men." He thought Smit would have the most appetite for a fight if they should encounter the unexpected. "Next will be Jason's strike force, which will split off from the main body when we pass Ash. Then Dad's group. Then Fallon's. Fallon will be at the rear of the column and will communicate with Mack's scouts, who will trail in the same formation as Hop's men. Group leaders will stay in line of sight as much as possible. In the unlikely event we encounter armed resistance, I'll signal to the leaders what to do. Probably we shall meet no difficulties, but the first rule of the march is to anticipate. Be prepared at all times, and stay alert to signals from your leaders. There is no need for strict silence, but cause no unnecessary noise and do not discharge your weapons unless and until you are engaged with hostile forces."

"Hop, start it off." Aleksandr nodded as the scouts started down the road, proud of their duty, and Aleksandr waited to give them a good start. He looked over the troops again. Felicity and the other women were marching with Fallon; Aleksandr hadn't thought it necessary to mention them in his address to the troops. He glanced over at Jason. The lanky hunter was now burdened with two weapons as well as two bandoliers. Aleksandr had insisted he take one of the high-powered old rifles he had brought with him, and Jason had insisted on carrying the 12-gauge shotgun as well.

"Now," Aleksandr said to Smit, and the mountainous blond nodded to his men. They began the march toward Hamp.

EVEN THOUGH THE ROAD on both sides of the cracked ancient highway was smooth, Aleksandr soon was sweating as heavily as Smit, and by the time they climbed the long steep hill into Ash sometime after mid-afternoon, his legs were weary. But he still wanted to press on into the evening, if necessary, to reach the site he and Jason had agreed on. So he simply waved to Jason and his men as they separated from the main body of troops, who resumed at once the ground-eating pace that came so naturally to the hilltown Chasers.

From what he could tell, the men seemed cheerful. They were together in greater numbers than ever before, strong enough to fear neither bandit nor Jonnie, and all the decisions were left to men whose judgment they as yet had no reason to doubt. Their morale is good, Aleksandr thought, but it will either be better or nonexistent after their first battle. The words of the Roll of Humility began going through his mind, begging for success by the backward way of asking for the grace to handle it properly.

He called a halt for a meal while there was still more than two hours of daylight left. Chasers tended to eat early, he knew; more to the point, Aleksandr's legs were about to give out. He forced himself to stroll to the rear of the column and back, however, before he sat to eat, and he tried to look as fresh as most of them genuinely seemed. They were in good spirits and perfectly willing to push on. Most of them were decidedly unimpressed by the quality of food in the tins he had shown them how to open, but they were not inclined to complain about minor inconveniences away from camp, and most had a small container of potato lightning. Until he detected any signs of drunkenness, Aleksandr would allow such comforts. The men themselves were their own best disciplinarians when there was any possible danger afoot.

It was getting dark by the time they completed their hike, and Aleksandr hurriedly assigned the men their places for the night. The scouts were brought into camp to sleep, as they had had to be particularly alert all day, and volunteer teams of other experienced woodsmen were set up to alternate guard watches. No campfires were allowed, but as Jonnies rarely forayed at night and reliable sentries were posted, Aleksandr allowed smoking, drinking, and socializing on a quiet scale. He knew the men were tired and soon would be asleep, and he had already warned them that they would be mustered at the first gray glow of light in the morning.

He called the leaders together at an open patch in the woods, a few meters up the hill from the road. First he asked for reports, and neither Hop nor Mack had seen anything unusual during the march. The worst problem had been remembering the order against shooting, as Hop's men had come upon four or five tempting deer in a meadow by the road. Neither Fallon nor Smit nor Dad had anything on his mind by way of complaint, nor special insight into what their men might be concerned about. Everyone was ready and willing, reluctantly willing, to fight.

"Very well," Aleksandr said. "Here's the battle plan." He could feel the sudden tension bind them all, sharpening their senses and their wariness. Aleksandr himself was excited. It was the excitement of the warrior chief, and nothing was quite so exhilarating, he thought. "I'll show you placement of the troops in the morning. It should be quite a simple matter. All that's necessary is thorough and safe concealment, and every hill-towner I've met is an expert at that." The group leaders smiled, and a feeling of confidence began to hum alongside the tension.

"What we're doing," Aleksandr continued, "is setting up an ambush. Our aim is to neutralize superior forces, gain a victory, undermine the enemy morale, and put them on the defensive.

"Broadly, the situation is this. Jason and the strike force are on the other road to Hamp setting a similar ambush. Their assignment is to take as few risks as possible, but attempt to confuse and halt, if possible, any Jonnie advance. Our reasoning is that the last time the Jonnies moved in force, they divided their soldiers into two units, one using each road. We don't have the manpower to successfully engage both units. So the strike force will try to delay, decimate, and possibly halt the Jonnies in its area. The strike force ambush is situated at a protected bend in the road, and it's really not far away, as at this point the roads come close together." They now were camping, in fact, not far from where Aleksandr's helicopter had crashed.

"For sure," Hop said quietly. "By the time you finish your pipe I could be to the other road. Done it often."

"Right. Meanwhile we'll take on the unit using this road. They probably won't outnumber us by much. We'll be positioned here on the hillside, with the open road below. After we open fire, they won't have anywhere to go but down on the other side of the road to where that stream is. If they can get that far across the stream into the woods, we'll let them go. We don't want to risk any casualties in pursuit.

"Advance and rear scouts will remain in place, well concealed. The approach of troops will be signaled to us in the usual way. We'll let the Jonnie scouts pass by. They'll be your meat, Mack, if they're in range."

"We'll see to it they're in range," the rear scout leader promised.

"I anticipate," Aleksandr went on, "that some of the Jonnies will run down to the stream and into the woods. Others will retreat back on the road. That's where you come in, Hop. Pick off as many as you safely can, but no unnecessary risks, understand?"

"Never took a risk yet."

The Russian laughed. "Now, two important things to stress to your men. If the Jonnies charge us up the hill, and I don't think they'll be stupid enough to do that, hold concealment until the last possible moment. Don't get excited and run out to get a better shot or anything. The shots will be good enough, and chances are that few, if any, of the Jonnies could get up to our places in one piece.

"The other thing is that I expect that the combination of surprise and their lack of experience in dealing with organized resistance will make the battle short. Some of your men might not even get one clean shot. Skirmishes of this nature tend to be very brief and very confusing. None of your men must take the chance of giving chase. There will be Jonnie wounded and prisoners. We must treat them properly. I'll signal the end of the battle, at which point firing must cease except in self-protection, and Dad's men and I will carefully move down to the road, keeping lines of fire open if they become necessary."

"What will the signal be?" Dad wanted to know.

"The same signal as the start of the battle. Don't begin firing until a flash bomb explodes in the middle of the Jonnies. When another goes off in the woods across the stream, stop."

"Now, this is somethin' I look forward to," Smit said. "Are we lining up the same way we marched?"

"Just about. I'll show you in the morning. Your people will be on the hillside closest to Hamp, but Fallon's men will be next and then Dad's so his people can drop down to the road and make sure all's clear after the battle."

"Well, now." Fallon said, just to gain attention. They all listened. "Seems good. But how do you know the Jonnies 'll come along here soon in any number?"

"I can't be sure, of course," Aleksandr admitted. "But my thinking is that somehow they're going to hear that the hilltowners are planning to fight back, and they'll want to strike first. If they don't come along that road tomorrow or the next day, we'll have to march down toward Hamp and try something else. But I think they'll come, and soon."

WHEN ALEKSANDR SAID HE thought the Jonnies would come soon, he was almost praying. The first full-scale fight had much better chances of success if it could be held on ground and terms chosen by the Russian; he didn't want to take the hilltowners into battle against the better-disciplined Jonnies until they had been blooded and had won at least a small victory. Even for only two days of waiting, Aleksandr knew, it might be very difficult to keep his troops on duty and in concealment.

But he had hardly hoped the Jonnies would come as soon as they did. They must have left Hamp at dawn, the same dawn the hilltowner ambush was in place. And that confirmed Aleksandr's suspicion. One way or another, the Jonnies had heard of the men organizing to do battle with them.

The signal was relayed back by Hop's sentries in midmorning. The excited waving caught Aleksandr's eye at once and he began his own relay signaling: Jonnies coming, and a lot of them.

The day was sunny but hadn't turned warm yet, and for the most part the troops were standing in small groups, quietly talking. But they too caught the urgency of the signals and quickly settled in their places on the hill, where trees and boulders provided ample concealment but left various lines of fire open toward the road.

It seemed to Aleksandr that it was an eternity before anyone appeared along the road, but it really was only minutes. The usual four scouts, two on each side of the road. They weren't looking about with any particular caution—they were in a hurry, and their task obviously was simply to guarantee that the road was clear. They were wearing lightweight green jackets and carried their rifles carelessly, not looking for trouble. Aleksandr formlessly prayed that all his troops would obey orders and let the scouts pass; inexperienced troops were likely to shoot at the first movement they saw. But the hilltowners were excellent hunters and understood the principles of Aleksandr's trap perfectly. The scouts passed and were now Mack's worry now. Aleksandr took one of the flash bombs from his right thigh and fitted it to the Mayakovsky assault rifle. He switched the weapon to its auxiliary mode, then took a kneeling position behind a boulder. The Mayakovsky was pointed at a patch of road that didn't stay empty for long. The greencoats flooded into Aleksandr's line of fire, and the Russian was trembling with excitement. He had risked his career and even his life for this moment.

He waited until the grimly silent column had passed along the shaded road far enough that he estimated the vanguard was directly under the guns of Dad and his men. Aleksandr then took careful aim and pulled the trigger.

It was as though he had unloosed the string that held the world bound together.

As the flash bomb exploded, the hillside to Aleksandr's right and left erupted with a chain of rifle fire that could not have been resisted even by a troop of men who had been prepared for an attack. The Russian officer switched his rifle from auxiliary to automatic and prepared to run off a clip at the Jonnies below, but he stopped at the last moment. The sound of a burst from the powerful assault rifle would carry through the din, and he could see that the first volley had done the job. It would be good for hilltowner pride to know that their own rifles had been enough. He switched back to auxiliary, attached another flash bomb, and settled in to watch the battle.

It was over before most of his men had taken three shots. The roadside was littered with Jonnie dead and wounded, and those who dropped into defensive firing positions rapidly saw the hopelessness of their struggle. Some ran back along the road they had just traveled, dashing through the gauntlet of rifle fire provided by Smit and his men. The greencoats couldn't have known that once past the ambush, they still would be in peril from Hop and his advance sentries.

Other Jonnies, some dropping their weapons, ran away from the hilltowners' fire, down to the brook and across to the forest beyond. Not all of them made it.

The warrior's ecstasy, the clash of arms, made the moment vivid and prolonged for Aleksandr, who had been trained to sharpen his perceptions in combat. In truth, however, the eruption of the hillside into rifle fire lasted only a moment, and the few Jonnies who returned fire sized up the situation very rapidly and took to their heels. An officer who had tried to rally his greencoats stood haranguing them, waving his rifle. It was a short rally, as one of Fallon's men cut him down with a well-aimed bullet. The Jonnie troops then had everything to fear in front of them and no more to fear behind them, and their feet suddenly developed minds of their own.

Aleksandr's estimate was that there had been about one hundred Jonnie men; his sixty or so had routed them with ease. He could see no sign of further opposition from the road below, so he aimed at a large facing of rock near the brook and squeezed off the flash bomb. The din of battle rapidly subsided. The hilltowners were proving more capable of discipline than the Russian officer had expected. For a moment, Aleksandr thought with surprise that he heard the Jonnies still firing; then he realized that the wind had carried a sound from the direction where Jason had prepared his own ambush. So they had been right about the division of the Jonnie troops.

Switching his rifle back to automatic and leveling it down the hill before him, Aleksandr stepped out of cover and began a cautious descent.

"Smit! Send someone to Hop and have him come back and report. Be careful on the way. Get the rest of your men into defensive position to protect us in case any of the Jonnies decide to come back." Smit immediately nodded to a young fellow, who scurried along the hillside to where he could cross the road and find Hop. Smit then fanned his men out facing back toward Hamp. "Fallon! Keep your men in position for the moment. Dad! Send someone back to fetch Mack, and be careful about it. Send someone else up the hill to get the women. The rest of you come with me to check what's left of the Jonnies."

He didn't need to look closely at the men to tell that they were swollen with pride and power, and soon he could see that the vanquished had no spirit left. He heard scrambling behind him on the hill and saw to his annoyance that Felicity had not waited to be summoned but had come as soon as the firing stopped. He put aside his irritation, however, for he could hear the cries and groaning of the wounded.

"Dad!" Aleksandr shouted a little louder than necessary, ignoring Felicity. "Any wounded?"

"Nothing worse than a couple of wet britches." His huge sons guffawed.

"Fallon! Any wounded?"

"Two. Nothing serious."

"How about your people, Smit?"

"One wounded, one clean dead. Stood up to take a better aim."

"How bad is the wound?"

"Pretty bad, in the side."

"Come on," Aleksandr said to Felicity, heading toward Smit's men. "I'll be right back, Dad. You people guard the prisoners."

Smit's wounded man wasn't badly off; the bullet had passed through without damaging any major organs. Aleksandr popped an ampule of antibiotic-painkiller from the medicine kit into the wounded man's arm and swabbed the ingress and egress wounds, then left Felicity to plaster on the bandage and follow behind him to Fallon's wounded. One leg wound. One arm wound. The wounded men could be moved up the hill to recover out of harm's way; he'd leave Jen to care for them for a day or two.

By the time he'd returned to the road, Hop and Mack were on hand to give their reports, but first Aleksandr, Marth and Jen attended to the Jonnie wounded. Several were hopeless without prompt surgical care; the Russian without consultation used a different kind of ampule on those. As a stopgap, the antibiotic-painkiller and a bandage had to do for the rest. Most would survive easily, Aleksandr judged.

It was time to do a tally.

"What happened to their scouts, Mack?"

"Four dead. All stood still as a listenin' deer when they heard the shootin' start. We knew how they'd be comin' up the road, so we each knew which to shoot. Bullets worked real good, too." Aleksandr already had heard a number of awed comments about the quality of the ammunition: These men wouldn't settle for hilltown manufacture ever again.

"How did your men do, Hop?"

"Killed five of em on the run. They didn't stop to look around, just ran faster. Nicked a couple of em too, I think."

The tally on the road and by the stream showed Aleksandr the dimension of the victory. There were fourteen Jonnies dead, twenty wounded, and eighteen unharmed prisoners. Added to Hop's and Mack's totals, the figures meant that easily more than half the Jonnie force would not be returning to Hamp. And the hilltowners had suffered one dead, three wounded. Already he could feel the new confidence of his men; and it was aided by the sight of the battered, helpless and frightened Jonnie prisoners.

"Hop," Aleksandr ordered, "take your scouts over to Jason's position. Be very cautious. But I want to know what happened there. Tell him if all's well we'll meet his group down where the roads come together." Hop signaled to his men and left, cutting across the stream and into the woods without needing to pause to seek a path.

Brukov turned to his commanders. "We want to get out of here as quickly as we can. No use letting the Jonnies know where we are. Dad, you organize the uninjured prisoners to dispose of the bodies. Fallon, have your men collect all the Jonnie weapons and ammunition. We want to be ready to move as soon as Hop gets back."

One of the uninjured Jonnies had identified himself as the troop's medical officer, and Aleksandr gave him a free hand with the wounded greencoats.

Smit's men were in position, and Aleksandr sent Mack back to his scouts with instructions to be alert. They would be signaled when it was time to move out.

After a brief inspection of Smit's men—in the aftermath of battle they were euphoric, laughing and passing around containers of potato lightning, and the Russian gently reminded them to be cautious and on guard—Dad led three of the greencoats over to him. "These here want to talk, Cap'n."

And talk they did. The three were brothers named Wells, Seth and Arb, and only the latter was wounded, a minor scrape on the arm. It was Seth, a handsome young man with a soft, pleasant voice, who served as spokesman.

"We want to join you," were the first words spoken by Seth, and Aleksandr immediately gave the three young men his full attention.

Like many of the Jonnies, Seth said, he and his brothers, along with other men they knew, were in the service of the Reverend only because it was a simple way of guaranteeing food, housing and security. The religious fanatics really weren't too numerous among the troops. Most were failed farmers who had grown weary of battling the elements—and the recent vicious raids on the hilltown camps had been extremely unpopular among the brothers and their friends

"Were you on your way to attack again?" Aleksandr asked.

"Killin' was the business this time," Seth said with no emotion in his tone. "Word was the camps was gettin' set to fight. Go get em first, that was the word."

"How did these stories start that the Hilltowners were going to fight?"

Seth shrugged. "Just talk." He seemed to be telling as much as he knew, and Aleksandr reminded himself that he had started talk of fighting the Jonnies before going back to base, and that had been some time ago.

Aleksandr went on to question the men closely about the organization of Hamp and the Jonnies, and all three confirmed his suspicion that there was a certain amount of antagonism between the Reverend and the Steward.

"Each one thinks he's got it in special with God," Seth said, and his companions laughed in agreement.

The Russian was convinced of their sincerity, and the information they gave him was valuable. "If you're willing," he said, "here's what I want you to do. Seth, you and Wells collect your rifles and go off down the road back to Hamp as though you escaped from our ambush. No Jonnie who was here is going to guess any different. Say you hid out in the woods until things quieted down. Once you get back to Hamp, try to line up those people who agree with you. Be very careful. It's a dangerous plan. But if we know we're going to have help inside Hamp once we attack, we can plan accordingly. You'll have to come back for instructions—say tomorrow night. Can you do that?"

"Unless he sends us off somewhere," Seth said. "Maybe even then we could do it.

"Good. And Arb, since you're wounded..."

"It ain't bad. I can get back to Hamp too."

"I'm sure of it," Aleksandr said, "But Seth and Wells can take care of that job. We need you here. We can't afford to leave adequate guards with the Jonnie prisoners. There are almost as many of them as of us. There must be Jonnie believers among them."

"I don't think so," Wells said. "They was all with the other troop over to the other road with the Steward. Not many here talk much about it. They're scared. But I don't think they like the killin' any better'n us."

"Well, that's your job, Arb. Talk to them, make sure they know we don't want to harm anyone who doesn't want to harm us, and make sure they keep away from Hamp for a few days."

Arb nodded thoughtfully. "Long as we got food, no one is like to go back."

"Good. We'll have to take our chances then."

Aleksandr agreed on a meeting place with Wells and Seth, let them fetch their rifles, and sent them off with an escort so that Smit's perimeter guards didn't decide to kill some more greencoats.

By then, Hop and his men were back, with the men of Jason's strike force calmly following behind.

"I told you they were to use the other road," Aleksandr snapped at Hop.

"Hold on, Cap'n," Jason cut in before Hop could reply. "Jonnies are runnin' on that road, and they might stop to get mean if we follow too close. Better we're all together."

"Well," Aleksandr said, unwilling to acknowledge that a direct order had been ignored, "what happened over there?"

"You figured right, Cap'n," the grinning Jason said. "They come along, right enough. Wind was goin' your way so we couldn't hear if you was shootin'. We just laid up in them rocks where the road goes through that notch in the hill. We just started shootin'. Every round went off. They was a lot more'n us, a lot more, but we didn't get one scratch. Steward was there tryin' to get em to take a run at us, but we was just poppin' rounds into em. They just kind of crawled off backwards."

"Do you think they went back to Hamp?"

"Well, I guess. You told us not to follow, take no chances, so we didn't. And flup, but I wish I got that Steward. I tried, twice, but he never stood still in the open, runnin' like a deer in the woods, he was."

The emotional let down after the excitement of battle hadn't yet come to Jason, Aleksandr could see. Each moment of the fight was still living before his eyes.

"How many did you you get?" the Russian asked.

"Didn't count. More'n one of em dead for every one of us alive, though."

"What about their wounded?"

"Killed em. Not like this crowd you got here." He nodded toward the Jonnie prisoners huddled along the road.

"Killed them? Jason, I know how you feel about losing Sue, and I can't really blame you for what you did to that farmer..."

"Killed Jobey, too."

"I know that Jason, but I'm saying the killing's got to stop. It's one thing in battle, but after the fight is over, you just don't execute prisoners."

Jason shrugged. "Couldn't take em with us. We hid their rifles and supplies."

"I've already discovered, Jason, that many Jonnies are perfectly willing to desert the Reverend and the Steward and join with us. You'll only terrify them into loyalty toward the Jonnies if you slaughter helpless prisoners."

Jason reluctantly nodded agreement; though it was plain he wasn't convinced. Aleksandr knew that once these hilltowners decided that a man was an enemy they were a long time thinking him a friend again. And it was better to kill an enemy than to let him do the kind of things the Jonnies regularly did to the hilltowners. It would take time for that enmity to die out, but getting rid of the Reverend, the Steward and the core of fanatics around them would speed the day.

"Well," Aleksandr said, suppressing a sigh, "let's get organized and get out of here. I don't want the Jonnies to know where we are."

‹ *Chapter Eighteen* ›

ALEKSANDR BUILT CAREFULLY toward the final assault on Hamp. The next two days he kept his troops on the move, swinging around the perimeter of the Jonnie stronghold. At night they camped in a strong defensive position, guarding against the extremely unlikely chance that a desperate and enraged Reverend might try a sneak attack. If he had, his forces would have been chewed up as decisively as at the first battle.

There were roast pigs the second night, almost a celebration by the increasingly confident warriors. The Valley farmers, sensitive to the winds of change, were being discreetly cooperative. They donated the pigs and potatoes. Aleksandr tried to discourage drinking, though some tippling couldn't be avoided. Overconfidence and laxity could be worse than timidity in a soldier. But most of the hilltowners seemed sensible and a little edgy; they were not in the habit of celebrating a victory before it was won. Their lives had taught them harsher lessons.

The Jonnies didn't venture out in force during those two days, but Aleksandr kept the pressure on. The greencoat defectors Wells, Seth and Arb had provided him with a thorough briefing on the location of Jonnie sentry posts and the routes and schedules of routine Jonnie patrols. Jason and his strike force were assigned the task of forcing the withdrawal of sentries to Hamp proper, and they undertook their chore with efficiency. Aleksandr stressed the need to minimize casualties among the hilltowner troops, so Jason and his men took no unnecessary chances. But they sniped at sentries from a distance, killing a couple of Jonnies and wounding several more. By the end of the second day it was apparent that there would be no more sentries posted on the outskirts of Hamp.

The town became an unwalled fortress.

At the same time, Aleksandr detached Fallon, Smit and Dad with their men in separate ambushes along the paths normally patrolled by the Jonnies. Each ambush stayed in place a couple of hours only; no use boring the men or wasting too much of their time. But several times Jonnie patrols did materialize, and in each instance they suffered casualties while inflicting virtually no punishment on the well-concealed hilltowners. The quick retreat of the Jonnie patrols made it obvious that they were neither inclined nor ordered to be aggressive, and Aleksandr found it necessary to remind his irregulars that the enemy still was armed and dangerous, and that troops were never so fierce than when defending their own territory, especially their own encampment.

But there was no dampening the enthusiasm of the hilltowners, and in truth Alexander was glad. The battle for Hamp was not simply, or even primarily, a clash of armed men. It was foremost a matter of conflicting ideas of autocratic rule by a madman or consensus government under the guidance of the Russian Imperial Mission. It was essential not just to kill Jonnies, but to convince the survivors, as well as the farmers and other Chasers of the area, that they would be better off with the Reverend and the Steward and their most loyal followers dead or gone. And to win that battle, the battle of conviction and will, it was necessary for the hilltowners to have and to display high spirits and unflagging confidence.

Aleksandr tried to restrain his excitement—he constantly mumbled to himself the Roll of Humility and the Roll of Abasement—but he was quite certain that he was about to achieve the dream he first had while recovering from the ankle injury he suffered in the helicopter crash: He was going to lead an ignorant but decent people into a good, safe way of life, perhaps even into Shared Grace.

He was troubled only by Felicity—her penchant for blasphemy, her insistence on powerful perceptions that were wrong, disturbing and frightening. By contrast, the thought of Lyalya and their complete sharing of every understanding was infinitely soothing and irresistible. It was, after all, in Russia that Aleksandr could be appreciated for his discoveries of the true nature of Chaser Two and be rewarded for gathering those aimless souls into a productive community. It was Lyalya who could understand that; Felicity only fought against reality with a distorted vision of her own.

Fortunately, he was busy with the business of war. He saw little of Felicity, and when he did deal with her he adopted the aloof manner of the commander. Somewhat to his annoyance, she didn't seem to mind. Her dark, thin form still moved with electric energy—still attracted and excited him, he acknowledged—but she seemed to smile more, joked easily with the wounded men she treated where once she would have scowled and treated injuries with furious resentment. She was softer and gentler in her ways, and seemed willing to let Aleksandr go about his duties without spending time with her.

He was right, perhaps, to be proud that he had come to a greater understanding of the natives of Chaser Two than any other Russian, Aleksandr told himself, but he would never understand Felicity.

THEY MET WELL AFTER dark in one of the abandoned sections of Hamp, Wells and Seth in their greencoats and Aleksandr with his assault rifle at the ready, confident that there was no betrayal and most likely no real danger even if they were discovered. Hop and his scouts were spaced around the meeting place as an added precaution.

"No need to worry, Cap'n," Wells said as they exchanged greetings. "No Jonnies around here."

"Too busy arguin' with each other," Seth said, grinning.

"That's what I want to know," Aleksandr said. "Tell me everything."

"Well, it's risky for us," Wells cautioned. "We've got ten others who'll come over when they get the word. There prolly a lot more, but we only asked them we was sure of. Ask the wrong one and we could get shot."

"Quite right. Don't take any unnecessary chances."

"Reverend had two fellas shot," Seth added. "Caught em trying to run off."

"Have there been many deserters?"

"A few." Wells shrugged. "Most of em don't know whether it's worse to take their chances with the Reverend or try to get out. You can get killed either way."

"Wait a few days and Reverend and the Steward will prolly kill each other and you can just march in," Seth said.

"Are they quarreling, then?"

"Yup."

Wells nodded in agreement. He was quite a young man, but seemed to discipline himself to speak as one of wise years. "Got their men lined up, too. Steward thinks Reverend messed things up, and they all ought to get out while they can, move somewhere else. Reverend says it's all Steward's fault for lettin' the Russ get away." He grinned at Aleksandr. "He says we stay and fight, and the God Jonathan Edwards will smite the Devil.

Like Seth said, they'll prolly smite each other first."

"I don't think we can just wait and trust to luck," Aleksandr said. "We must attack. It's a question of timing."

"It's about as bad as it's goin' to get now," Wells said. "Some 'll fight, but some won't. It 'll be the same a week from now."

"Perhaps you're right. How many Jonnie troops would you estimate there are now?"

Wells thought a moment. "They put the women and kids in them big houses up the hill. They know you ain't comin' that way. They're all in by the church and them buildings there."

"I see," Aleksandr said, suppressing his impatience with the indirect answer, so characteristic of the nonconformist Chasers.

"But men with rifles," Wells mused. "Prolly about the same as we marched with the other day, wouldn't you say, Seth?"

"Sure. Same as we marched with. Different men, though."

"That's enough to put up a good fight," Aleksandr said. Some more recruits had joined his hilltown brigade, but not enough to bring the total up to a hundred. And the Jonnies would have the advantage of a defensive position.

"Figure ten of em 'll be with us and not fightin'," Seth noted.

"That's right," Wells said. "And half the rest 'll crawl away and just try to keep alive till the shooting stops."

"That makes the odds better," Aleksandr agreed.

"Reverend figures you're goin' to have to come after him. Plenty of food there," Wells explained. "He's stayin' in the church and them buildin's there, praying all the time. Don't even have patrols out no more. He figures the Lord will help."

"All right," Aleksandr said, his mind made up. "Listen carefully, you two. We'll come in the dawn after this, at the very first light. Not a word to anyone. Tell the people who are with you to meet at the houses on the hill where the women and children are, but don't tell them why and don't tell them anything until tomorrow night."

"They'll guess," Wells said.

"Let them, but tell them to keep their guesses to themselves. When you get to those houses, stay together and stay alert. And when you hear the shooting start, take off those green jackets and get rid of them. Guard the women and children. None of my troops will be up there. If any Jonnies come, capture them if you can or kill them if you must. We'll send any prisoners up there without their rifles, and you keep them under guard until we can sort things out. If someone comes along who is running away from the fight, take away his rifle and make him sit, but don't give him any trouble. A lot of these Jonnies will be happy to see the Reverend and the Steward gone, if you fellows are any measure."

"That's how we favor, right enough," Wells said. "But them that ain't is goin' to fight, no mistake. They won't be runnin'."

"We'll give them all the fight they can handle, I promise you that," Aleksandr said.

THE PALE LIGHT OF THE moon was cooperative, and Aleksandr had his troops on the move before dawn, walking quite openly along the road toward Hamp. Jonnie patrols had ceased, as Wells and Seth had reported. Hop's scouts were well ahead of the main body of men and would give adequate warning if anything were out of the ordinary.

Aleksandr had decided that his men were too keyed up, and the enemy too confused, to attempt a siege. He might lose the advantage if he tried to wait out the Reverend. His men could lose their edge, might even drift away. The Jonnies could regain their confidence, perhaps surprise the hilltowners and win a skirmish or two. No, the battle had to be joined now, and he kept to the schedule he had given Wells and Seth.

They slowed and became more cautious as they reached the abandoned buildings, some of them in rubble, that constituted the greater part of the town of Hamp. The inhabited portion of the town was relatively small, mostly the church, jail and other buildings around the large cleared space that once, evidently, had been a commercial center but now was an open common.

Aleksandr checked the sky. The light that heralded dawn was glowing.

To cross the common toward the buildings would be to invite discovery, as the Jonnies surely had guards on duty, so Aleksandr ranged his troops in concealment. Dad's men were strung out up the hill toward the place where Wells and his men presumably were hiding now with the women and children. Aleksandr was with Smit's men, directly across the way from the main fortress of the church. Fallon and his troops were spread along toward Aleksandr's right, curving with the concealment of the buildings in the direction of the rear of the church and its companion structures. Jason and his strike force were further yet to Aleksandr's right, and were in position to cut off retreat from the church. Their assignment was to capture the jail, which commanded a sweep of the rear of the Jonnie position and would provide a strong outpost to defend against the flow of a retreat.

Dawn was at hand, and Aleksandr felt the fearful nervous thrill of battle about to begin.

He reached to his thigh and lifted one of the armor-piercing "slams" to the muzzle of his rifle and clamped it in place, checking the switch to make sure the function specified auxiliary. Just then he heard a spatter of rifle fire from behind the church. Evidently Jason had begun his attack. There was a rapid scuttle of sounds and shadows across the way as the Jonnie guards reacted to the sound of gunfire from the direction of the jail.

Aleksandr braced the Mayakovsky against a protruding stone of the building that concealed him. He aimed carefully at a window on the first floor of the church. Gently he squeezed the trigger. The recoil pounded his shoulder at the same instant that the church window exploded with a roar, and Aleksandr heard his men yelling as they opened fire. He switched his rifle to automatic, aimed at the same window, and poured a clip into the smoking hole. The smooth loud purr of the rifle as it almost instantaneously spewed out thirty rounds was peculiarly satisfying to Aleksandr. He felt almost as though he were on a target range as he casually released the metal clip, listened without looking down as it clattered to the broken concrete flooring beneath his feet, and drew a full clip from the rows on his chest and clicked it into place. He'd wait to fire again until he saw how the battle developed.

The Jonnies now were returning fire from the church and two adjacent buildings, but the sporadic shots were fewer, less intense than Aleksandr had expected. He gazed slowly and thoughtfully around the area; perhaps the Reverend had dispatched a body of troops to a nearby post to be brought up from the rear of the invaders when the inevitable attack came. It was possible, and the possibility was dangerous. The Russian saw Mack and his men a short distance down the shadows and gave a low whistle. Mack looked up and Aleksandr waved, bringing the scout on the double.

"Either some of their men are holding their fire to try to lure us in, or else they have troops posted elsewhere and they might show up at the wrong time," Aleksandr said to Mack, who was crouching behind a crumbled brick wall. The Russian had to speak loudly to defeat the din of rifle shots.

"They don't seem to be putting up much of a fight," Mack agreed.

"That's what worries me. Split your men into two groups. Send one behind our flanks on the east side and the other on the west side. Sweep the back streets from the outside in toward the middle. Have a man stay at an observation post if you find a spot where you can see a distance. And get back here in a hurry if you spot any Jonnie activity."

Mack trotted back to his men and they split into two groups and set off at once.

Aleksandr turned his attention back to the exchange of fire across the town common. He saw a blur in the shadows near the buildings on the flank protected by Dad's men, and the hilltowners poured out rounds with a new urgency. Some of the Jonnies—probably the entire contingent at that post—had decided to try to escape into the shadowy streets and buildings, up the hill where Aleksandr and Jason had escaped from prison what seemed a lifetime ago.

There was no telling from where he was how many of the Jonnies had escaped and how many had fallen, but it didn't really matter. The fact that the flank position now was deserted or nearly so was the key.

He gathered himself for a run toward Dad's position, but he didn't need to give directions. He saw a rush of his troops across the far end of the common and into the vacated Jonnie position. Now the hilltowners had a stronghold within the Jonnie defenses. Aleksandr smiled at the quick reaction of Dad's men. All the troops had quickly come to respect the value of military discipline, and all showed an initiative and willingness to act decisively that was truly uncommon. A couple of months' training with modern weapons and they'd be the equal of any troops under the Russian Imperial Mission banner.

Rifle fire erupted from the building where Dad's men had entered, and Aleksandr knew they were beginning a deadly sweep toward the stronghold of the church.

The Jonnie rifle fire was still light, and Aleksandr suspected some kind of trap or other deception, but still he knew that prompt action was necessary. The Jonnies couldn't be allowed to grow confident in their defense, and they ought to be engaged with sufficient vigor to prevent them from organizing against the slow advance of Dad's men. It was time to take a chance. Aleksandr attached another "slam" to his rifle, flipped the function switch to auxiliary, and took careful aim at a doorway across from Fallon's men on the other flank. When it exploded into a gaping hole, scattering bricks and mortar a dozen feet around, Aleksandr waved toward Fallon's position. His men were already on the run, half of them having provided an advance fusillade and following as soon as they reloaded. Aleksandr saw three of them fall, but the rest reached the building.

Aleksandr could sense the eagerness of Smit's men—they wanted to join their fellows in the assault. He heard a crackle of rifle fire from the building Fallon's men were occupying, and the shouts of men coming together in hand-to-hand combat carried on the damp dawn air. It was time. Aleksandr switched to automatic and ran another clip off into the doorway across the common from his position, punched another clip into place, and nodded to where Smit sat watching him. "Wave them on," the Russian called, and Smit's huge frame rose with surprising speed as he signaled his men and then ran forward himself without waiting to see who might follow.

A bullet sang past Aleksandr's ear, and a man next to him fell, but the rush to the church was so swift, and the images glimpsed by his frantic bobbing eyes so disjointed, that he had no sense of danger until he reached the wall of the building. A green-clad form suddenly appeared at a window that had been raggedly enlarged by the first "slam," and before Brukov could raise his Mayakovsky the figure fell backward. Smit nimbly propelled his bulk through the opening, his reloaded rifle still pointing in the direction of the bullet just spent.

Two more of Smit's men entered the church through the opening before Aleksandr could leap in. By the time he entered, firing had stopped. Three greencoats sprawled on the floor in the casual postures of death and two more, one of them bleeding from a shoulder wound, were prisoners under guard in a corner. Smoke and the smell of firing were in the air, and Aleksandr's heart was pounding.

"Others went in there," Smit said, panting after his furious exertion. He motioned to a heavy oak door across the large room. "I heard a bolt go home."

"We'll give them a little surprise," Aleksandr said, switching to auxiliary and lifting another "slam" from his thigh. He turned to the prisoners as he attached the rocket to his rifle. "You there. Not all your troops are fighting. Where are your reserves?"

The wounded Jonnie was grimacing, absorbed in his own pain, but his terrified companion swallowed hard and found his voice. "No reserves. Steward had a fight with the Reverend, called each other devils. Steward wanted to go south, find some place else. Reverend wanted to kill the Russ devil." He looked hard at Aleksandr. "Steward took his men and left at midnight, went south."

"It is enough to make a cat laugh," Aleksandr cursed. He had been so sure of the course of events that he hadn't even put out patrols! Well, let the Steward go, as long as he went away and stayed away.

He turned back to the prisoner. "Is there another exit from the room behind that door?"

"Out to the common from the back." The prisoner no longer was afraid; he was enjoying his role as an important person whose information was sought by the Russian, devil or not.

Suddenly Aleksandr realized that the room behind the door must be the chamber of the Reverend, where he and Jason had been so uncivilly interrogated. The other door would exit right into the bullets of Fallon's men. The Jonnies were trapped. "Is the Reverend in there?" he snapped at the prisoner. The prisoner gulped and nodded.

"All right, men," Aleksandr said. "This will explode in

toward the other room. There shouldn't be much danger in here, but stay back against the walls and get in there when it goes off. They'll be stunned for a moment."

Smit silently motioned his men into arrangement along the walls, and a flash of pride went through Aleksandr. Now only an oak door between him and the achievement of his goal.

Aleksandr raised the rifle and aimed at the center of the door, just where the double roll of metal studs showed where the primary fortification on the other side would be. He squeezed the trigger and the room screamed with noise. The door ripped sideways off its heavy hinges and plaster billowed out through the opening. Smit hesitated only a moment before dashing through the door at the head of his men.

There were shots and a crash, the dust still stirring as Aleksandr entered the room, his rifle back on automatic and nosing menacingly before him. Smit was on the floor holding his leg.

"Flup, Cap'n, it's not bad. I just can't move much till I get bandaged. Missed my shot so I had to thump him one." Smit's rifle lay butt-end toward a greencoat who was face down on the floor, the side of his head a pulp. Two other greencoats sprawled where they had fallen under the explosion of the "slam" or the subsequent bullets of Smit's men, two of whom, Aleksandr now saw, were uneasily pointing their rifles at a man with fiery eyes sitting with his hands clenched tensely on the desk in front of him. The Reverend wore his green robe. The sepulchral voice that chilled Aleksandr at once began:

> 'Tis commonly so, that just before God appears for any
> remarkable salvation and comfort of his people, they are
> reduced to the greatest, their distress the most; and so
> their necessity of divine help most clearly and
> remarkable.

"We shall see about God's allegiances," Aleksandr said coldly. Smit's men, guarding the Reverend, shuffled their feet, lowering their rifles but remaining in place.

There was a clatter outside and Aleksandr turned to see Hop and Jason enter the room, their weapons at the ready. Jason was carrying the 12-gauge shotgun, his rifle apparently abandoned in favor of the short-range effectiveness and automatic capacity of the ancient hunting weapon. He was grinning exultantly, but Mack entered right behind them and spoke first.

"Looked as good as we could," Mack reported. "Don't see any other Jonnies around, but left my men and they'll come runnin' if they spot somethin'."

"Thanks, Mack, but I think I've discovered the answer to the scarcity of opponents," Aleksandr said. He looked toward the tense, statue-still figure of the Reverend, becoming more statue-like indeed as the plaster dust settled. "It seems the loyal Steward took his troops last night and left the Reverend to fend for himself."

"That's what I heard from a prisoner just now, Cap'n." Hop said.

"God will destroy him," the Reverend suddenly boomed out. "He is no steward but the very instrument of the Devil." His eyes rolled upward.

> Calamities that are very small in comparison of the
> universal temporal destruction of the whole world of
> mankind by death, are spoken of as manifest indications
> of God's great displeasure for the sinfulness of the
> subject; such as the destruction of particular cities,
> countries, or numbers of men, by war or pestilence.

"Cap'n," Jason said happily, plainly ignoring the Reverend as both incomprehensible and what the hilltowner would call ear-elephant, "Cap'n, I found Sue and she's all right. She was in the jail cause she give em so much trouble. She's just all right." His grin became even wider.

Aleksandr slapped him on the shoulder, grinning himself,

and started to congratulate his friend on his good luck when he heard the single word: "Doom!"

He turned to see the Reverend, who was standing now. "Doom to the Steward that was and doom to you, but I shall live a thousand years!" Again the possession took him.

> *And it is to be observed, that the means and inducements to virtue, which this age enjoys, are in addition to most of those which were mentioned before, as given of old; and among other things, in addition to the shortening of man's life, to 70 or 80 years, from near a thousand.*

Aleksandr could scarcely understand the meaning of the words, and he glanced away as he tried to think of what to say. But a sudden rustle of movement brought his attention back to the Reverend.

"DOOM!"

A huge ancient pistol of a type Aleksandr had never seen before appeared from beneath the Reverend's green robe and pointed straight at the Russian. Before Aleksandr could raise his Mayakovsky there were two booms, almost simultaneously, and he saw the flash from the muzzle of the Reverend's pistol.

The Reverend's body rose and crashed backward and Aleksandr spun to the side with a sharp flash of pain.

"Cap'n, you all right, Cap'n?" Jason hovered anxiously over him. His shotgun had sounded just as the Reverend's pistol roared.

"I don't know," Aleksandr said, though the words didn't come out clearly.

"Here, let me see," Hop said, kneeling beside him. "You're a little messy but you're all right. Felicity can fix that in no time."

The pistol bullet had grazed the left side of his cheek, nicking his jawbone painfully but not shattering it. There was blood, but no serious wound.

"Just sit while I get Felicity or one of the others," Jason said, trailing words behind him as he raced out. Aleksandr sat stunned, not even trying to say anything more. Vaguely he heard a few scattered shots, and Hop said comfortingly, "They're just finishing up, Cap'n. Almost all over."

"Flup, Cap'n," Smit said cheerfully from across the floor, "You ain't even shot as bad as me, and I ain't bad at all!"

Very shortly, Jason reappeared with his sister. "She was already halfway here," he said jubilantly.

"Supposed to stay back," Aleksandr mumbled in halfhearted reprimand.

"Shup," she commanded sternly, her dark eyes grave with worry. She swabbed his jaw line efficiently. "It's not bad," she said with relief, and busily set about readying a bandage.

"I tole him I was hit worse," Smit said, "but wouldn't you know the Cap'n gets first treatment, at least from this nurse."

"Shup, Smit," Felicity said without any acknowledgement of Smit's humor. "You're next."

"Oh, don't hurry. Might as well look at the Reverend first."

"Jason already saw to him," Hop said. "He's all fixed up just perfect."

"That's enough," Felicity said, but she smiled at Aleksandr as she finished bandaging him. "There. It wasn't bleeding much. You ought to be able to talk now."

"Thank you, Felicity," was all he cared to say at first. He rose to his feet somewhat tentatively and looked over at the shattered form of the Reverend.

"Only Perfect God can count the shadows and know their meaning," Aleksandr said in words from the Roll of Humility.

He looked over at the two Jonnie prisoners. Perhaps it was his imagination, but he thought he read in their features relief at the lifting of the cloud represented by the Reverend.

Felicity now was busy with Smit. "You men," she said. "A

little scratch and you fall down and start crying."

"Just our way of makin' the women to come runnin'," Smit said, but Felicity refused to be baited.

"The bullet went through clean. There's no damage to speak of. You can walk all the way back to Coe if you want."

"But real slow," he said.

"Slow," she agreed.

"With the withdrawal of the Steward's men," Aleksandr mused, turning from Smit and Felicity and wandering back into the first room they had entered, "it really wasn't much of a fight. A little anticlimactic."

"Flup," Jason said, following him. "Seemed like a fight to me."

"Oh, of course. I didn't mean... what's that?" He suddenly froze, his senses attentive. He walked to the opening in the wall that he had enlarged with his rocket. The sound was clearer by the second. "It's helicopters," he said. "I haven't even activated my locator yet. That's quick."

The beat of the rotors grew, and all eyes turned to the south as a formation of five Stavrogins came swinging up over the crumbled buildings. They flew no more than two hundred feet above the ground and moved, now that they approached their destination, with some deliberation, as a man might who wished each step to fall on a marker.

Aleksandr's regiment of hilltowners was beginning to gather on the common, and the sound of approaching helicopters drew even more men out of the buildings. Some of the hilltown warriors were escorting Jonnie prisoners up the hill, others were simply lounging and discussing the one-sided battle just past. Only the men who volunteered to help Marth and Jen and Felicity patch up the wounded and sort out the dead were showing any urgency.

By now the morning was well begun, the sun beginning to practice its blinding tricks as it eased over the tops of buildings and through the slots between them, and the promise in the air was for the clear warmth of an early summer day. An auspicious sign for a new era, Aleksandr thought.

He started to step out through the wall to the common to greet the helicopters. He frowned as he endeavored to scramble through the rubble while maintaining the measured pace and erect posture proper to his uniform and his stature as the conqueror of Hamp, the organizer and leader of a new force on behalf of the Russian Imperial Mission. He regretted the indignity of his hastily bandaged jaw. But as he made his way he saw the two flanking helicopters suddenly swing wide, one toward each end of the open area over which the hilltowner troops had dashed such a short time ago, and Aleksandr reacted with immediate horror. He recognized the fantail formation, a standard Mission maneuver. Before the shout of surprised warning could escape his lips, however, all five helicopters opened up with the large-caliber machine guns, the three middle Stavrogins settling to the common to disembark troops.

The scream of ricocheting bullets was louder than the sound of the machine guns, and intermittent screams from the men who moments before had been lounging on the common were louder yet. The fantail formation was designed to saturate an area with machine gun bullets as thoroughly as possible without catching Russian craft or troops in a crossfire, and the effect was certain to be devastating. Aleksandr had thrown himself at once behind the rubble, and he rolled deeper into the recess of the room, clinging to the wall for maximum protection.

"Felicity! Stay in there!"

"I'm safe, Aleksandr," she cried back, seemingly already accepting this new catastrophe.

Jason was at the other side of the opening, also protected by the wall. "Stay down, Jason," Aleksandr shouted. He frantically pulled out his locator; irrationally praying that if he acted quickly enough the damage could be prevented. The damage was already done.

"Sue!" Jason suddenly yelled, and he leaped to his feet.

"You can't..." Aleksandr began, but Jason already was dashing to the inner room where Felicity and Smit and the others still were. Aleksandr knew he was heading for the other door. "Jason, stay here!" He knew that the call was fruitless, and he jammed the locator again and again with vicious urgency, as though the small, innocuous transmitter bore a measure of the guilt that was engulfing him. Each activation of the locator should flash a light and sound a buzzer within the helicopters as the finders automatically switched on.

Only seconds had passed, yet Aleksandr when at the Academy had memorized the rate of fire of those large-caliber machine guns; multiplied by five, the numbers became staggering. And even if his intellect hadn't known the numbers, his ears could give him a working approximation. He punched the locator again as though it were his enemy.

Aleksandr thought he heard one of the machine guns stop. He tensed himself in the dusty rubble, listening hard. Abruptly, there was only one of the weapons firing, and it stopped almost at once. An eerie silence fell, and as his ears adjusted Aleksandr picked up the lower harmonic of the moans of wounded men. Absurdly, a rifle shot rang out, and Aleksandr scrambled to his feet and yelled, "Stop, stop," hopelessly battling the noise of the machines.

He stumbled out through the opening and screamed again, "No more firing." The Russian troops must not have even noticed the rifle shot, or surely they would have begun again.

The three central Stavrogins had just settled as Brukov emerged from the church, and troops were beginning to pour out. Short, stocky, swarthy troops in full battle gear; the Indimex regiment. They were arranging themselves in position, and plainly were tense with the unfulfilled need for battle. They carried Mayakovsky assault rifles like Aleksandr's own, but evidently the order to cease firing had been relayed to all the ships. They weren't firing, though the desire was clear enough. They stayed by the helicopters, their sleek rifles sweeping back and forth across the buildings they faced.

Crumpled heaps of cloth and flesh dotted the common, and a few of the figures writhed and emitted indecipherable but all-too-human noises.

"Felicity!" Aleksandr yelled back behind him. "Get Marth and Jen! Quick!" Trembling with rage and frustration, tears already beginning to fill his eyes, Aleksandr turned back toward the helicopters, uncertain as to whether he could even control his voice. One of the flanking helicopters then angled back and swiftly dropped onto the common before him. More Indimex troops popped out in guard position, and behind them scrambled the figure of Colonel Dalstroi.

"Aleksandr! Praise God you're safe. Our prayers are answered." Brukov strode toward his base commander, feeling something like relief at having an object for his wrath, no matter how kindly his feelings toward Colonel Dalstroi had been in the past. "My colonel, what is the meaning..."

"We had heard you were dead, Aleksandr. We had an intelligence report that you and your troops had been ambushed. Naturally we decided to retaliate at once."

"Colonel, you have retaliated against my troops. These men you have slaughtered have just defeated the Jonnies and liberated the town of Hamp for the service of the Russian Imperial Mission.

"My dear Aleksandr!" The colonel was aghast. "I'm so terribly sorry. What a horrible mistake! We'll help them at once, of course. But how wonderful that you yourself..."

"I suspect they'd rather help themselves. Just hold the

General's killers back." He shot a contemptuous glance at the impassive Indimex troops and turned on his heel, leaving his insulted commander speechless and immobile.

Aleksandr could hardly control his own walk as he went to where Felicity was administering to a hilltowner gasping on a patch of ragged grass. Part of the man's stomach was hanging out, and Aleksandr could see that he had little chance of survival. As he drew nearer he saw that the wounded man was Moe, the curly haired owner of the bird dog, Smoke, who had so enlivened his hunting sessions with Jason. The tears started again to his eyes.

"Felicity..."

"Not now, Aleksandr. We must be quick."

She had popped an ampoule into Moe as Aleksandr had taught her, and now was swiftly taping his abdomen. Marth and Jen had also emerged from the rubble and were scurrying from one shattered figure to another.

Aleksandr straightened up and looked at the buildings. Surviving hilltowners were emerging, slowly, quietly, and with great caution. They all held their rifles at the ready, and their eyes were fixed unwaveringly on the Indimex troops before the helicopters. They could have no illusions about their chances, but they were spoiling for a fight every bit as much as the Indimex regiment. They had been blooded in battle, and won; they had learned a discipline, and gained confidence; they had learned how to obey, and when to take the initiative. They had become soldiers, and now they had been surprised and betrayed. They reacted as soldiers would. Aleksandr's hopeless pride tore in his breast. None of them looked at him; not for leadership, not in reproach. He wore the same battle uniform and had carried the same weapons as the poised, unafraid soldiers they eyed across the common.

Aleksandr saw with a shock the lifeless body of Dad sprawled a few bodies away from where Felicity worked, and next to it the equally dead frames of two of Dad's sons. Above them stood another son, alive and staring at the troops with hard eyes like the other men. Impossible!

Hop trotted up breathlessly, the only moving figure besides the nurses.

"Cap'n, Felicity. Jason wouldn't stop back then. He ran right out." He didn't need to say more.

"That should do it, Moe," Felicity said, though the bandaged man could hear nothing. Aleksandr's frozen horror at Hop's words lasted only a moment. Felicity rose and he joined her in following Hop in an awkward run, skirting bodies.

Hop led them around the side of the church, toward the door where Jason and Aleksandr had entered in captivity.

They saw the body as soon as they turned the corner. He had been caught by a burst as he dashed out of the door toward the jail, and Sue was already at his side, on her knees and crying silently. She held a lifeless hand in her own and pressed it to her cheek. Jason was on his back, a leg awkwardly broken beneath him. His eyes were open but saw nothing. Aleksandr began reciting the Roll of Shared Grace.

Felicity kneeled on the other side of the body from Sue. Tears ran from her eyes, too, but neither woman sobbed. Sue was rocking back and forth slightly in rhythm to unsounded moans.

"Oh no," Aleksandr said softly in flat hopelessness, unable to continue his prayer. "Oh no."

"Leave us, Aleksandr," Felicity said.

He turned and wandered, numb with grief, back toward where Colonel Dalstroi stood.

"Poor fellow, this was quite a mess" the colonel said. "All in all, however, regrettable as it is, the aim is accomplished. You've done the job, and quite admirably. A faulty bit of intelligence complicated things at the end, but that's no mark against you. It was all done brilliantly, I'd go so far as to say."

"Colonel, we may have undone much of it here."

"Nonsense, my dear Aleksandr. Naturally, you're distraught. Been wounded, too, I see. But it will be put right easily enough. We'll clear out and let them tidy, and soon enough we'll be back with goods they'll be glad enough to get. My word on it, Aleksandr."

"I can only hope you're right, my Colonel. And you'd better board up these troops again before trouble starts."

"Of course. Nothing to be done here, anyway. We'll re-establish liaison when things have calmed down. Might be another job for you, eh? Climb on my ship and we'll patch you up proper." The Colonel nodded sympathetically toward Aleksandr's jaw, where indeed the bleeding was starting again.

Brukov hesitated. "Go back now?" he asked, as though of himself.

"Of course. This job's done, and done well, too. There'll be notice of you even in Moscow for this, my dear fellow."

"Yes," said Aleksandr, not even hearing his colonel, "Yes I suppose I must."

"Operation Grainrail is safe here, thanks to you. Now we can get about it," the Colonel said.

"One moment, Colonel," Aleksandr said, and turned to go back to Felicity. He walked faster and faster and soon was running.

Felicity now was comforting Sue, but she released the grieving woman when she saw Aleksandr approaching again. Sue's eyes didn't move from the fallen form of Jason.

"Felicity. Felicity, I must go. I..."

"Hush, Aleksandr. Say nothing more. I know. Now it is better that you go."

"Felicity I..."

"Not a word more." She put her arms around him and held

him gently, her face against his chest. "Don't promise, don't lie, nothing that might ever be false. You were never false, Aleksandr. I know that. You must go, Aleksandr, my love. You've done all you can. Go before it gets worse. Go back to your Russia. I can't go with you, Aleksandr, so don't think of it. Remember me always." She squeezed him fiercely. "You must always do that."

"Felicity..."

"Remember me always and Jason too." Aleksandr involuntarily let a sob escape. "Aleksandr, don't regret what can't be helped or changed. My place is here, as yours is in Russia. I know how you love Russia, Aleksandr. You will be happy there. You could never live here. But remember me."

He kissed the hair on the top of her head and turned blindly away from her. Everything that was unsaid and unresolved, all that he felt in her that he didn't understand, it would have to wait, perhaps forever. He couldn't stay now, and there were no more words to be said.

"Come, my boy, into the helicopter with you," Colonel Dalstroi said as he approached. "I know it's been hard for you, but we must be off. After all, they *are* only Chasers, they'll be all right after a bit. Get on in."

Aleksandr ducked into the Stavrogin and the colonel turned his back to the troops. "Up and out!" he shouted, accompanying his words with vigorous hand signals. He then moved briskly into the helicopter himself as the troops began their orderly filing into the craft, alert sentries waiting until the last moment. Before the machine even lifted into the air the regimental doctor in the Colonel's helicopter had begun working on Aleksandr's jaw, so he didn't even see the common and the town of Hamp receding into the past below him.

But Felicity watched the helicopter, her eyes not leaving the one into which Aleksandr had disappeared. The machines made a fearful clatter and raised the dust of the rubble, then shot away at a low angle, arrogantly swift and sure. She watched as the sound faded and the helicopter became a dot and then disappeared.

She had loved Aleksandr for his knowledge, the knowledge that had awakened her. She knew she could never live up to that knowledge or to the longings of her own soul. Already an adult, she barely was learning to read. There was too much for her to learn.

Her tears of grief—for the loss of Jason, for the just as certain loss of Aleksandr—were not bitter tears. Aleksandr had given her the flame, though he seemed neither to understand nor forgive its light and heat. She put her hand to her belly and smiled as the last of the formation of helicopters died away and as the survivors left behind in the sweet air of early summer began to pull their lives together again. Aleksandr's flame lived in her belly. It would be a boy, she was sure, and the boy would nurture that flame and master that light. He would be a True Chaser, a lord of earth and air, a challenger of God. She would see to it.

Author's Afterword

In imagining a possible future, I have borrowed not only Oswald Spengler's celebrated central thesis about the decline of the West, but his passing suggestion that a successor culture might arise in a liberated Russia. The novel also makes use of Spengler's discussion of the qualities inherent in Western and Russian souls, though obviously I am responsible for the attempt to portray them through characters and dialogue. Any vulgarity or superficiality is mine, not Spengler's.

There is no system of clues within the text to provide the date when the events occur. I named Captain Brukov's sidearm the Pushkin Series 2100 as a suggestion that the events might be taking place 150 years or so from now, and other details support a reading of the near future. I wanted to stress how rapidly change is upon us and how complete a metamorphosis the world can undergo in a short period of time. But it would be just as acceptable, and perhaps more plausible, to imagine the novel taking place 500, 700, or even 1,000 years from now.

In the matter of knowledge and technology: It seems reasonable to me to imagine a dominant new culture that spurns technology while still relying on technology's advantages in a limited way. Such unholy jobs as manufacturing could be left to mechanically gifted but soul-exhausted slaves in or from Old Europe. What's more, the knowledge that survives the crash of a civilization is selectively absorbed and re-discovered by later peoples. Much of what is now known might be ignored as inadmissible or irrelevant or simply untrue, especially early in new cultures. In the Middle Ages it was known with scientific certainty that the world was round, yet educated sailors sailed a flat sea.

A vigorous culture can easily dominate a spent civilization, and do so with utter arrogance and unquestioning belief in its destiny. It is only when a civilization begins to fade that its self-confidence and dominance dwindle; then there is more appreciation of the values of the subject peoples and less ability to dominate them. The idea of establishing the residents of Old Europe as superior and even necessary slaves was suggested by the discussion of the Ottoman Empire's Christian slaves in Arnold Toynbee's "A Study of History." Infidel-born slaves were trained for and entrusted with the highest public positions, even to the exclusion of the Muslim-born.

The occasional use of the Russian language, with which I am unfamiliar, varies according to my whim. The word *samogon*, as an example, is used at face value; it means "bootleg vodka." At the other extreme, I simply made up the word *stroza*. I deliberately distorted the word *kulak*, which means or meant "rich peasant"—one of the class persecuted early in the Soviet regime. I use it to mean the lowest class of peasant, because I was struck by an altered Russian attitude toward the word expressed by Nadezhda Mandelstam in her memoirs and because Aleksandr Solzhenitsyn in "The Gulag Archipelago" suggested that "by 1930 *all strong peasants in general*" (his italics) were being called kulaks.

I did not presume to invent the precise nature and scope of the Russian religion-to-come, but kept in mind a new version of Christianity—very different from most of today's varieties, but probably no more different than contemporary Christianity is from the religion in its early forms.

I also think it consistent with our knowledge of the world today to imagine that an ignorant people could embrace religions based on cruel misunderstandings of discrete texts.

Finally, I meant the narrative to combine, and sometimes chide, the qualities of an old-fashioned frontier adventure yarn and the traditional Russian novel. I tried to take the point of view of a popular Russian writer of the even more distant future, a writer spinning out a tale of historical fiction about the early days Russian attempts to civilize North America. Such an author, with advantage of historical hindsight, could afford to depict the brashness and the shortcomings of his nation's trailblazers, and could also afford to admire members of the burned-out civilization whom they encountered during their adventures. Such a future author would keep foremost in his mind the need for his book to entertain.

L. Michie, Buckland, Massachusetts, 1982